AMBER EVE

Highland Getaway

Also by Amber Eve:

The Heather Bay series

The Accidental Impostor
The Accidental Actress
A Scottish Cozy Mystery
Impostor Bride
The Actress Unscripted

Standalones

The Love Curse
The Book Feud
Cool Girl Summer

AMBER EVE

Highland Getaway

Black&White

Black&White

First published in the UK in 2026 by Black & White Publishing
An imprint of Bonnier Books UK
5th Floor, HYLO, 105 Bunhill Row,
London, EC1Y 8LZ

A CIP catalogue record for this book is available from the British Library.

Paperback ISBN: 978-1-78530-898-7
eBook ISBN: 978-1-78530-899-4

1 3 5 7 9 10 8 6 4 2

Typeset by IDSUK (Data Connection) Ltd
Printed and bound in Great Britain by CPI (UK) Ltd, Croydon CR0 4YY

At Bonnier Books UK, we are committed to publishing sustainably.
Find out more here: bonnierbooks.co.uk/sustainability
The authorised representative in the EEA is
Bonnier Books UK (Ireland) Limited.
Registered office address: Block B, The Crescent Building,
Northwood, Santry, Dublin 9, D09 C6X, Ireland
compliance@bonnierbooks.ie
www.bonnierbooks.co.uk

*To my parents, who have always known I would one day
'grow into myself'.*

Chapter 1

I'm not quite sure how it happened, but at some point in the last twenty-four hours, I seem to have been granted the gift of invisibility.

At least, I think that's what it is. It's the only explanation for the way everyone I've encountered since I left London this morning has seemed to look *through* me rather than *at* me; and it's definitely the only explanation for the fact that I'm currently trapped in a train toilet somewhere in the Scottish Highlands, on my way to change my life.

Or I will be if I can just get out of this damn toilet.

Right now, though, that's looking pretty unlikely; mostly because of the whole 'gift of invisibility' thing, which is the reason no one noticed me come in here a few minutes ago – and also the reason no one's going to notice when I don't come back out again.

It's more of a curse than a gift, actually, now I come to think of it.

'Um, hello?' I call out, as the train lurches to a halt at what I'm assuming is my stop. 'Can anyone hear me?'

I press my ear against the jammed toilet door, desperate for a response.

Silence.

Which isn't all that surprising, I suppose, even without the invisibility cloak I appear to be wearing; unlike the packed train that brought me from London to Edinburgh, the two carriages that have trundled the rest of the way to the little village of Glenmuir were empty except for me, an extremely disgruntled ticket collector and a woman with long purple hair, who may or may not have been a witch.

If I didn't know better, I'd be starting to think I'd somehow died on the way to King's Cross this morning, and this new-found invisibility of mine is my punishment for what I did in order to come here. Like, because I cheated my way into an exclusive getaway to a Scottish castle, I'm now doomed to walk the earth as a ghost for evermore. Just my luck, really.

'Hello?' I yell, starting to panic at the thought of eternity in a public toilet. 'Could someone help me?'

Still nothing.

'*Please?*' I add, for good measure.

The silence is making me sweat. The toilet door is still wedged shut, no matter how hard I try to push against it.

What's more, I'm pretty sure Glenmuir is the last stop on this line. If I can't get the toilet door open within the next few minutes, I'm going to be carried all the way back to Edinburgh . . . and then, presumably, brought back *here* again if I still can't get out. It could be days before anyone finds me. It could be *weeks*. I could easily spend the rest of my life being shuttled around the Highlands in a toilet, surviving only on water from the handbasin, and that half-bag of Haribo I bought at Edinburgh Waverley.

The thought of becoming some strange kind of toilet-dwelling ghost is all the motivation I need to get out of here before the train leaves again. With a low, guttural kind of roar that I didn't know I had in me, I take a step back, then throw myself at the toilet door as hard as I can. Then I do it again, the resulting pain a timely reminder that joining a gym was going to be one of my New Year's resolutions this year, but here we are in June already, and I can't even break down a door without wanting to cry.

(Although, to be fair, *who can?*)

There's a loud cracking noise as if something's breaking, but there's no time to figure out whether it's me or the train, because the next thing I know, the door's swinging open and I'm flying forward, still doing the weird roaring sound as I'm carried by my own momentum back out into the carriage, and then through the open door, and into the arms of an extremely surprised-looking man who's standing on the platform.

'Oh, my God, I'm so sorry,' I gasp, trying to extricate myself from his grip, but failing miserably on account of all of the bags I have slung over my arms, which keep getting in my way.

'Whoa, there,' the stranger says, grinning down at me in amusement as he helps me get back to my feet. 'I know it's probably every man's dream to have beautiful women throwing themselves at him, but maybe we could at least introduce ourselves first?'

My cheeks instantly start burning, and I drop one of my bags through sheer embarrassment. I know he's probably just trying to be polite and smooth over an awkward situation, but I've instantly lost the power of speech. I'm not used to getting compliments; especially not ones that come from men with cheekbones so sharp you could grate cheese on them.

Well, it figures that if I'm going to make a fool of myself, I'm going to do it in front of someone who looks a bit like he's been carved out of marble, doesn't it?

'Er, Rosie, is it?' he says, realising I'm in no fit state to answer him. 'Rosie Summers? Headed to the Chrysalis?'

'Yes! Yes, that's me. I'm Rosie Summers,' I say, grasping gratefully at the conversational straw, while trying to pretend I haven't just had to peel myself off his chest. 'And yes, I'm supposed to be going to the Chrysalis hotel. For the launch event? Do you know it?'

The stranger smiles again, skin crinkling around eyes that are such an unusual shade of brown they almost look golden in the late-afternoon light. The gold-brown eyes are paired with reddish-blond hair and a light sprinkling of stubble on a very square jaw, and the overall effect is enough to make my cheeks burn even more than they were already.

Leave it to me to basically throw myself at the most handsome man in the Highlands; which is what this guy *surely* must be?

'Aye, I know it,' he says, in a soft Scottish accent which carries more than a hint of amusement. 'I work there actually. Hunter Stuart,' he adds, holding out a hand. 'Gardener, chauffeur and man of all work, at your service. Literally, I mean; I've been sent to pick you up and bring you back to the hotel.'

'Er, hi,' I squeak, shaking his hand, and hoping to God mine isn't quite as sweaty as it feels. Behind me, the train chuffs its way back to life and prepares to pull away again in the direction it came; leaving me alone on the tiny platform with this Hunter Stuart, and . . .

'Is that a *wolf*?' I gasp as a huge black shape comes bounding towards me, wagging a tail that looks roughly the size of a small tree. 'Do they still have *wolves* in the Highlands?'

'Stevie? No, Stevie's no wolf.' Hunter chuckles, grabbing the beast by its collar. 'He's just a pup. He gets a bit too excited when he meets someone new. Don't you, Stevie?'

He ruffles the creature's neck, and I look at them both doubtfully. Stevie looks way too big to be a 'pup', while Hunter is tall and muscular, with the kind of rugged good looks that makes him seem like exactly the kind of man who might keep a wolf as a pet.

I grip my phone tightly in my pocket, very aware that I'm about to get into a car on my own with this stranger – and his wolf – in the middle of what appears to be the exact middle of nowhere.

'Your . . . your dog's name's Stevie?' I ask, feeling like this is probably a safer question than, *Are you planning to abduct me and have your wicked way with me?* which is what I *really* want to ask him.

'Aye. Well, it's actually Stephen, but that's his Sunday name,' he replies with a grin. 'So I just call him Stevie. Anyway, we best get going; they'll be expecting you back at the hotel by now. I was starting to think you must have missed the train or something.'

'Yeah, I, er, got locked in the toilet,' I admit. 'With half a bag of Haribo.'

'Right. I see,' says Hunter, looking about as impressed by this nugget of information as you might expect. 'Well, let me take your bag then, and I'll get it into the car. Oh.'

He pauses, looking down at the collection of luggage I've brought with me, which includes one suitcase, and all of the other bags I could possibly find.

'Well, you definitely don't travel light, do you?' he says, throwing the suitcase effortlessly over his shoulder and swooping the rest of the bags up in one arm. 'Or were you planning to stay all summer?'

He turns and strides off down the platform to where I can see a beat-up old Land Rover waiting for us.

'No, just the four days,' I reply, having to jog to keep up with him. My stomach gives a painful little lurch at the reminder that four days is exactly how long I have to change my life. 'I'm just here for the press stay. Four days, then the launch party at the end, the invitation said?'

'That's what they tell me,' Hunter confirms, reaching the car and putting my bags inside. 'Right. Well, jump in then,' he adds, opening the passenger-side door for me. 'It's a bit of a mess, I'm afraid. I'm more used to transporting plants than people, but I was the only person available to meet this train, so you're stuck with me, I'm afraid.'

He grins again, and my mouth goes dry.

'Oh, that's . . . that's *fine*,' I reply, clambering inelegantly into the car, and wishing I'd worn something a little more practical than the dress and sandals that seemed like the *perfect* travel outfit at home, but which are hopelessly out of place next to Hunter's jeans and work boots. 'I'm happy to be stuck to you. *With* you. Um, I mean, thanks for picking me up.'

Hunter's lips quirk slightly. 'No bother,' he says, starting the engine.

I sit there silently as we pull away from the little station and out into a narrow road, which is lined on each side with gorse bushes covered with beautiful little bright yellow flowers. I'd expected Scotland to be cold and dark – especially this far north – but the sky above us is bright blue, and the sun seems nowhere near setting, even though it must be close to dinnertime by now.

'So, you're a gardener?' I say, the vivid yellow of the gorse reminding me of Hunter's earlier comment.

'Among other things,' he replies. 'I do whatever needs doing. The plants are the bit I like most, though. They don't expect anything from me, except for me to look after them. And you're an *influencer*?' he adds, giving the word an emphasis that suggests he thinks it's made up.

'Um, yes, that's right,' I reply, shifting uncomfortably in my seat. 'I'm here to cover the launch of the hotel, and get some photos and videos of it before it opens. I think there's a few of us here this week?'

I think of the email that popped into my inbox unexpectedly, just a few days ago, my stomach lurching again with something that could be either guilt or excitement – or possibly just the results of the speed at which we're hurtling down this impossibly winding road.

Your transformation is about to begin! the message said, in perky, PR speak. *You and a group of other lucky influencers have been hand-selected to attend the exclusive pre-launch event at the Chrysalis Resort and Spa in the beautiful Scottish Highlands. Come and join us on a life-changing journey of reinvention!*

Well, I mean, how could I say no?

'Aye,' says Hunter, and this time there's no mistaking the hint of disapproval in his tone. 'The rest have already arrived. They all had a lot of luggage, too. I think you're the winner, though. I can tell you like shopping.'

He gives a dry chuckle and jerks his head towards the back of the car, where Stevie the wolf is sitting slobbering next to my many bags, looking almost as if he's laughing at me. They *both* look like they're laughing at me, actually; a realisation that takes me right back to high school, and the time I walked out of the girls' bathroom with my skirt tucked into my knickers.

'I do like shopping,' I say, with as much dignity as I can muster given that I'm clinging onto the grab handle for dear life as we bounce along the single-track road at a speed that makes me wonder what'll happen if we meet someone coming in the opposite direction. 'It's . . . well, it's my happy place. Shops, I mean.'

I don't bother telling him I feel like this because every shop I enter has the potential to change my life; that I'm always just one purchase away from becoming a whole new 'me' – a version of myself that stood up to the school bullies, and went on to become a raving success at . . . something I haven't quite figured out yet.

Someone whose boyfriend absolutely would *not* have chosen to dump on her birthday three weeks ago, having first of all stood her up at her own party.

I'm definitely not telling him that bit.

'Your *happy place*?' Hunter says, speaking in an 'I've seen it all now' kind of tone that makes my shoulders tighten in indignation. 'A *shop*?'

'Yes, a *shop*,' I reply, my instinct to defend myself triggered by the amusement in his voice. 'And I suppose yours is the top of a mountain, or . . . or the middle of a lake or something?'

He shrugs easily. 'Anywhere without people is fine by me,' he agrees. 'We call them lochs, though, not lakes. And you'll need to wear something a bit warmer than . . . well, *that* . . . if you want to see any of them while you're here.'

His eyes flick over to me, and travel down from my floaty dress to my strappy sandals, in a way that makes it clear that I might have been invisible to everyone else I've encountered so far today, but this man can definitely *see* me.

Maybe a little bit too well, actually; it could just be the guilt talking, but it feels almost as if those clever golden eyes of his can see not just the unsuitable outfit choice, but the reason for it, too. As if he knows I'm just pretending.

'I don't expect hiking clothes would look nearly as good in photos, though,' Hunter adds with a smirk.

And there I am, right back in school again; always wearing the wrong thing, and being the butt of everyone's joke because of it.

'I'm getting the feeling you don't much like influencers, for some reason,' I say, bristling at the slight.

'I don't know any well enough to like or dislike them,' Hunter replies dismissively. 'I just think there are better things to do with your life than take selfies and post them on the internet so people can "like" them – or whatever it is you do it for.'

He snorts, as if to underline his point, and my skin prickles with the familiar shame of being looked down upon – and I'm not talking about his height, either.

'I don't do it for "likes",' I retort. 'I do it because—' I trail off, struggling to find the right words.

The truth is, I might not do it – or *want* to do it, rather – for 'likes' exactly, but I did start my Instagram account for validation; to feel like I fitted in somewhere at last. That I'm finally being accepted. That, sure, all the girls in my class might have followed me home one day, chanting insults and hitting me with rolled-up umbrellas – the schoolgirl's weapon of choice – but *now* they'll want to follow me on Instagram instead, because, hey, look at me now! Look how much I've changed!

Am I good enough for you yet? Do you like me now?

I get the feeling a man like Hunter Stuart, who looks like he's never endured so much as a second's worth of bullying in his life, wouldn't really understand that though.

'In this case, I'm doing it to promote the hotel you work for,' I tell him instead. 'So that, when it opens next week, it'll be inundated with bookings, and make lots of money. Then you get to keep your job, and I get to keep mine. Which is what this is, by the way – a job, just like any other.'

I raise my eyebrows and give him what I hope is a suitably pointed look, feeling proud of myself for having somehow pulled off this little speech. It's not often I manage to stand up for myself.

'Fair,' Hunter says, agreeably enough, bringing the car to a stop in front of a set of giant iron gates. My stomach does a little wriggle of nervous anticipation as I notice the words 'the Chrysalis' above them in a swirly script, which looks a bit like a butterfly's wings.

'To be fair,' he goes on, pressing something on the dashboard that makes the gates swing silently open, 'I've never seen influencers in action before, so I don't really know what the "job" involves. I guess it's going to be an interesting few days for me.'

'Um, yeah,' I agree, my stomach wriggling even harder as the car starts back up again and moves through the gates. 'Me too.'

You have no idea just how 'interesting' it's going to be for me . . .

We travel silently down a long tree-lined driveway with a large turreted building at the end, which comes looming out of the surrounding forest in a way I tell myself is not at all creepy, even though it *is* just a little bit creepy.

We're here.

As the email said, my 'journey of transformation' is about to begin.

It's just a shame I wasn't actually invited on it . . .

Chapter 2

I knew as soon as I got the invitation that it wasn't meant for me.

It couldn't be, really; I'm not an influencer after all. I'm just a girl with an Instagram account and a shopping habit, who takes photos of her outfits and posts them online. And that might have got me 2,038 followers – not that I'm counting – but it's not nearly enough to grant me influencer status. I'm not sure I've ever influenced anyone in my *life*, actually (not unless we're counting my ex-boyfriend, who I definitely 'influenced' to dump me . . .) which is why, as soon as the email arrived, I knew it had to be a mistake.

Well, that and the fact that my name isn't Rosie Summers, either, like Hunter Stuart thinks it is.

It's Rosie Winter.

Which is an easy mistake to make, I suppose; although only if you've never seen the *real* Rosie Summers, who's blonde, beautiful, and looks like she might have bullied me in high school.

Rosie Summers is a bona fide influencer, with the follower numbers to prove it, and brand deals coming out of her ears.

Rosie *Winter*, on the other hand is . . . well, me.

So I'm not sure how it happened, but somehow the Chrysalis invited the wrong Rosie to their influencer retreat. Which is the point at which any *sensible* person would've hit reply on the email and told them exactly that. No harm, no foul.

But no one has ever accused me of being sensible. And, the fact is, when the invitation arrived, it caught me at a particularly low point. A 'just been dumped by the man I thought I'd spend the rest of my life with' point. An 'I need to move out of the flat we shared, even though I have nowhere to go' point. An 'I hate my job, but I can't afford to leave it' point.

You get the point, I'm sure.

With five days to go before the lease on the flat ran out, I went to my happy place – the retail park – and bought myself a beautiful red cashmere sweater with what was left of my overdraft.

No, it *wasn't* the most sensible thing I could've done, under the circumstances. But, when I bought it, I really thought that sweater was going to change my life; in the same way I think all new purchases will have the power to do that. I remember standing there in the shop, stroking it lovingly, and thinking about how, when I put it on, I'd be transformed into someone completely different; someone deserving of this beautiful item of clothing that I couldn't really afford, but also couldn't live without.

Someone who wasn't about to become homeless in five days' time.

It was as I walked out of the shop that the email arrived from Luna Stone, inviting me – well, inviting Rosie Summers – to the Chrysalis; leaving four days from the date on the email.

'"A journey of reinvention",' it said.

A chance to run away from my life, and find myself a better one. A chance to step into Rosie Summers' life, and find out what it's like to be one of the most popular women on social media.

The kind of opportunity that might never come along ever again.

And, well, also somewhere to live for a few days once I'd handed back the keys to the flat.

'Was this *you*?' I asked the sweater, peeking into the bag. 'Are you made of some kind of magic?'

And that's why, instead of hitting the 'reply' button and letting them know they'd got the wrong person, I'm currently sitting outside a Highland castle, with all of my fingers crossed, and all of my worldly goods – literally – crammed into the bags behind me.

But now I feel so sick with nerves that I can't even begin to imagine what I was thinking when I decided to go ahead with this plan. Or what I'm going to do when the truth inevitably comes out. I mean, it's not like anyone other than Hunter Stuart, who clearly avoids social media, is going to mistake short, mousy-brown me for the model-like Rosie Summers, is it?

'Are you OK?' asks Hunter, looking at me curiously from the passenger seat as I stare anxiously through Stevie's ears and up at the hotel, which, the website informed me, is a converted eighteenth-century castle, and the family seat of the Glenmuirs, who still own it today.

'Um, sure,' I reply, in a voice that sounds unconvincing, even to me. 'It's just . . . it's very *imposing*, isn't it?'

In the photos online, the Chrysalis looked straight out of a fairy tale; all turrets and ramparts, with grounds stretching all the way down to the sea, which I can hear crashing against some unseen shore as I get out of the car. As I look up at it from the bottom of the sweeping stone staircase that leads to the front door, though, it somehow looks more like the setting of some kind of Gothic horror; one with mad-women in the attic, and a dungeon where . . .

On second thoughts, let's not even *think* about the possibility of there being a dungeon. Or what might happen in it to women who come here under false pretences.

'It's a bit more modern inside,' says Hunter, joining me. 'We've been working on the renovations for months now. Come on, let's get you checked in.'

I follow him reluctantly into the hotel's reception area, Stevie padding soundlessly behind us like a shadow, and Hunter carrying my many bags as easily as if they weigh nothing.

The main lobby is vast and imposing, with a chequerboard tiled floor and a wide staircase leading up to a gallery landing above us. Chesterfield sofas are dotted around, creating cosy little seating areas, and there's a log fire blazing away merrily, even though it's June. The reception desk sits to one side of the stairs, with an enormous stuffed stag's head mounted above it, and it's being presided over by a man so handsome that he almost looks like he's been AI generated.

And here I was thinking Hunter Stuart must be the most handsome man in the Highlands.

Striking though he is, it's the couple AI man is currently speaking to who claim my attention. I've never met them in my life, but the woman has shiny dark hair and a red-lipsticked smile which is almost as familiar as my own reflection, while her husband is equally recognisable, with his dark-blond hair combed up at the front, and a very large camera slung around his neck.

'Oh, my God,' I breathe, clutching Hunter's arm in shock. 'It's the Fosters!'

'The who?' he says, looking pointedly at the fingers burrowed into his fleece jacket.

'The Fosters,' I reply, watching as the couple in question appear to argue with the man behind the desk. 'Bex and

Daniel. They're one of the most popular YouTube couples in the country. They have over a million followers.'

'Never heard of them,' says Hunter, with an infuriating shrug. 'D'you want me to leave this stuff here, or will I?'

'Shh,' I hiss, trying to listen in to the conversation at the reception desk.

'I'm sorry, sir,' AI man is telling Daniel Foster, in a tone that doesn't sound even remotely apologetic. 'But your name definitely isn't on my list. *This* is my list.'

He holds up a sheet of paper with just a few typewritten lines on it.

'See?' he goes on, his Scottish accent contrasting with his Mediterranean looks. 'No men. Just the ladies.'

'I understand that,' replies Daniel Foster, with what's presumably supposed to be a winning smile. 'But I'm sure you can make an exception for us. My wife and I come as a package, you see. We're the Fosters?'

He puts an arm around Bex, and they both look expectantly at the man in front of them, who just stares back at them as blankly as Hunter did when I told him the same thing.

Beside me, Hunter's mouth twitches as if he's trying not to laugh.

'What's going on here?'

There's a sudden click-clack of stilettos on tiles as a very slim woman who looks to be in her late forties appears. She has dark, chin-length hair cut into a chic bob, and I could swear the temperature in the room drops a few degrees as she comes clacking up to the little group by the desk.

'Is there a problem, Dante?' she says sharply, making it sound like if there is, it's about to get a whole lot worse.

'No problem,' replies Dante, his eyes narrowing at the sight of her. 'Just a gatecrasher. I'm dealing with him, though.'

'A *gatecrasher*?' says Bex, her green eyes widening in shock in her porcelain face. Combined with the red of her lips, she looks a bit like Snow White; if Snow White had been in the habit of shopping mostly at Harvey Nichols. 'You're calling Daniel a *gatecrasher*?'

Stiletto lady's head whips round so fast I'm amazed it doesn't make her dizzy.

'Bex Foster!' she coos, her whole attitude changing abruptly. 'And Mr Bex! Well, isn't this a wonderful surprise?'

'No,' says Dante bluntly. 'It's not. I have a list. See?'

He holds the list in question out again, and the woman bats it away impatiently.

'Sabrina Bates,' she says, shaking hands with each of the Fosters in turn. 'I'm head of PR for Glow Media, who the Chrysalis have hired to manage their launch. And I know Daniel wasn't *technically* invited to this event,' she goes on, glancing at her colleague behind the reception desk, 'but of course we'd be delighted to have him join us, wouldn't we, Dante?'

She glares at the man, who immediately returns her look with exactly the same level of ferocity. I can't help but like him for it.

'No,' he says again, shaking his dark mane of hair for good measure. 'I said no. And I'm the manager of the hotel; you're just the manager of the PR firm. So I win.'

'It's not a competition, Dante,' Sabrina Bates hisses, leaning in to him. 'The Fosters are the biggest influencer couple in the UK. Having them both here would be excellent publicity for the hotel. You *do* want this launch to be a success, don't you?'

She bares her teeth in something that's presumably supposed to be a smile. Dante bravely bares his own – very white – teeth in return, then shrugs again, before sliding a room key reluctantly across the desk to Bex, who snatches it up as if she's afraid he might change his mind and take it back.

'Room number five,' he says, refusing to meet Sabrina Bates in the eye. 'I'll have someone take your suitcases up for you.'

'And, in the meantime, if you'd both like to come with me, we can have a quick chat about our plans for your stay,' says Sabrina warmly. 'I can't tell you how pleased we are to have you both on board for this launch. It's going to be so exciting.'

She turns on her stiletto heels and clacks away again, the Fosters following obediently behind her. Now it's my turn.

I clear my throat nervously as I step up to the reception desk.

This is it.

This is the moment I'm about to be unveiled as the impostor I am, and sent back home again – not that I have a home, as such, to go to – before I even have a chance to change my life.

When I decided to accept the invitation, even though I knew perfectly well it wasn't mine to accept, my vague plan was to just style it out; to pretend to be as surprised as anyone else to find that I *hadn't*, in fact, been invited to stay at a freaking castle for four days, in exchange for coverage on my Instagram account. As Dante looks up at me, though, his dark eyes registering the slightest flicker of surprise as I approach, looking absolutely nothing like the *real* Rosie Summers, it occurs to me that I should really have thought this through a little more thoroughly. No one's going to believe I'm an influencer, are they? No one's going to think that I belong here; because I don't.

And now I'm about to prove it.

For a split second, I think about turning and running away, just heading straight back out of those double doors and making for the hills I saw from the train on the way here. Well, mountains, really. Very large ones, with snow-capped peaks and jagged sides that I wouldn't last more than a few minutes on in my strappy sandals and stupid dress.

On second thought, maybe the mountain life isn't for me after all.

Which means it's back to plan A: style it out and pretend to be a successful influencer, who has just as much of a right to be here as anyone else.

What could possibly go wrong?

'Hi,' I say brightly, pulling my shoulders back in an attempt at confidence as I hand Dante the booking confirmation that came with the email. 'I'm Rosie, checking in.'

Chapter 3

It's the ghost who saves me.

I mean, it's probably not an *actual* ghost, obviously. As I hand Dante the slip of paper bearing a name that isn't mine, though, a flicker of movement from the gallery landing above me catches my eye, and I glance up just in time to see a small, shadowy figure go darting away, as if it's afraid to be seen.

Or, at least, I *think* it was a small, shadowy figure. It is pretty dark up there.

'Is this place haunted?' I blurt out, gazing around the vast space, which is opulent if not just a little gloomy, thanks to all the dark wood panelling that covers the walls, and the flickering light from the fire.

'Haunted?' says Hunter from behind me. 'Well, not *really*. Just the usual kind of thing. Strange noises in the night, ghostly figures in the halls, cold spots . . . just your average eighteenth-century castle, you know?'

I look over my shoulder at him, trying to figure out if he's for real, but it's impossible to tell whether the hint of a smile on his face is sarcasm or sincerity.

'There are no ghosts at the Chrysalis,' Dante assures me, his perfect brow creasing with annoyance at the very suggestion that there could be something wrong with his hotel. I get the distinct feeling that if there were ghosts here, they'd be afraid of *him*, rather than the other way around.

'Unless we're counting Sabrina Bates,' he adds under his breath. 'And she's more of a vampire than a ghost.'

All the same, as he takes the booking confirmation from me and quickly scans it, the frown doesn't leave his face, and his eyes keep flicking up towards the landing where the 'ghost' – or whatever it was – had appeared. He's so distracted by it that he doesn't bother asking me for any ID, or even a credit card (although maybe they don't do that for these influencer retreats? I wouldn't know . . .), and although my heart feels like it's beating so loudly it could easily be the star of an Edgar Allan Poe story, no one seems to hear it but me, so that's a relief, too.

'Right, that's you all checked in,' Dante says, still with one eye on the upstairs landing. 'Room Six. I'll have your bags taken up for you and unpacked. Perhaps you'd like to try out the spa while you wait?'

'Oh. I . . . uh, yes, I . . . I guess so. That would be lovely,' I stutter, amazed to find that not only is no one going to challenge my presence here, I've somehow managed to find myself in the kind of hotel where you don't even have to unpack your own suitcase. 'If it's not too much trouble, that is? I'm happy to just sit here and wait, if it is?'

'It's no trouble,' says Dante. 'Agnes will show you the way.'

He presses a button on his desk, which makes a young woman with long red hair and big brown eyes appear from a door behind him, as if by magic.

'I'll leave you to it then,' says Hunter, looking relieved to be able to hand me over to someone else. 'Have a nice stay, Rosie.'

'Thanks,' I reply, surprised by the way my heart sinks at the thought of him leaving so quickly. He might not like influencers much, but now that he's going, I feel suddenly quite defenceless in this (possibly haunted) castle.

Luckily for me, however, Agnes turns out to be refreshingly normal, and chatters away in her charming Highland accent as she leads me down a maze of corridors on the ground floor of the castle, all of them long and seemingly identical, with tall, arched windows which look out on a landscape that's gradually turning golden as the sun starts to go down at last. It's evening now, but it's still light this far north, and the castle grounds look soft and hazy in the dusk; the distant mountains a silvery blue-green which makes me think of wizards and fairies, and all of the stories this land must hold.

'Where is everyone?' I ask Agnes, as we turn down yet another echoing corridor. 'The place is so empty. Where are all the other guests? I mean, I know the hotel isn't properly open yet, but the invitation said something about other influencers, and so far I've only seen two of them?'

One of whom wasn't even supposed to be here; a bit like me, in fact.

'There *are* no other guests,' says Agnes solemnly, her eyes wide in the dim light of the hallway. 'It's just you and the ghosts.'

I stop in my tracks, my heart beating a tattoo in my chest, which only slows down when Agnes starts giggling uncontrollably.

'Sorry,' she says with a mischievous grin. 'I couldn't resist. Your face! You were so freaked out!'

'Agnes!' I splutter. 'Don't do that to me! You almost gave me a heart attack.'

'Sorry,' she says sheepishly as we start walking again. 'It's OK, though; there aren't any ghosts. Well, not as far as I know, and I've lived in the village since I was a wee girl. They only invited five influencers this week, though. You're kind of like the test crew. I think the idea is that, as well as getting the chance to take photos and stuff without other folk in the background, you also get to try everything first, so if there's any problems, we find out before the *real* guests arrive. A bit like Danger Night at the funfair, when you get to test out all the rides for free, because there's a risk you might die on them?'

I swallow nervously, but there's no time to reply because, as Agnes speaks, we emerge into a courtyard with a giant chess set in the middle, which we cross, before re-entering the building through a large door leading into what I guess is the modern extension.

'This was finished just a few weeks ago,' says Agnes, producing a set of keys which she slides into yet another door. 'Caused a right stir in the village; you'd think it was a skyscraper they were building, not a swimming pool, the way some of them carried on. I think it's lovely, though. Look.'

She pushes open the door and I find myself facing a large pool, set in the middle of a building made almost entirely of glass. There's a Jacuzzi bubbling away at one end, and a sauna at the other, and I can feel the tension that's been building up all day slowly start to seep out of my body at the sight of it all.

'You're the first person to try it,' says Agnes, looking as proud as if she'd built it with her own hands. 'I'm really jealous, actually.'

'Oh!' I say, remembering something. 'I don't have my swimsuit with me. It's still in my suitcase.'

'Och, it's no bother,' says Agnes reassuringly. 'We have gift bags for everyone; they have bikinis in them and everything.'

She goes over to a low bench by one of the windows and collects a posh-looking cardboard gift bag with the name

'Rosie Summers' on the front, along with a thick, fluffy robe and a matching pair of slippers.

'You should find everything you need in there,' she says cheerfully, handing me the bag, which I take, feeling like I'm stealing it. 'Now you go and enjoy the sauna. You look like you could be doing with a bit of relaxation.'

I return her smile, guilt gnawing at my stomach at the thought of deceiving her – and everyone else, for that matter.

I really should have thought this through before I decided to go ahead with it. I'm just not sure I'm cut out for the impostor life. If nothing else, it's surely going to give me a stomach ulcer.

Guilt aside, though, the sauna does look rather inviting with its clean, woody smell and pristine surfaces. So, once Agnes is gone, I head into the changing room and reach into the gift bag, which contains an entire set of luxury toiletries, plus a small, red garment which turns out to be a bikini.

At least, I *think* it's a bikini. It's so tiny it looks like it was made for a doll rather than a human, and it's all the confirmation I need that Rosie Summers and I definitely aren't the same size, because my breasts are barely contained by the top, and I have a horrible feeling they're about to break free at any second, which . . . surely it's not *supposed* to look like that?

Is it?

Getting the thing on is a workout in itself, and once it's done, I'm tempted to take it right back off again and just accept that I am *not* Rosie Summers, and never will be. Quite apart from that, though, it's also kind of weird having the entire pool building totally to myself. Nice . . . but still weird. The blank windows that surround the pool reflect my own, unflattering image back at me, and I turn away, spooked by the knowledge that anyone who happens to be out there will be able to see me standing here, lit up as if I'm on a stage. The thought makes me feel suddenly self-conscious, so I step quickly into the sauna and close the door firmly (but not *too* firmly; I haven't forgotten what happened on the train . . .) behind me before I shrug off the robe, tugging the too-small bikini bottoms out of my butt cheeks as I go.

I place the towelling robe on the seat before lowering myself onto it, my eyes fixed on the door that leads to the pool, ready to leap into action if it so much as budges.

But the door remains closed. And, after a few minutes, my eyes start to close too, lulled by the heat and soothed by the steam until the next thing I know, I'm back out in the courtyard, playing a game of chess against Hunter Stuart, while Sabrina Bates and Dante, the handsome hotel manager, look on, holding up score cards. I'm just about to pick up my queen to deliver a devastating checkmate when I'm interrupted by a loud bang, and my eyes snap open just in time for me to see the sauna door fly open and Hunter Stuart's reddish-blond head appear around it.

For a split second, I think I'm still dreaming, then the strap holding my bikini top up abruptly gives way, releasing the girls into the world, and I realise this is no dream; this is a *literal nightmare* – one in which I'm caught half-naked in a hotel sauna by a tall, handsome near-stranger, and it doesn't work out anything *like* all of those romcoms I've read would have you believe.

I let out a small, involuntary squawk of horror as I attempt to stuff my runaway breasts back into the bikini top, but it's no use: the thing's well and truly broken – not

that it was covering much of me to start with – so I leap up and throw the robe around me instead.

'Why did you barge in like that?' I demand, turning to Hunter with my cheeks flaming and sweat dripping off the end of my nose. 'You could have at least knocked!'

'I *did* knock,' protests Hunter, whose voice is also a little shaky, as if he's had a very big shock. 'I was knocking for at least five minutes. And shouting. But you didn't reply, so I had to come in to check on you. You've been in there for almost an hour. We were worried. You could've been dead for all we knew.'

'I wish I *was* now,' I wail, close to tears. 'Wait. *We?* What do you mean "we"?'

By way of answer, Hunter clears his throat awkwardly, then steps aside, giving me a clear view of the pool area behind him.

There, lined up almost exactly as they were in the dream that was so rudely interrupted, are Sabrina Bates, Dante and lovely Agnes, the housekeeper. Even Stevie the dog has turned up to witness me emerging topless from the steam.

I tighten the belt of my robe self-consciously, my head swimming from the heat of the sauna.

Have I really been in there for as long as Hunter says I have?

'Er, Agnes came to get you when she realised how long you'd been in there, but she couldn't get the door open,' says Hunter, looking at his feet. 'So Dante sent for me, to help get you out.'

'But . . . that can't be right,' I protest, refusing to believe this whole 'stuck door' thing could've happened to me *twice* in one day. 'I checked the door when I got in and it was fine. So how could it possibly have been stuck?'

'That's beside the point,' says Sabrina Bates, her voice cutting across the room like a knife. 'What I'd like to know is what you think you're doing here?'

'I . . . um . . . having a sauna?' I reply, like a contestant on a quiz show who's blatantly just guessing the answer.

Sabrina shakes her head and folds her arms across her chest, one high-heeled shoe tapping impatiently at the tiled floor.

'No, I mean, what are you doing *here*, at the hotel?' she demands frostily. 'Because one thing's for sure: you certainly weren't invited, were you?'

Chapter 4

Sabrina marches me back across the courtyard and through the hotel, still dressed in my towelling robe – although she does allow me to slide my feet back into the slippers first, which I suppose is something to be grateful for.

That's the *only* thing to be grateful for, though, because the jig is well and truly up. I just don't know how they found out – yet.

And now I'm about to be kicked right back out of the castle, having travelled all the way to the Highlands – and been locked in a toilet in the process – just to spend an hour in a sauna, before heading right back home again.

As journeys of transformation go, I'm not sure I'll be recommending this one to my followers, all things considered.

All the way back along the maze of corridors, I try to work out a solution but there just isn't one. This is all my own fault and, whatever happens next, it's going to be exactly what I deserve.

Just as I'm telling myself things can't possibly get any worse, we finally reach the reception area, and find it filled with people. Bex and Daniel are there, of course, both of them looking glamorous in evening dress, and standing next to a short, blonde woman, who I recognise as Millie Mitchell – a TikToker who's best known for making dance videos with her cockapoo, Gigi. (Who *doesn't* seem to be present this evening, thankfully, so at least that's one less person – well, dog – to witness my humiliation.)

On Millie's other side is Zara Harris – a tall Black girl with high cheekbones and a figure like a runway model – and sitting on her own in a chair next to the fire is Yasmin Hussein, her glossy black hair slicked back into her trademark ponytail, and a pair of designer sunglasses perched on top of her head.

It's like a Who's Who of British influencers. It would actually be pretty cool, really, if I wasn't wearing a dressing gown that's threatening to come apart at any second, and a pair of papery hotel slippers at least three sizes too big for me.

Oh, and if I wasn't about to be revealed to be a dirty rotten liar, obviously.

A nervous-looking woman with curly brown hair and thick glasses is standing by the reception desk, looking like she's about to throw up, and I swear she gets paler still as she catches sight of Sabrina coming towards her, one hand still firmly grasping me by the elbow.

'Well, here she is – our impostor,' she says, letting go of me and squaring up to the curly-haired woman. 'What do you have to say for yourself, Luna?'

The room falls silent, everyone turning in our direction to see what's going on. Over by the fire, I hear someone stifle a laugh, and when I catch sight of my reflection in the mirror behind the reception desk, I instantly understand why.

My face isn't just red, it's a startling shade of bright scarlet – the kind that would probably glow in the dark. If the electricity went off right now, they'd be able to use me to light their way back to their rooms. My hair is plastered to my skull with sweat, and mascara runs in two black rivers down my cheeks, making me look like one of those

scary clown dolls my sisters used to torment me with when we were kids.

'You, er, might want to, um, adjust your towel thing a bit,' says Hunter in a low voice from behind me. I glance down and, sure enough, my robe is gaping open, which at least explains the giggles that are coming from influencer corner over there.

'I'm *so* sorry, Sabrina. I've no idea how this has happened,' squeaks the brown-haired woman, who I'm guessing must be the Luna Stone whose name was on the email inviting me here. Well, inviting *Rosie Summers* here. Sabrina is presumably her boss – which means at least I'm not the only person in the room experiencing some extraordinarily bad luck today.

'Oh, *I* know how it happened,' snaps Sabrina. 'You've invited the wrong person, Luna. It's the only explanation.'

'But I checked all the names you gave me,' replies Luna, sounding like she's about to burst into tears. 'I'm sure they were right. Wait, let me just find my list.'

She flips through her notebook, then holds it up, her hands trembling as she shows her boss the page.

'See?' she says, the relief evident in her voice. 'Rosie Summers. Just like you said. That's who this is. Is . . . isn't it?'

She looks at me with sudden panic, and I smile encouragingly at her, even though there's really not a whole lot to feel encouraged about here. Even Stevie, the wolf-dog, looks like he'd rather be somewhere else.

'Is that *really* Rosie Summers?' I hear Millie Mitchell whisper in a plummy accent which suggests she probably grew up riding ponies and spending summers on Daddy's yacht. 'She's put on a lot of weight since her last video, hasn't she?'

She's speaking in a low voice, which I'm obviously not supposed to hear, but my heart plummets to the soles of my feet anyway, and I cross my arms protectively over my body, as if to hide it, tears prickling at the backs of my eyes.

I might have left high school long ago, but I'm not sure it ever really left *me*. Not if the shame currently flooding my cheeks is anything to go by.

'No, idiot,' hisses Bex Foster, sounding nothing like she does on YouTube, where her entire shtick is based around being the best friend who lives in your phone. 'Of *course* that isn't Rosie Summers. Rosie Summers is *pretty*. And much taller. That's definitely not her.'

'But it was *supposed* to be Rosie Summers?' confirms Millie, who appears to be one of those nice-but-dim girls who're only ever vaguely aware of what's happening. 'Well, that would make more sense, I suppose.'

Everyone nods solemnly, me included. It *would* make a lot more sense if the *real* Rosie Summers was here, instead of me. It would also mean I wouldn't be having to stand here, listening to people discuss me as if they think I can't hear them.

As if I really am invisible.

So far, so painfully familiar.

'So, who are you?' says Sabrina, her eyes narrowed with suspicion as she looks from me to Luna and back again, trying to figure out which one of us she should blame for this mess. 'What are you doing here? This is a private event, and you weren't invited to it.'

'Um, I'm Rosie Winter,' I say quickly, not wanting the timid-looking Luna to get the brunt of her boss's obvious ire. 'And I *was* invited. Look.'

I reach into my pocket for my phone but, of course, it's not there; it's back in the changing room at the pool. Which means I can't show them the email I was sent; the

one that, in my defence, was just addressed to plain old 'Rosie', rather than to Rosie Summers. It was only when I opened the attached booking reservation that I realised who it was *supposed* to have been sent to; but by then, of course, it was too late – physically, I might have been packing up my stuff in a cramped London flat, but mentally I was already on my way to the Highlands. And, by that stage, the thought of turning back was too much to bear.

It still is.

'I did get an email,' I say quietly. 'An invitation to the hotel.' This is technically true. It's just not the *whole* truth, is all.

'Oh, my God,' says Luna, slapping one hand to her mouth as she scrolls frantically through her phone with the other. She looks up at us all with large, anxious eyes.

'Your email addresses are almost the same,' she says, looking as terrified as I feel right now. 'Except yours starts with *"rosie.w"* and hers starts with *"rosie.s"*. I think I . . . I must have sent it to the wrong Rosie.'

There's a tense silence, during which I realise I'm starting to feel a bit woozy, although whether it's from the fact that I just fell asleep in a sauna or the sheer terror of facing Sabrina Bates in a bad mood, I'm not quite sure.

Given the choice, I think I'd rather face the sauna, though. At least it only had the potential to almost kill me, as opposed to completely humiliating me, like Sabrina so clearly wants to.

'The S and the W *are* very close to each other on the keyboard,' says Zara Harris, looking at her own phone as if it's a crucial piece of evidence in a trial. 'The W's right above the S. It would be a pretty easy mistake to make.'

'Exactly,' says Luna, looking relieved.

'Very true,' I add, just a beat too late.

I smile hopefully around the room, even though I can tell by the look on Sabrina's face that there isn't much point in trying to win anyone over here; I'm about to be sent home in disgrace. That's if I don't faint first, from this weird, light-headed feeling.

I can't believe I convinced myself I'd get away with this. How on earth could I have been so stupid?

'How could you be so stupid?' snaps Sabrina, echoing my thoughts so perfectly that I think she's talking to me, until I catch sight of Luna's pale face, and realise she's feeling even worse than I am about all of this. 'You *know* how important this launch is, Luna,' Sabrina goes on. 'It has to be *perfect*. We can't afford to mess this up. God! I can't believe you've done this.'

'That's enough,' says Hunter Stuart, speaking softly but firmly. 'We don't speak to people like that here.'

Beside him, Stevie gets silently to his feet, looking even more wolf-like in this Gothic horror show of a setting. I really want to applaud them both – or give a small cheer at the very least – but the memory of Hunter walking in on me in the sauna is still so painful that I can't even bring myself to look at the man, let alone do something that might make him look at *me*.

(Also, I'm so light-headed after my lengthy stint in there that I'm afraid to move my head in case I faint. So there's that, too.)

'And who might you be?' Sabrina says haughtily, looking him up and down as he stands there in his muddy work boots and worn-out jeans, looking almost as out of place as I do, and yet still somehow completely at ease.

'Oh, I'm nobody,' Hunter says easily. 'But I'm sure I speak for everyone when I say you're being unfair to them both. It sounds like it was an honest mistake.'

OK, now I *do* want to look at him, so I can show him how grateful I am for this defence that I absolutely do not deserve. But he's too busy watching Sabrina to return my glance.

'It was,' says Luna, with a tremulous smile in Hunter's direction. 'It really was, Sabrina, I promise. Summers, Winter . . . Like Zara said, it's an easy mistake to make. Don't you think?'

Sabrina looks like she really wants to disagree with this, but Hunter shifts on the spot, as if to remind her of his presence, and she closes her mouth again.

'OK,' she says, with a theatrical sigh. 'Luna . . . I mean, *we* invited the wrong Rosie. So now we just have to invite the *right* Rosie. Yes?'

'Um, no,' says Luna in a whisper. She holds up her phone. 'I just checked her Instagram,' she goes on. 'Rosie Summers is at another spa hotel. In Iceland. Apparently she's landed some big campaign for WanderNest – you know, the hotel chain?'

There's an audible intake of breath at this piece of news. Dante in particular looks like he's about to explode at the sheer audacity of someone deciding to visit a hotel that isn't his. For a moment, I almost forget I'm the cause of all this drama, then I happen to catch Hunter's eye in the mirror, only for him to swiftly look away again, casually reminding me of my ongoing humiliation.

'Wait!' says Luna frantically, with the air of someone about to save the day. 'I was just thinking, Sabrina. Maybe it's a *good* thing that we have the wrong Rosie.'

Sabrina's lip curls in derision. To be honest, I'm not exactly loving the title 'Wrong Rosie' myself, but it's better than the many alternatives I can see lined up on Sabrina's lips, so I let it go.

'No, seriously,' Luna's saying now, her eyes lit up with an almost religious fervour as she fights for her job – and possibly her life, if Sabrina Bates really is as fearsome as she seems. 'Think about it. We don't have an *average* girl yet, do we? And people love seeing an average girl in these campaigns. It reassures them that they could do all the things they see the influencer doing, too. So, maybe Rosie could be our Ms Average?'

'Hold on a second,' I interject, not sure I like the sound of this any more than I liked the Wrong Rosie thing. But Sabrina's nodding again, her teeth bared in what she presumably thinks a smile looks like. 'People do like *average*, for some reason,' she says, pronouncing the word as if it's an ancient enemy she's been locked in a feud with for decades. 'I suppose it could work.'

'You can't be serious?' says Bex Foster, who's wearing a long black evening gown that makes her look like the star of a film noir. 'You're not paying this . . . impostor person . . . the same as you're paying us, are you?'

Wait: they're all getting *paid* for this? To stay in a luxury – albeit possibly haunted – hotel for *free*?

Wow.

There was definitely nothing in the email I was sent about getting paid; a thought which seems to occur to Sabrina at the same time as it does to me.

'We do need five influencers for the competition,' she says thoughtfully. 'And we've kind of maxed-out the budget already, now that we have Mr Bex here on board. Oh, it's not a problem,' she adds gushingly, turning to the Fosters. 'You know we're absolutely *thrilled* to have you both here. But because Bex and Daniel share an account, they can only really count as one influencer,' she goes on, speaking almost to herself now. 'So I suppose it would be helpful to have a fifth person who wasn't going to cost much.'

Beside me, Hunter shuffles his feet against the tiled floor. 'That hardly seems fair,' he points out mildly. 'If you're paying everyone else, you should surely be paying Rosie, too?'

'Oh, no, that's OK,' I gasp, too dizzy now to think straight. 'I don't need money. I mean, I *do* need money, but . . . um, I wasn't expecting to get any for *this*. So if I'm allowed to stay, that's absolutely fine by me. Being allowed to stay would be all the payment I need.'

My voice is shaking by the end of this short speech; I'm so horribly aware of everyone's eyes on me that it's all I can do to get the words out. But the fact is, I didn't come all this way, and pretend – albeit briefly – to be someone else just because I fancied a trip to the Highlands. I did it because I *need* this. I need this opportunity to change my life, just like the email said it would. I mean, I'm a twenty-nine-year-old office manager who hates her job, and just got dumped. I don't have anywhere to live. I had to max out my credit card to buy that bag of Haribo at the station, and my next direct debit is going to bounce so hard it might hurt someone. Probably me.

So yes, I *do* need the money, as it happens. But, even more than that, I just need a *break*. I need the 'life-changing journey of reinvention' the email promised. And, now that I'm here, I'm not about to let myself be bullied out of it.

For once.

'It's also probably worth remembering that Rosie's just had quite an ordeal in the sauna,' Hunter says, politely refraining from mentioning the fact that he had quite the ordeal himself when he walked in on me. 'She could've been seriously hurt. You're lucky she's not threatening to sue the hotel for negligence.'

'Oh, no, I wouldn't want to—' I begin, stopping abruptly when he elbows me sharply in the side. 'I *am* very thirsty,' I say instead, truthfully. 'And is it just me, or is the room a bit wobbly right now?'

'Here.'

Zara Harris appears at my elbow and hands me a bottle of water in a Chrysalis-branded glass bottle; a small act of kindness which would be enough to make me cry if I wasn't basically just a dried-out husk of a person at this point.

I take the bottle and practically pour it down my throat, gasping in pleasure at the icy coolness of it. I'm not acting – I really am so thirsty I was considering drinking from one of the vases of flowers that are dotted around the foyer until Zara stepped up – but the sight of me guzzling away is the final straw for Sabrina, who gives a single nod, followed by her signature evil glare.

'Dante?' she says, looking at the hotel manager, who's been watching all of this silently, but in a way that suggests he's taking notes in his head for later. 'It's your call. What do you want to do here?'

Dante's dark eyes move slowly up and down my sauna-flushed body, finally landing on my mascara-streaked face. I can almost feel myself shrinking under his gaze. There's no way this man's going to let me stay here. Unless . . .

'I say we let her stay,' he says at last, with a shrug which tells me he's only doing this because he knows it'll annoy Sabrina, and not because he actually wants me here.

No one actually wants me here; a thought that would be more than enough to make me leave of my own accord, if I wasn't too weak with dehydration to make it further than the front door.

'Fine,' Sabrina says, waving her hand dismissively at me. 'You can stay. You've missed dinner, though, so you'll have to make do with room service. Dante will get someone to show you to your room.'

My shoulders sag with relief as everyone stands and starts gathering their things, ready to leave.

'Oh, I almost forgot,' Sabrina adds, spinning on her heel and addressing the room at large. 'Breakfast is at 9 a.m. sharp tomorrow. And we need everyone there, because we'll be giving you the details of the competition. We couldn't do it at dinner because not everyone was there.'

She looks pointedly at me, then turns and strides off, Luna trotting at her heels in the same way Stevie does with Hunter. After a few muddled seconds, the rest of the influencers follow her, and Dante steps back behind the reception desk, leaving me alone with Hunter, who turns around to face me, his arms folded defensively over his chest.

'That wasn't a mistake, was it?' he says bluntly, glancing over at Dante to make sure he can't hear us. 'The invitation. You knew it wasn't meant for you, didn't you?'

'I . . . um . . . it was just addressed to "Rosie",' I begin weakly, but he cuts me off.

'I asked if you were Rosie Summers back at the station,' he says. 'You said you were. Why? Why did you lie?'

I look up at him, grabbing onto the back of a nearby chair in order to keep myself upright.

What am I supposed to say to that? How do you explain what it's like to want to run away to someone who lives in a place like this, and seems so sure of who he is, and what he's doing with his life, that I'm willing to bet he's never once lain awake at night trying to come up with an escape plan?

But *I* have.

And this is it. This is my escape plan; random and ill devised though it may be.

'I just needed a break,' I tell him in a croaky voice that's only partly due to the dehydration. 'And I don't mean a holiday; I mean I needed a *chance*.'

'To do what?' His arms are still crossed, but there's a genuine curiosity in his tone that gives me the courage to go on.

'To be someone else,' I say simply. 'Some*where* else. This place claims to be able to do that.'

Through the window behind him, I can see the tips of the distant mountains, now a soft pink to contrast with the greenish-blue of earlier. The clock on the wall tells me it's past ten o'clock, but there's still light in the sky and magic in the air.

I'm not lying when I say I believe coming here could change my life.

It kind of *has* to.

'Aye,' says Hunter, following the direction of my gaze. 'The Highlands have a way of changing people. I would know.'

He bites his lip, as if he's trying to stop himself saying something else. I really want to ask him what it is, but, before I can find the courage to actually do it, he whistles to Stevie, who comes bounding over from where he's been curled up in front of the fire.

'Well, I'll leave you to it,' says Hunter, abruptly bringing the conversation to an end. 'Make sure you drink plenty of water. You're going to need it.'

Without waiting for a response, he turns and goes striding towards the double doors of the hotel, Stevie at his heels. I stand there for a second, wondering what I said that made him want to get away from me so quickly, until another thought arrives to wipe Hunter Stuart completely from my mind.

What was it Sabrina said to all of us before she went clacking off in her spindly heels earlier?

Competition?

Didn't she say something about a *competition*?

Chapter 5

With Hunter gone, Agnes shows me to my room, which is on the third floor of the hotel, and accessed via at least four different corridors, plus a narrow set of winding stairs, which I'm almost certain I'll be falling down at some point.

I keep my eyes peeled for any sign of ghosts as we make our way through the old castle, but, with the exception of a few of those creepy oil paintings which look like the eyes of the person are following you all the time (one of them looks a lot like Dante, the hotel manager, actually, which makes it even creepier . . .), everything seems fairly normal: in a 'five-star hotel that used to be a castle' kind of way.

Room number six turns out to be in one of the turrets I briefly saw from the driveway, and I coo with delight at the perfectly round room, which has a four-poster bed, and a free-standing bathtub with little gold feet next to one of the windows.

'There's an en-suite shower room through here,' says Agnes, opening a door to reveal a modern bathroom with a rainfall shower and double vanity. 'And this is the wardrobe. It's one of those walk-in ones.'

I sit down on the end of the bed, not sure if my legs are weak from dehydration or just plain excitement.

I can't believe all of this is for *me*.

'The turret rooms are our best suites,' Agnes adds, seeing the look on my face. 'They're super-expensive.'

'I bet,' I reply, lovingly stroking a soft tartan blanket that's draped over the end of the bed.

'Well, I'll let you get some sleep,' Agnes says kindly, seeing me fail to stifle a yawn. 'Your stuff's all been unpacked for you, so you can just relax.'

I watch as she gives a cheerful little wave and leaves the room, before turning back to the bed, which looks so inviting that I waste no time in climbing into it, a bottle of water from the mini fridge clutched firmly in my hand, so I can attempt to rehydrate from a horizontal position.

It's been one hell of a day.

Tomorrow, though, will be better. Tomorrow I'll wake up refreshed, ready to start over. Tomorrow my 'journey of reinvention' will really begin.

Because, let's face it, it's not like it can possibly be any worse.

* * *

The next morning, I wake up to find my makeup imprinted on my pillow, my tongue stuck to the roof of my mouth and a scene straight out of a movie outside my bedroom window.

The room I'm in is at the back of the hotel, and it looks out over a vast formal garden and down to the sea. The sun's just coming up, and the water shines silver in the early-morning light, a solitary seagull soaring high above the waves. The grounds themselves are perfectly symmetrical and it's still early enough that there's a light dusting of morning dew over everything, creating an ethereal, other-worldly effect that doesn't seem quite real. There's even a small, perfectly manicured maze in the centre of the grounds, which I make a mental note *not* to enter, because, the way my luck's being going so far, I'd probably never find my way out of it.

After a quick shower, during which I use each of the expensive toiletries in turn, I put on my best jeans and the new red cashmere sweater I bought the day I got the invitation to the Chrysalis: the magic one, that promised it was going to change my life.

Well, let's just hope it was right about that.

After a final look in the mirror to make sure I don't have lipstick on my teeth, I let myself out of the room, trying my best to remember the directions Agnes gave me to the hotel dining room last night. But it's no good. After five minutes of walking up and down apparently endless corridors, all of which seem absolutely identical to me, I realise I'm hopelessly lost.

Shit.

What do I do now?

I really don't want to be late for breakfast – especially not after the way Sabrina warned us all to be on time – but I'm pretty sure I'm just going around in circles here, and getting nowhere. Quickening my step, I march down the corridor, trying doors at random in the hope that one of them will lead to the staircase I remember from last night. Most of the doors have room numbers on them, and are obviously guest rooms, but finally I come across one that creaks slowly open when I try the handle, with a noise that reminds me of the sound I made when I was trying to get out of the train bathroom yesterday.

Yes, it would appear I really am going to be reliving that moment for the rest of my life, then.

Shaking my head to get rid of the memory, I step quickly through the doorway, and find myself in a large, but cosy room, with a snooker table at one end, a huge TV at the other, and lots of comfortable couches grouped around coffee tables in between. The walls are lined with bookshelves – the kind that you need a ladder to reach the highest shelves – and the windows all look out onto the same view of the sea I have from my room, only from a different angle, in which white-tipped mountains are just visible further along the coast.

The sun's fully up now, but a light mist has come in from the sea, wreathing the building in fog and making it feel a bit like we're floating in a cloud.

How magical.

I step forward for a closer look, and am just about to snap a quick picture of the view with my phone (which Agnes kindly retrieved from the changing room for me last night) when someone clears their throat loudly, making me jump.

'Looking for something?'

I spin around to find Hunter Stuart silently watching me from a high-backed chair by the fire. He's wearing a dark-coloured fleece and jeans, which blend in so well with his surroundings that I didn't even notice him when I walked in.

'Sorry,' I say, my entire body cringing as I remember the last time I saw him. 'I was looking for the dining room. I'm a bit lost.'

'I can see that,' he replies gravely. 'The dining room's on the ground floor. This is the library. Well, it *was* the library. It's now what they're calling the "den". It's where guests can come to relax and "mingle".'

He says the word 'mingle' the way I say 'diet' – as if it's personally offensive to him. I kind of get the impression Hunter Stuart isn't a man given to mingling, somehow.

And now here *I* am, blundering in and destroying his peace and quiet.

'Sorry,' I say again. 'If you could just tell me how to get to the dining room, I'll—'

'You need to stop apologising all the time, Rosie Winter,' Hunter says, getting to his feet. 'You've been apologising since you got here. You apologise just for existing.'

'I've been messing up since I got here,' I point out. 'Since *before* I got here, in fact. So I've had a lot to apologise for.'

He shrugs. 'Maybe. Not all of it was your fault, though. You didn't send yourself that email by mistake, did you? And you weren't the one who jammed the sauna door shut, either.'

'Jammed? It wasn't jammed, was it?' I frown, trying to make sense of this. 'No, it wasn't,' I go on. 'I distinctly remember checking to make sure I could open it, because I didn't want to get stuck in there, like I did in the train toilet.'

'That's what I thought,' says Hunter. 'But the door was definitely stuck when I tried to open it. I had to force it open to get you out.'

I look up at him, my heart skittering nervously in my chest.

'What are you trying to say?' I ask quietly. 'You . . . you think someone did it deliberately?'

My legs feel strangely weak again, just like they did last night when I almost died in the sauna.

OK, I didn't almost *die*.

But I *could* have.

And the thought that someone in this hotel might have been responsible is making me feel like I might just die again; only this time from fear rather than dehydration.

And before anyone gets to see my magic red sweater, too.

'No, no,' says Hunter, making a gesture with his hands as if he's batting away the thought. 'No one here would do something like that. The door must be faulty. I'll take a look at it this morning. Wouldn't want anyone else getting stuck in there. Anyway, come on; I was just about to get to work, so I'll drop you off at the dining room on the way.'

I follow him out of the library/den, wishing he hadn't ended the conversation about the sauna door quite so abruptly. Because I know he was trying to reassure me, but I somehow don't feel reassured. All I feel is a horrible sense of foreboding; and it only intensifies as we make our way through the castle, and back down to the lobby, where Dante is standing behind the reception desk, his jet-black hair and smooth-skinned face making him look a lot like Dracula.

Could *Dante* have locked me in the sauna?

No. That's ridiculous. Why would he, after all?

Why would anyone?

I roll this thought around in my mind as Hunter leads me through the lobby and into yet another corridor, before stopping so suddenly that I walk right into him.

'Whoops! Sorry,' I say, quickly removing my foot from his ankle. 'I was in another world, there.'

'Apologising again, Rosie Winter?' he says with a smile of amusement. 'Didn't I tell you to stop that? Or at least save the apologies for when you've actually done something worth apologising for.'

'Sor— Right. Got it,' I reply. 'Got any other advice for me while we're here?'

Hunter looks at me speculatively.

'Well, since you ask,' he says. 'You might want to try valuing yourself a bit higher. You caved way too quickly last night on the payment thing. If everyone else here is being paid to take a few photos, why shouldn't you?'

'Because I'm not a real influencer,' I remind him, much as it pains me to do it. 'I'm not even supposed to be here, remember? And I don't have nearly as many followers as the rest of them. So I'm not as valuable to the hotel as they are.'

Hunter's eyebrows twitch, but I can't tell whether he's surprised or just amused by this.

'That's only true if you judge your "value" in terms of followers,' he replies, in an unmistakably sarcastic tone. 'Which is a really weird way to make yourself feel bad for absolutely no reason. Look, all I'm saying is, don't sell yourself short, Rosie,' he adds, in a softer voice. 'Everyone has value. Even Sabrina. Well, probably.'

'Is this a pep talk?' I reply suspiciously. 'Or a motivational speech? Because you kind of ruined it with the ending, if so.'

'Just a bit of friendly advice,' he replies, shrugging. 'You can take it or leave it. It's no skin off my nose. I don't even have an Instagram account, so I'm the least "valuable" person here, according to your way of thinking.'

I open my mouth to argue with this, because it's absolutely *not* what I meant, but he pushes the doors open before I can speak, revealing a large, formal dining room; the kind you always see in period dramas or stately homes, with a single, long table in the centre of the room, and a chandelier dangling above it. I'm sure I remember seeing another restaurant on the hotel's website too – a more normal-looking one, with lots of smaller tables to seat different groups of people – so this must be the room they use to host private functions.

Like influencer press stays, for instance.

The room falls suspiciously silent as I enter; a sure sign that the small group of women (and one man) seated around the table have just been talking about me, and one that's painfully familiar to me from my school days.

So, we're off to a great start, then.

'Isn't that your granny's sweater, Bex?' says Daniel Foster suddenly; a statement so utterly random that it takes a moment for me to realise he's referring to me, as I stand there awkwardly in the doorway. 'Is she wearing your granny's sweater?'

'Oh. My. God,' squeals his wife. 'She *is*. I can't believe this. You're wearing my granny's sweater,' she tells me. 'That's so funny.'

I look down at my outfit, confused to be thrown into a conversation about grannies and their clothing choices.

'Um, no, it isn't your *granny's*,' I explain, tugging self-consciously at the sweater in question and wondering if I've stepped into some kind of alternative reality. 'It's *mine*. I bought it. I didn't steal it.'

'Oh, no, of course not,' says Bex, her eyes wide with innocence. 'And I think it's a really bold choice, actually. I mean, it's not easy pulling off an old lady sweater like that, but you're just over here rocking it anyway, aren't you? Well done, you.'

She smiles sweetly and I open and close my mouth uselessly, not knowing what to say to this. I genuinely can't tell whether she's being nice or if she's just a straight-up bitch. And, either way, she's just made it very clear that the outfit I so carefully picked out is completely *wrong*.

'You can't call it an "old lady sweater",' points out Zara Harris, from the other side of the table. 'That's ageist, Bex.'

'No, it isn't,' Bex replies, tossing her glossy hair over her shoulder. 'Some old ladies are very stylish, Zara. I meant it as a compliment. I think it's very brave of Wrong Rosie to try to pull off something like that. I would *never*.' She smiles again, and this time there's no mistaking her meaning.

'Well, I think it's rather nice,' says Daniel gallantly, as if he's trying to make up for his wife's now-blatant bitchiness. Bex glares at him, and I look down at my 'lucky' sweater, which is turning out to be not-so-lucky after all, and then back up at Bex; who's *also* turning out to be a bit of a disappointment, as it happens. On social media, she always seems so *nice*; the kind of girl you can easily imagine being best friends with. And yet, here she is, somehow managing to make me feel like I'm fifteen again, and turning up at school in my sister's hand-me-downs, or something my mum had unearthed from the depths of a charity shop, because she couldn't afford to buy us new clothes.

I glance over my shoulder, hoping Hunter might have some more words of wisdom for me, but he isn't there. He must have slipped off at some point during the whole 'granny's sweater' conversation. It's hard to blame him, really. Instead, to my mounting horror, the doors swing open again and Sabrina Bates comes through them, wearing something that looks like it's made of papier mâché, but which is presumably high fashion.

'Oh, good,' she says brightly, looking around the room. 'You're all here. Is everyone ready to hear about the competition?'

Chapter 6

A few minutes later I'm sitting at the oversized dining table with an equally oversized cooked breakfast in front of me while Sabrina confirms my worst fear: this isn't just a cushy little all-expenses paid hotel stay I've landed – it's a competition.

And, even worse than that, it's a *popularity* competition.

'Right,' says Sabrina, pouring herself a cup of black coffee and waving away the waiter's offer of food as if it's the most ridiculous suggestion she's ever heard. 'Let's do some quick icebreaker exercises first, shall we? Just to get to know each other, seeing as we're all going to be effectively living together for the next few days.'

Excellent: that's two of my worst fears checked off, and we're not even finished breakfast yet.

'Do we *have* to?' says Millie, pouting. 'I think we already all know each other, don't we?'

Everyone nods eagerly, especially me.

'I don't do icebreakers,' says Yasmin Hussein, speaking for the first time. 'My agent should have told you that.'

She's wearing her dark glasses perched on top of her head this morning, and her skin is so flawless she almost doesn't look real. I seem to remember there were rumours of her being invited onto some kind of reality TV show a few months ago, so I expect this is all a bit beneath her, really.

'Look,' says Zara, in her matter-of-fact way, pushing her cloud of hair out of her eyes. 'We do all know each other – well, all except Rosie. And I think Rosie's well and truly broken the ice already, so . . .'

Every eye in the room swivels to me.

'It *would* be nice to get to know Rosie a little better, though, wouldn't it?' says Bex innocently, a glint of mischief in her eye which Sabrina totally misses; probably because she doesn't seem to be particularly familiar with the concept of normal human emotions. 'Maybe *she* should do the icebreaker?'

'OK, OK,' Sabrina sighs, refilling her coffee cup, having drained the last one already. 'Why don't you tell us a bit about yourself, Rosie?'

I reluctantly put down my cutlery, hoping to God I don't have egg on my face – literally or otherwise.

'Um, well, I'm Rosie Winter,' I begin, wondering if I should stand up, as if I'm giving a presentation at work, then deciding against it. 'As you know. I'm from London, and I'm an office manager. I, er . . . that's it, really.'

I pluck a slice of toast off my plate and take a bite, wracking my brain for something vaguely interesting I could tell them about myself, but it's no use: I've got nothing here. I'm fairly sure they're not going to want to hear about my siblings' kids, for instance, whom I spend most of my time with when I'm not at work – or, well, *shopping* – and they definitely won't want to hear about how I'm going to have to sleep on my sister's couch if I can't find somewhere else to live soon.

So, yeah: there's really not a lot to tell about my life right now. Or nothing *good*, anyway. Which is, of course, the main reason I'm here.

'Wait. You have a job other than Instagram?' says Millie, her little rosebud mouth forming an 'O' of astonishment.

'Well, yeah,' I reply, tearing chunks out of the poor piece of toast. 'I . . . haven't been on Instagram very long, really. I'm not like all of you.'

Bex gives a 'you don't say' kind of snort, and I'm actually relieved, for once, when Sabrina interrupts, having presumably heard enough about me for one lifetime.

'Right,' she says, putting her coffee cup down so firmly I'm surprised it doesn't break. 'Let's get on with it, shall we? So, as you all know, you've been invited here to do some pre-launch social media publicity for this wonderful hotel, which officially opens to the public next week. What you *don't* know, though,' she adds coyly, 'is that when we came up with the agenda for this week, we decided to make things a little more interesting, with an exciting competition.'

She pauses so everyone except me can 'ooh' and 'ahh' obligingly. I just sit there with a horrible, sick feeling in the pit of my stomach, which I'm pretty sure is only partly due to the speed at which I just inhaled my breakfast.

Well, I did miss dinner last night . . .

'Luna?' snaps Sabrina, looking at her assistant, who's watching her as if she's hearing all of this for the first time, along with the rest of us.

'Oh. Right,' says Luna, plucking an iPad from the table in front of her and holding it up so we can all see it. 'Welcome to the Face of the Chrysalis Contest.'

She pushes a button, and the screen bursts into life, photos and video clips of the hotel scrolling across the screen, accompanied by a voice-over explaining that the Chrysalis is looking for someone to be the face of the brand: someone who'll spend a full year under contract with the hotel, staying there one weekend every month (all expenses paid, naturally . . .) and creating content to promote the Highland's most popular wellness retreat.

'We just put in that last bit to make it sound good,' says Luna, putting the iPad down again. 'It hasn't actually opened yet so we don't really know if it's going to be popular, but—'

'Luna!' snaps Sabrina again. 'Of *course* it's going to be popular. Especially with all of these amazingly influential people on board.'

'And Rosie, too,' says Bex, beaming as if she's paying me a compliment.

Sabrina beams around the table as if she's bestowing a very great gift upon us all. Although she's obviously making an effort to be a bit less abrasive than she was last night, her strained smile and jerky movements suggest an undercurrent of stress that would almost make me feel sorry for her, if she wasn't so incredibly difficult to like.

'Now,' she goes on. 'The details. It's pretty straightforward, actually. All you have to do is what you usually do; take photos, make videos, post them on your socials. We've given each of you a unique referral code to give to your followers, and at the end of the week, the person – or couple – who've referred the most bookings will become the face – or faces – of the hotel. It's as simple as that. The codes are in the information packs Luna's handing out now. Oh, and you'll find an updated itinerary for the stay in there, too: we've made a few changes since we put together the last one.'

Luna gets to her feet and makes her way around the table, distributing glossy, cardboard files, which contain some printed information about the hotel, along with its key messages ('Let the Highlands heal you'; 'Rest, rejuvenate, rediscover'; 'The start of your next chapter'), some 'talking points' and, of course, our unique referral codes. Mine is 'ROSIESUMMERS'. I'm sure that won't be confusing for people at all.

Sabrina smiles again as we all rifle through our information packs, although this time most of her energy is directed at Bex and Daniel, and there's no mistaking who she's expecting to become the faces of the hotel.

'Sounds great, Sabrina,' says Bex, looking smug.

'But let's talk figures,' adds her husband, leaning forward and making a little pyramid with his hands, which he stares at her over the top of like a James Bond villain. 'You said the winner would get a year-long contract. So, how much are we talking?'

'I thought you might ask that,' replies Sabrina, producing a piece of paper, which she slides across the table to Daniel and Bex, who look at it, then slide it over to Yasmin. She passes it to Zara, who passes it to Millie, who's about to pass it back to Sabrina when I clear my throat to remind her I'm still here, and she reluctantly hands it to me instead.

Well, I know I have absolutely no chance of actually winning this thing, but I have to admit, I'm curious to know how much a contract like that would be worth. Like, would it be enough to pay the deposit on a new flat, say, or just enough to—

'Holy shit, you must be kidding me!'

I don't even realise I've spoken out loud until I feel everyone's eyes upon me yet again, and I look up to see them all staring.

'Sorry,' I mutter, looking down at the figure written on the piece of paper, which would not only let me rent somewhere on my own, but pay off my credit card, too. 'Is this real, though? Because this is . . . wow.'

This is a life-changing amount of money; not for a *normal* person, you understand, but certainly for someone like me, with a shopping addiction that's landed her in tons of debt and a dead-end job that doesn't even come close to paying for it all.

With the money from this contract, I could clear my debts, and find somewhere to live. I could leave my job and try to figure out what I actually want to do with myself when I'm not having to spend all my time doing a job I hate.

(I could also buy that really nice coat I've had my eye on, but it seems wrong to bring that up right after the whole 'paying off the debt caused by my shopping addiction' thing, so let's just stick with the life-changing bit for now. The coats can come later.)

'It's not going to be *you*, though, is it?' says Bex, voicing the thought that's surely on everyone's mind. 'Because you're not actually an influencer, are you?'

She treats me to another one of her sugary, fake smiles, and a tiny spark of anger ignites somewhere in my chest.

I can't believe how different she is from her online persona.

I guess at least I'm not the only person here who's been pretending to be someone she's not.

Bex might be a toxic nightmare, however, but the fact is, she isn't *wrong*: it's definitely not going to be me who wins this thing. Not unless I actually *do* somehow manage to completely change my personality in the next four days; which now seems about as realistic a prospect as the stupid idea I had of me and Bex becoming friends.

'Does anyone have any questions?' asks Sabrina. 'No? Well, then. Let's go and create some content.'

There's a scrape of seats as everyone gets to their feet, ready to leave.

'Oh, one last thing,' calls out Sabrina, raising a hand to stop us. 'You're free to enjoy the hotel and the grounds,' she says, 'but please make sure you stay out of the private areas, which are all clearly signposted. I'm not sure if you know this, but the hotel is owned by Lord Glenmuir, who I believe has quite a fearsome reputation, and he's made it very clear that he doesn't want anyone wandering around the family's private quarters.'

'A lord?' says Millie immediately. 'Really? Is he single?'

'A widower, I believe,' replies Sabrina. 'He's eighty-two, though,' she goes on. 'So I'd be very surprised if he was in the market for a new wife.'

'I wouldn't be,' says Zara in a low voice that only I catch. 'Boys will be boys, right? Even old ones.'

I smile, my interest piqued at the thought of the curmudgeonly old lord tucked away somewhere in the castle, maybe looking down on us all from one of the turrets.

I wonder what he thinks of all of this? The pool, and the sauna, and the . . . is that a hot tub I can see on the other side of this window? A huge one, with a view out over the ornamental gardens and maze?

It is.

This really is a beautiful hotel. And although it's worlds away from my life in London, and almost everyone I've met so far has been needlessly hostile to me, I'm still grateful to be here, influencer competition and all.

I really wish I had a shot at winning that.

Wouldn't it be amazing to come back here every month and really enjoy the place without having to worry about competing with the fellow guests to be the face of an ad campaign?

But, right now, that's what I'm going to have to do if I want to earn my keep, and not be kicked out, like I almost was last night. And, as much as I know the odds of winning are definitely not in my favour, I can't help but feel just a *little* bit excited as we all file out of the dining room and go our separate ways.

The Chrysalis describes itself as a place of rebirth and reinvention, and that's exactly what I'm going to get out of this. A whole new me. A *right* Rosie to replace the wrong one who arrived here.

And, even if I don't win the competition, at least I'll have fun trying.

Right?

Chapter 7

Wrong.

I will *not*, as it turns out, be having much fun trying.

Or not so far, anyway.

First of all, it takes me a good twenty minutes to find my way back to my room, and I only manage it in the end by enlisting the help of Agnes, who kindly shows me the way, and tells me she'll try to draw a map for me when she has a spare moment.

Once I get to the room, though, I pull off the red 'granny' sweater and wrench the wardrobe doors open only to find, like Mother Hubbard herself, that the cupboard is completely bare.

'Where are my clothes?' I demand seventeen minutes later, having somehow made my way back down to the lobby, where Dante looks at me as if I'm hurting his eyes.

'You're . . . wearing them?' he says, looking pointedly at the wretched sweater, which I was forced to hurriedly put back on again, considering it's now one of the only things I have. 'Which is certainly an improvement on last night, I must say. I've been meaning to speak to you about that, actually. I know you'd just arrived, but the Chrysalis *does* have a strict dress code and we do ask that guests be fully clothed at all times. Robes don't count, just FYI. Not outside of the spa area.'

'Thanks for the fashion advice,' I snap, the stress of the moment making me forget to apologise for once in my life, 'but I don't mean *these* clothes. I mean the ones in my room. They're not there. They're . . . g-gone.'

I started off strong, with an assertive, *I will take no shit from you* tone that would've made Hunter Stuart proud if he'd only been here to see it. But I end on the kind of muffled wail that would make even a *banshee* proud, and that's not exactly the impression I was hoping to make here.

Luckily, though, it at least makes Dante take me seriously.

'Gone?' he says, his handsome face arranging itself into a frown. 'What do you mean they're gone?'

'Just that,' I tell him, managing to get a grip of myself again. 'I went into my room to get changed, and the wardrobe is empty. Someone's taken all my clothes.'

Dante pulls a face that suggests he very much doubts that anyone would want my clothes.

'Are you sure?' he asks. 'Were you definitely in the right room? Agnes mentioned you keep getting lost?'

'This is the only key I have,' I tell him, holding it up. The rooms at the Chrysalis all have old-fashioned locks rather than swipe cards, and the room number is clearly visible on the tag. 'Surely it won't let me into any other room but mine?'

'No. It wouldn't,' Dante says, picking up a phone from the reception desk and pressing a button on it. 'Look, leave it with me. I'm sure it's just some kind of misunderstanding. I'll look into it for you.'

He turns away to mutter something into the phone, leaving me standing there with my mouth hanging open as I wonder what to do next. I can't even imagine what kind of 'misunderstanding' could result in all of my clothes vanishing over breakfast.

No, that seems more like something someone must have done on purpose.

But who?

And, well, *why*?

The thing is, everyone connected with the influencer campaign was already at breakfast when I arrived; sure, Sabrina was a few minutes late, but not late enough that she'd have been able to get into my room without a key, and steal all of my clothes. Which just leaves the hotel staff. Lovely Agnes, who I refuse to believe is capable of messing with anyone, let alone a guest. Dante, who *has* been pretty sneery about my dress sense, to be fair, but whose surprise at the Mystery of the Missing Clothes seems genuine. Or . . .

'Hello again. Still here, are you? They haven't kicked you out yet?'

Hunter Stuart.

'Oh. It's you,' I say, turning to face him, then almost falling over as a giant ball of fur in the shape of Stevie the wolf-dog comes barrelling at me.

'Er, aye. It is. Have I done something to justify that frosty response?' Hunter replies, his brow creasing in confusion.

'I don't know. *Have* you?' I shoot back, the dignified effect I was going for somewhat ruined by the fact that Stevie's currently trying to wash my face with his tongue.

'Sorry,' I mutter, seeing the confused look on Hunter's face, and realising I have absolutely no proof that he's the clothes thief either. 'I'm just having a bad morning.'

I quickly fill him in on the influencer competition, and the missing clothes drama.

'I see,' he says gravely as I reach the end of my sorry tale. 'So you reckon someone wants you out of the picture, then? A sabotage attempt, to ruin your chances of becoming Miss Chrysalis?'

'Er, no, not really,' I reply, taken aback. 'That sounds a bit far-fetched, don't you think? They're content creators, not the Mafia. And it's not "Miss Chrysalis" either, it's just a silly competition.'

'One with quite a lot of money at stake, though,' points out Hunter, stroking his chin thoughtfully. 'I'd be watching my back, if I were you. And my bed.'

'My bed? Wh—What's going to happen to my bed?'

'Well, you might find a horse's head in it one of these nights,' he replies seriously. 'Maybe even tonight.'

'Do you really think so?' I breathe, my palms sweaty at the thought that I might have inadvertently gotten myself embroiled in the kind of drama I'm more used to watching on TV than participating in.

'No, of course not,' says Hunter, with a grin that shows a row of very white, even teeth. 'That would be insane. This is the Scottish Highlands, Rosie, not 1940s Sicily.'

He chuckles quietly to himself, and my sweaty palms start itching to strangle him.

'You're not funny, you know,' I say fiercely, finally managing to get Stevie off me. 'And this might be a big joke to you, but it's important to me. I need my clothes. I can't just wear the same outfit for four days.'

Especially not one Bex Foster described as an 'old lady sweater'. That's exactly the kind of misstep that made me spend my teenage years being referred to as Raggedy Rosie, or sometimes Rosie the Reject, depending on which of my three sisters' hand-me-downs I was wearing that day.

I do *not* want to go back to that time, but that's exactly what it's going to feel like if I can't find my clothes, not to mention the fact that, unlike everyone else here, who presumably just packed enough for the four day stay, *I* had to bring everything I own, on account of having nowhere else to store it all.

I haven't lost just a few outfits here; I've lost literally *everything*.

And there's absolutely no way I can afford to replace it all.

'No, that would be a true disaster, right enough,' says Hunter, who's wearing almost exactly what he had on yesterday. 'Social death. I'm not sure how you'd live with yourself.'

He grins, and I scowl back at him. I might have guessed Mr I Hate Influencers wouldn't understand the seriousness of the situation.

'At least it'll give you an excuse to go to your "happy place", though,' he says teasingly, making scare quotes around the words. 'So that's a bit of good news, no?'

'This isn't about shopping, Hunter,' I reply, a little too sharply. 'Whether you like it or not, your clothes say something about you. They're how people judge you. And I . . . I don't want to be judged.'

My voice shakes a little as I say this, and Hunter blinks at me in surprise.

'Look, relax; I'm sure your stuff'll turn up soon,' he says, scratching his head awkwardly. 'It can't have gone far. Maybe one of the housekeepers took it by accident when they were cleaning the room.'

'How many are there, do you know?' I ask, wondering how anyone could 'accidentally' steal clothes. 'Housekeepers, I mean.'

'Oh, at least a dozen, I think,' Hunter says vaguely. 'But there's only three on duty this week, because there's just you lot staying for now.'

'And Lord Glenmuir, presumably,' I say, remembering. 'Hey, what's he like?' I go on, still curious about the man rich enough to own an entire castle. 'You must have met him?'

'The Laird? Aye, I've met him all right,' Hunter says, scratching his head as if he doesn't really want to answer this question. 'Cranky old bugger he is. I'd try to keep out of his way if I were you.'

'Right. Well, I guess I can cross him off my list of suspects,' I say gloomily. 'I just wish I knew what's happened to the clothes. I really need them so I can take photos of the hotel.'

'You're going to dress the hotel in clothes?' Hunter's eyebrows shoot almost into his hairline, but the smirk tugging at his lips is cheeky – a private joke just between me and him.

'No,' I reply, returning the smile in spite of myself. 'The clothes are for me. I need to take photos of myself enjoying my stay here. For the contest, you know?'

'Ah. Right. But you're *not* enjoying your stay here, are you? What with the missing clothes, and the jammed sauna, and that Becky one prancing around like she owns the place.'

'Bex,' I correct him. She might be a tough nut, but I believe in showing respect to others, even if they don't necessarily show you any. 'Her name's Bex. And enjoying myself isn't really the point. The point is to make it *look* like I'm enjoying it, so that my followers think *they'd* enjoy it too.'

'A lofty goal,' observes Hunter. He's about to say something else but right at that moment there's a clatter of heels, and Bex and Daniel appear, both of them wheeling matching, monogrammed suitcases, which I instantly covet.

'Are you checking out?' I ask, surprised.

'Of course not, Wrong Rosie,' replies Bex chirpily. 'We didn't get a shot of us arriving last night because the light was all wrong, so we're going to recreate it now. Are you ready, Daniel?'

By way of answer, Daniel unzips his suitcase and produces a tripod with a camera attached to it, and a set of studio lights, which he begins setting up in the foyer.

'Give me strength,' mutters Hunter, his mouth twitching with suppressed laughter.

For Bex and Daniel, though, this is no laughing matter. I watch, fascinated, as they set their professional-looking camera up on the tripod, then go outside with their suitcases, only to walk back through the front doors a few seconds later, cooing with appreciation as they pretend to see the interior of the hotel for the first time.

They do this another five times before I finally get bored and turn to Hunter . . . who isn't there. Once again, he's managed to disappear on me, almost as if he was never there to start with.

Or as if he were a ghost.

The thought reminds me of the figure I thought I saw on the stairs last night, but I shake off the chill that runs through me at the memory and head out into the hotel grounds, muttering a quick apology to Bex and Daniel for ruining shot number six in the process.

Once outside, I walk down the steps, then turn and look up at the hotel.

The building is so beautiful it almost doesn't seem real, with old stone walls rising up from the immaculate grounds and turreted rooftops which remind me of Rapunzel's tower; although hopefully without anyone trapped inside them. The long driveway stretches out before me, and, through the mist which is still hovering over everything, I see Zara and Millie taking it in turns to photograph each other posing in front of the gates at the bottom of it.

Which reminds me why I'm here.

Ignoring the feeling of foreboding that's still following me, I find a large stone in the driveway and prop my phone up against it, switching on the self-timer, then racing back to the top of the stairs to pose for the camera. I keep on doing this until I'm red in the face and uncomfortably sweaty, but when I scroll back through the photos in my camera roll, I realise I've got the timing all wrong, and most of the shots just show me either racing towards the steps with my backside the main focus of the photo, or reaching out to pick up the camera again, looking like I have five chins.

This influencing business is much harder than people think it is.

There's not much I can do about it, though, because Zara and Millie have finished their photo shoot at the gates and are now making their way towards me. I really don't want them to witness my pathetic attempts at content creation so I hold up the phone and snap a quick selfie with the castle in the background. When I check the shot, I see that the castle appears to have dropped in from the set of a Disney movie, while I look a lot like someone's thumb got stuck in front of the lens. It's too late, though; the influencers are almost upon me, so I turn and make my way around to the back of the building, uploading the photo to my feed as I go.

Just checked in to the hotel of my dreams for a bit of rest, rejuvenation and rediscovery, I type into the caption box, feeling pleased with myself for remembering to add one of the key messages from the information pack. *So far, the Highlands are everything I hoped for and more!*

Then I tag the hotel and add my #ROSIESUMMERS tracking code, before hitting publish, with a heavy feeling of doom in my chest that's completely at odds with the perky caption I've just typed.

So far, the Highlands actually *aren't* 'everything I hoped for and more'. In fact, so far my stay at the Chrysalis has been one humiliation after another.

I can't admit that to my Instagram followers, though. That's not going to win me the competition; or any friends, for that matter. So I'm just going to have to pretend to be having the time of my life, instead. What's that they say about faking it until you make it?

That's what I'm going to have to do.

The back of the hotel is even more impressive than the front, with the grounds leading down to a little private beach which is covered with the kind of flawless white sand I didn't think existed outside of the Caribbean, let alone in Scotland. It's peaceful out here, so I take my time as I wander among the flower beds, stopping at one point beside a large, circular pond, the surface of which is so still it looks almost like glass.

I'm just thinking how amazing it would look in a photo, and how annoying it is that I don't have a handy Instagram husband, like Bex does, to take one for me, when the sound of chopping breaks the silence, and I follow it instead, down one of the narrow gravel paths that wind between the flower beds, and all the way to the entrance to the maze, in front of which I find Hunter Stuart attacking a defenceless little tree with an axe.

'Oh no, don't!' I cry out before I can stop myself, making Hunter stop abruptly, the axe still raised above his head. The position has made the T-shirt he's wearing ride up, showing a thin slice of a very toned stomach which makes my mouth feel strangely dry. The fleece top he had on earlier this morning is lying by his feet, and there's a slight sheen of sweat on his brow in spite of the early morning chill. He looks like some kind of outdoorsy action man – part lumberjack, part Highland warrior – and I lick my lips nervously, trying not to stare at the way the muscles in his arms flex as he lowers the axe.

'Stop what?' he asks, in a dangerous tone, glowering at me.

'Um, well, stop attacking that poor tree,' I reply, pointing at it stupidly. 'It's so cute; like a little Christmas tree.'

'It's like a falling-down Christmas tree,' Hunter replies grimly. 'One that would probably break you in two if it fell on you, Rosie Winter.'

'Oh. I . . . didn't realise,' I say, wondering if he absolutely *has* to sound quite so pleased at the prospect.

'It got damaged in the big storm we had last week. If I don't take it down, it'll take someone *else* down in the next one, and then we'll get ourselves sued,' he goes on, raising the axe again as if he's done with this conversation. 'So I'm not sure "cute" is the word I'd use for it.'

'Got it,' I mutter, feeling like the silly city girl he so obviously thinks I am. 'It's a killer tree, not a cute one. I'll bear that in mind.'

I'm just about to slink off again, having annoyed him for long enough, when something occurs to me.

'Er, I don't suppose you'd do me a quick favour, would you?' I blurt, crossing my fingers tightly behind my back for luck.

Hunter lowers the axe again with the air of a man whose patience is being sorely tested.

'Depends what it is,' he replies warily. 'And how quick it is. Some of us have real work to do here.'

'Oh, it'll be quick,' I assure him, wishing I hadn't asked if this is how he's going to be. 'Seconds, really. All I need you to do is take a photo of me next to that lake over there. One photo. Well, maybe two if the first one doesn't work out.'

'I'm a gardener, Rosie, not a photographer,' Hunter points out, his mouth settling into a straight line. 'Wouldn't you be better off asking one of the influencer lot?'

'No. I don't trust them,' I confess. 'I don't really trust anyone in this place.'

'Not even me?' he asks. 'Am I still on the list of suspects, then? Och, don't look at me like that,' he goes on. 'I know you were thinking I might have done the clothes-stealing thing earlier.'

'Well, you *do* like winding me up,' I point out. 'And you know how important my clothes are to me. I don't think you'd have shut me in the sauna, though,' I add, shivering at the memory. 'That wouldn't be a very good joke, would it?'

A small line appears between Hunter's eyes.

'No, it wouldn't. The door was just stiff, though,' he says, sounding almost as if he's trying to convince himself as much as he is me. 'I went over and took a look at it this morning. It's probably just because it's brand new. There's bound to be some teething problems.'

I nod, remembering what Agnes said about 'Danger Night', and how we influencers were basically a test crew, here to help the hotel iron out any potential problems before launch day.

Well, you have to hand it to me, I've definitely done that.

'So, will you take the photo for me?' I ask, desperate to change the subject.

I hold out my phone and he takes it with a world-weary sigh.

'Lead the way, then,' he says, putting his axe carefully down on the ground. 'Let's get this over with.'

Chapter 8

Twenty minutes later, I'm on my way back to the hotel, feeling much better now that I've flicked through the surprisingly decent photos Hunter Stuart took of me standing by the lake, with both the castle and my red-sweatered self perfectly reflected in its mirror-like surface.

Maybe this jumper *is* made of magic, after all?

Or maybe the magic comes from . . . but no. I will *not* think of Hunter Stuart the way I thought of my cashmere sweater when I found it; as if he, too, is something with the potential to change my life. I'm only here for four days, after all. I'll never see him again after that. And there's no point kidding myself he'd be interested in the 'average' girl, when he's clearly so far above average himself: I know from experience that's not how it works. You can trust the girl who got dumped on her birthday to tell you that.

'Have you found my clothes yet?' I ask Dante as I walk back into the hotel lobby, which is now mercifully empty of influencers.

'Yes. Yes we have, actually,' replies the manager, raising one eyebrow like a cartoon villain.

'Seriously? But that's fantastic,' I exclaim, hardly daring to believe my change of fortune. 'So, where were they?'

'They were in the wardrobe,' replies Dante, staring at me impassively. 'The one in your room. Where you left them.'

'But . . . no, that can't be right,' I say, confused. 'The wardrobe was empty. I saw it with my own eyes.'

'Maybe you should book an eye test when you get home?' suggests Dante, drumming his fingers impatiently against the desk. 'It sounds like you need one.'

'I do *not*,' I reply indignantly, even though I actually *do* need to book an eye test, as it happens. I might be short-sighted, but my eyesight isn't bad enough for me to think the wardrobe in my room was empty when it was, in fact, full . . . which means someone in this hotel is definitely messing with me.

And I'm determined to find out who it is. Ideally before I fully morph back into my much younger self, the way I almost did in the dining room this morning, when my response to Bex's low-key bullying was to want to burst into tears rather than to fight back.

I don't want that to happen again. I don't want to be *that* person again; not after all these years, and . . . well, all of the things I've *bought* that person, in my ongoing bid to make her less of a target to people like Bex Foster and her sidekicks.

That's why I need my clothes back. Because I'd never admit it to someone like Hunter Stuart, who thinks I'm just a superficial shopaholic, but clothes are my armour – and sometimes a disguise. And, right now, I've never been more in need of both of those things.

'You need to do something about this,' I tell Dante, pulling myself up to my full height – all five foot five of it. 'You need to launch an investigation.'

'An *investigation*?' he replies, not even bothering to hide his amusement. 'To find out who *didn't* take your clothes?'

'But someone did take them,' I insist, refusing to allow him to gaslight me on this. 'They must have.'

'And then brought them back again?' says the manager. 'So, this mystery person basically just took these clothes of yours for a walk, did they?'

'I . . . don't know what they did with them,' I say, faltering in my conviction. 'Or why they brought them back. But I know it happened, and now you need to find out who it was.'

'I hate to break this to you,' says Dante, with a world-weary sigh, 'but I'm a hotel manager, not Miss Marple. If you'd like to call the police and report your clothes as *not* missing, then by all means, go ahead. I'm sure they'll send someone over in a few days. We don't exactly have a large team of police at our disposal this far north.'

He pushes the phone on the desk towards me, and I push it right back at him, frustrated beyond belief.

'I know I'm staying here for free,' I say, with as much dignity as I can muster, 'but I'm still a guest. And I'm . . . well, I'm *upset*.'

To my horror, my eyes obediently fill with tears, as if to prove this. Fortunately, though, it seems that a crying woman is the very last thing Dante wants to have to deal with (well, the second-last thing; the mysterious case of the missing clothes being the first . . .), and he carefully rearranges his expression into one of concern.

'Of course, of course,' he says, trying to sound reassuring. 'Look, why don't you go up to your room and relax? The kitchen's about to send up some afternoon tea to everyone soon. And I'll, er, have another word with the staff about the . . . other thing.'

'Thank you,' I say quietly. 'I would appreciate that.'

I turn and march towards the staircase, hesitating as I reach it.

'Third floor, second corridor on the left,' says Dante helpfully.

'Thanks,' I say again. 'Sorry.'

Then, groaning inwardly at the needless apology, and feeling grateful that Hunter Stuart at least isn't here to witness it, I go slinking off in what I hope is the direction of my room.

*   *   *

It takes me just fifteen minutes to find my way this time (which I'm quite pleased about, because it means I've shaved two minutes off my previous record), and a mere thirty seconds to cross the room to the wardrobe, which, sure enough, is filled with clothes, just as it was when I left the room this morning, before breakfast.

'You've got to be kidding me,' I groan, flicking quickly through them to make sure everything's there. 'Don't get me wrong, clothes, I'm pleased to see you all again, but I really wish you could tell me where you've been.'

The clothes just hang there silently, though, with absolutely no signs of where they've been, or what they've been up to. I throw myself onto the bed and allow myself to lie there for a bit, wallowing in my misery, and wondering if I might have a brain tumour, or some other affliction that's making me see things – or *not* see things, as the case may be.

I *am* starting to talk to my clothes, after all, and that can't be a good sign, can it?

Eventually, though, there's a knock at the door, and I haul myself up to answer it to Agnes, who's carrying a tray laden with what she tells me is a Highland-themed afternoon tea. As well as a wide selection of scones, there are also tiny haggis bonbons, miniature bagels filled with smoked salmon and something Agnes describes as Cullen

Skink tartlets, which she assures me taste much better than they sound.

'Wait,' she says, as I raise one to my mouth, ready to put this to the test. 'Aren't you supposed to be taking photos of this kind of thing?'

I lower the tartlet guiltily.

'It's a good job you're here,' I tell her, picking up my phone instead. 'I'm not exactly doing a great job of "influencing", am I? It didn't even occur to me to take a photo of it rather than just eat it.'

'Och, you'll soon get the hang of it,' says Agnes, smiling reassuringly. 'Here, I can help you, if you like.'

She spends a few minutes rearranging things on the tray, then gets me to sit behind the table and pretend to be eating one of the little cakes, while she takes some photos with my phone.

'Just pretend, mind,' she says sternly, instructing me to move to where the light's apparently more flattering. 'You don't want to smudge your lipstick by actually eating it.'

I do as she says, feeling horribly self-conscious as I pretend to tuck into the food, my stomach rumbling in protest the entire time. I've been an influencer for less than twenty-four hours, and I'm already getting tired of all of the pretending I'm having to do.

'Have *you* ever considered being an influencer, Agnes?' I say, taking the phone back at last and scrolling through the photos. 'You're much better at this than I am.'

'Och, no,' she says, with a pleased smile. 'I want to be a vet. It's all I've ever wanted to do. That's why I took this job, actually; I need to save up as much as I can, for university. Even if I go to the nearest one, I'll still have to live there during term time, and it costs a fortune.'

She chatters away for a few minutes, telling me about how she's wanted to work with animals since she was a little girl, and I absent-mindedly chew on a scone as I listen to her, feeling ever so slightly envious about how certain she is about what she wants to do with her life, and how she's going to do it.

It must be nice to feel like you have some kind of purpose; a reason to get out of bed in the morning because you really *want* to, rather than just because you *have* to.

That's exactly the kind of thing I'm looking for; and the kind of thing I'm hoping this trip will help me find.

A few minutes later, Agnes leaves, and I'm just about to tuck into my afternoon tea at last when I happen to glance out of the window just in time to see Bex and Daniel down in the castle grounds below us.

Bex has gone full Fairytale Princess, in a red evening gown with a huge tulle skirt which floats dramatically around her as she runs in slow-motion through the mist-covered grounds, while Daniel attempts to film her on both the GoPro and his camera at the same time.

I watch entranced, the spread in front of me forgotten. The red dress contrasts sharply with Bex's pale skin and dark hair, while the length makes it look almost as if she's floating in it. I can already imagine the comments this is going to get when she uploads it, and I'm just about to turn away in defeat and go and eat my feelings of envy about all of this (because that's *got* to be better than actually *experiencing* them, right?) when the scene abruptly ends, with Bex stopping in her tracks and holding out her hand for the camera to peer at the shots Daniel's taken on the screen at the back.

I take a step closer to the window, my breath misting up the glass as I press my nose against it. I can't hear what they're saying, but they're obviously arguing now, their body language tense, and a frown on both of their faces. After a few, clearly fraught, minutes, Bex turns on her heel and marches back towards the castle, leaving Daniel standing there on his own, his posture somehow resigned, as if he's seen all of this before.

Well, that *was weird.*

Still thinking about Bex and Daniel, and how different the reality of them is from the highly edited version I follow on YouTube, I polish off my tea in record time, then spend the rest of the afternoon looking at flat rental websites online, hoping – and failing – to find something that doesn't require at least one month's rent upfront. There's absolutely nothing, though (well, it's hard to find a place to rent when your budget is approximately zero . . .), so I give up at last, and open my wardrobe door to find something to wear to dinner – which we're having in the library tonight, according to my itinerary for the stay.

Someone's added a handwritten note next to this item saying 'dress to impress', so, after a bit of thought, I select a sequined slip dress and team it with a pair of sparkly stiletto sandals: a look which says, *I might never get the chance to wear this outfit again, so you better believe I'm going to make the most of it.*

And also *Please let me sit with you.* Which, let's face it, is the *real* message I'm hoping to get across tonight.

I stare at my reflection in the mirror on the back of the wardrobe door, a tiny thrill of excitement running through me. I love dressing up; I always have, ever since I was a little girl. Back then, it felt like magic to me; almost as if I was slipping into another world, or another life, just by changing my clothes. It still does. The life I chose *these* clothes for, though – the sequinned, sparkly ones that are currently making me look like a human mirror ball – is one I don't actually *live*; which is why it's so thrilling to me that I'm getting the opportunity to wear them, and in a *castle* of all places.

'Wow. Nice outfit, Wrong Rosie,' says Bex as I step through the door and into the softly lit room, which is filled with the glow from the log fire, and the murmur of voices, all falling silent the moment I appear.

I soon realise why, too; because, when I turn around to thank Bex for the unexpected compliment, I find her standing there smirking in jeans and a T-shirt, with her hair pulled back in a simple but elegant ponytail and minimal makeup. On the sofa behind her, Millie is sipping champagne while wearing a bright pink tracksuit, and even Sabrina has exchanged her usual high-fashion look for something soft and flowy that may or may not be nightwear.

'Are you off out somewhere?' asks Millie in her nice-but-dim way. She's sitting next to Yasmin (in what looks like a pair of black silk pyjamas) and Zara (in leggings and an oversized sweater), and they all look at me in my sequinned dress and what now feels a lot like clown makeup, as if I'm the evening's entertainment.

'Um, no,' I stammer, feeling my cheeks turn red. 'I'm just . . . I'm just . . .'

I'm just getting it wrong again, is the truth of the matter. Wrong Rosie, Wrong Outfit.

Wrong, wrong, wrong.

'She's just been doing a photo shoot in the ballroom,' says a voice from behind me.

I turn around to find Hunter Stuart standing framed in the doorway, still in his jeans and work boots, but with the fleece jacket now covering his washboard abs again, much to my relief. 'I opened it up for her earlier. She obviously didn't have time to change before she came here, did you, Rosie?'

'That's . . . that's right,' I reply, blinking. 'I was in the ballroom. Taking photos. Of myself. In the ballroom. For the contest.'

'I think they got it,' whispers Hunter, his lips brushing my ear in a way that makes my entire body tingle unexpectedly. 'You can stop talking now. I would recommend it, actually.'

'Thank you,' I whisper back, trying not to think about how good he looks, his hair slightly messy from being outdoors all day, and his eyes twinkling merrily. 'That was really nice of you. I was dying there.'

I fight the impulse to lean into the reassuring bulk of him. He might think I'm an idiot, but Hunter Stuart is still the kind of man who could very easily break my heart, given half a chance. And having my heart broken by a Highland heartthrob definitely isn't on my agenda for the next few days.

'Aye, it seemed like real life-or-death stuff right enough,' he replies, his mouth twitching, as he gestures for me to follow him to a quieter corner of the room, where no one can overhear us – not that anyone seems to be listening to us, anyway, now that my over-the-top outfit has been explained.

'So,' Hunter goes on, looking me up and down and making my insides feel confusingly fizzy. 'If a person's clothes tell you a lot about them, what is it that *this* says about *you*, then?'

'It says I'm an idiot,' I reply crisply, my cheeks turning even redder, if that's possible. Then I remember the note on the itinerary. 'Actually, no, I'm not. Well, I *am*, but . . .

it's just, I'm sure the itinerary I was given said "dress to impress". I'm certain of it, actually – I never forget anything involving clothes. And that bit had been added in by hand, too, so it stood out. I wish I'd brought it with me.'

I open my little beaded evening bag and peer inside, as if the itinerary might have magically appeared inside it, the same way my missing clothes appeared right back where I'd left them.

'Oh, that reminds me,' I tell Hunter, snapping the bag closed again. 'You'll never guess where my clothes were.'

He raises one hand and rubs the stubble on his chin sceptically as I give him a quick rundown on my fluctuating wardrobe situation, omitting both the bit where I started talking to my jumpers and the thing about the potential brain tumour.

'Are you *sure* they weren't there the first time you checked?' Hunter says as I finish. 'Were you definitely looking in the right place?'

'Of course I'm sure,' I reply indignantly. 'I know I might seem a bit . . . fluffy . . . to you, but I'm not stupid. And I don't make stuff up.'

'Right,' he says, sounding unconvinced. 'It's just . . . well, you *are* a bit "fluffy", as you put it. And it's a big room. There's a lot of, um, *doors* in it. And you do keep getting lost.'

'Not in my own room,' I reply with dignity. 'And there might be a lot of doors, but there's only one walk-in wardrobe, so I don't think I could've mistaken it for the bathroom, somehow, if that's what you're suggesting. If there's one thing I know about, it's wardrobes: trust me. And if there's something else I know, it's that none of this stuff that's been happening is random, Hunter. Someone's messing with me on purpose.'

'And the murderer is in the room with us now,' says Hunter, his eyes wide as he pretends to scan the room.

'Maybe.' I look around at the influencers, who're all chatting in their little groups. 'But I can't rule out the possibility of it being someone from the hotel, either. It would've been much easier for a member of staff to have gotten into my room while I was at breakfast. They're the ones who have access to it.'

I look up at him, wondering if he'll show any sign of guilt at this, but he just shrugs in that hard-to-read way of his.

'It would've been easier for one of this lot to change the itinerary you were given, though,' he points out, indicating the influencer group with a slight nod. 'So, if I had to guess, I'd say it was most likely Professor Plum, in the billiard room, with the lead pipe.'

'You're infuriating, you know that?' I begin, but before I can go any further, the library door opens, and hotel staff start filing through it, all carrying trays laden with food and drinks.

'Right, well, I'll leave you to it,' says Hunter, looking relieved at the interruption. 'I only came in because I thought you lot would be in the dining room again and I'd have the place to myself. Apparently not, though.'

He turns to leave, and then hesitates, looking back over his shoulder at me as if he's trying to make up his mind about something.

'You look very nice, by the way,' he says at last, his voice a little hoarse. 'So whatever that dress is saying about you, I . . . well, I agree with it.'

Then he ducks quickly out through the open door of the library, looking like he's surprised even himself with his words, and is now trying to get away from them as fast as possible.

He's definitely surprised *me*, that's for sure.

'I . . . thanks,' I say to the door as it closes behind him, my cheeks reddening at the unexpected compliment.

But Hunter's already gone, leaving me alone with my tormentors.

I really wish he'd stayed, though; and not just because of how adorably awkward he looked when he told me he liked my dress, but because I don't care what he says, I'm still convinced someone in this room is messing with me.

And I guess now is as good a time as any to put my theory to the test.

Chapter 9

After dinner, which is served tapas style, with lots of little grazing plates which only Luna and I eat (the influencers are all too busy taking photos, and I'm not sure Sabrina knows *how* to eat – I've certainly never seen her do it . . .), we all sit down to compare notes on our day's work; at which point it emerges that the other influencers have racked up over 150,000 'likes' between them on their Chrysalis-themed content, and I've lost ten followers – although there *are* a few comments about how 'cosy' my jumper looks, so at least that's something.

Take that, Bex Foster: my sweater is *magic, after all . . .*

Zara and Millie's photos all feature them posing in bikinis around the pool and spa; the ones they took at the gates all having been ruined by me being in the background, apparently. Yasmin, meanwhile, has gone for a stunning black-and-white shot in which she reclines gracefully in the bathtub in her room, which has been filled to overflowing with bubbles. Her hair is piled up on top of her head in a way that would look messy on anyone else, but which is effortlessly sophisticated on Yasmin, and she's holding up a glass of champagne while looking dreamily out of the window behind the tub, which has been thrown open, the white gauze curtains framing the view through the window as if it's an oil painting.

It's Bex's photo, however, that gets the most attention, and, it has to be said, it deserves it. Daniel has somehow managed to capture his wife mid-leap, at a moment when both of her feet are off the ground, making her appear to be floating through the air, her hair fanning out around her, and the hotel rising up in the background like a paid actor in the Bex Foster show.

'Oh, I didn't really do anything,' she says modestly as Sabrina fusses around her, wondering aloud if the hotel should use the photo in its advertising campaign. 'It's Daniel who does all the hard work.'

She simpers up at him, and he takes her hand, harmony apparently well and truly restored between them. Either that or they're just very good actors.

I swallow hard, thinking about my ex, who didn't ever look at me the way Daniel Foster looks at Bex. I don't think anyone's ever looked at me like that.

'Well, I have an excellent model to work with,' Daniel replies, confirming that he really is the perfect husband. 'Oh, if you do want to use the shot commercially, Sabrina, we'll have to chat about licensing, obviously,' he adds, snapping abruptly back into business mode. 'Let's get something in the diary, shall we?'

'Of course, Mr Bex. Let's set it up now,' Sabrina says eagerly. 'I think we're done here, aren't we? Luna, come over here, would you?' she calls out sharply to her assistant. 'I need you to check my calendar.'

She goes striding over to join the Fosters on their sofa, signalling that the meeting is adjourned, and everyone else drifts over to the back of the room, where a tray of champagne has been set up on a table by the window, along with some crisps and other nibbles. The wine I had with dinner has already started to go to my head a little, so champagne's the last thing I need right now, but I get up and follow them anyway. Well, wouldn't now be the perfect time to do a bit of detective work, and see if I can figure out whether any of them might be the clothing criminal? Or the sauna sealer?

Actually, on second thoughts, maybe this isn't such a great idea after all, if the champagne's going to make me start behaving like I'm in an episode of *Scooby Doo*.

Nevertheless, I wander casually over to the window where Zara and Millie are still comparing the various photos from today, and Yasmin's still pretending she's not actually a part of this group at all.

All I have to do is find out where they all were when the incidents in question happened. And maybe also try to establish whether any of them are evil enough to want to lock someone in a sauna and leave them to their fate.

That should be easy enough, shouldn't it?

'Bex's photo is *ah-may-zing*,' sighs Millie enviously as I select a glass of champagne and attempt to insert myself into the group without attracting too much attention to myself; which is tricky, really, on account of me looking like a giant disco ball.

'It really is,' says Zara, selecting the image from the Fosters' Instagram grid and tapping to open it. 'I guess that's what happens when you marry a professional photographer, though.'

'It's gorgeous,' I agree, sidling up to them, emboldened by the large gulp of champagne I've just had. 'Slightly sinister, though, don't you think?'

'Sinister?' Millie tilts her blonde head to one side in surprise, like a spaniel. 'Whatever do you mean?'

'Oh, nothing really,' I say, airily. 'It's just . . . don't you think the red dress looks a bit like a splash of blood against the misty sky?'

I widen my eyes innocently, although, inside, I'm already cringing at how completely unsubtle my attempt to establish evil tendencies in my fellow influencers is.

'Oh, yes,' says Millie, leaning over Zara's photo to get a closer look. 'I suppose I see what you mean. Sort of.'

'And is it just me, or does it look like she's running *away* from someone, rather than *to* them?' I go on, warming to my theme. 'Almost as if she's being *chased*?'

'I think it's just you,' says Zara dryly. 'It's supposed to look like a scene from a fairy tale, not a horror story.'

'The original fairy tales are very similar to horror,' murmurs Yasmin, shocking us all into silence with the reminder that she can actually speak. 'They're very dark. *Very* dark.'

'That's right.' I nod, looking at her through narrowed eyes. She's dressed head to toe in black, as usual, and keeps reaching up as if to adjust her sunglasses, only to realise she's not actually wearing them for once.

'Like in "Hansel and Gretel",' she says. 'When the witch is literally fattening the children up to eat them. Or the one where the stepmother murders her stepson and cooks him into a stew.'

Yasmin pops a glacé cherry into her mouth from a bowl by the drinks tray.

'Then she serves it to his father,' she adds, matter-of-factly. 'I think about that a lot, you know. Well, bedtime for me, I think.'

Without another word, she slings her bag over her shoulder and heads for the door, swerving to avoid the group on the sofa as she goes.

The three of us stare after her, open-mouthed.

'My favourite fairy tale is "Cinderella",' says Millie, in a small voice. 'It's just about shoes, and handsome princes.

I'm not sure I'd like these other ones. They seem a bit . . . bloody.'

Zara pats her reassuringly on the arm and starts going through the Instagram photos again to distract her. I sip my drink thoughtfully as I watch them.

Zara and Millie were out by the gates when I was taking my first set of photos, and then at the pool later. And I know Bex and Daniel were in the lobby, then the gardens all afternoon. Which means Yasmin is the only one of the group who was unaccounted for at the time the clothes must have been returned to my room.

But how would she have got her hands on them in the first place? And why would she want them?

'This is really good, actually,' says Zara, interrupting my chain of thought as she scrolls past the 'thumb face' selfie on my feed and stops at the photo Hunter took for me by the pond. 'I wish I'd thought of it.'

'Thanks,' I reply, blushing. 'Not that it's done me much good, though. It didn't get anything like the reaction yours did. And I lost ten followers.'

'Oh. Well, you know . . . they're probably jealous,' Zara replies, looking unconvinced. 'People can be a bit funny like that.'

'That's true,' agrees Millie. 'I don't even read the comments on my posts anymore; they just make me feel horrible about myself. Someone once messaged me and said I was obviously evil, just because I said I don't watch the news. But the news is, like, *really sad*, you know? And I'm not evil. I'm really not.'

She sniffs loudly, and Zara pats her on the arm again, while I nod uselessly, mentally striking Millie off my list of suspects. She's way too childlike to be capable of doing anything to intentionally mess with someone.

'Of course you're not,' Zara says soothingly. 'Why don't you go and sit down; I'll bring you another glass of fizz.'

Millie nods tremulously and goes to sit by the fire.

'She *is* evil, though,' Zara tells me with a wink, grabbing another couple of glasses.

'Sorry, did you say evil?' I put down my empty glass and pick up a full one, convinced I must have misheard.

'Oh, yeah,' says Zara, nodding. 'You should've heard her earlier, talking about how she was going to win this competition. Totally cut-throat. She might look like a little doll, with all that baby pink stuff she wears, but trust me; the only doll Millie's like is Chucky. You know, the one who—'

'Murders,' I reply, my entire body cold despite the heat from the fire. 'Yeah.'

'Oh, not just that,' says Zara cheerfully. 'Chucky *tortures* first. And so would Millie. Trust me.'

'I . . . but she seems so harmless,' I protest, taking a much larger gulp of my drink than I meant to. 'Surely it can't all be an act?'

'All of this is an act, Rosie,' says Zara, indicating the room at large. 'You know that, right? None of it's real. That's not champagne Yas is drinking in that photo of hers; it's just fizzy water. You can't tell because she's made the shot black and white. And Millie and I were absolutely freezing in those shots in the spa. I can't believe this is what passes for spring up here.'

I want to add that Bex and Daniel looked like they were about to break up when I saw them in the grounds earlier, but it feels strangely disloyal for some reason (plus, I'm still not sure I can trust Zara, either . . .), so I say nothing.

Zara's right, though. Everyone here is putting on an act of some kind, whether it's just for the content they'll post on social media later or for those of us they have to interact with in real life. I'm doing it myself, standing here in my completely unsuitable dress, and posting Instagram captions telling everyone about what a great time I'm having, when, actually, I'm not sure I've ever felt more alone or out of place: and I went to an all-girls school where everybody hated me, so I speak from some experience, here.

And all of this, of course, is going to make it so much harder for me to try to figure out who's responsible for the things that have been happening to me since I arrived here – if *anyone* is. Because, now I think about it, I'm starting to wonder if Hunter's right, after all.

Maybe the sauna door *was* just stuck? Maybe I *did* somehow get confused about the location of my wardrobe? Maybe the handwritten note on my itinerary said, 'DON'T dress to impress', and I just read it wrong? Because that would definitely make a lot more sense, considering that most people currently in the room with me look like they've come from either an exercise class or a pyjama party.

Wait.

The note on the itinerary.

At least that's one thing I can find out for sure, isn't it?

'You know the itineraries for the week we were given this morning?' I ask Zara. 'Did, er, yours have anything on it about a dress code for tonight?'

Zara looks at me blankly.

'A dress code?' she says. 'No, there was nothing about a dress code. I asked Luna earlier, though, and she said just to wear something comfy, so . . .'

She indicates her leggings (which, naturally, look amazing on her model-like legs), then drifts over to join Millie by the fire. I quickly drain my glass, then put it back on the tray before heading for the door, feeling glad for once that

I'm seemingly invisible again, which means no one so much as glances in my direction as I go.

Back in my room (just five minutes to get there this time – a new personal best), I cross quickly to the dressing table, looking for the printed itinerary, which I remember leaving there just before I started getting ready for dinner.

Well, I *thought* I remembered leaving it there.

It's definitely not there now, though, so, firmly shaking off the feeling of foreboding that's returned with a vengeance, I start to search the rest of the room instead.

Over the next half an hour, I practically turn the place upside down in a bid to find the itinerary: I even look inside the bathroom cabinet, and in the pockets of my clothes (which are, thankfully, hanging in the wardrobe, exactly where I left them).

But it's not here.

No matter how hard I search, or how many times I tell myself that it *has* to be here, that I *know* it's here, eventually I'm forced to give up and admit defeat.

The itinerary has vanished into thin air.

And now I have yet another mystery to solve.

Chapter 10

I check my bed carefully for horses' heads, then climb into it so I can lie awake overthinking for a while, before falling into a dream in which Millie Mitchell is chopping down a Christmas tree, which turns into Bex Foster as I watch.

Bex falls to the ground, bright red blood pooling around her like the tulle of her dress, and I awake with a start to a mysterious tapping on the window.

Oh, please God, no. Not a mysterious tapping on the window now. Anything but that, I'm begging you.

I pull the covers aside and slip cautiously out of the giant bed, hoping that this is going to turn out to be one of those weird waking dreams; which are terrifying, sure, but still *just dreams*.

But no: a quick pinch of my forearm confirms that I'm very much awake – and now the tapping is coming from the door of the room, rather than the window.

I pause halfway across the bedroom floor and listen carefully, but all I can hear is my own heart hammering wildly in my chest, almost deafening me with the sound of abject terror. So at least I know what *that* sounds like now.

This is definitely the last time I accept an invitation to a wellness retreat; because, to be completely honest, this place is making me feel anything *but* 'well'.

Tap.

Tap.

Tap.

I listen closely, pressing my hands against my chest as if that'll persuade my heart to pipe down a bit.

Yes, the sound is definitely coming from the door. Which is *sort of* a relief, because that means it most likely has a human source, whereas the only thing that could possibly have been tapping on my third-floor window would be . . . well, nothing good, let's put it that way.

If the tapping is coming from an actual person, though, that means it's probably the *same* person who's been tormenting me in all of these other ways, too; and that thought is enough to propel me across the room, a small shriek of combined terror and outrage escaping my lips as I wrench open the door to find . . .

. . . nothing.

Well, of *course* there's nothing. That's just par for the course with me and this place, isn't it? Although . . . wait. Is that . . . ?

I squint down the corridor, wishing I was wearing my contact lenses, because I'm almost blind without them.

At the opposite end of the hall, something small and white flickers into view, the gloom of the long corridor making it look almost like it's floating.

Unless, of course, it *is* floating?

I take a cautious step forward and peer into the darkness, not sure whether my blurrier-than-usual vision is due to my poor eyesight, the champagne I had earlier, or if I'm about to faint.

Please don't let it be the last one.

My legs start to sag beneath me as the ghostly figure of a child begins gliding silently down the corridor; and not just *any* old ghostly child, either, but a little ghostly *girl*.

And everyone knows those are the scariest kind, don't they?

If you'd asked me before I came to this hotel what I'd do if faced with the ghostly figure of a creepy little girl in a long white nightgown, I'd have laughed and told you not to be silly, there's no such things as ghosts.

If you asked me the same question at any point after this exact moment, however, I'd now be able to tell you with some degree of confidence that what I'd actually do is *scream*.

Loudly.

And also rather squeakily, actually.

The door behind me slams shut with a very loud bang, indicating that I'm now locked out of my room, too, as if I didn't have enough to deal with right now.

'Shhh!' hisses the ghost, starting to run towards me. 'Stop making so much noise! You're going to wake everyone up. They'll be mad.'

I sag weakly against the door, doubting the proof of my own eyes.

Ghosts can't *talk*, can they?

Or run?

The thing is almost upon me now, and as it – *she* – approaches, I notice that what appeared from a distance to be one of those long, old-fashioned nightgowns the Victorians were so keen on, is actually a white towelling robe with the hotel's logo sewn onto the front. There's one just like it hanging in my bathroom right this second. Which means . . .

'Hello,' says the decidedly flesh-and-blood little girl shyly as she reaches me. 'I'm Hannah. Why are you screaming?'

* * *

A few minutes later, I'm walking Hannah back to her apartment in the staff quarters, her little hand tucked trustingly into mine as she chatters on about her day, and this one kid in her class called Billy, who once tried to climb out of the window, and got stuck halfway out and upside down.

I feel like Billy and I would have a lot in common somehow.

'Hannah, were you knocking on my door earlier?' I ask gently, interrupting her.

She looks up at me: big blue eyes set in a pretty little freckled face, and framed with long white-blonde hair which reaches almost to her waist.

'Sorry,' she says, not looking remotely sorry. 'I just wanted to see you close up. You're the lady who was in the hotel reception in her bathrobe, aren't you?'

'Well, yes,' I agree reluctantly. 'That was me. I was . . . well, it's a long story.'

'You looked really funny,' Hannah says gleefully. 'Your face was all red. And you had all this black stuff under your eyes.'

'Were you watching, then?' I ask, remembering the flicker of movement I'd thought was a ghost on the landing when I arrived.

Hannah nods cheerfully.

'Oh, yes,' she says. 'I like watching people. I used to do it all the time in the olden days.'

'The . . . the *olden* days? How long have you . . . *lived* . . . here?' I stutter, my body cold again with renewed tension, as I wait for her to reveal that she's been walking these corridors for two hundred years now, luring innocent guests to their doom.

'Oh, *ages*,' replies Hannah seriously. 'Weeks and weeks. I'm seven and a half now, and when came here when I was only seven and a bit.'

'Right,' I say, relieved. 'And that was before the castle was turned into a hotel?'

'Yes,' says Hannah. 'The olden days. And the only people who lived here were builders, and decorators and stuff. It's much better now. There was a lady who looked like a princess outside earlier.'

'Yeah, that was Bex,' I tell her. 'She's very . . . princessy. Is this where you live?'

We've stopped outside a large wooden door marked 'STAFF', which Hannah immediately pushes open. I hesitate, remembering what Sabrina said this morning about not going into the private areas of the building. The last thing I want to do is risk incurring the wrath of the cantankerous old Lord Glenmuir; and, let's face it, that would *also* be very much on brand for me this week, so I dig in my heels, determined not to cause any more trouble.

'I think I better just leave you here, Hannah,' I tell the little girl gently. 'I'm not allowed to go any further. You know how to get back to your apartment from here, don't you?'

'Of course I do,' she says scornfully. 'I know how to get everywhere. I told you, I've lived here for ages. I want you to come with me, though, Rosie. Please,' she adds beseechingly, her eyes very wide. 'I did a drawing of you after I saw you in the lobby. I really want to show you.'

'Maybe you could show me tomorrow?' I suggest. 'It must be way past your bedtime by now. It's definitely past mine.'

'I'm scared,' says Hannah, who doesn't look like anything scares her. 'I need an adult to look after me.'

I sigh, knowing perfectly well that I'm being shamelessly manipulated, but also knowing I'm probably going to let her get away with it, because who could refuse a cute little girl who claims to be scared?

'OK,' I say, relenting. 'But very quickly, OK? I'm not supposed to be here.'

'It's fine,' Hannah replies, forgetting she's supposed to be scared as she grins at me. 'You're with me.'

Taking my hand again, she pulls me through the door, which – surprise, surprise – leads to *another* corridor. It's darker here than it is in the public parts of the hotel, and I'm relieved to find we only have to walk a short distance before stopping outside yet another door, which Hannah unlocks with a key she pulls from the pocket of her dressing gown.

'You have a key to get in and out?' I ask, surprised. 'I assumed your parents were in the apartment, and you sneaked out?'

'I just live with my daddy,' she replies sadly. 'And he's busy working. So I have a key.'

'Oh.'

I'm not quite sure what to say to this, but I definitely don't feel comfortable leaving her on her own now, so I allow her to lead me into the little apartment, which is small and mildly chaotic, with a large number of books piled on the various surfaces and a small mountain of laundry rising up precariously next to an ironing board, which has been set up in front of the TV. There's a couple of acoustic guitars lined neatly up against the sofa, and almost as many vinyl records as there are books scattered around.

'Let me show you my drawing,' says Hannah, dashing off excitedly towards what I'm assuming is the door to her bedroom. A few seconds later, she's back again, handing me a sheet of paper on which she's drawn a very round person with a magenta face and two thick black lines under the eyes. The circle-woman's mouth is wide open, showing an extremely large set of tonsils, and she appears to be completely naked.

'Very accurate,' I tell her, smiling in spite of myself. 'I love it.'

'You can keep it if you like,' she replies, pleased. 'I can always do another one.'

'Well, thank you very much, Hannah,' I reply, folding up the drawing and slipping it into the pocket on the front of my pyjama top. 'I'll treasure this. Now, I think it's probably time we got you into bed, don't you? It's very late.'

Hannah puts up a token protest at this suggestion, but allows me to accompany her to her room (which is much tidier than the rest of the flat, and decorated with bright pink bedding and cushions) and tuck her into bed.

'You will stay, won't you, Rosie?' she says pleadingly, as I finish arranging her staggeringly large collection of stuffed animals around her in an order that corresponds exactly to her extremely detailed instructions. 'You're not going to leave me on my own, are you?'

I look at her sceptically. I'm pretty sure she isn't even the tiniest bit scared of being on her own but, at the same time, it doesn't feel right to just leave her here.

What was her father thinking of, leaving a seven-year-old girl alone at this time of night?

Making up my mind to hang around at least until I can ask him this question myself, I smile reassuringly at her.

'Sure,' I tell her. 'Now get to sleep.'

I turn to leave, but then another thought occurs to me, prompted by the thought of Hannah being the ghost I thought I'd seen when I arrived.

'Hannah?' I ask, halfway through the door. 'You didn't go into my room this morning by any chance, did you?'

'Your room?' She peeks at me over the top of the covers. 'What do you mean?'

'Oh, it's nothing, really,' I reply, not wanting to scare her. 'It's just . . . I thought I'd lost some of my clothes for a bit; but then they turned up again. It was quite funny, really. I wondered if you might have moved them? You know, as a prank? You can tell me if you did,' I add quickly. 'I won't be angry.'

'I'm not allowed to go into the guest rooms,' Hannah replies, shaking her head vehemently. 'I'd get into so much trouble. And I couldn't, anyway. Dante always locks the spare keys away. He has a special box he keeps them in.'

'Ah, I see,' I reply, filing this piece of information away in case I need it later. 'Oh well, never mind. I just wondered if you might know anything about it. It was probably just me being silly.'

'Probably,' says Hannah, snuggling back down. 'Either that or Dante took them. He's always sneaking around.'

'Is he?'

'Oh, yes. I see him sometimes. He doesn't see me, though.'

She gives me a cheeky wink, and I smile back before closing the bedroom door, already thinking about how to find out what Dante was up to today; because while I can think of no earthly reason why he'd want to mess around with a guest's clothes, the fact remains, *someone* did it.

And wouldn't the man with access to all the spare room keys be the number one suspect?

Chapter 11

I'm standing at the ironing board in Hannah's living room a few minutes later, working my way through the pile of laundry that's been left there, when the door to the corridor opens and Hunter Stuart appears, rubbing his eyes as if he's just come off a particularly hard night shift; which is strange, really, because he's a gardener, and I'm pretty sure they don't work at night.

It's not as strange as the fact that he's here at all, though; and, judging by the surprised look on his face as we stare at each other, he's thinking exactly the same thing about me.

Trust him to turn out to be Hannah's father.

'Can I ask what the hell you're doing in my flat?' says Hunter evenly, recovering first. 'And at my ironing board?'

'I don't know,' I reply smartly. 'Can *I* ask what the hell you were thinking, leaving a little girl on her own in the middle of the night? Because I think that's a bit more important than you and your ironing, don't you?'

Hunter glares at me.

'Not that it's any of your business,' he says, 'but Hannah's not on her own. Agnes is with her. Or she's supposed to be, anyway. That's what I'm paying her for.'

He looks around the room, as if he's expecting to see the housekeeper hiding in a corner somewhere. Unfortunately for him, though, it's just me. And also Stevie, who comes bounding towards me joyfully, proof that at least *someone* in this place is pleased to see me.

'Agnes isn't here,' I tell him, stating the obvious. 'And Hannah didn't mention her, either. She was completely on her own. I found her in the hallway outside my room.'

I don't bother mentioning that I thought his daughter was one of the Undead. It doesn't seem like the kind of thing a parent would want to hear, somehow.

'Great,' says Hunter, rubbing his eyes wearily again before coming all the way into the room and dropping into one of the armchairs, pushing a stack of books aside first. 'I swear to God, I'm going to kill that girl. Not literally,' he adds, meeting my startled gaze. 'You can stop looking at me like that, Rosie Winter. Seriously, though, this is the second time Agnes has promised to keep an eye on Hannah, then disappeared. I bet she's down in the cellars. Dante told me he thinks someone's been helping themselves to some of the booze down there. Apparently there are quite a few bottles missing. We think some of the younger staff might be meeting up there after their shifts.'

He runs a hand down his face, and I feel a flash of sympathy for him. I don't suppose it's easy, being a single parent. Especially when people keep letting you down.

'You didn't mention you had a daughter,' I say, turning back to the ironing, just to give myself something to do.

'I didn't realise I was supposed to tell the guests my life story,' Hunter replies. 'Dante must have missed out that part of the job description. Would you mind putting my underpants down, by the way? I don't normally show women my underwear until I know them a little better.'

I glance down at my hands as if I'm seeing them for the first time, and, sure enough, I'm holding a pair of bright yellow boxer shorts with tiny pineapples printed on them.

I drop them as if I've been scalded by the fabric.

'I . . . didn't have you down as a fruit-print kind of guy,' I blurt out, saying the first thing that comes into my head, as usual.

'Well, funnily enough, I wasn't expecting you to come into my flat and start rummaging through my pants,' replies Hunter. 'Or I'd have looked out something a little more sophisticated for you.'

'I wasn't "rummaging through your pants",' I retort. 'I didn't want to leave Hannah on her own, and I decided I might as well tackle some of this ironing to pass the time while I waited for you to come back. *Some* people would describe that as "being nice", just FYI. But *you*—'

'Sorry, Rosie,' he says quietly, holding up a hand to stop me. 'I'm sorry. It's been a long day, and I'm . . . I'm pretty pissed off at Agnes, but I shouldn't be taking it out on you. I appreciate you looking out for Hannah. And doing the ironing. I've been meaning to get around to that for ages; there just never seems to be time.'

'It's fine,' I tell him. '*Now* who's the one doing too much apologising?' I add, feeling like I should at least attempt to continue with the sparring that's become customary between us. Now that I look closer, though, I can see dark shadows under his eyes and a small line between his brows, which I have a sudden, inappropriate urge to smooth out with my hands.

'Sorry. Again,' he says, with one of those unexpected grins of his. 'You must be rubbing off on me. Can I offer you a wee nightcap before you go, by way of thanks for looking out for Hannah?'

'A wee *nightcap*?' I ask, imagining myself in one of those long hats with a pompom on the end that people used to wear to bed.

'A dram,' Hunter clarifies. 'A glass of whisky. It's what some people call a nightcap, Rosie.'

I blush again.

'Of course. I know what a nightcap is,' I say, wondering what it is about this man that makes me start talking nonsense every time I see him. 'It's been a long day for me, too.'

I haven't actually answered his question, but Hunter gets up anyway and goes over to a sideboard, from which he produces a bottle of whisky and two glasses.

'Here,' he says, handing me one. 'This is a good cure for a bad day.'

I stare down into the glass, unconvinced. I'm more of a wine person, really. But I'm curious now about how Hunter Stuart came to be living alone in a remote hotel with his seven-year-old daughter, so I raise the glass and take a much larger gulp than I really should have; a fact I instantly regret when I start choking and spluttering, my throat seemingly on fire as the liquid appears to burn its way right down through my body.

'And you're telling me people drink this stuff for *fun*?' I say, when I finally recover the power of speech. 'Seriously?'

'People do a lot of strange things for fun, Rosie Winter,' says Hunter – a statement that makes me glad of the dim light in the room, because I'm suddenly blushing from head to toe. He's already finished his drink, and he picks up the bottle to pour himself another, holding it out to me first.

'Um, no thanks,' I reply, shaking my head. 'I think one was enough for me.'

'It's a bit of an acquired taste,' he replies, taking the glass back to his armchair, where he sits down, looking a little more relaxed than when he arrived, although there's a deep weariness in his posture that makes me wonder what kind of work it is he's been doing that's kept him out so late.

Sensing me watching him, Hunter raises his eyes to mine, and I'm very aware of the fact that all I'm wearing is a pair of very short, silky pyjamas, which probably isn't the *most* appropriate outfit I could've come up with for this: not that I knew that 'this' was going to involve drinking whisky with an incredibly attractive and only moderately infuriating man, while the daughter I didn't know he had sleeps in the next room.

So, for once, this mistake *isn't* my fault.

Seeing me tug self-consciously at my top, Hunter gets to his feet, plucks a dark blue hoodie from the top of the laundry pile and hands it to me.

'Here,' he says gruffly. 'Stick that on. It'll, er, warm you up. Not as much as the whisky, mind, but still.'

'Thanks.' I take it gratefully and zip it over my PJs, trying not to think about how ridiculous I must look in a sweatshirt that comes halfway to my knees, and probably makes me look like I'm naked underneath it. 'I should probably get back to my room, though. I . . . Oh no, wait.'

I slap a hand over my mouth, remembering the way the hotel room door slammed shut behind me earlier.

'I think I might be locked out,' I admit guiltily. 'The door closed behind me when I went into the corridor. They lock automatically, don't they?'

'Aye.' Hunter nods. 'They do.' He chuckles. 'You have a real talent for getting yourself into scrapes, don't you?'

'This one wasn't totally my fault,' I point out. 'Hannah knocked on my door.'

Hunter grimaces.

'Did she? Ach, I'm sorry. I think she just wants someone to talk to. It's a lonely old place for a little girl.'

'And for a bigger one, too,' I say ruefully, thinking about the way Bex Foster expertly managed to freeze me out at breakfast this morning. 'Hannah really wasn't bothering me, though. Well, OK, I *might* have briefly thought she was a ghost, but I soon figured it out. And she was very sweet; I was happy to talk to her. I . . . well, I know what it's like to be lonely, even when you're surrounded by people.'

'Really? You're not making friends with the other influencers, then? I'd have thought you'd all have loads in common, what with the shopping, and the selfies, and all that?'

Hunter smiles to soften his words, but they sting nonetheless.

'I thought I'd make friends with them all, too,' I reply, perching on the end of the sofa. 'Or I hoped I would. I was really excited about getting to meet them all, but . . . well, they're nothing like the way they come across on their socials. None of them are. And it's not all about "shopping and selfies" by the way,' I can't resist adding. 'I *do* think about other things as well, you know.'

'Oh, aye? Like what? What does Rosie Winter like to do when she's not shopping?'

'I . . . um . . .'

I look around the room, as if for inspiration. Going by the guitars, and all of the records he has lying around, it's not hard to guess that music is one of Hunter's interests; history, too, judging by the books I can see on the shelf. But me . . .

I wrack my brain, trying to think of something I do, other than going to work and coming back home again. I don't think watching true crime on Netflix, or going to the pub with my friends counts as a hobby somehow, but, other than those things, I'm coming up painfully empty here. My entire adult life so far has basically been spent working to pay for all of the things I want to buy . . . which

I never really have the opportunity to enjoy, because I'm too busy working to pay for them.

I have a feeling there has to be more to life than this; I'm just not totally sure what it is, yet.

'I don't really know,' I admit, thinking about Agnes, and how certain she was about her future. 'I guess that's what I'm here to find out.'

Hunter looks at me intently; which is such a novel experience for me and my invisibility cloak that I have to fight the impulse to glance over my shoulder, just to make sure there isn't someone standing there who's more deserving of this kind of intensity.

'What do you do for work, then, when you're not pretending to be an influencer?' he asks, the softness of his tone making me feel like he's genuinely interested, and not just making polite conversation; another novelty for me.

I tell him about my boring office job, which I called in sick to in order to come up here, and he chuckles when I admit I'd sometimes rather *be* sick than have to spend one more day sitting in that temperature-controlled box with a view of the car park.

'Well, if it's a big change you're looking for, you've come to the right place for it,' he says, toying with his whisky glass. 'You've already seen what *my* office looks like.'

He tilts his head to indicate the window, which, like mine, looks out across the sprawling grounds of the estate, and down to the deserted beach beyond. There's still a faint touch of light on the horizon, despite the lightness of the hour. I'm starting to think it must never get properly dark here; instead, time just stretches out, as if there's plenty of it to go around, and it's never going to run out.

It makes me feel almost light-headed from the sense of space and . . . well, *freedom*, it inspires. In a place like this, I could be anything I wanted to be.

I just have to figure out what, exactly, that is first.

'Don't *you* ever get lonely, though?' I ask, in a blatant attempt to find out where Hannah's mum is, or if there's anyone else in the picture. 'You don't miss being around other people?'

'I think most people are overrated, Rosie,' he says simply, putting the glass down and getting to his feet. 'Hannah and Stevie are more than enough for me.'

I nod as if I completely get this, although my heart sinks slightly; both from the admission that he doesn't seem to have room for anyone else in his life, and from the fact that he's obviously getting ready to kick me out of his apartment.

And just when I was starting to enjoy his company, too.

'Look, I better go and find a spare key for you,' he says. 'Dante's basically nocturnal, as far as I can tell, but even he has to go to bed sometime. I'll go and catch him before he clocks off for the night, if you wouldn't mind waiting here for a minute? I'd take you with me, but I don't want Hannah to wake up and come looking for me.'

'Oh, no, of course,' I say, sitting back down. 'No problem.'

'Help yourself to another drink while you're waiting,' he says over his shoulder as he leaves. 'If you think you can handle it.'

I snort with amusement at the transparent attempt to goad me, like I'm Marty McFly being called chicken. All the same, though, as the door clicks softly closed, I find myself reaching for the bottle anyway, painfully aware of a shift in the atmosphere of the little room.

Offering me one drink could just have been an act of politeness on his part; a way to thank me for looking after his daughter while he was gone. Offering me a second, though . . . well, *that* almost sounds like he wants me to stay longer.

Does he though? Or is that just wishful thinking on my part?

I look at the bottle of whisky, as if it might possibly answer my question.

I guess it wouldn't hurt to hang around a little longer and have another tiny sip.

Chapter 12

Stevie watches with interest as I tip up the bottle and allow the smallest amount of the amber liquid possible to dribble into my glass, then take an experimental sip, looking curiously around the apartment at the same time.

I deliberately didn't look too closely at my surroundings earlier, because it would've felt too much like snooping. Now that I know the place is *Hunter's*, though, and that he has a daughter, but apparently no wife or girlfriend, my 'intrigue sensor' has been triggered, and I shamelessly want to know why the two of them are on their own.

Tragic dead wife?

Bitter custody battle?

Witness protection programme?

I scan the room quickly, but all I can gather from the general chaos is that Hunter wears brightly coloured underwear, and really needs to get a cleaner.

There's no evidence of any feminine touch at all, though, and I'm just trying to figure out why that pleases me as much as it does when the door opens and Hunter appears again.

'Got it,' he says, holding up a room key. 'I see you decided to brave the whisky again?'

'I did,' I reply, holding up the glass to show him. 'It tasted a bit better this time. Either that or my taste buds have just been destroyed by it.'

'I told you it would grow on you,' he says. 'Everything OK here while I was gone? No more ghostly wanderings from Hannah?'

'Nope. Not so much as a peep from her. And I didn't *really* think she was a ghost earlier,' I add, knowing Hannah will probably be telling him all about my hysterical reaction as soon as she wakes up in the morning. 'It was just a bit spooky after everything else that's happened since I got here. I'm starting to feel like I'm in an episode of *Scooby Doo*.'

'Well, I'm happy to assure you that Hannah's very much alive,' Hunter replies, refilling my glass without asking. 'And her mother's alive, too,' he adds. 'Just in case you were wondering.'

'Oh, I wasn't,' I assure him, even though I absolutely was. I take another sip to give me an excuse to look away.

'She lives in Edinburgh,' he goes on, smiling in a way that tells me he knows exactly what I was thinking. 'We'd originally intended to try to share custody, but she travels a lot for work, so Hannah ended up with me. Not that I'm complaining, mind you. I love having her here; I just worry that she'll be lonely stuck in a mouldy old castle without any other kids to play with.'

'That must've been really hard,' I say, surprised that he's being so open. I guess that whisky really does loosen the tongue. 'Breaking up when you have a child, I mean?'

I'm hoping the question will prompt him to say more about the mysterious ex – and *why* she's a mysterious ex – but Hunter's face just takes on an odd, closed expression, as if he's said too much already.

'Ah, well, it is what it is,' he says, in a tone that tells me story time's over, as abruptly as it began. Shame. 'Another dram?'

'Definitely not.' I cover the top of my glass with my hand. 'I should probably be going, actually. It's late.'

'You're sure you won't be too scared of the ghosties to make it back to your room?' he replies, but there's a twinkle in his eye, which I know means he's just teasing.

'No, it's the human residents of this place I'm scared of,' I reply, getting reluctantly to my feet. The whisky I've drunk has left me feeling pleasantly fuzzy around the edges, but not so much that I don't know a bad idea when I see one; and falling for a man who lives hundreds of miles away would definitely be a bad idea, even by my standards – and I say that as someone who recently pretended to be an influencer in order to blag her way into a free hotel stay.

'You still think someone's out to get you, then?' Hunter asks, hitting on the one topic of conversation guaranteed to make me stay.

'Um, I'm not sure,' I reply, sitting back down beside him and trying not to think about how good he smells: like woodsmoke and salty air. 'I can't imagine why anyone *would* be, really; especially not if they've seen the kind of content I'm coming up with for this competition. It's not like I'm a big threat to any of them. But then, someone definitely moved my clothes; I just can't accept that I imagined that. And then there's the thing with the itinerary.'

I tell him how I searched my room for the piece of paper with the note on it, watching him closely the whole time for any sign of guilt. But Hunter just listens quietly, then shrugs in that way of his.

'It's a slip of paper, Rosie,' he says. 'It's really easy for a piece of paper to go missing. They fall down cracks. They get mixed up with other documents. The fact that you haven't found it yet doesn't mean someone's stolen it.'

'I know. And if it was just that, I wouldn't give it another thought,' I reply. 'I'd think I'd just mislaid it. But there's also the fact that mine was the only copy with that note added to it. Zara told me hers didn't say anything about dressing to impress. Someone wrote that on mine deliberately, then took the paper from my room so I couldn't prove it. I'm sure of it.'

'OK,' says Hunter, leaning back. 'Say someone did. What's the point? Just to make you dress up when no one else was? So? Why does that matter?'

'Oh, it matters,' I mutter darkly. 'I know it probably seems trivial to you—' he nods briefly, not even bothering to deny this '—but it made me feel stupid and out of place. And I *hate* that.'

He fixes me with that intense gaze again, and for once there's no mockery behind it.

'You try very hard not to feel out of place, don't you?' he says softly.

'Very,' I agree, the whisky I've drunk making me brutally honest. 'I've been trying all my life. It never works, though. I think I'm doomed to always be the "wrong" Rosie – at school, at work . . . and now here, too.'

Hunter reaches out and tops up my glass again without asking.

'Is that what it's all about then?' he asks. 'The shopping? The obsession with wearing the right thing at all times? It's not about standing out for you, like it is with all the rest of them, is it? It's about fitting in.'

I pause, struck by the insightfulness of this observation, especially coming from a man who barely even knows me.

'I grew up poor,' I tell him, deciding to trust him with something I've never really admitted to anyone else. 'With three older sisters and a mum who was on her own and couldn't afford to buy us new things. All of my clothes were hand-me-downs. Everything was at least two years out of date. And I went to a school where that kind of thing mattered far too much, so, needless to say, I didn't exactly fit in. And, yeah, I guess now I try to shop my way out of the feeling of being a perpetual misfit. I always feel like if I can just find the right outfit, or the right piece of furniture, or . . . the right thing . . . then my life will be perfect. And it never is, but I still keep trying. I know how stupid that sounds, trust me.'

'It doesn't sound stupid, Rosie,' says Hunter. 'But no one's life is perfect. Not even those women you're trying so hard to be like.'

I think about Bex and Daniel, arguing in the grounds; Millie's big blue eyes filling with tears when she spoke about some of the horrible comments she gets.

Maybe he's right.

Although, right now, I'd still rather have their lives than mine. At least that way I'd have somewhere to live when I leave here. And be able to take a sauna without worrying someone might try to kill me.

'So, who's the number one suspect?' Hunter asks, his eyes twinkling with mischief. 'Oh, come on, don't pretend you don't have a list. I can tell you do.'

'So far I'm thinking either Sabrina or Dante,' I reply, secretly grateful for the opportunity to air these thoughts rather than just obsessing endlessly over them in private. 'They've had the most opportunity. Oh, and neither of them particularly wants me here, do they? Especially not Sabrina. She hates me. And Dante's not exactly warm, either.'

'He's got a lot on his plate,' says Hunter, carefully. 'It's a big responsibility, running a place like this. The Laird puts a lot of pressure on him. And, just between you and me, I don't think Sabrina's business is doing too well, either. So she probably has a lot riding on this launch, too. I wouldn't take anything they say too personally, you know? Stress does funny things to people. And, like I say, no one's life is perfect. Not even mine, even though it looks it.'

He grins, gesturing at the towering pile of laundry behind him.

'I guess not,' I reply, thinking about him trying to raise his daughter on his own while living in the picturesque middle of nowhere. 'Although this place does seem pretty perfect to me, at least. It's so beautiful. I always thought I was a city girl, but scenery like this could easily change my mind.'

'Aye, well, I'm not much of a city person myself,' Hunter replies, taking another sip of his drink. 'Too many people for my liking. Out here you can hear yourself think. There's a freedom you don't get in the city. You can be yourself here. If you want to, that is.'

'Oh, I do,' I reply, captivated by the picture he's painting of Highland life. 'I *do* want to be myself.'

Or, at least I *think* I do.

'Maybe not this *exact* version of myself,' I qualify, an image of me emerging, tomato-faced from the sauna, popping suddenly into my head. 'But a better one. The version of myself I'm going to be once I've finished figuring out who she is, exactly.'

And once the Chrysalis has worked its magic on me.

'Well, there's nothing like being out there in nature to focus the mind,' Hunter says quietly. 'And you wouldn't be the first person to come to the Highlands to "find" themselves.'

'You know, *you* should be the face of the Chrysalis,' I tease, struck by the solemnity of his tone. 'You're the perfect advert for it. You're making me want to quit my job and just stay here forever.'

'Aye. Me too,' he replies, a faraway expression stealing into his eyes. 'I, er, I wish *I* could stay forever, I mean. Not you. Although you'd be very welcome to stay too, I'm sure. If you wanted to, obviously.'

He quickly picks up his glass, then sets it down again when he realises it's empty, and I smile at how flustered he is, in spite of his rugged, man-of-few-words act.

'Wait, what do you mean you wish you could stay too?' I ask as the words in question sink in. 'Don't you live here?'

I indicate the room around us, with all of its signs of life.

'For now, aye. I don't know how long we'll be staying, though,' Hunter replies, stroking Stevie's head as the huge dog jumps up beside us, folding his long limbs underneath him on the couch. 'It depends how well the launch goes, really. Everything's riding on that. If the hotel doesn't do well, it's not going to stay open for long; and if it doesn't stay open . . . well, it's back to Edinburgh for me and Hannah.'

'But . . . you said you hated the city?' I protest, trying to imagine him squashed into a crowded bus, or sitting trapped behind a desk somewhere, when everything about him screams of fresh air and wide open spaces.

I just can't do it, though. It wouldn't work. He'd be as out of place as I've always been – although something tells me Hunter Stuart wouldn't try nearly as hard to make himself fit in.

'Oh, I do,' he replies, nodding. 'If it was up to me, I'd never go back. But we don't always get the things we want in life, do we?'

His voice is sad, but resigned. I want to argue with him – to tell him that *of course* we should all get the things we want most, whatever they happen to be. But, then again, that's the kind of talk that just made me spend £120 on a sweatshirt everyone made fun of, so I guess I can't really talk here.

'I suppose not,' I say, reaching out to stroke Stevie's furry body, and finding myself stroking Hunter's hand instead.

'Oops. Sorry. Too much whisky, I think.'

I snatch my hand quickly back, and our eyes meet for a fleeting moment, which sends a hot shiver running deliciously down the length of my body.

Uh-oh.

'I think it's time we got you to bed,' says Hunter, a line that makes my knees suddenly weak, for reasons I don't think I can blame on the alcohol this time.

'Oh, I . . . um . . .' I splutter awkwardly, heat flooding my cheeks as I try to figure out what to say to this. And what I *want* to say to it.

'*Your* bed,' Hunter clarifies, his face almost as red as mine is, as he gets quickly to his feet. 'It's getting late, I mean. You should be sleeping by now.'

He holds out his hands to help me up, and I briefly wish I could just sink into the sofa and disappear down the side of it, like a lost coin.

'Right! Yes! Of course!' I say instead, giving a large, theatrical yawn. 'Just what I was thinking, too!'

I take his hands – which are large and warm, and a little bit rough from all of that manual labour he does – and allow him to gently pull me upwards, staggering slightly as I find myself back on two feet again. There's a brief moment where I overbalance and end up leaning against his hard chest, my cheek pressed up against his sweater, then another moment in which time seems to briefly stand still. Then Hunter's arms cautiously wrap themselves around my body and I allow myself to relax into him, breathing in the woodsy, spicy scent, and allowing some of the tension I've been carrying around since I got here to seep out of my body.

'Rosie,' he whispers softly, his breath warm in my hair. 'Are you sleeping?'

'Nope,' I say brightly, pushing back against him until I'm upright again. 'Totally awake. Bushy-eyed and bright-tailed. No, wait . . .'

'Come on,' Hunter says, chuckling. 'If you're not sleeping now, then you definitely should be.'

I follow him meekly to the door of the apartment, where he pauses and looks down at me, that line back between his eyes again.

'Will you be OK getting back to your room?' he asks. 'I'd come with you to make sure, but I can't leave Hannah.'

'Oh, no, honestly, I'm fine,' I insist, taking the key he's holding out for me and making a monumental effort to sound as fine as I say I am. 'It's just along this hallway. Um, isn't it?'

'It is,' says Hunter. 'You can't miss it. Well, *you* probably could, but . . . look, it's right down the hall. Come back and get me if you can't find it.'

'I can look after myself,' I say proudly, but, thanks to the whisky, it comes out sounding more like, 'I had a look at your shelf' – which is technically *true*, but probably not particularly reassuring.

'Well,' says Hunter, clearing his throat awkwardly as he holds the door open for me.

'Well,' I reply, stupidly, wishing I hadn't drunk quite so much whisky.

He looks down at me, his caramel-coloured eyes dark in the dim light of the corridor outside his apartment, and I'm horrified to find myself tilting my face up to him, as if I'm waiting for him to kiss me.

What was that about not falling for a man who lives hundreds of miles away?

'Um, I should be going, then,' I mutter, stepping quickly backwards and almost landing on Stevie's tail in the process. 'Thanks for the drink.'

'Thanks for ironing my underpants,' Hunter replies seriously, his mouth quirking very slightly at the corner. 'It was a big help.'

'Oh, any time,' I assure him. 'I'm really good with pants.'

And, with that immortal line hanging in the air between us, I turn and practically run in the direction of my room – which I find relatively quickly this time. It's only once I'm on the other side of the wooden door, though, that I remember what Hannah said earlier about Dante keeping the room keys locked away somewhere.

So, if that's the case; how come Hunter was able to get me this one?

Chapter 13

I wake up late the next morning, and only just manage to get myself showered, dressed, and out onto the hotel driveway as the rest of the influencer party are boarding the minibus, which is taking us to the nearest village, for what the itinerary vaguely describes as 'sightseeing / content creation'.

'You missed breakfast, Wrong Rosie,' says Bex, in her sing-song voice as I climb on board just as the engine starts up. 'We were starting to think you might be stuck in the sauna again. Or that you'd given up on the competition already and gone home.'

I do my best to ignore her as I start to make my way down the aisle, determined not to let her get to me. Because, whether Bex and the rest of them like it or not, the fact is, I *haven't* given up *or* gone home. And I might not stand the slightest chance of winning this contest, but that doesn't mean I'm not going to try.

And the more Bex and co. try to convince me I'm the 'wrong' Rosie for the job, the more determined I am to become the *right* one.

I can do this.

I will be cool. I will be calm. I will be the very picture of a successful influencer, who doesn't need the approval of Bex Foster, or anyone else.

And I will start right now.

I continue on down the aisle, somehow managing to keep my balance until the bus suddenly makes a sharp turn at the end of the hotel driveway, forcing me to reach out and grab the nearest headrest with both hands to stop myself falling flat on my face.

'What the hell?' splutters the headrest, coming to life at the exact moment I realise it isn't actually a headrest at all. No, it's an actual *head* – Daniel Foster's to be exact – and it's looking up at me with so much horror that, for a split second, I wonder if I've somehow managed to wrench it right off its body.

The head looks at me. I look at the head, its cheeks scrunched together between my palms and the lips forming a perfect 'O' of shock.

'Sorry!' I gasp, letting go at last. 'I'm so sorry, I—'

Before I can go on, the bus makes another turn, which, once again, knocks me off balance, making me sit down sharply . . . on what turns out to be Millie Mitchell's lap.

Millie and I shriek simultaneously into each other's surprised faces, and I jump back up again, just in time to see Zara's shoulders shaking with laughter, and Bex holding up her phone, filming the entire little show I've just put on.

Great. I'd have hated for *this* moment to go unrecorded.

Muttering yet another apology, I throw myself into the nearest empty seat and lean my forehead against the window, staring out at the passing scenery as I wait for my nervous system to stabilise itself, and everyone on the bus to stop laughing at me; which takes much longer than really seems necessary.

Trust me to turn even the simplest of tasks – like getting onto a bus, say – into a comedy show.

The sky outside the window is a moody dark grey this morning, to match my mood; purple rain clouds obscuring the craggy hilltops, and making the landscape look like a watercolour painting – little stone cottages set in miles of unspoilt countryside, with views out over the coastline we're following. Just as we reach the outskirts of Glenmuir village, though, which is a few miles north of the hotel, there's a break in the clouds, and a feeble ray of sunshine breaks through, sending a rainbow shimmering into the damp air. The bus fills with the sound of camera shutters as everyone oohs and ahhs at it in unison, all scrambling to get the very best photo for social media, while I just sit there, nose pressed against the glass as I watch the light change in front of my eyes.

It might be windswept and remote, but I think I understand what it is that Hunter sees in this place. There's something secret and wild about it, as if it's a place from some long-forgotten story that couldn't possibly exist in the same universe as the humdrum city streets I'm used to, and as I sit there watching it slide past the window, my heart rate finally starts to slow to a more normal pace.

It would be very easy to feel at home here.

It's just a shame I'm never going get the chance to.

'OK, everyone,' says Sabrina, getting to her feet as the bus comes to a stop at the edge of a little harbour, which is lined with cafes and restaurants, some of which have bunting hung around their windows, and tables and chairs arranged invitingly outside. 'As you know, the purpose of today's trip is to show your followers a bit of the local area, and make them want to see it for themselves, by booking a stay at the Chrysalis. I'm thinking *quaint*. I'm thinking *authentic*. I'm thinking haggis, bagpipes, tartan; you know the kind of thing.'

'I'm thinking bullshit,' mutters Zara from the seat behind me. Sabrina glares at me as if it was my fault, and then very deliberately turns her back on me to address the rest of the bus.

'You have two hours here to do your thing,' she says, 'so, off you go. Let's really make that content *sing*.'

'It's not very big, is it?' says Millie, as we file off the bus – me waiting until last, so there's no chance of me grabbing onto any more heads as I pass them. 'I don't think it's going to take us two hours to look round it, somehow.'

She's probably right. But as we split up to go our separate ways, Zara and Millie teaming up again so they can take each other's photos, I can't help but feel excited at the prospect of getting to explore the place. There's a split second when I find myself wishing I had someone to wander around with but, then again, I know that if my ex and I were still together, and he was here with me now, I'd have felt like I was on my own anyway, so maybe it's for the best that he isn't.

As I said to Hunter last night, sometimes the loneliest place is the middle of a crowd; or, in my case, when you're with someone who barely even notices you're there. And at least this way I get to do whatever I like, without having to worry about someone else, or feel the weight of his disinterest bearing down on me.

I take a few photos of the pretty little harbour, then head for what I'm assuming is the centre of town. Sure enough, the narrow street I head down opens out into a small, open square, which is filled with market stalls, from which vendors are selling a dizzying array of goods. The mouth-watering scent of fish and chips wafts over from a food truck parked at one side of the square, and there's a buzz of chatter and life as tourists mix with locals, all enjoying my very favourite thing: shopping.

'Oh, this is gorgeous,' I say, stopping at one stall and picking up a little gift basket filled with things like hand soap and shower gel, all beautifully presented and tied up with a bright red bow.

The stallholder straightens up from a box she's been unpacking, and I give a start of recognition at the sight of her long, purple hair and forget-me-not eyes.

It's the 'witch' I saw on the train; looking even more witch-like up close.

'All handmade right here in the village,' she says proudly, holding out a little glass jar for me to inspect. 'Here, try this one; it helps ward off evil.'

I'm not sure about its evil-repelling properties, but the cream smells exactly like a sunny day at the beach, while the one after that is a mixture of spices and woodsmoke that reminds me of Hunter Stuart.

Not that I've been thinking about Hunter Stuart, you understand.

Well, not *much*.

'I'll take one of each,' I tell her, knowing there's no way I'm going to be able to pick a favourite. 'And, um, two of this spicy one. I don't suppose you take credit cards, do you?'

I'm half-expecting her to say no, but she produces a card-reader without comment, and I hold my breath as the transaction goes through, praying I'm not up to the limit on my card yet.

'You know, you should try selling these at the hotel,' I say thoughtfully as the woman hands me a little paper bag with what I'm assuming is her name – Isobel Lamb – on the front. 'You know, the Chrysalis? It's in this old castle, not far from here.'

'Aye, I know the place,' says the woman shortly. 'We all know that place.'

'Oh. Right,' I say, surprised at the change in tone. 'Well, it's just, I'm staying there for a few days, and the bathrooms are filled with products, which are all very nice, but not nearly as nice as these. I was thinking maybe you could approach them and see if they'd stock your stuff instead? I bet they'll get through tons of toiletries once the hotel's properly open; you could make a fortune from it. And it'd be nice for the guests to be able to try some locally made products, rather than the kind of thing you can get anywhere.'

I beam at her, pleased with myself for having come up with this idea.

'Aye,' says the woman, clearly meaning 'no'. 'That'd be a good idea right enough . . . if the new laird wasn't too far up his own backside to be bothered with the likes of us. Isn't that right, Ian?'

'That's right, Izzie,' says the man at the stall next to hers, who's been blatantly listening in to the entire conversation, without even pretending otherwise. 'Up his own arse, so he is.'

I squint at them both in surprise. The man – Ian – has short, yellow-blond hair, rosy cheeks and very blue eyes. His stall is a riot of colour, selling fresh produce like carrots, turnips and leeks, which leads me to believe he's from one of the nearby farms.

Miss Marple would certainly be proud of me, with these deduction skills of mine.

'The new lord . . . I mean laird?' I venture cautiously. 'What happened to the old one, then? I thought he was still living up at the castle?'

Izzy snorts, her craggy, sharp-nosed face creasing with amusement.

'Oh, aye, he is,' she says. 'He's probably still up there, pacing the corridors like an old ghoul. But it's his nephew who's in charge these days. Or great-nephew, it must be, I suppose. Whatever he is, he wants nothing to do with us villagers; that's one thing I can tell you for sure.'

'Now, the *old* laird,' says Ian, putting some parsnips into a brown paper bag and handing them to a customer as he speaks. 'He was a different kettle o' fish. A bit of a devil, mind, but always keen to do his bit and send some business our way. But since they decided to turn the place into a hotel, that all changed. Everything has to come from wholesalers now, to keep the price down. They buy nothing local anymore.'

'But that's terrible,' I say. 'That's one of the best things about travelling somewhere; getting to try all the local produce. Can't you speak to him? Set up a village meeting or something?'

'Chance would be a fine thing,' says Ian, his good-natured face clouding. 'He doesn't even live here. I don't think he's even visited the place. He's just a toff from Glasgow.'

'It's thought he might be a Nuckelavee,' says Izzie in a low voice, leaning close as if imparting a secret.

'Now, it's only thought that by *you*, Izzie,' points out Ian. 'Don't go scaring the lass.'

'A Nuckelavee?' I say, hardly daring to ask. 'What's a Nuckelavee?'

'Why, a Nuckelavee is one of the very worst things there is,' says Izzie dramatically. 'A bringer of plagues, droughts and misfortune; particularly to the fishermen and farmers. They normally come from the Orkney isles, but this one comes from Glasgow, which is even worse.'

'It *has* been a bad year for us farmers,' says Ian glumly. 'Nuckelavees or not. We used to send hundreds o' tatties up to the castle every year, when the old laird was in charge. And now nothing. It's had a big effect on the farm. I even tried to turn one of the fields into a pumpkin patch this year, but it was too muddy for it to work. The wee ones kept getting stuck. And it was turnips we were selling, not pumpkins. The wee ones always used to carve turnips at Halloween, but these days it's pumpkins they want. It's all Americanised now, isn't it? I blame that Justin Bieber.'

'He's a Nuckelavee,' says Izzie, as if that settles it. 'I told you so.'

'Justin Bieber?' I ask incredulously. 'But that's—'

'Not Bieber,' Izzie interrupts. 'Well, actually, he might be one as well. I'll have to consult the cards. But no, I meant the new laird. *He's* the Nuckelavee. Destroying the crops and bringing chaos to all.'

'I think he's a property developer, actually,' puts in Ian. 'That's what I heard, anyway.'

'Aye, that's what they all say,' mutters Izzie darkly. 'He'll be planning to sell the place the first chance he gets. Nuckelavees and property developers – they're all the same.'

'I'll buy some tatties from you, Ian,' I say, hoping to change the subject. 'Wait, actually, tatties are potatoes, aren't they? On second thoughts, that's maybe not such a great idea: I don't really have anywhere to store them in my hotel room. Or cook them. I don't think Dante would like the thought of me trying to roast them over the fire, somehow.'

'If it's the Dante I'm thinking of, then no, he certainly would not,' says Izzie tartly. 'Ideas above his station, that one. The village was always too small for him and his big ideas.'

'Now, now, Izzie, I don't think that's quite fair,' Ian puts in. 'I was speaking to Dante's mother just the other day, and she was telling me what a big help he's been to her. Paid to have her roof fixed after that big storm, apparently. She reckons that new job of his has been good for him.'

'Aye, I bet it has if he can afford to pay for things like that.' Izzie sniffs. 'Still, it's good that he's helping out,' she adds, relenting slightly. 'Maria's been on her own for as long as I can remember. She'd never have been able to fix that roof herself.'

Their conversation moves on to other members of the village and the damage their houses apparently sustained in the last big storm, and I listen idly as I browse the little stall, eventually selecting a particularly fine turnip, and a couple of leeks, which Ian assures me will keep until I get back home, after which I'll be able to make a fine soup with them; or even something called a 'clapshot' that I don't dare ask about.

I nod confidently, then, with their permission, shoot some more video of them both serving customers, and chatting about village life, for what Sabrina will surely think is a nice bit of local colour when I edit it into an Instagram Reel later.

'I know you don't think he'll see you,' I say as I'm preparing to leave, 'but I honestly think you should come up to the hotel and ask to speak to the Laird about getting his nephew to start buying his stock from the village again. You never know, he might listen.'

'Aye, and Ian here might grow wings and fly,' snorts Izzie.

'Just have a think about it,' I tell them both. 'Wouldn't it be worth it? Not just for you two, but for the rest of the village, too. There must be other local businesses that could benefit from working with the hotel?'

'Aye, there's plenty,' says Izzie. 'It's just a question of getting someone up there to listen to us. Maybe if I made one of my persuading potions?'

'Now, Izzie, we've talked about this before,' says Ian quickly. 'Remember what happened with the church minister?'

Much as I wish I could stick around to hear the end of this story, I've been standing here chatting for much longer than I meant to, so I leave them to argue it out between themselves, and with my bag of vegetables in one hand and my toiletries in the other, I make my way back to the harbour, still buzzing with the pleasure of shopping, even though it was for vegetables rather than clothes.

Still, shopping is shopping, and I'm just wondering if there might be time to pop into one of the little gift shops I spotted earlier before the bus leaves, when I reach the harbour and stop abruptly in my tracks, realising there's something different about it: or something *missing about it*, rather.

No.

No, *this can't possibly be right.*

I'm at least ten minutes early.

But the bus is gone.

Chapter 14

'Do you believe me now?' I say a short while later, as Hunter's Land Rover pulls up at the harbour and I jump into the passenger seat, shooing Stevie out of the way first. 'They *hate* me, Hunter. All of them. Well, at least one of them. Why would they have driven off without me if they didn't?'

'Now, there's nothing to suggest they left you behind deliberately,' Hunter replies, checking his mirror before pulling out onto the main road. 'I'm sure there must be some explanation. You didn't get stuck somewhere again, did you? Because, no offence, you seem to have made a bit of a habit of that.'

'I didn't get stuck anywhere,' I reply, annoyed. 'I was just at the market; there was nowhere to get stuck. And I was definitely at the pick-up point on time, Hunter. I was even *early*. They just drove away and left me. Come on, that *has* to have been deliberate. Even you have to admit that.'

'The driver wouldn't do that,' says Hunter. 'He wouldn't dare. It's more than his job's worth to leave a guest behind.'

'He probably didn't even notice I wasn't there,' I say glumly. 'That happens to me a lot.'

'I find it hard to believe anyone wouldn't notice you, Rosie,' Hunter replies, his eyes fixed firmly on the road, so I can't tell if he means this, or if he's just trying to cheer me up, but either way a blush colours my cheeks. 'And I can't imagine why Sabrina and co. would want to leave you behind on purpose, either.'

'You obviously never went to an all-girls school,' I reply, reaching over to pat Stevie on the head as he nudges at me with his nose for attention. This wolf-dog is more like a puppy; and he's really growing on me. 'Women can be absolutely brutal to each other, trust me. And they don't even need a reason for it, either.'

My shoulders thrum with tension at the thought of all of the other things I've been deliberately left out of, and I have to force myself to relax them.

'Well, in this case, they definitely don't have one,' says Hunter gallantly. 'Unless it's something to do with the vegetables. What are you planning to do with those, by the way? Are you going to make soup?'

'Oh!' I look down at the turnip on my lap, and the leeks poking out of the top of my brown paper bag Ian gave me. 'No, I bought them in the village. I don't actually know what I'm going to do with them – Ian said something about a "clapshot"? – but the people selling them were so nice I wanted to buy something. Can you believe the hotel doesn't buy any local produce at all? Apparently, everything comes from giant wholesalers down in the Central Belt. Isn't that wild? It's so they can save money, Izzie says.'

Hunter glances at me curiously.

'What else did you find out from Izzie and Ian, whoever they are?' he asks.

'Ian's a farmer,' I tell him, picking up the turnip so I can admire it. 'Although he's worried he might have to sell up if things don't improve for him soon. And Izzie is a witch. A green witch, I mean,' I add quickly, as the Land Rover swerves towards the side of the road. 'She makes things from natural ingredients. Here, smell this.'

I pull out some of the little bottles I bought from the market and thrust one under his nose.

'It reminded me of you,' I say without thinking.

The car swerves again.

'That'll be why it's so disgusting, then,' Hunter comments, pulling a face as he recovers control of the Land Rover. 'What other types of snake oil did this witch sell you?'

'Um, just that,' I tell him, not wanting to admit to the little tub of gel that Izzie described as a 'love potion', and insisted on giving me for free, saying I looked like I needed it.

I'm still not sure what she meant by that.

'They did tell me a ton of stuff about the village and the castle, though,' I go on quickly, before we can get back to the subject of me buying lotions that remind me of burying my face into Hunter's jumper last night. 'And about the Laird. Did you know that he's basically a prisoner in the place now? And his posh-boy great-nephew is running the show from Glasgow?'

'Is that right?' Hunter comments, his tone infuriatingly neutral.

'So Izzie says. Everyone hates him, apparently. They're convinced he's going to try to sell the hotel the first chance he gets. Ian said he was a right arsehole who only cares about money, so that's definitely the kind of thing he'd do. Have you met him?'

'Your pal Ian? Or the arsehole nephew?'

'The arsehole,' I confirm. 'Izzie says that if she hadn't pledged to do no harm, she'd make a tincture for his tea, to make him a bit less tight-fisted. She doesn't think she could do it without potentially killing him, though, unfortunately.'

'Well, that's a shame.' On the steering wheel, Hunter's own fists seem to tighten, although a smile plays around his lips.

'It's not funny, you know,' I say, turning to look at him, and almost headbutting Stevie in the process. 'The stuff they make is really good quality, *and* it's all made locally. The hotel should be buying it. They could even have a little shop in reception or something, selling different things from around the area.'

I hold up the turnip and the bottle of Eau de Hunter again, as if to prove my point.

'Maybe I'll have a word with Dante when I get back,' I go on thoughtfully, when Hunter doesn't answer. 'He's the manager, surely he must have some say over what kind of products are bought?'

'Maybe. Why are you so invested in this, though?' Hunter asks, his eyes flicking in my direction. 'Or is it just that you enjoy shopping so much that you want to shop on behalf of the hotel now, too?'

'I *do* think about things other than shopping, you know,' I remind him, annoyed. 'I told you that last night. And I'm not *invested*, particularly; I just want to help.'

I don't want to tell him this, but his constant jibes about shopping and selfies have been making me think a bit more about what it is, exactly, that I want to get out of this stay – these four days in the life of an influencer. And I'm still not totally sure what the answer to that is, but I *do* know it has to be something more than just that. I don't want to influence people to be like me; constantly buying things they don't actually need, as if it'll make up for the things they *do* need, but which aren't actually for sale. Like love, say. Or that elusive sense of belonging that I'm starting to realise doesn't come courtesy of a cashmere sweater or sparkly dress; no matter how fabulous.

I want to make a difference.

And maybe this is a good place to start.

'Izzie and Ian are the first people who've been nice to me since I got here,' I say instead. 'Well, other than you and Agnes. And, yes, you too,' I add, laughing as Stevie nudges me with his nose to get my attention. 'I'd just like to do something for them in return.'

'Fair enough. I'm just not sure pestering Dante to buy their stuff is the best way to go about it,' says Hunter. 'I told you how much pressure he's under. I don't really fancy your chances of convincing him to buy hand cream, or whatever that stuff is.'

I clutch my shopping bags a little tighter, annoyed by how dismissive he's being of my big idea. It reminds me of my ex. He always thought my ideas were stupid, too; that's if he even bothered listening to them.

And I haven't even got onto the subject of the Nuckelavee yet. Or told him about the hand cream that repels evil.

'Laugh all you want,' I say, opening up the bottle of lotion again so I can have another sniff. 'But yes, convincing Dante to shop locally for the hotel *is* the best way to go about it, actually. And it could be good for the Chrysalis, too. People want to experience local culture. They don't want to travel to the Highlands and just see the same old things they can find in any Travelodge in the country. They want quality produce that's made in the place they're visiting.'

'Aye, and all that stuff comes at a price,' Hunter replies. 'Which the hotel has to be able to afford if it's going to survive. Tourists might like local products, but they don't always like the price tag that comes with them.'

'Well, that's why I'm here, isn't it? To influence them. And if there's anyone who can persuade people to shop, it's me.'

I cross my arms stubbornly over the bag of leeks. I may be down to just over two thousand followers now, but that's still two thousand people who might see one of my posts and decide to come to the hotel.

That has to count for something?

'Well, I for one have every confidence in you, Rosie,' Hunter says, in an amused tone which makes me want to throw my turnip at him. 'I'm sure the Chrysalis is very lucky to have you out there *influencing* on its behalf.'

'It's lucky to have all of us,' I retort. 'And so are you, Hunter. I know you think influencers are stupid, and vapid, and obsessed with shopping, but if you and Hannah want to be able to stay here in the Highlands, you need the hotel to be a success as much as anyone else. And having us all doing our best to promote it could help it do that.'

'Hey, now, I didn't call you stupid *or* vapid,' he protests, the amused tone gone. 'I would never say anything like that, Rosie.'

'No, but you *do* think it, don't you?' I challenge him.

'Not about *you*,' he says after a pause. 'I can see you're neither of those things. You *do* like shopping, though.'

I shrug, because there's no point arguing with that one.

'Look,' he says in a gentler tone. 'You're right. I do want the hotel to be a success. I want to be able to stay here. I want Hannah to grow up somewhere with enough space to run wild when she feels like it, without worrying about who she might be disturbing. So I'm sorry if I sounded a bit . . . well, sceptical . . . about what you do. I didn't mean to.'

'It's not really what *I* do,' I admit. 'I'm not even supposed to be here, remember? But it *is* what Bex and the rest of them do. And this is an amazing place, Hunter,' I go on, twisting around in my seat so I can see his face. 'It just needs the right publicity, so people know it's here. And once they do, they'll want to come and see it for themselves. I just know it.'

'And you think you and your pals are the right people to give it that publicity?' The amused tone is back, although he's doing his best to hide it.

'Maybe,' I reply, with a defiant tilt of the chin. 'We can't just let the arsehole nephew sell the place, can we? We have to defeat him.'

This seems like an excellent line for me to exit the car on, only I forget about the turnip and have to go back to get it, and I'm not sure a turnip is *quite* the prop I need for my big moment. Not even a particularly large and tasty one, which Ian assures me this one will be.

It's the best I can manage under the circumstances, though, so, holding the turnip in both hands so I don't drop it, I make my way up the steps that lead to the castle, feeling like Erin Brockovich or . . . or Moana, say.

OK, maybe not like either of those.

But as I stride into the lobby, giving Agnes a breezy wave as I march past her at the reception desk, and then another one as I pass her for a second time, having realised I'm going in the wrong direction, I walk with a renewed sense of purpose; because now I'm not just here to get a few spa treatments while taking part in a competition I have no chance of winning. Or even to have myself the journey of transformation I was promised.

No, now I'm here to save the hotel from the property-developing Nuckelavee from Glasgow who wants to sell it to the highest bidder; and, not only that, but to save dozens of people's jobs in the process.

And if that's not a lofty goal, as Hunter sarcastically put it, then I don't know what is.

Chapter 15

Back in my room, I conduct my now customary search for horses' heads and missing clothes, then, finding everything in order, I settle down in a seat by the window to edit and post some of the photos and videos I took this morning in the village.

There are quite a few of Izzie and Ian, and not too many of me; but the village looks picturesque in the sunshine that finally broke through the clouds, and the shots of the market stalls have actually turned out quite well – or as well as photos of vegetables *can* turn out – so, all in all, I figure my bid to save the hotel by influencing people to come to the area is off to a good start.

According to the fresh copy of the itinerary Luna pushed under my door this morning (this one without any notes relating to dress codes, I notice . . .), this afternoon's activity is a picnic on the beach; which sounds lovely until I realise we'll be getting there on horseback.

In the rain.

Putting down my phone halfway through a video edit, I get reluctantly out of my comfy chair and stare out of the window at the tiny drops of water that are suddenly obscuring the view, in a stark contrast to the sunshine of earlier.

The guidebooks really weren't joking when they said the weather changes every fifteen minutes here, were they?

The combination of pouring rain plus horseback riding presents me with the kind of sartorial dilemma that's going to be no fun at all to solve (as opposed to the dinner-plus-dancing kind, which *are* pretty fun to solve), so I spend a stressy half-hour or so in the walk-in closet in my room, emerging at last looking like Nanook of the North, in a tight pair of jeans and a large, puffy jacket which I'm just going to have to hope is waterproof.

This is not going to look good in photos, unfortunately, but there's not much I can do about it, so I head stiffly downstairs, where, of course, I find everyone else waiting for me, looking like they're about to be photographed for a magazine shoot. Bex, in particular, has gone all out in a long, flowy white dress, which she's accessorised with a chunky knit jumper, which I fully expect her to describe as 'rustic' in the resulting Instagram caption.

'Ooh, another brave outfit choice, Wrong Rosie,' she coos, in her pretending-to-be-nice tone. 'Can you even bend your arms in that jacket?'

'Almost,' I mutter, a tiny bead of sweat starting to trickle down my back, because it might be raining, but it's also strangely humid. 'And it's just plain old Rosie, thanks.'

'Oh, you're not *that* plain,' Millie assures me earnestly, as we all file out of the door and onto the driveway where, of course, I find out the rain has stopped already, rendering my waterproof jacket completely redundant. '*Or* old. I bet you're only about thirty-five, aren't you?'

'I'm twenty-nine,' I tell her, making a mental note to update my skincare as soon as I can afford it. 'That's not what I meant, though. I really hate the way everyone – well, Bex, really – keeps calling me Wrong Rosie and going on about how I'm supposed to be the "average" one. It's . . . *unkind.*'

Following Sabrina, who's wearing a long leather trench coat, like some kind of international spy, we turn and walk around the side of the castle, towards the grounds, where I can see Hunter Stuart standing waiting for us with a group of stocky little Highland ponies beside him.

Oh, please tell me he's not going to be around to witness this, too. That's all I need.

'Look,' says Millie, falling into step beside me as we crunch our way across the gravel to where Hunter's waiting. 'The Wrong Rosie thing. You need to lean into it. Own it. Embrace it, even.'

I look at her doubtfully. I'm not sure I really *want* to lean into average. To embrace 'ordinary'. And I *definitely* don't want to keep on being referred to as Wrong Rosie for the rest of my stay here.

'The thing is,' says Millie with a sigh, 'you need a gimmick, right?'

'I do?' I raise an eyebrow.

'Yes, of course, silly. Everyone needs a gimmick. Take me, for instance. I'm the plus-sized one, right?'

I look at her doubtfully. She might not be the slimmest of the women here, but I'm not sure I'd have described her as plus-sized, either; which makes me wonder how people who are *actually* plus-sized would be described in this influencer world, and who *they're* supposed to be influenced by?

'Just in social media terms, obviously,' she says impatiently. 'It's my gimmick. And I'm also short; so that's *two* gimmicks.'

She smiles proudly, and I nod, not quite knowing what to say to this. She *is* quite short, I suppose. It's weird to hear someone's natural body type referred to as a gimmick, though.

'So, maybe being average is *your* gimmick,' Millie goes on importantly, as if she's imparting some great wisdom to me. 'Maybe that's the thing that will set you apart from everyone else. Think about it.'

She smiles brightly, and I nod again, wondering how on earth I'm supposed to stand out by being average. Isn't that a bit of an oxymoron? And what if I don't *want* to have to have a gimmick? What if I just want to be myself, and not have to put on some act all the time? What then?

'OK, this is where I leave you,' says Sabrina, saving me from this train of thought as she addresses us from the front of the group. 'This gentleman—' she gestures towards Hunter, whose name I can tell she's forgotten '—will be taking over from here. And Luna will be on hand if you need anything.'

'Aren't you coming with us, then?' says the assistant, who looks even more terrified than usual.

'God, no,' says Sabrina, looking horrified at the thought. 'I don't do horses.'

'Me neither,' says Daniel Foster, who's carrying his camera and tripod again. 'I'll be keeping my feet firmly on the ground; it'll be easier to take photos of Bex that way.'

'That's not fair,' puts in Zara. 'None of the rest of us have someone to take photos of us on the ponies. You being here gives Bex an unfair advantage.'

'You and Millie have been taking each other's photos too,' points out Yasmin, surprising everyone into silence again, simply by speaking. 'That's not fair either.'

'You could've paired up with Wro— with Rosie,' shoots back Zara.

'Enough bickering, everyone,' interrupts Sabrina. 'Luna will take photos of all of you. Luna, you can stay on the ground to do it, with Mr Bex.'

Luna looks as relieved as if she's just had a last-minute stay of execution. I can't really blame her; I've got that feeling of foreboding hanging over me again, and I actually *like* horses. I hate to think how much worse this would be if I didn't.

'Right, then,' says Hunter, clearing his throat to get everyone's attention. 'If you could all choose a pony each, I'll just quickly go over some safety information before we get started.'

We all move forward, some quicker than others. I select a sturdy little black gelding who has big, hairy fetlocks and the name Bramble embroidered onto the browband of his bridle. He turns and looks at me solemnly through his long lashes as I approach, and I stroke his velvety nose, enjoying the familiar, horsey smell of him.

Hunter walks around to the front of the group and gives a characteristically short speech about all sticking together and not making any sudden noises while Luna hands out safety helmets, which Bex and Millie both refuse to wear, until Hunter growls at them and threatens to cancel the expedition altogether.

'Fine by me,' says Bex, sounding close to tears. 'That thing's going to completely ruin my hair. It'll look shit in the photos.'

'Maybe Bex could just take hers off for a few minutes?' says Daniel, stepping forward with the air of a man who's here to save the day. 'Just until we've got the shots we need. Then she can put it back on again? How does that sound?'

'No,' replies Hunter bluntly. Everyone waits for him to say something else; then, when he doesn't, Daniel clears his throat importantly, preparing to take charge.

'Just leave it off for now, babe,' he says to Bex. 'We'll get the shots first, then—'

'I said no,' says Hunter, through gritted teeth. 'Did you not hear me?'

'I *heard* you,' replies Daniel, making a face which suggests that listening to Hunter is physically painful to him. 'But what I'm *suggesting* is that Bex just—'

'What *I'm* suggesting is that Bex just wears the safety helmet, or she doesn't come on the ride,' says Hunter, his face thunderous. 'Do I make myself clear?'

'Oh, for goodness' sake,' spits Daniel, turning to Sabrina for backup, only to find she's not there, having already stomped off in the direction of the hotel. 'This is ridiculous. How are we supposed to get decent content if you're going to force them all to dress like LEGO people?'

Bex starts to cry quietly.

'I'm not here to help you create content,' says Hunter, folding his arms across his chest and widening his stance as if to say *don't even think about messing with me*. 'I'm here to look after you all, and make sure everyone stays safe. These are live animals, not photo props.'

I'm about to object to being referred to as an animal, live or not; then I realise he's talking about the ponies, and close my mouth again.

'Oh, please, they're just like a bunch of big dogs,' says Daniel, rolling his eyes.

'Big dogs that could kill you,' replies Hunter pleasantly, sounding like this wouldn't bother him *too* much, were it to happen. Daniel glares at him as if *he* might be the one doing the killing. Hunter smiles easily back, until Daniel finally backs off, shrugging as if he doesn't really care whether his photos are ruined or not.

'Just keep the hat on for now, babe,' he calls over to Bex, making sure Hunter hears him. 'I'll have a word with

Sabrina later and sort something out. Maybe we can organise a private trek or something.'

Hunter gives a snort that sounds a lot like a curse word.

'If you could all put your helmets on,' he says, ignoring Daniel, 'we'll make a start. The picnic baskets are already waiting for us on the beach.'

Everyone dutifully puts on their helmets (which, to be fair, do make us look a bit like LEGO people . . .), then Hunter goes around and helps everyone mount, spending a particularly long time with Millie, who keeps shrieking and kind of draping herself over the saddle with her perfectly shaped butt in the air.

I swear she's doing that deliberately.

'Do you want a leg-up?' Hunter says from behind me as I gather Bramble's reins in one hand, and attempt to get my foot into the stirrup, hampered by my slightly too tight jeans, which are restricting my movement much more than I thought they would.

'Nope, I'm fine, thanks,' I reply breathlessly, attempting to scramble into the saddle. 'I can do it. I used to take riding lessons when I was a kid. I totally know what I'm doing.'

I attempt to raise my foot even higher, and am *almost* there when a loud ripping sound fills the air as the seam of my jeans gives way.

Oh, my God.

Blushing furiously, and with shrieks of laughter echoing in my ears, I tug my jacket self-consciously down over my suspiciously breezy rear, glad for once that I decided to wear my 'big pants' this morning. Before I can look down to verify this, though, there's a movement from behind me, and Hunter picks me up, lifting me as easily as if I *wasn't* wearing all my clothes at once, and placing me in the saddle as if I'm a doll.

It's strangely hot, actually; although I suppose that *could* just be the thick jacket I'm wearing.

'OK,' says Hunter, taking a step back so he can see us all. 'Unless anyone else has some drama they'd like to unleash, we'll be on our way.'

He goes to his own horse and springs smoothly into the saddle.

He would.

The rest of us fall into line behind him (me sticking to the back of the line, so no one has to look at my butt) as he sets off at a slow walk, taking a gravel path around the outskirts of the castle's ornamental garden, then following it down to the white-sand beach beyond.

'That's it, Bex,' yells Daniel, who's been following along behind us with Luna, both of them snapping away on their cameras as they keep up easily enough with our snail's-pace progress. 'If you could just look over your shoulder and give us a smile.'

Bex does as she's asked, although there's a murderous look in her eye which reminds me of the day I saw her arguing with Daniel in the grounds. Her long dress drapes over her pony's back in a way that may not be practical, but which will look amazing on camera, and her hair is in an intricate, long braid down her back. If it wasn't for the solid black helmet perched on top of her head, she'd look like some kind of Highland princess; which I suspect was exactly the effect she was going for before Hunter stepped in with his pesky safety requirements.

'Almost there,' calls Hunter, twisting around in the saddle to address the short line of riders behind him. 'We'll have our picnic on the beach, as planned, but we'll have to be quick; I don't think the rain's going to hold off for long.'

I look up at the darkening sky, wishing it had occurred to me to buy an umbrella in the village earlier; it would probably be a lot more useful to me than a turnip, that's for sure.

The thought of the village, however, reminds me of the incident with the bus earlier, and how it drove off without me.

Hunter thinks there must be some kind of reasonable explanation for it.

I'm not so sure.

But I guess there's only one way to find out. And I know exactly who I'm going to ask.

Chapter 16

I urge Bramble forward until we're level with Zara, who's riding a grey pony, and trying to take a photo of the beach through its ears.

'Hey, what happened with the bus earlier?' I ask, deciding I might as well get straight to the point. 'You all drove off without me.'

Zara looks over at me, her curly hair cascading over her shoulders, and still somehow looking good, even when trapped under the unflattering safety helmet .

'Oh. Yeah,' she says uncomfortably. 'Sorry about that. It wasn't deliberate. It was—' she lowers her voice and I have to lean forward to hear her '—it was Bex.'

'Bex? I might have guessed,' I reply grimly. 'She really has it in for me, doesn't she?'

'No, it wasn't anything to do with you,' Zara replies in a whisper. 'I don't know what happened, but she came back to the bus in tears, and Daniel insisted he had to get her back to the hotel right away. He was really pushy about it. And, of course, Sabrina'll do anything to keep the two of them happy, so she told the driver we had to leave. We were almost back at the hotel before we realised you were missing.'

'Right. Well, that figures too, I suppose. The invisible woman strikes again.' I lean forward and ruffle Bramble's mane in an attempt to hide my hurt at this additional proof of how little impact I make on people.

'The what?'

'Oh, nothing,' I reply, trying to shake off the melancholy that's descended on me like a blanket. 'That's . . . that's strange about Bex. I wonder what's going on with her?'

'It's probably to do with her birthday,' says Zara, as if stating the obvious.

'Her birthday? What's that got to do with anything?'

'Well, it's next week, isn't it? And Bex hates her birthday. She gets really moody in the run-up to it.'

'No, she doesn't,' I reply, confused. 'She always makes a massive fuss about it. Remember last year when she had that big party to celebrate her twenty-fifth? Bex didn't stop posting about it for at least a month.'

Zara's shoulders shake, and after a second, I realise she's trying not to laugh.

'You didn't *really* think Bex turned twenty-five last year, did you?' she says, finally getting herself under control. 'Rosie, Bex is at least thirty-six. At *least*.'

'Seriously?'

I stand up in my stirrups, trying to get a better look at Bex, but all I can see is that long braid, which, now I come to think of it, is at least twice as long as her hair was this morning.

'Did she somehow get extensions in the village?' I ask incredulously.

'It's a clip-in,' replies Millie from behind me. 'She brought it with her. She has a few of them. And I think she's thirty-seven now, Zara. What's this about an invisible woman, though? Is the castle *haunted*?'

'Only by me,' I reply, distractedly. 'I can't believe Bex has been lying about her age. I had no idea. And thirty-seven isn't even old.'

'It is if you're trying to get collaborations with brands that mainly cater to women in their twenties,' says Zara, shrugging as if this is a well-established fact that everyone should know. 'A lot of them won't even consider you if you have to scroll too far to get to your birthday when you're filling in their online forms. So she lies. We all do; just not all about the same things.'

I'm about to ask what it is *she* lies about to land brand collaborations when Yasmin's pony comes to a halt in front of me, and I have to grab the reins to stop Bramble before he barges right into it.

'OK, everyone,' says Hunter, jumping down from his horse. 'This is where we stop.'

We all scramble off our ponies and onto the sand, where a small group of picnic baskets have been laid out on rugs, not too far from the shore.

The rain starts falling again halfway through the picnic, however, which, once again, appears to be of interest to the influencers only as a photo prop, rather than as actual sustenance.

'You're not going to take any photos, then?' asks Hunter, looking at me through the drizzle as we sit together on one of the blankets, my stomach rumbling loudly at the sight of the miniature pork pies and selection of cakes which I don't dare touch for fear of disturbing the careful way they've been arranged to look good on social media. 'I thought that was why you were here?'

'I'm not exactly dressed for a photo shoot,' I reply, not wanting to tell him the real reason I'm not moving from the blanket is that I can't stand up without flashing everyone through the hole in my jeans. 'I don't think I'm going to be influencing anyone to "shop my style" somehow.'

'There you go again, worrying about what you're wearing,' Hunter replies. 'Do you ever just relax and enjoy yourself, Rosie?'

'I'm enjoying myself now,' I point out. 'How could I possibly fail to enjoy being in a place like this?'

I hold out my arms in an expansive gesture that takes in the beach itself, plus the castle standing proudly behind it, looking particularly Gothic this afternoon against the slate-grey sky. It really is a magnificent building; and the beach is picture perfect, even in the rain.

I'm not surprised he wants to stay here; I've never been to Edinburgh, but I can't imagine any city competing with the wild beauty of the Highlands, somehow.

'We'll have to think about getting back to the hotel soon,' says Hunter, frowning as he looks up at the rapidly gathering clouds. 'This weather isn't going to get any better, and the woman from the stables we borrowed the ponies from will be coming to pick them up soon.'

'I think you might have some trouble persuading this lot to leave,' I reply, looking down the beach to where Zara and Millie have removed their shoes and socks to take photos of each other paddling in the shallow water. The temperature has dropped sharply since we left the castle, and they both look like they're about to pass out from the cold; and Bex, who's now riding along the beach, hard hat conspicuously missing, is slowly turning blue from it.

I'm just wondering if I should try to persuade Hunter to take some photos of me sitting on the blanket – which is the best I can really hope to do, given the jeans situation – when the sound of raised voices comes drifting across the sand, and I look up to see Sabrina and Dante storming towards us through the drizzle; or what passes for storming when you're walking across sand in stilettos, like Sabrina is. So, a kind of slow-motion angry plod, then.

It's the 'angry' bit that makes the hairs on the back of my neck stand on end. Because I may not know Sabrina very well – I don't think she's said more than maybe six sentences to me in total since I got here, and almost all of them have been accusing me of something – but I have a horrible feeling that if she's angry about something, it's probably me.

'Oh, my God,' whispers Luna, lowering the camera she's using to take photos of all of us as she catches sight of her boss battling with the sand.

Or it could be Luna.

Please let it be Luna.

'What the hell is this supposed to be?' Sabrina demands as she reaches us, holding up an iPad to show what is unmistakably my Instagram grid.

Nope, it's definitely me.

Thought so.

'Well?'

Everyone edges closer, trying to see what's got Sabrina so worked up that she's risked her designer heels in this weather. Zara and Millie come padding over in their bare feet, and even Bramble the pony pauses in the act of chomping on a sandwich from the picnic basket to listen in.

Once we're all within earshot, Sabrina taps quickly on the screen, and a video starts playing; one I recognise immediately as the piece of footage I was in the middle of editing when I was distracted by the rain outside earlier.

Oh no.

Please don't tell me I somehow managed to hit 'publish' rather than saving it to drafts?

The video starts off innocently enough, with some arty shots of the colourful fruit and veg piled high on Ian's stall, before cutting to Izzie, who's holding up some of her hand creams, and speaking earnestly about how the ingredients are all gathered locally, by the light of the full moon. (I meant to edit that bit out, actually.) Then there's a short, blurry clip of my face in the reverse camera, before we go back to the market square, which looks vibrant and bustling.

'This is really boring,' says Bex, her teeth chattering as she sits on her pony at the back of the group. 'Why are we watching this, Sabrina?'

'Wait,' says Sabrina, her tone grim. 'Just wait.'

The camera reaches the last stall, then swoops forward in a move I recognise, with a sinking heart, as being what happens when I forget to hit the 'stop' button on the video, and put the phone back in my pocket while it's still filming.

This time, though, the phone doesn't simply end up filming the lint in the corner of my pocket. No, it remains in my hand, now pointing at my feet as I walk back across the square, towards Izzie and Ian.

'I'll take one of those turnips,' I can be heard saying, although the shot is still of the ground. 'And maybe some leeks, too.'

'That'll be much better for you than the muck they serve up at the Chrysalis,' says Ian from off-camera. 'They brought in some fancy chef from London, so I heard.'

'Aye. I bet it's just those tiny wee portions o' fancy stuff they give you,' chimes in Izzie's voice. 'Is that right, Rosie?'

'I'm not sure,' replies a voice that's unmistakably mine. 'I haven't had a proper dinner at the Chrysalis yet. I got locked in the sauna on the first night and missed it. I could have died, according to the handyman.'

'You never did!' says Izzie, scandalised.

The audio is interrupted at this point by a loud rustling sound as Ian puts the leeks into a paper bag, but it comes back just in time for me to be heard saying, 'And I was almost naked, too!'

The screen goes blurry again as I raise my hand to take the bag of leeks, the camera swooping dizzyingly around until the video finally ends on a shot of Ian holding up a particularly phallic-looking cucumber. 'This is what we think of the new laird,' he says with a devilish grin, the scene cutting out just before we can find out what he means by that – although, judging by the looks on everyone's faces, the message is pretty clear as it is.

There's a long, horrified silence as everyone on the beach tries to figure out the appropriate response to what they've just seen. Even Millie seems lost for words for once, and just stands there looking from face to face, desperate for a cue.

'Well?' says Sabrina again, wiping raindrops off the screen of her iPad with her sleeve, before fixing me with a gaze that makes my blood run cold. 'I assume there's some explanation for your decision to post this absolute travesty of a video?'

'It . . . wasn't actually a decision,' I reply shakily, wishing I was still sitting on the blanket, because my legs have gone all wobbly again. 'It was a mistake. Surely you can see it's been posted by mistake? I was in the middle of editing it . . . I was just going to post the bit with the scenery in it, and nothing else . . . but . . . I guess I got distracted. And I, er, somehow must have uploaded the entire thing.'

'For God's sake,' mutters Dante, reaching up to push his dark hair out of his eyes. 'I knew we shouldn't have let her stay. She doesn't have a clue what she's doing.'

'Well, *I* know that,' replies Sabrina shrilly. 'It wasn't my decision, *Dante*.'

'Well, I didn't know she was going to pull a stunt like this, did I?' the hotel manager snarls back at her.

'I just wanted to help,' I say in a quiet voice as they square up to each other. 'Some of the villagers told me the hotel might close if the launch doesn't go well, and I was trying to save it by . . . by showing some of the local colour.'

'Aye, because that's all we needed,' says Dante. 'For a tourist from London, who's never been to the Highlands in her life, to spend five minutes here and decide she alone knows how to "save" us.'

He holds his fingers up and makes scare quotes. It would be quite amusing, if only he didn't look quite so much like an angry Ken doll.

Oh, and if the anger in question wasn't directed at me, obviously.

'I'm really, really sorry,' I say pleadingly, looking from him to Sabrina and back again. 'I honestly didn't intend to post it. But look, I'll delete it right away,' I add, brightening as the obvious solution to all of this hits me. 'And the good thing is that it was just me who posted it, and no one ever sees what I post, anyway. I only have 2,012 followers, and most of them don't even use . . . Oh.'

I stop speaking as Sabrina thrusts the iPad in my face and I see the number of hearts at the bottom of the video.

'Twenty thousand likes,' says Sabrina. 'And it's already been shared multiple times.'

'Really?' says Millie, finding her voice at last. 'Oh, well done, Rosie. That's amazing.'

'It's not amazing,' spits Dante, doing the waggly-finger thing again. 'It's a disaster. She made the food sound terrible with the "tiny wee" portions we apparently serve, then said she almost died in the sauna. Who's going to want to stay here after hearing that?'

'Maybe . . . people who are on a diet?' suggests Millie brightly. 'That could work.'

By way of response, Dante lets out a groan so hollow that it startles the ponies. Bex's steed whisks its tail in alarm, and takes a step backward, making Bex grab onto its thick mane in fright.

'I hope you realise what you've done,' Dante says, his voice rising as he turns to face me through the drizzle. 'This kind of bad publicity could make the hotel fail before it's even open. We could all lose our jobs.'

I open and close my mouth uselessly, feeling like I'm in one of those nightmares where you're trying to scream but nothing comes out.

'Do you have nothing to say for yourself?' shrieks Sabrina, so shrilly that Bex's horse takes another step back from us all, whickering nervously.

'Stop shouting,' screams Bex, shouting louder than anyone. 'You're scaring this thing. It's going to throw me off.'

She jerks the reins roughly, and the little pony's eyes widen, showing the whites.

'Be quiet, Bex,' yells Daniel, just as loudly as his wife. 'And stop pulling its hair. You'll scare it.'

He takes a step towards the animal, his hand raised. It looks to me as if he's planning to grab hold of the bridle to stop it moving any further away, but the pony obviously thinks differently, and when it sees Daniel's hand looming towards it, it whinnies again in fright, then turns tail and goes galloping off down the beach, Bex clinging helplessly to its neck, her white dress billowing around her like a ghost in a wind tunnel.

For a second, no one moves, and then Hunter and I both spring forward, running for our ponies. I reach Bramble first, and scramble up into the saddle, accompanied by another loud tearing sound as the seat of my jeans rips even further.

There's no time to think about that now, though.

Bex's pony is bolting along the shoreline, headed for the cliffs at the end. I know it'll keep going now until something stops it, and, for Bex's sake, it would be much better for that thing to be me than either a very jagged landing on the rocks, or an extremely wet one in the sea; especially given that she's not wearing her safety helmet. So I turn Bramble's head towards the shore and urge him forwards, praying I haven't forgotten everything I ever learned during that pony-mad summer I spent hanging out at the local stables when I was twelve.

Surely it's just like riding a bike, though?

Isn't it?

Chapter 17

It is not, it turns out, anything like riding a bike.

Bikes are significantly smoother, for one thing; and a whole lot easier to control. Plus, there's virtually no chance of a bike deciding it doesn't want you on its back any more and randomly tossing you into the ocean. But horses? Horses have minds of their own – as Bex has just found out.

Fortunately for me, though, Bramble doesn't seem to be particularly interested in getting rid of me (which makes him the only one here who feels that way, but this isn't the time to dwell on that . . .), and instead allows me to urge him first into a lolloping canter that feels a bit like being on a rocking horse, and then into a slow gallop, his thick mane streaming out behind him as he takes off in pursuit of Bex, who's still clinging valiantly onto her pony's neck.

I'm vaguely aware of the sound of hooves thundering on the sand behind me, and a lot of shouting from the group by the picnic blanket, but I'm too busy concentrating on staying in the saddle to pay much attention to anything else. Rain rushes into my face as we fly over the wet sand at the edge of the water, spray from the sea mixing with the steady downpour in an icy cold froth. It's quite exhilarating, really, with the wind snapping at my face and the rhythmic pounding of hooves echoing in my ears. For just a moment, I allow myself to forget about everything else – the chaos behind me; the sheer horror of the video; Ian holding up that cucumber – as I lean forward in the saddle, the wild beauty of the beach stretching endlessly ahead.

'Rosie! Look out!'

Hunter's voice reaches me just as I spot Bex up ahead, her pony moving more slowly now that the initial fright has passed. It's still showing no signs of stopping, though, and Bex looks like she might slide off at any second, so I close my legs around Bramble's burly sides and encourage him to speed up until we're just behind, and then almost level with them.

'Hold on, Bex,' I yell, the words whipped away by the wind as soon as they leave my mouth. She turns her head towards me, her eyes wide in her pale face as, with a last burst of effort, Bramble finally gets close enough for me to lean forward and grab hold of the other pony's reins.

It takes me a few seconds – which feel like hours – but eventually the pony starts to respond to the pressure on the reins, slowing down to a canter, and then dropping into an exhausted walk, its head low, as if it's just realised what it's done, and is embarrassed by it.

I know how you feel, little pony. I know how you feel.

'Rosie! Bex!'

Hunter's horse comes crashing towards us through the shallow water just in time for him to catch Bex, who slides out of the saddle as soon as the pony stops, looking very much like a fairy-tale princess falling into the arms of her handsome prince, as he rescues her from the wicked witch.

Trust Bex to look good even when she's falling off a horse.

I climb clumsily down from Bramble's back, very aware of the large rip in the seat of my jeans, now that the initial panic is over.

'Is she OK?' I ask, shivering as my feet land in the frigid water.

'No,' says Bex plaintively.

'Aye,' says Hunter, who's still holding her easily in his arms, making me feel ridiculously jealous, considering that she's just escaped mortal peril. 'Aye, she'll be fine. We best get her back indoors, though; she's had the fright of her life, and she's absolutely frozen. Can you bring the horses?'

'Sure,' I reply, deflated by the lack of any reaction to my daring rescue. Surely that was worth a bit more than just, *Can you bring the horses?*

It looks like that's all I'm going to get, though, so, stifling a sigh, I somehow round up the three ponies and set off along the beach behind Hunter and Bex, who I'm pretty sure could walk on her own if she really put her mind to it, but who appears to be content to lie there, curled against Hunter's strong chest as I trail along behind them, forgotten once more.

The invisible woman indeed.

* * *

Fortunately for me, Sabrina and Dante are too busy flapping anxiously around Bex to pay much attention to me as we all make our way back to the beach.

'She needs to see a doctor,' demands Daniel, who snatched his wife from Hunter's arms as soon as he saw her in them but turned out to be not quite strong enough to carry her the rest of the way to the hotel and had to put her down halfway there. 'Somebody call a doctor.'

'I'm fine, Daniel,' says Bex quietly. 'Stop making a fuss.'

'No, I agree with Daniel,' interjects Sabrina, who's clearly more worried about potentially being sued than she is about Bex and her ordeal. 'Dante, call a doctor.'

'From where, the 1930s?' snaps Dante. 'I don't know what it's like in London, but doctors don't make house calls out here, Sabrina. You'll have to take her to the hospital; the nearest one's in Inverness. Or I think there's a vet in the village that might agree to take a look if you're desperate.'

We've reached the entrance of the hotel by now, and they continue to squabble among themselves all the way into the lobby, Bex now loudly protesting that she does *not* want to be taken to the vet.

'Here, I'll take those,' says Hunter as I pause at the bottom of the steps. He reaches for the reins of the three ponies, which I'm still towing along behind me. 'The van from the stables will be coming to collect them all in a few minutes.'

I hesitate, reluctant to go inside to face the consequences of my first and last viral video; the one that just guaranteed me an early exit from the hotel, like the first person to be voted off a reality TV show.

I silently hand Hunter the reins, then stand watching as he collects the rest of the ponies from Zara, Millie and Yasmin, who follow the others into the hotel, Millie wondering aloud if anyone else thinks the vet will put Bex to sleep once he's had a look at her.

'That was a brave thing you did, earlier,' Hunter says without preamble as he turns back to me. 'Stupid, mind. But brave.'

'Oh. It was nothing, really,' I reply, wishing he hadn't added the 'stupid' bit, but basking in the compliment nonetheless.

'And surprising,' adds Hunter, ruining the moment somewhat. 'I didn't think you had it in you.'

'I have quite a lot *in* me that you don't know about, I'll have you know,' I reply with dignity. 'And I told you I used to take riding lessons.'

'Aye, but then you couldn't even get on without help,' he points out. 'So I didn't really expect you to go charging off like that. Anyway, like I said, well done.'

'You *didn't* say "well done",' I can't resist pointing out. 'You said I was stupid but brave.'

'And you are,' he says, nodding. 'All the same, though, you should be proud of yourself. Bex is lucky you were there.'

I open my mouth to say I'm sure he'd have rescued her if I hadn't, but discover I'm too flustered to speak, so I just close it again, my cheeks flaming red in spite of the cold air that's biting into every inch of exposed skin.

'You better get yourself inside and warm up,' says Hunter, seeing me shiver. 'Oh, and also,' he goes on, with a wicked little twinkle in his eye, 'I can see your arse through that rip in your jeans. So you might want to get changed before anyone else sees it.'

With a yelp of embarrassment, I walk backwards up the steps to the lobby, then, finding it mercifully empty, turn and run for my room, relieved to discover I've finally managed to memorise the route to it, just before I'm inevitably made to leave because of that stupid cucumber video.

I open the door and head straight for the closet to peel off the now-ruined jeans, which, just as Hunter said, must have been giving everyone around me an absolute eyeful; especially Hunter himself, as I raced along the beach in front of him on horseback.

Maybe it's actually for the best that I'm probably going to be asked to leave this place sooner rather than later. Even though I have absolutely nowhere to go.

It's only as I exit the walk-in wardrobe, fully clothed once more, that I see it.

Sitting in the exact centre of the four-poster bed, in a spot in which I definitely didn't leave it, is the turnip I bought from Ian at the market earlier.

And sticking out the top of it is a very sharp knife.

Chapter 18

'Knife in the turnip! Knife in the turnip!' I shriek, barging into Hunter's apartment a few minutes later, turnip in hand. 'Look! There's a knife in the turnip!'

'There's a what in the *what*?' yells Hannah, jumping up from the sofa and coming running towards me, closely followed by Stevie.

'Er, nothing,' I say, quickly putting the turnip behind my back. 'It's nothing. Just a . . . just a joke between me and your dad.'

I shoot Hunter what I hope is a meaningful glance, and he heaves a weary sigh as he gets to his feet.

'Hannah, can you give Rosie and me a few minutes to chat?' he says, patting his daughter on the head as he approaches us. 'Maybe go and do some drawing in your room?'

'Ooh, yes,' says Hannah. 'I was going to do another one of Rosie, wasn't I?'

She scampers happily off, and I produce the turnip from behind my back, holding it up so Hunter can see the knife still sticking out of the top of it.

'Er, there's a knife in the turnip,' I say again, more quietly now I know Hannah's next door. 'See?'

'So I gathered. That's not a knife, though,' says Hunter, matter-of-factly as he takes the turnip and examines it. 'That's a dirk.'

'A . . . dirk?' I look at him suspiciously, wondering if he's winding me up again, like when he tried to tell me the hotel was haunted.

Which I'm starting to think it *is*.

'Aye. A dirk. It's a kind of ceremonial dagger.'

'Oh. Right. Well, that's absolutely *fine*, then,' I reply, a little hysterically. 'If I'd known it was just a *dirk*, I wouldn't have bothered you.'

I reach for the turnip, but he holds it up just out of my reach, even when I stand on my toes.

'Calm down,' he says. 'Where did you find this?'

'On my bed. Right in the middle. And before you say it, yes, I'm sure I was in the right room, and no, I definitely didn't leave it like that myself. Wait, don't do that,' I add with a gasp, as he takes the knife – sorry, the dirk – and pulls it out of the vegetable. 'You shouldn't touch it; it might have fingerprints on it.'

Hunter stares at me impassively.

'I don't think they're going to mobilise Scotland Yard over a turnip, Rosie,' he says bluntly. 'You've got some funny ideas about how the police work, do you know that?'

'Oh, come on, Hunter, don't give me that.' I fold my arms defensively across my chest. 'It's not *just* a turnip, is it? It's a turnip with a kni— with a weapon stuck in it. Even you have to admit, that's a pretty clear message, isn't it?'

I pause, waiting for him to come up with some kind of joke about turnips, and the kind of messages they might hold, but he just walks silently over to the sofa and sits down, still looking thoughtfully at the knife; which I just can't bring myself to think of as a 'dirk'.

'OK,' he says, after a silence that seems to go on forever. 'The missing clothes was one thing, but this . . . I can see why this would upset you. It's . . . well, it's not very nice, is it?'

'Not *nice*? That's one way of putting it,' I reply, incensed. 'It's an outright threat, Hunter, *and* it proves beyond doubt that someone's been going into my room. You can't possibly think I did this myself by mistake, can you?'

'No. No, I don't think you did it yourself, and I don't think it's a mistake, either,' he replies, in a soothing tone, which I can imagine him using to speak to Hannah when she's mid-tantrum. 'I *do* think there's a possibility that it's supposed to be some kind of practical joke, but—' he holds up a hand as I start to protest this '—even if it is, it's not funny, and it has to stop. Right now.'

'Oh. Right, well . . . good,' I reply, surprised he isn't trying to argue with me, or convince me I'm wrong. 'I'm glad we're on the same page. It . . . it really scared me, Hunter. Whoever did this must *hate* me. I just don't feel safe knowing someone's going around stabbing turnips just to get at me.'

Hunter holds up the turnip in question again, and we both stare at it, as if it might start speaking and reveal all the answers.

'Leave it with me,' he says at last. 'I'll speak to Dante. This is really his domain more than mine.'

'Um, yeah,' I reply, sitting down beside him on the couch with a soft *whump*. 'Sorry, I should probably have gone to him first. It's just . . . well, you're the only one I trust.'

'And you *can* trust me, Rosie,' he says, his face serious. 'I'll get to the bottom of this. And I'll make sure it doesn't happen again. You're safe here, I promise.'

For a second, I think he's going to reach out and hug me; I even raise my arms slightly in anticipation of it, but just as he leans towards me, there's a loud bang, and Hannah comes bursting back into the room, making Hunter and I spring guiltily apart.

'Look, Rosie,' Hannah says, handing me a piece of paper. 'I finished my drawing. What do you think?'

This time, the drawing depicts a perfectly round person balanced precariously on top of what looks like a very large, very deformed, dog-type animal. The person's legs are the same blue as the denim of the jeans I was wearing earlier, but there's a huge pink blob at the top, which I guess is supposed to be . . .

'That's your bum,' says Hannah happily. 'Daddy told me all about it.'

'I, um, told her about what happened on the beach,' says Hunter, looking uncharacteristically embarrassed. 'With Bex, and the ponies.'

'And my bum,' I add, kind of enjoying his obvious discomfort.

'No! I . . . well, I . . . I might have mentioned it in passing.'
He's actually blushing now.

This would almost be fun, if it wasn't happening because I flashed everyone on the beach. And also because of the whole turnip-and-dirk thing, which, to be totally honest, makes it hard to laugh at *anything*, really.

'Er, I think I'll go and try to catch Dante now, actually,' Hunter says, getting quickly to his feet. 'I'll take Hannah with me. D'you want to wait here for us?'

'Um, if that's OK with you?' I reply. 'I don't exactly fancy the thought of going back to my room on my own, when there's—'

Hunter shoots me a warning glance, his eyes flicking down towards his daughter.

'When there's so much fun I could be having here,' I finish instead. 'Isn't that right, Hannah?'

'Oh, tons,' replies Hannah. 'Have you ever played Minecraft before? Because I can teach you when we get back, if not.'

They head for the door, Hunter carrying the turnip in one hand and the dirk in the other. I notice he leaves Stevie behind, though, and I can't help but feel reassured by his doggy presence because, silly though it might sound to be freaked out by a turnip, of all things, I am, nevertheless, fairly freaked out by this *particular* turnip, which I guess is never going to make it into that soup Ian insisted on giving me the recipe for now.

Shame.

I feel safe here with Stevie, though; and with Hunter, too, when he gets back. The question is, though – just how safe am I going to be once I head back to my room on my own?

* * *

By the time Hunter and Hannah get back, I've given up on pacing the living room floor and have set up camp in the kitchen instead, where I'm busy making a sauce to go with the pasta I found in the back of one of the cupboards.

'Wow. What happened in here?' says Hunter, standing in the doorway, still with the turnip in his hand. 'Have I been robbed?'

'I hope you don't mind,' I reply, looking up from the stove. 'I wanted to do something to keep my mind off . . . well, *things* . . . while I was waiting for you to get back. I hope this is OK?'

'Aye,' Hunter says, running a hand through his hair as he gazes around at the gleaming surfaces of the little kitchen, which betray the fact that it was slightly more than just a quick tidy-up. 'Aye, this is just fine by me. You really didn't have to do all this, though, Rosie.'

'Oh, it's no problem,' I assure him, dishing the pasta into bowls. 'I like cooking. And cleaning, actually. It's quite therapeutic.'

I hand him a bowl of pasta, hoping he won't figure out the *real* reason I decided to cook dinner, which is that I wanted to try to delay the moment when I'll have to go back to my room on my own, knowing that the turnip stabber might reappear at any moment.

'You're not having any?' he asks, watching as I take the second bowl to Hannah, who's playing Minecraft in the living room, before returning to clear up.

'Oh. Well, it's your food,' I say. 'I didn't like to just help myself to it.'

'Och, come on, Rosie. You cooked it, *and* you cleaned the kitchen – I think we can spare you a wee bit of pasta in return,' Hunter replies with a grin. 'This is *really* good, by the way,' he adds through a mouthful of food. 'I didn't realise you were such a good cook.'

'It's just cheesy pasta.' I shrug, dishing up a bowl for myself. 'I have a bunch of nephews and nieces who're permanently starving when I babysit for them, so it's good to have something quick I can make for them.'

'Well, you're welcome to cook for me and Hannah any time you like,' Hunter replies, sitting down at the little kitchen table. 'Especially if it's always as good as this.'

'So, did you speak to Dante?' I ask, taking a seat opposite him. 'What did he say? Did he have any ideas who might have access to my room?'

Other than Dante himself, obviously. And presumably literally everyone else who works here.

'Ah. Right. Dante. I couldn't find him,' Hunter admits, rubbing his head bashfully. 'I'm sorry, Rosie. I looked everywhere – that's why I was gone for so long – but there was no sign of him. It's his night off, mind; he's probably gone to the pub in the village.'

'Oh. That's a shame,' I reply, struggling to imagine Ken-doll Dante sitting in a rustic village pub, when he looks more suited to a spooky old turret, say. Or a coffin. 'I was really hoping to get to the bottom of this. Although, if it was Dante who did it—' I nod at the turnip, which Hunter has placed on the table, thankfully minus the dirk '—I don't suppose he'd just admit to it, would he?'

'I suppose not,' agrees Hunter. 'I can't imagine Dante being behind this, though. He wouldn't want to risk the hotel's reputation – or his own. This job's a big deal to him. It's basically his entire personality. You saw how he reacted to your video.'

'Um, yeah,' I reply, cringing at the memory. 'Hannah told me he's always "creeping around" the place, though. I mean, doesn't that sound suspicious to you?'

'He's the manager of the hotel,' Hunter replies, sounding infuriatingly unbothered by this nugget of information. 'What Hannah sees as "creeping around" is probably just him keeping an eye on things. It's his job. And it would be pretty strange for him to sabotage it by terrorising a guest, wouldn't it? Come on, Rosie, you have to admit, that's pretty far-fetched, even for you.'

'Maybe,' I say, refusing to concede the point. 'Or maybe if the hotel's that important to him, he'd think nothing of trying to scare off someone he saw as a liability to it? I mean, how well do you really know him, Hunter?"

I twirl my fork absent-mindedly in my spaghetti, more convinced than ever that Dante is the dark force behind all of the things that have been happening since I got here.

'I know him well enough, I suppose,' Hunter says, helping himself to some more pasta. 'I know his mum moved here from Italy before he was born. Apparently she fell in love with a Scotsman, but it didn't work out, so she ended up having to raise Dante on her own. I think she worked here in the castle at one point, too.'

'As, like, a scullery maid or something?' I ask, suddenly feeling a bit more sympathetic to Dante now that I know he was raised by a struggling single mum, just like I was.

Hunter snorts so hard I think he's about to choke on his pasta.

'I don't know how old you think Dante is, Rosie,' he says at last, 'but I'm pretty sure he's around my age. This would've been the 1990s, not the nineteenth century. I don't actually know what his mum did here, but I don't expect it was cleaning the grates, or whatever it is you're imagining.'

'OK, OK,' I reply, blushing. 'So, what else *do* you know about him, then?'

'Er, that's it, really,' Hunter admits. 'Men don't really have deep and meaningful conversations with their colleagues, Rosie. We just talk about the weather, and sometimes football.'

'So, I'm guessing you don't know anything about the rest of the staff, either?' I say, disappointment making my shoulders sag in defeat. 'Agnes? The guy who drives the minibus? *Anyone?*'

'I haven't been here all that long, really,' he says apologetically. 'No one has; it's a brand-new hotel, so we haven't had a lot of time for staff *bonding*. And I spend most of my time out in the grounds. So I know everyone about as well as I need to, but not much more than that yet. None of them strike me as the kind of people who'd go around sticking dirks into turnips as a warning, though, so . . . I'm not much help here, am I?' he finishes ruefully. 'I'm sorry, Rosie, really. I wish there was something more I could tell you. I'm almost as much of an outsider here as you are, though.'

'Oh, I doubt that very much.'

I chew my bottom lip, anxiety rising as it occurs to me that I might *never* find out who's behind all of this now – especially if I do get kicked out of the hotel first thing tomorrow morning, like I'm expecting to. And even though it technically won't matter anymore by then, I hate the idea of the mystery being forever unsolved.

'Try not to worry,' says Hunter. 'You're safe here. Hannah and I will look after you. And I'm sure Sabrina and Dante will see the funny side of the cucumber video eventually. What is it they say? "All publicity is good publicity"?'

'That might be what they *say*,' I point out, starting to clear away our plates. 'But it's not what anyone actually *thinks*. I was supposed to be influencing people to come to the hotel; not to *avoid* it.'

'And it's important to you, this influencing thing, isn't it?' Hunter asks, getting up to help me.

'I *thought* it was,' I tell him ruefully. 'I didn't get to be popular in high school; I guess I thought I could make up for it by being popular on the internet. But it turns out I'm not particularly good at that, either. And I'm not sure I really *want* to be anymore. I'm not sure I want to be like Bex, or the rest of them. And after speaking to Izzie and Ian at the market, I just . . . well, I just thought that if I'm going to influence people, maybe I could do it over something more important than clothes. I thought if I could do something to make people want to come to the hotel, then that would help save your job – and Dante's, and Agnes's, and everyone else's. And, OK, I messed up by posting the unedited video rather than the version I'd planned, but I didn't do it on purpose. Lesson learned, though; at least I'll be happy enough to go back to being invisible again after this.'

'You're only "invisible" because you *make* yourself invisible,' Hunter points out, rummaging in the fridge until he finds a bottle of wine. 'Buying the same clothes as all the rest of them; trying to act like them and be like them. That's what makes you invisible, Rosie. Er, not that I think you *are* invisible, obviously. *I* always notice you, anyway.'

My cutlery clatters loudly against my plate after he says this. Did he mean that how I think he meant it? But before I can say anything, he holds up the bottle, looking as flustered as when Hannah mentioned my bum earlier.

'Um, wine? As a thank you for dinner?'

'Sure,' I reply, mentally calculating how long I could conceivably stretch out a glass of wine for, so I have less time to spend in my room. 'You were saying? About it being hard not to notice me when . . .?'

I widen my eyes innocently as Hunter takes a couple of glasses out of one of the cupboards, keeping his back turned for longer than is strictly necessary.

'You were going to say it's hard not to notice me when I'm always inadvertently flashing you, weren't you?' I go on when he doesn't answer. 'Admit it, you were, weren't you?'

'No, not all,' he insists, pouring the wine rather sloppily. 'I hardly ever think about what happened in the sauna. And as for your . . . bum . . . well, I'm far too much of a gentleman to think about that, either. Not that it isn't a bum worth thinking about, obviously, because it very much is. Um, from the very little I've seen of it, because I haven't been looking. It's a very fine bum, though. I think.'

'Relax,' I reply, smiling as he hands me a glass of wine. 'I'm just teasing. You can stop saying the word "bum" now. Listen, though, I was thinking; you have access to the room keys here, don't you?'

'I do. Why do you ask?'

'I want to change rooms,' I blurt out. '*Now*, preferably. I don't want to go back there, Hunter. Not even for the night. Not now I know for sure someone's been going in there. I'm . . . I'm scared. I know how stupid that sounds because it's just a turnip, but I am.'

I pause, waiting for him to make fun of me, but instead, his face softens.

'Oh, Rosie,' he says, taking a step towards me. 'You're not stupid, OK? I shouldn't have said that about you earlier. And I'm not surprised you're a bit shaken by . . . well, all of it. I can't give you a new room, though; or not right now, anyway.'

'You can't?' I know my voice sounds kind of weak and pathetic, but I can't bring myself to care. I just want to be able to go to sleep tonight without worrying about waking up to find a dirk stuck in my own *head*.

Not that I'd be very likely to wake up under those circumstances, I suppose.

'No, I'm sorry. It's not that I don't want to,' he assures me. 'It's just, none of the other rooms are ready yet. They haven't been cleaned, or even decorated yet. It's just the ones that are being used this week that were prepared for guests. Everything else is still under dust sheets.'

'Oh, I don't care about that,' I reply, relieved. 'I can make up a bed myself. And I don't mind a bit of dust, either. As long as the door locks and I know no one but you knows where I am, that'll be fine by me. It's probably going to be just for tonight, anyway, so it's fine.'

I look up at him hopefully.

'No, Rosie,' he says gently. 'It's not fine. I can see how scared you are over this; and I'm sure you're perfectly safe, but I want *you* to be sure of that, too. I don't like to think of you lying awake worrying that someone's going to get into your room. No, you can stay here tonight. At least you know no one's going to get past Stevie. Or me, for that matter.'

He grins in a way that I know is supposed to reassure me, to make me feel safe. And, actually, it works. Even though I barely know this man, I *do* feel safe with him. For all he likes to pretend to be a misanthrope who just wants to be alone with his mountains and his plants, I can see how much he cares about Hannah; not to mention the way he raced after Bex earlier today.

Whether he'd admit it or not, Hunter Stuart is clearly a man who cares about people. And, just for tonight, it's very tempting to let myself pretend he cares about *me*.

'Oh! I didn't mean . . . I wasn't trying to . . . I couldn't possibly . . .' I mumble, awkwardly, worried that he's just offering out of politeness. But he holds up a hand to stop me.

'Relax, Rosie,' he says with a grin. 'It's no problem. Look, you can take Hannah's room; she can come in with me. There's plenty of room – well, as long as you don't mind sharing with all of those soft toys she collects. Then we can speak to Dante in the morning and try to figure out what to do about this business with the dirk. I'll help you, I promise.'

'Are you sure?' I reply, still torn between relief and awkwardness at the thought of staying here overnight. Then

I catch sight of the turnip again, and I decide to go with relief.

'Absolutely,' says Hunter firmly. 'I'm afraid you're going to have to play Minecraft for a bit, though; I don't think Hannah's going to take no for an answer.'

'Fine by me.' I smile, my stomach doing an odd little flip of either excitement or nerves as I get up to start clearing the table.

I'm spending the night with Hunter Stuart.

Maybe my luck really *is* about to change, after all.

Chapter 19

We spend the next couple of hours sitting cross-legged in front of the TV, Hunter and I sipping wine, while Hannah attempts to explain what a 'creeper' is, and why we don't want to encounter one. Then, when she finally gives up, I take over and casually thrash them both at Tetris, making a mental note to thank my sisters later for bringing such a large amount of children into the world who can practise this stuff with me and keep me on my toes.

'I would never have guessed you'd be so good at video games, Rosie,' Hannah exclaims, when she gets up to get ready for bed. 'You were rubbish at Minecraft earlier.'

'Rosie's full of surprises,' observes Hunter with a slow smile in my direction that suggests he's not just talking about Tetris.

'Um . . .'

'She cooks a mean pasta, too,' he goes on.

'And performs daring rescues on horseback,' I put in, feeling like I might as well keep mentioning this, seeing as it's probably the most impressive thing I'll ever do.

'And shows people her bum,' shrieks Hannah, putting a quick end to the conversation.

'Teeth, Hannah,' says Hunter, tipping the last dregs of the wine into our glasses. 'You're in with me tonight; Rosie's going to be taking your room. That's if you're sure you wouldn't be more comfortable in my bed, Rosie?'

He pauses, the wine bottle hovering above my glass as he looks at me questioningly.

'And I'd take the couch?' he clarifies, seeing the look on my face.

'No, um, I'm sure I'll be fine in Hannah's room,' I reply, my cheeks growing hot under his gaze.

'Well, as long as you're sure,' he says with a shrug which suggests it doesn't matter to him where I sleep; a fact that's considerably more disappointing to me than it should be.

Fortunately for me, Hannah chooses this moment to provide a distraction by effusively bidding us both good-night, and, by the time she's safely tucked up in bed, I'm behaving more or less like a normal person again.

Well, by my standards, anyway.

'Feeling a bit more relaxed now?' Hunter asks, handing me my wine glass again. 'Now that you know you're not going to be stabbed in your sleep?'

'I didn't *seriously* think that would happen,' I protest, even though that's exactly what I thought. 'I just got a bit spooked by it, that's all. You don't really expect to find a knife in your bed, do you? Especially not in a five-star hotel.'

'No, that's definitely four-star treatment,' agrees Hunter. 'I'd be leaving a strongly worded review if I were you. Don't though – I'm begging you. I don't think Dante would survive that.'

'I still have him down as the main suspect,' I tell him, sipping my wine. 'It's not normal to be as passionate about your job as he seems to be.'

'You just think that because you hate yours,' Hunter points out. 'Some of us are quite happy with what we do, believe it or not.'

'So, who do *you* think's doing it, then?' I ask. 'It has to be someone. Even if you can explain away the other stuff, that . . . dirk . . . didn't get itself into my turnip on its own, did it?'

'Ach, I don't know, Rosie,' Hunter admits. 'I'm still inclined to think it's some kind of stupid prank that's gone too far. Whoever it is probably doesn't even know how much it's getting to you.'

'Don't do that,' I say quietly, staring into my glass. 'Don't try to minimise it. I hate that. I know you're just try-ing to reassure me, but . . . I'd rather you didn't.'

'OK,' he replies carefully, after a pause. 'Am I allowed to ask why?'

'My ex,' I say, swirling the wine around in the glass. 'Adam. He was always trying to tell me I was wrong about stuff. Always trying to play down my fears, or my worries.'

'Rosie, I wasn't . . .' Hunter says softly. 'I would never try to do that. But I'm sorry it came across that way. I really was just trying to make you feel better.'

'I know,' I tell him, flushing. 'Sorry, I think I've probably had too much wine. I know you were just being nice.'

'And you're being *too* nice again, by apologising all the time,' he points out. 'Even when you have absolutely nothing to apologise for.'

'Sor— um, OK. And thanks for saying that; I appreciate it.'

'So, this Adam,' he says, leaning forward and resting his chin on his hands. 'What other things do I have to hate him for?'

I laugh in spite of myself.

'Oh, nothing, really,' I reply. 'Adam isn't a bad guy. He just wasn't the *right* guy, that's all. He's not worth hating.'

'Nope, too nice again,' Hunter cuts in. 'Give me something to work with here, Rosie. At least tell me he hogged the remote all the time. Or squeezed the toothpaste in the middle.'

'He was in a fairly committed relationship with the remote control,' I admit. 'Much more than he ever was with me.'

'And?' Hunter raises his eyebrows comically. 'There must be more than that?'

'Well . . . he would sometimes finish watching a TV series that we'd started together without waiting for me,' I say, warming to this game.

'No!'

'And then he'd talk about it in front of me. With spoilers.'

Hunter puts his face in his hands and pretends to weep.

'Go on,' he says through his fingers.

'He was always late for everything. Especially when it was something we'd arranged to do with my family. Or my friends. He just didn't seem to see them as particularly important. I once asked him to come to one of my sister's birthday dinners, and he genuinely couldn't understand why I expected him to come, or what it had to do with him. It was like he didn't see us as a couple.'

Hunter lowers his hands, and I notice he isn't laughing anymore.

'Then, when it was *my* birthday this year,' I tell him, 'I decided to throw a party; which I never normally do, because I don't like the attention. But my best friend talked me into it, and I thought, why not? Why *shouldn't* I get to feel special for once?'

I pick up the wine glass and take a huge gulp.

'Adam didn't turn up,' I say into the glass. 'Well, not until the party was almost over, anyway. Said he forgot about it. He just . . . *forgot* about me.'

'He forgot? Seriously? He forgot your *birthday*?' Hunter almost spits out his wine.

'Yup.'

I swallow the rest of mine in a single gulp.

'Rosie, that's shit,' says Hunter quietly. 'That's really, really shit. I hope you told him where to go after that?'

'That's the thing,' I admit, staring back into my wine glass. 'I didn't. I accepted his apology, and I tried to pretend it was fine; that it was my fault for thinking I needed some big celebration just for having been born. Then he dumped me anyway, for being "high maintenance". That's why he'd come round.'

'He dumped you *on your birthday*?'

He says it quietly, but there's an undercurrent to his words that makes me feel like I'm hearing this piece of news for the first time. And, when he says it like that, I can suddenly see how awful this actually is, and how little I deserved to be treated like that.

'Rosie,' says Hunter, taking the glass out of my hands and putting it down on the floor. 'You know how messed up that is, right? You know it's not stupid or weird to expect your partner to remember your birthday, or come to your party?'

'I know it *now*,' I reply, blinking frantically to stop myself from crying. 'But at the time, it was easy to believe he was right.'

'Well, he wasn't,' Hunter says, taking both of my hands in his and looking me right in the eye, in a way that should be uncomfortable, but somehow isn't. 'He was completely and utterly wrong. You *do* deserve to be celebrated. And you deserve to be with someone who knows that; not someone who hogs the remote control and tries to make you think you're not important.'

I blink, my breath catching in my throat. His hands are warm and steady, and he's looking at me as if he actually *sees* me; which is unusual, to say the least.

'There's also the TV thing,' I remind him, swallowing down the lump that's risen in my throat. 'That was pretty annoying, too.'

'Very annoying,' agrees Hunter. 'I'm serious, though, Rosie. Never let anyone convince you that you're not special. Not Bex, not Sabrina and definitely not this Adam eejit.'

'I'm not totally sure what an "eejit" is,' I confess with a smile. 'But thanks. I'll . . . I'll bear that in mind.'

'You don't need to thank me,' he says. 'Just promise me you'll try to assert yourself a bit more. Stop letting other people try to tell you who you are.'

'Noted.'

We look at each other, the air between us humming with something unspoken.

'So, what about you and Hannah's mum?' I venture at last. 'Did she hog the remote, too? Forget to replace the loo roll when it was done?'

Tell me all the ways I should hate her, I'm begging you.

A shadow of emotion flickers across Hunter's face, and I worry I've broken the spell we've been weaving together by saying something I'm not supposed to. But then he looks me in the eye and smiles softly.

'No, nothing like that,' he says, rubbing the stubble on his chin thoughtfully. 'And she never forgot anyone's birthday, either. Hannah's mum's the most organised person I know; it's why she's so good at what she does, I suppose.'

'What does she do?' I ask, relieved that he hasn't just shut me down, like he did the last time I tried to bring up the topic.

'She's a corporate event planner,' he replies. 'Which means she's constantly travelling for work. That's why it didn't work out between us: she was just never there for us to make a go of it. She was married to her work.'

He laughs without humour.

'She must miss you both, though,' I say, thinking of this super-organised, jet-setting career woman, who sounds like the exact opposite of me, in every way. 'If she's travelling so much.'

'She misses Hannah.' Hunter shrugs. 'Takes her on amazing holidays every chance she gets, to make up for not being here for her the rest of the time. I'm not sure she misses me, though. She doesn't really know me well enough to miss me.'

'She . . . she doesn't?'

I reach for my wine glass again, wondering how this can possibly be the case.

How can she not know the man she shares a child with?

'Hannah wasn't planned,' Hunter says, grinning at my confusion. 'Sienna and I had only been seeing each other for a few weeks when she got pregnant. We wanted to keep the baby, but we both knew by then we didn't want to keep each other. And Sienna wasn't ready for a family. She loves Hannah – I know she does – but she loves her work too. I told you some people do.'

That shadow crosses his eyes again, and I put my glass back down and reach for his hands, the way he took mine a few minutes ago, when I was talking about Adam.

'Well, Hannah's lucky to have you, then,' I say, squeezing them gently. 'Because I happen to think you're pretty great; even when you keep mentioning my, um, wardrobe malfunctions.'

'I happen to think your "wardrobe malfunctions", as you put it, are pretty great too,' he replies, his voice a little hoarse all of a sudden. 'Especially the one in the sauna.'

I cringe at the memory.

'Oh God, that was so embarrassing,' I say, letting him go so I can cover my face with my hands. 'I don't think I'll ever get over it.'

'I know I'll never *forget* it,' replies Hunter, chuckling softly. 'I hope I never do, anyway; it was easily one of the best sights of my life.'

'Really?' I blink at him through my fingers.

'Really,' he confirms, pulling my hands gently away from my eyes. 'You're glorious, Rosie. Absolutely glorious.'

His eyes flicker down to my lips and, all of a sudden, the room feels smaller, and far too warm. My pulse quickens as he shifts closer.

'Rosie,' he says, his voice barely above a whisper.

'Yes?' My thoughts are a jumbled mess as he leans in, his face just inches from mine.

'If you don't feel the same, tell me now,' he says, his forehead almost brushing mine. 'Because I really want to kiss you, and if I wait any longer, I'm not sure I'll be able to stop myself.'

I hesitate for the briefest of moments. Then, instead of pulling back, I close the gap; my lips meeting his in a kiss that's every bit as surprising to me as it is to him.

Hunter freezes for a split second before his hands slide up to cup my face, deepening the kiss with a tenderness that makes my knees weak. His thumbs brush over my cheekbones, slow and deliberate, as if he's trying to memorise me by touch. His lips are soft, and they taste like red wine; the sensation so intoxicating I barely notice the way my hands have found their way to his chest, my fingers tracing the taut muscles that lie just beneath the thin fabric of his shirt.

'I've been thinking about this ever since I saw you in that sauna,' he murmurs huskily as he breaks the kiss for a fraction of a second. 'You have no idea what you do to me, Rosie.'

His lips find mine once more, and I sigh with pleasure as he pushes me back against the cushions on the sofa, completely abandoning myself to the moment, until . . .

'Dad! Daddy, can I get a drink? I'm really thirsty.'

I'm so wrapped up in Hunter and what's happening between us that it takes a few seconds for Hannah's voice to filter through, but when it does, Hunter and I jump instantly apart, both of us looking instinctively towards the – thankfully still closed – door.

'Um, I best be going,' I say, getting reluctantly to my feet.

'Aye. I suppose you should.'

Hunter follows suit, smiling so widely at me that I almost reconsider my decision to leave. But then the bedroom door creaks open, and Hannah peeks around the side of it, taking the decision out of my hands.

'Well, 'night then,' I say over my shoulder as I walk towards the door of her room.

'Goodnight, Rosie Winter,' replies Hunter. 'Sleep well.'

As the door of Hannah's bedroom closes behind me, though, I have a funny feeling that I'm not going to be getting much sleep at all.

Chapter 20

I wake up in Hannah's little single bed the next morning with Stevie draped over my legs, a fluffy rainbow bunny on top of my head and the memory of Hunter's kiss still on my lips.

Did that actually happen, or did I dream it?

I lie in bed for a few minutes, feeling pleasantly fuzzy and warm from the memory, and wondering if there might be an opportunity for an action replay at some point.

Like today, maybe.

Who knew my journey of reinvention would involve meeting someone like Hunter? Someone who tells me I'm special, and kisses me like he believes it? Oh, and who . . . lives in the far north of Scotland. In a castle where someone stabs turnips just to prove how much they hate me. There *is* that to consider, too.

I push Stevie off my legs and get out of bed, silently slipping out of the T-shirt Hunter gave me last night and into my clothes. Hunter's door is closed, and although I hover outside it for a few seconds wondering if I should at least knock and let him know I'm leaving, in the end, I slink off quietly, not wanting to wake him.

The thought of going back to my room doesn't seem nearly as scary in the light of morning as it did last night, but I take my time heading back there anyway, still thinking about Hunter, and how he lives in a hotel that's approximately six hundred miles from London; and I know because I googled it last night, before I went to sleep.

But no, I'm not going to think about that right now.

I'm not going to think about Hunter at all, in fact. I'm going to think about . . . hot tubs. Yes, hot tubs. Because I'm sure I remember something on the itinerary about this morning being a spa day, where we'd get to sample all the various treatments the hotel has to offer, and I have to admit, that *does* sound rather nice.

If only Sabrina and Dante decide to let me stay here long enough to find out.

I'm still thinking about the hot tub as I make my way back to my room (only now I'm thinking about Hunter being in the hot tub *with* me; which isn't exactly helping with the whole *not thinking about him* thing . . .), but I stop in my tracks when I reach it and find the door standing wide open, and a tiny flicker of movement inside which can mean only one thing:

There's someone in my room.

Again.

And, this time, I'm finally going to find out who it is.

'Aha!' I yell in a crazed voice, adrenalin making me brave as I burst into the room like a clumsy superhero. 'Caught in the act!'

There's a shrill scream as Bex jumps up from where she's been sitting on the edge of the bed, looking beautiful and fragile, in a *hand me my smelling salts* kind of way.

'Bex? What are you doing here? How did you get in?'

I eye her warily, then glance around the room to make sure everything's as it should be.

'Sorry,' she says in an unusually subdued tone as she sinks back onto the bed. 'One of the housemaids let me in; she was in here cleaning when I arrived. I hope you don't mind? I just wanted to thank you for what you did yester-day. You know, on the beach?'

I nod cautiously, my heart sinking at the revelation that not one, but *two* people have been in my room without me knowing about it.

I'm never going to figure out who the turnip stabber is at this rate.

'Seriously,' Bex goes on, oblivious to my distress. 'I owe you one, Rosie. I could have died out there.'

'You probably wouldn't have,' I say, coming over to sit next to her. 'You'd have landed on sand, so it wouldn't have been too bad. I've fallen off loads of times and I'm still here. Unless you landed on your head, obviously. I suppose you could've broken your neck that way. Or your back. That would've been bad, too. Um, anyway, I'm glad you're OK, and not, you know . . .' I trail off, realising my nerves are making me ramble. 'You *are* OK, aren't you?'

'Oh, I'm fine,' she says, rubbing her arms and staring at the floor. 'I was cold more than anything else, and that was my own fault. The vet said to just rest up and stay warm.'

Her pretty face arranges itself in a pout.

'I also wanted to apologise for how I've been since we got here,' she says, in a voice so quiet I think I must have misheard at first. 'The whole "Wrong Rosie" thing,' she goes on, still looking at the floor. 'I know you didn't like that, but I kept doing it. I was just being horrible. I'm sorry.'

'It's—' I'm about to assure her it's fine, but then I remember what Hunter said about asserting myself, and I straighten my shoulders, figuring now's as good a time as any to make a start on that.

'I appreciate the apology,' I say instead, wishing he was here to see me.

'I'm really *not* horrible,' Bex says, looking up at me, her eyes swimming with tears – which are so unexpected coming from someone like her that I momentarily forget we're supposed to be in the middle of a heartfelt apology here. 'Honestly, I'm not. I just . . . I've been having some issues.'

'Do you want to talk about it?' I ask, remembering the argument I saw her having in the grounds yesterday. 'Is it Daniel?'

'Daniel? No. No, Daniel's a sweetheart,' Bex replies, wiping her eyes. 'No, it's me. It's all me. We've been trying to get pregnant,' she goes on in a rush. 'But it hasn't happened yet, and honestly, I'm starting to think it might not happen at all. It's been making me quite . . . well, *emotional*, I suppose.'

'Well, that's understandable,' I reply, touching her lightly on the hand. 'It can take a bit of time, though, can't it? Trust me, I have three sisters, and not one of them has a filter, so I . . . well, I know quite a lot about this, for someone who doesn't have kids herself.'

'That's the thing, though,' she says tearfully. 'I don't *have* a lot of time. I'm . . . well, I'm a bit older than the rest of you, Rosie.'

For the first time since I met her, Bex looks embarrassed. I arrange my face into what I hope is an appropriately surprised expression, not wanting to let on that Zara's already dropped this particular bombshell.

'That's why this Face of the Chrysalis contest is so important to me,' Bex continues earnestly. 'Because we've been saving up for IVF, but God, it's so expensive, Rosie. So expensive it feels like we're never going to get there. What if we never get there?'

She turns her wide, panicked eyes towards me and, for the first time since I stumbled across her YouTube channel a few years ago, I realise Bex Foster is just a human being, like the rest of us. An unfairly attractive, and occasionally kind of annoying one, sure, but still, just a human. And, right now, she's a human who needs a little bit of kindness.

'Of course you'll get there,' I tell her, patting her tentatively on the arm, as if she's one of the ponies from yesterday's beach ride. 'Your content's amazing, Bex. Everyone knows that. You're going to win this contest; and even if, for some reason, you don't, I'm sure the hotel will still pay to use some of your photos in their advertising.'

I'm not sure of this at all, actually; especially after everything Izzie and Ian had to say about the hotel's future with the bawbag nephew in charge. Right now, though, Bex looks so miserable that I mean every word.

'Thanks, Rosie,' she says, hugging me impulsively. 'You're being so sweet, and I know I don't deserve it after the way I've been treating you. I think it's just the stress of it all. It's making me a bit crazy, really. And my period's due, too, so I suppose it could be hormonal. Oh, by the way,' she adds, brightening as she pulls away, 'I know you probably think no one wants you here after that weird cucumber video, but it's OK: I spoke to Sabrina and Dante, and they want you to stay. Well, actually, they *didn't* want you to stay at first.' She tilts her head thoughtfully. 'They both wanted you to leave. But I told them that if they kick *you* out, they'll have to kick me out too, and they obviously don't want to lose *me*—'

'Obviously.'

'—so it's all agreed: you're staying.'

She beams at me, pleased with her work.

'Thanks,' I reply, not sure if I should be happy to be staying, or worried that Sabrina and Dante only agreed to it under duress. 'That's . . . great.'

'It was the least I could do after you saved my life,' Bex says, getting to her feet. 'I wouldn't *actually* have gone, obviously, because I do really want to win the competition, but they don't know that, so it all worked out. I'll never forget what you did, though, Rosie. Never.'

I watch as she heads for the door, still pale, but looking a little more like her old self now that she's got this apology out of the way. She sounds totally sincere but, then again, she always sounds sincere in her videos too, and now I know how fake they are.

'Um, Rosie,' Bex says, halfway through the door. 'Can I ask you a favour?'

'Sure,' I reply, hoping it's not going to be anything to do with Sabrina or Dante, both of whom I'm still scared of.

'You won't post that video, will you?' she asks, sounding almost shy. 'It's just, it would be so embarrassing for me. I really don't want my followers to see it.'

'Video?' I frown, wondering if we're talking about the cucumber again, and what it has to do with Bex and her followers. 'What do you mean?'

'Oh. Haven't you seen it yet?' she replies. 'Luna sent it to us both, earlier. She took it yesterday, on the beach.'

I pull my phone out of my pocket, and she gives a little shriek of horror at the sight of it.

'No, don't watch it in front of me,' she begs. 'I'm just going, anyway. But please, Rosie; don't post it, OK? I feel silly enough about it already.'

She leaves, and I immediately open up my email app, scrolling quickly past a bunch of Klarna payment reminders and sale notifications until I find the message from Luna.

'Thought you both might like to have these,' she's written, attaching a selection of photos from yesterday's excursion, which I scroll through quickly, until I reach the video Bex mentioned, which turns out to be the full, unabridged version of her, Hunter and I all thundering along the beach, Bex screaming her head off and looking a lot like a wet tissue, while I come riding bravely to the rescue, at an angle which, thankfully, makes me look fully clothed. It ends with a short clip of Daniel struggling to pick Bex up on the beach after Hunter was forced to release her, and Bex yelling that she's not *that* heavy, her usual Little Miss Perfect act completely forgotten as she screams at her husband.

For the first time since it happened, I allow myself a moment of pride over how I leaped into action yesterday. Hunter said he didn't think I had it in me – and the truth is that *I* didn't, either. And yet, here's the proof, captured on camera, that I'm not always the 'wrong' Rosie.

Sometimes, in fact, I'm the really quite *right* one.

Chapter 21

The spa morning I'm apparently going to be allowed to join now (thanks to Bex) includes breakfast, according to my new itinerary, so after a quick shower, I put on my swimsuit and dressing gown, before having a look around the room to make sure no more dirks have turned up while I was gone last night.

Everything looks totally normal, though; so much so that as I lock the door behind me and make my way downstairs, I start to feel a little silly for being so scared.

It was just a turnip, after all.

Maybe it *was* just some kind of practical joke, like Hunter said?

The thought of Hunter gets me thinking about *kissing* Hunter again, and I wander in a pleasant daydream through the pool area (deliberately not looking in the direction of the sauna, in case it triggers some kind of flashback), and outside again to the hot tub, which sits on a wide wooden deck, looking out over the gardens to the sea beyond; the kind of view that makes you stop in your tracks just to gape at it.

'Rosie! There you are at last!' yells Bex, who's already in the water with the other girls, wearing a complicated-looking bikini with so many straps that it reminds me of one of those cat's cradle things. Daniel, I notice, is still fully clothed and hovering on the deck with his giant camera in hand, and I quickly slip out of my robe and into the warm water before he can point it at me.

'Here,' says Millie, handing me a plastic glass filled with what turns out to be Buck's Fizz. 'There's some toast and pastries in the pool building too, if you're hungry.'

I take the glass, and look out at the view. The sky is a vivid bright blue this morning, as if it's just been washed after yesterday's rain, and the mountains stand out sharply against it. It's so beautiful it's almost hard to believe it's real, but I've already learned how quickly the weather can change up here, so I lean back against the headrest, determined to enjoy it while I can.

'It's gorgeous, isn't it?' says Zara, adjusting the strap of her bright red bikini.

'It's like we're actually inside an Instagram Reel,' agrees Millie, holding her blonde head carefully above the water so as not to ruin her makeup, which she's applied as thickly as usual, despite the fact that we're going to be spending the morning jumping in and out of the water, in between beauty treatments.

'Or like we're lobsters, being boiled in a pot,' adds Yasmin solemnly, adjusting her sunglasses. 'For dinner.'

The rest of us exchange nervous glances, but Yasmin doesn't appear to notice and, after a few seconds, everyone starts chatting as usual, while Daniel snaps away in the background. Now that Bex has decided she owes me one, and is being nice to me, the atmosphere of the group feels much more relaxed (or, at least, it does to me; I suppose this must be how it *always* felt to the rest of them), and we giggle and splash away, taking it in turns to pose for photos.

I sip my drink, listening in fascination as they all swap stories and anecdotes about their lives, which sound so different from mine that it feels almost as if I'm on some kind of anthropological study, which will have a voice-over from David Attenborough, earnestly observing that here we see the female influencer in her native habitat – a hot tub, with a steady supply of fizz.

Strange as it is to be sitting here with a group of women I'm more used to seeing on the pages of my social media feeds, though, for the first time since I got here, I actually feel like I'm part of things, rather than just a barely toler-ated observer. If it wasn't for the fact that my life back home is still such a disaster, I'd almost feel like one of them. And, just to prove it, yesterday's cucumber video might have almost got me ejected from the hotel, but it gained me an additional 1,023 followers before I got the chance to delete it, so things are finally starting to go well for me at last.

Naturally, then, the universe chooses this exact moment to remind me of what I said to Hunter last night about wanting to use my new-found influence for good, rather than for . . . well, *shopping*.

'Who's that?' says Zara, shielding her eyes with one hand and squinting in the direction of the castle. 'We're not expecting anyone, are we?'

I pop my head up out of the water like a baby seal to see a small group of people crunching their way over the gravel towards us. Izzie's in the lead, wearing a long purple cloak which swirls around her ankles dramatically. Ian's just behind her, looking like a cartoon version of a farmer, in wellies and a flat cap. With them is a small collection of what I'm assuming are other villagers, and, call me para-noid, but I have a funny feeling none of them are here for a social visit, somehow.

'Who are *they*?' says Millie curiously. 'They look like one of those pop groups from the seventies.'

'Well, I could be mistaken,' replies Zara dryly, 'but I *think* it's probably an angry mob?'

Just as she finishes speaking, Ian produces something that looks suspiciously like a shotgun from the folds of the waterproof coat he's wearing.

'Yup.' Zara nods, twirling a strand of hair around her finger. 'That's definitely an angry mob.'

'Don't shoot,' screams Millie in a panic. 'Please don't shoot!'

She scrambles frantically to get out of the hot tub, succeeding only in belly-flopping into the water face first, completely soaking her hair in the process and sending up a spray of bubbles that hit me full in the face, while somehow missing everyone else.

'Oh, my God, this is horrific,' breathes Yasmin.

'I know,' agrees Bex, still watching Millie. 'Look at her makeup!'

'Don't shoot,' shouts Millie again, emerging from the bubbles with mascara pooled under her eyes, and her lipstick smudged around the edges of her mouth, like a clown. 'Please don't hurt us!'

'Och, don't you worry,' says Ian, stepping forward with an embarrassed chuckle. 'Did you think this was a gun? It isn't a gun; it's just a walking stick that *looks* like a gun. See?'

He takes another step forward and everyone screams again. There's just time for me to notice Daniel Foster making a bolt for it around the back of the hotel, then Ian reaches us, holding out the 'gun' so we can see that it is, indeed, just a piece of carved wood.

'Inherited this from my granda, so I did,' he tells us. 'I carry it everywhere, on account of my dodgy knee. Got kicked by a horse when I was a young lad. It—'

'Aye, aye, enough about your medical issues, Young Ian,' says Izzie, gliding towards us like an apparition, her craggy face contorted into a fierce scowl. 'Oh, hiya, Rosie,' she says, smiling as she catches sight of me. 'We were hoping we'd see you here.'

'What's going on?'

There's a crunch of gravel underfoot as Dante appears, accompanied by Daniel Foster, whose face is pale with fear, and Hunter, who looks totally at ease, as if facing down angry mobs is all in a day's work for him. My stomach does a silly little flip-flop of pleasure at the sight of him.

'Well?'

The three men join us by the hot tub, Dante looking furious, and Hunter as impassive as always. At first I think he hasn't noticed me, so I sit up a little straighter, and am rewarded with a wide smile, and . . . did he just *wink* at me?

And what does it say about me that my entire body is now tingling with excitement, even though it's right in the middle of . . . whatever this situation is.

'It's an angry mob,' supplies Zara, helpfully. 'They haven't said why they're here yet, though.'

'Aye,' says Izzie, flicking her cape back to make it swirl around her body again. 'Aye, that's right. We're an angry mob. We're here to see the Laird.'

'We did call ahead,' puts in a very tall, extremely muscular young man, who has tattoos on every visible piece of skin. 'But there was no answer, so we thought we'd just chance it.'

'Look, they've brought backup,' whispers Millie, who appears to have regained her composure. 'They're really serious about this, aren't they?'

'Backup? Naw, that's just my wee brother, Callum,' says Ian, overhearing her. 'He's no' really bothered about any of this; he just wanted to see the influencer lot, and see if he can get any tips from them.'

'I've got 1.4 million followers on TikTok,' says Callum shyly. 'I started off doing stuff about tattoos, but now I mostly just lip sync to Gracie Abrams songs. Well, that and the odd dance routine, but we all do that, don't we? D'ye want to see one?'

'No,' says everyone simultaneously.

'Ooh, yes, please,' says Millie, one beat behind the rest of us. 'Well, maybe later, then,' she adds, sensing that this possibly isn't the time.

'I was *saying*,' hisses Izzie, glaring at Callum, 'that we're here to see the Laird. We want to speak to him about why the castle has stopped ordering goods from the village now that it's turned into a fancy hotel. We used to do a decent trade with this place – we all did – and we want to know what's changed. Other than the obvious.'

'The obvious?' Hunter frowns. At the sound of his voice, Stevie appears from the back of the group of villagers and comes padding softly towards his master.

'Aye. The bastard new laird,' says Izzie. 'The nephew, or great-nephew, or . . .' She trails off, her eyes wide with horror.

'Or bawbag,' says Ian, looking around to see what's upset her. 'That's the word you're looking for, Izzie, isn't it? It's bawbag.'

Izzie isn't listening, though.

'A Black Shuck,' she shrieks, pointing at Stevie. 'A Black Shuck! Beware the Black Shuck!'

'He's a Belgian shepherd,' says Hunter with dignity. 'With a few bits of something else in there, too.'

'Is he?' says Izzie, wrinkling her long nose in suspicion. She pulls a pair of spectacles out of her cloak and puts them on.

'Ach, so he is. It's just a dog, right enough, Ian,' she says. 'Sorry about that, everybody, false alarm.'

'She sees Black Shucks everywhere, this one,' says Ian, chuckling. 'The last one turned out to be just a very small cow, didn't it, Izzie?'

'You wait until you're my age, young Ian,' says Izzie fiercely. 'You'll be seeing Black Shucks everywhere, too. Harbingers of death, so they are. This one's just a Very Good Boy, though,' she adds, crouching down to pet Stevie, who immediately rolls over so she can scratch his belly. 'Aren't ye, Good Boy?'

'I don't know what a Black Shuck is,' says Millie eagerly. 'But there's an invisible woman in the castle. I heard Rosie talking about her yesterday.'

'I don't believe in ghosts,' says Yasmin vaguely. 'But I once read a book where a group of women were staying in a castle, and the locals butchered them all, one by one. Then they ate them.'

She makes a slicing motion across her throat with her finger, and we all stare at her, open-mouthed.

'I think about that a lot,' she says, shrugging. 'I'm not saying it's *definitely* going to be the same here, though.'

'Now, now,' says Ian, his cheeks red. 'No one's here to do any butchering or eating.'

'I could eat, to be honest,' says Calumn, hopefully. 'I've only had a protein shake since breakfast. Could you eat, Izzie?'

'Och, I suppose I could manage a wee something,' Izzie replies from her position on the ground next to Stevie. 'Just to be polite. Maybe just soup and a sandwich, say.'

'I'll have the full Scottish breakfast,' says Calumn. 'Vegetarian, if you have it.'

'Well, if everyone's eating,' begins Ian, 'I'm partial to the odd kipper. D'you do kippers?'

'Enough,' yells Dante, his voice cutting through the air like a knife. 'Would you all just be quiet and get off my property? This is completely unacceptable.'

'*Your* property?' replies Izzie, her eyes narrowed. 'This isn't *your* property, Dante Romano; it belongs to Lord Glenmuir. And that's no way to speak to your Auntie Izzie.'

'Sorry, Izzie,' Dante mutters, looking at his feet. 'She's not my real aunt,' he adds petulantly, under his breath. 'She's just one of my mum's friends.'

'Aye, and wait until I speak to her about this,' says Izzie, tapping a foot imperiously. 'Now, are you going to fetch the Laird for us, or does Young Ian here have to get out his gun again?'

'OK,' says Hunter, raising both hands in a placatory gesture as Millie resumes her screaming fit. 'That's enough, all of you. The Laird isn't going to be coming down to speak to you,' he goes on, his eyes flicking upwards to the top floor of the castle, almost imperceptibly. 'And he doesn't accept visitors in his private quarters, either. But if you'd like to come inside, I'm sure we can sit down together and have a chat about this. A calm one. Without any guns.'

'We can talk here,' insists Izzie, folding her arms in an *I won't budge* kind of way.

'*You* can do what you like,' announces Bex, standing up abruptly. 'I'm going inside. I'm not sitting in this hot tub while you all argue about whatever it is. My fingers are starting to go all wrinkly, and I hate that.'

She steps delicately out of the tub, water cascading off her perfect body as she goes. Everyone falls silent as she walks slowly down the steps and strolls casually over to a wooden hammock which we've hung our robes on, her head high, shoulders back.

'Did you get that, Daniel?' she hisses at her husband as she drapes the robe over her shoulders, influencer style.

'I'm coming too,' says Millie, getting up to follow her, clearly unaware of the clown makeup still smeared over her face. Nevertheless, Callum still turns bright red at the sight of them both, and then goes redder still when Yasmin follows suit, walking like a model in a runway show. After a few seconds, Zara heaves a world-weary sigh and does her own cat-walk, adding a sassy little head toss as she reaches for her robe, and then I reluctantly haul myself out of the water and go splashing clumsily across the deck, horribly aware of the fact that my swimsuit's giving me a wedgie, and Hunter's right there, watching me.

When I'm finally back in my dressing gown, however, I risk a quick glance in his direction, and see a broad smile on his face, which I shyly return.

Maybe this wasn't such a bad idea, after all?

'Right,' says Callum, clearing his throat importantly, once we're all gathered on the deck. 'So that's one full Scottish breakfast, one plate o' kippers, soup and a sandwich. Should one of us maybe be writing this down?'

'Come on,' says Hunter, his smile disappearing. 'Let's get everyone inside.'

Chapter 22

Ian persuades the rest of the villagers to go back home, assuring them that he, Izzie and Callum can take it from here, and then Hunter shows everyone to the library/den, where we all crowd around one of the coffee tables, as if we're about to have a business meeting.

'The thing is,' says Izzie, tucking into a toasted sandwich, which Dante has grudgingly had sent up from the kitchen. 'Business has been dire this year for all of us. We really need the boost that a partnership with the hotel would give us. It's a rural area, without a lot of opportunities for trade. Us local business owners need to work together; a rising tide floats all boats, and all that. And if the Bawbag isn't willing to even consider that, then I'm sorry, but there's only one option open to us.'

'A massacre?' says Yasmin, leaning forward in her seat, her dark glasses propped on top of her head.

Izzie shifts her chair a little further away from Yasmin's. 'No, I mean a curse. Obviously.'

'Now, Izzie,' says Ian, clearing his throat. 'We talked about this on the way here. We agreed there would be no curses.'

'It's too late,' mutters Dante, making everyone jump. 'I think this hotel is already cursed.'

He's sitting in a high-backed chair in a shadowy corner of the room, and the combination of his pale face and shiny black hair makes him look so sinister that Millie lets out another small squeal of fright at the sight of him.

She really is particularly highly strung this morning, even for her.

'Och, bite me,' says Dante, scowling at her, and then widening his vampire glare to take in the rest of us. 'I've had enough of trying to be professional with you lot. You're all completely off your rockers. And one of you is up to something. Don't even try to deny it.'

'Up to something? What do you mean, "up to something"?' says Daniel Foster, in the tone of a man who's trying to re-establish his authority after he ran off and abandoned a group of women to their fate earlier. 'Are you trying to accuse us of something? Because I'd like to know exactly what it is, if so.'

He pulls his GoPro out of his pocket and thrusts it into Dante's face, obviously intending to record him as evidence.

'Um, I think Dante's referring to the recent goings-on in the hotel,' I venture, seeing the hotel manager swat at the camera as if it's a particularly pesky fly.

'The goings-on?' says Bex blankly. '*What* goings-on? Am I missing something here? Is it something to do with the contest?'

'Well, it's just . . . some strange things have been happening since we got here,' I say, feeling stupid now that I'm about to talk about this in front of them all. 'To me.'

'Is it the invisible woman?' asks Millie excitedly. 'You still haven't told us about that? When did you see her, Rosie? Wait – *how* did you see her, if she's invisible?'

Her brow furrows as she tries to figure this out.

'Those from the spirit realm have ways of making their presence known,' says Izzie darkly. 'I wish ye'd told us about this yesterday, Rosie; I'd have brought some sage with me to flush her out. Is the spirit in the room with us now? Are ye able to make contact with it? D'ye want me to give it a try?'

'No,' I protest, seeing Millie's eyes flick nervously back to Dante, who doesn't help matters by giving her a Dracula-like smile which is just missing a set of fangs. 'No, there's no ghost, Izzie. The goings-on are . . . well, it's hard to explain.'

'Why don't you try us?' says a cold voice from the doorway. Millie screams again, then blushes as she realises it's just Sabrina, who's chosen this moment to join us, Luna lurking behind her, looking terrified as usual.

'Oh, good,' says Dante from his corner. 'It's the Angel of Darkness. That's all we need. Look,' he goes on, addressing Sabrina, who approaches us in her usual *army general* manner. 'This is your problem. You're the one who came up with the idea of a "pre-launch" event, or whatever you call it – I was just stupid enough to go along with it. Well, enough is enough. This is your circus, Sabrina, so you better look after your monkeys.'

'Who are you calling monkeys?' begins Daniel, but Sabrina waves him imperiously aside and turns to face me instead.

'You were saying?' she says, in a tone that would sound almost pleasant, if it wasn't her. 'Something about "goings-on", I believe? Why don't you enlighten us, Rosie?'

My stomach is churning so loudly it's probably going to be providing the soundtrack to the video Daniel thinks no one can see him filming, but every eye in the room is locked onto me, so I haltingly tell them about the missing clothes, the stolen itinerary and, finally, last night's turnip revelation; none of which sounds nearly as dramatic in my retelling as they all seemed at the time.

'Well, I never!' says Izzie in astonishment as my story comes to an end. 'Can you believe this, Ian? A dirk in the turnip!'

'It's no way to treat a turnip,' says Ian gravely. 'No way at all. That one would've made a fine soup, too.'

'Why didn't you tell us about any of this at the time, though, Rosie?' says Zara. 'I mean, we obviously knew about the thing with the sauna, but I thought that was just an accident. Wasn't it?'

'Yes,' says Hunter firmly. 'It was absolutely an accident.'

'Um . . . I'm not sure,' I say, staring at my feet in their paper spa slippers. 'I was starting to think it probably was, but then the turnip turned up with the dirk in it, and now I'm not sure. I'm not *sure* about any of it, though,' I add hurriedly. 'That's why I haven't mentioned any of it until now.'

'Oh,' says Yasmin, wrinkling her nose. 'Right. I just assumed you hadn't told us because you thought it might be one of us doing it.'

Millie gives a gasp of horror, and Daniel turns his camera on her.

'Well, it's the most obvious explanation, isn't it?' goes on Yasmin. 'We're all in a competition together. It would make sense for the person who wants to win it most to start bumping off the rest of us, one at a time.'

Everyone immediately looks at Bex.

'Oh, come *on*,' she says, putting her hands on her hips. 'You want to win as much as I do, Yas. How do we know it's not *you* who's been doing it?'

Everyone switches to Yasmin.

'No, that's a fair point,' she says, patting her hair in its slicked-back bun. 'It *could* be me. It could be any of us, really.'

'It's true that none of us have been particularly nice to Rosie,' puts in Zara. 'I don't think we can really blame her for suspecting us.'

'This is ridiculous,' says Sabrina, who's been listening to all of this with her arms crossed and one foot tapping impatiently. 'Of course we can blame her! This isn't some kind of murder mystery, for goodness' sake.'

'Isn't it?' says Yasmin seriously. 'Or is it just that the murder hasn't happened yet?'

The room falls silent, with the exception of Daniel Foster, who's still shuffling around, trying to get close-ups of everyone's faces.

'They thought it would be a relaxing break in a Highland castle,' he says in a voice-over tone. 'Then things suddenly took a darker turn . . .'

He thrusts his camera into my face and I push it away, my heart suddenly speeding up.

Could Daniel be the person behind the goings-on? I know he and Bex really need to make some money, after all. Maybe he thinks he can make some kind of found-footage-style spooky documentary and get rich that way? He does always have that camera on him . . .

'Gosh, this is thrilling,' says Millie breathlessly, shifting a little closer to Callum, who turns as red as the cooked tomato in his breakfast. 'It's like we're in a horror movie or something.'

Daniel and Bex exchange glances at this, and my spidey senses tingle alarmingly. What if they're *all* in on it? What if I've unwittingly become part of some kind of psychological experiment? Or one of those hidden-camera comedy shows?

'Have you seen any signs, Rosie?' says Izzie, seriously, interrupting my downward spiral chain of thought. 'Black

Shucks, stopped clocks, wailing winds . . . Anything like that?'

'Um, the wind *was* wailing quite a bit last night,' I say. 'I thought it was just stormy outside, though.'

'It *was* just stormy outside,' says Hunter firmly. 'There's an even bigger one forecast for tonight. And the sauna door *was* just stuck.'

'And the dirk?' I point out, annoyed that he seems to be trying to downplay my fears again, after everything we talked about last night. 'How do you explain that?'

Hunter opens his mouth and then closes it again, a sheepish look on his face.

'If I may,' says Luna timidly, from her position behind Sabrina. 'Can I ask if anyone else has experienced any of these goings-on? It's for our insurance,' she adds, as Sabrina spins to face her. 'We have a duty of care to the people we invited here. So, has anyone else found any dirks in their bed, say?'

Everyone shakes their heads except Izzie, who puts her hand up as if she's in class.

'Aye, I have,' she says brightly. 'Not since I was young, though. I actually wouldn't mind finding a dirk in my bed again.'

'I meant anyone in the influencer party?' says Luna, looking even more scared.

Everyone shakes their heads again.

'OK,' says Sabrina. 'I've had enough of this. We need to start getting ready for tonight. We're supposed to be going to the village fair, remember?'

'Where were *you* last night, Sabrina?' says Dante suddenly, leaning forward in his chair. 'I don't suppose you know anything about this business with the dirk, do you?'

'I don't even know what a dirk is,' replies Sabrina in a dignified tone. 'And, for your information, Dante, I was in my room all night, trying to pull together the details for the launch party tomorrow night. We were thinking of doing a big countdown to midnight, at which point we'll officially be into opening day for the hotel. So, it'll be like New Year's Eve, except, in this case, we'll be counting down to the hotel's first day of trade, rather than the first day of the year.'

She looks around at us all, as if she's expecting a round of applause for this idea but, unfortunately for her, everyone's still too focused on the goings-on to pay much attention.

Sabrina's shoulders slump. For the first time, I notice shadows under her eyes, which she's tried to cover with foundation; she must be under more pressure with this launch than I realised.

'Anyway, that's what I was doing,' she says. 'Luna will vouch for me, if you need an alibi. Won't you, Luna?' She gives a brittle kind of laugh, and turns to her assistant, whose eyes widen in terror.

'Um, that's right,' Luna says, her eyes very large behind her glasses. 'Sabrina was in her room all evening. I saw her.'

'She's lying,' says Zara in a whisper from beside me. 'I can tell. She doesn't have a clue where Sabrina was.'

I glance round at her, remembering what she said yesterday about how every one of them lies about something. I never did get around to asking what it is *she* lies about. And now it looks like I'll have to add Luna and Sabrina to my list of potential liars.

Is *everyone* in this hotel lying about something?

And, if so, do I have to include Hunter in that, too?

'Er, if no one has any objections, I'd quite like to get back to the subject of the hotel doing business with the village again,' says Ian, clearing his throat. 'That's why we're here, after all. This business with the turnips and the invisible woman is all very interesting, but it's not going to help us farmers, is it?'

'The Village People,' says Millie, snapping her fingers triumphantly as she stares at him. 'It's the Village People.'

'That's right, lass, we're people from the village,' says Callum gently, as if he's speaking to a very small child. 'We met you earlier, remember?'

'The *who*?' interrupts Zara. 'What are you talking about, Millie?'

'No, not The Who; I said it's the Village People. *That's* the seventies rock band the angry mob reminded me of earlier. You know, they had, like, a cop, and a cowboy, and stuff? Well, this lot has a witch, a farmer, a . . . I'm sorry,' she adds, looking at Callum apologetically. 'I don't know what you're supposed to be. I really like it, though.'

Callum turns so red his tattoos almost disappear.

'To come back to the discussion in hand,' says Ian. 'We would really like to speak to the Laird.'

'Well, you can't,' says Hunter bluntly. 'I already told you, he doesn't accept visitors.'

'He accepts visits from Dante,' says Izzie unexpectedly. 'I had tea with his mother last week – Dante's, I mean, not the Laird's – and she told me Dante and the Laird were as thick as thieves. Dante's his right-hand man, apparently. Well, according to his mum, anyway.'

Two bright spots of colour appear on Dante's high cheekbones, giving him an almost human appearance.

'I wouldn't say *that*,' he begins, but Ian interrupts, obviously wanting to get this meeting back on track.

'What if we put our request in writing?' he suggests. 'Would that work? Then maybe Dante here could make sure he gets it?'

Dante looks like he's about to say no to this, but then Izzie catches his eye.

'I suppose I could take him a note,' he says reluctantly. 'I can't promise he'll read it, though. He's not exactly the easiest person to deal with.'

'OK,' says Izzie briskly, wiping her hands on her skirt. 'That's settled. We'll hold off on the curse for now, until we can get a letter together outlining our complaints. I think we can give you twenty-four hours; maybe forty-eight.'

'Is this how curses always work, then?' asks Zara, raising her eyebrows.

'No, I normally go straight in with a curse, personally,' says Izzie. 'So they don't see it coming. I never let my enemies know rest.'

'Neither do I,' agrees Yasmin.

Everyone starts getting to their feet, Izzie and Ian squabbling among themselves over who should get the last piece of toast from the rack that came with breakfast, and the influencers chattering excitedly about the upcoming trip to the fair, my drama with the dirk already forgotten.

'Wait,' I say, raising my voice above the chatter, even as my nerves threaten to stop me. 'We didn't really talk about the goings-on, and what to do about them. Don't you think that's important? Someone put a dirk in my room – what if it happens again?'

But no one hears me; and, before long, the room's starting to empty out, everyone making their way to the door, the mysterious goings-on at the Chrysalis resort completely forgotten.

'You know what?' says Millie, distractedly, as the door swings closed behind them all. 'I actually think it was Fleetwood Mac they reminded me of . . .'

Chapter 23

Hunter's waiting for me outside the library as everyone leaves.

'Do you really think that was the best idea, bringing up the "goings-on"?' he says, using his fingers to make scare-quotes around the words.

'Yes. Yes, I do actually,' I reply, pulling my shoulders back. 'I should have mentioned it ages ago, really. I don't know why I didn't.'

I *do* know actually, and it's exactly as Yasmin said: it was because I was convinced one of them might be involved. Which still might be the case.

'I told you I would handle it, Rosie,' Hunter says. 'I told you I'd speak to Dante today, and we'd do our best to figure it out. But now you've taken it upon yourself to tell everybody someone's sneaking around trying to scare off the guests, which means—'

'Whoever's behind it will know we're onto them, and have the chance to cover their tracks,' I interject, slapping a hand over my mouth. 'God, I didn't even think of that.'

'Which *means*,' Hunter goes on pointedly, 'that you've just told a group of influencers about strange goings-on in the hotel. Do you really think you can trust them to keep that to themselves? Because, I don't know about you, but I don't think many people are going to want to stay in a hotel where they might find a stabbed turnip in their bed, are they?'

'Um, maybe?' I reply. 'If they like mysteries, possibly? Or . . . turnips? OK, OK, no,' I groan, covering my face with my hands. 'No, of course they won't. I didn't think of that, either. I don't think any of the influencers will try to publicise that, um, *aspect* of the hotel, though,' I add, brightening. 'They all still want to win the competition, so it would be pretty stupid of them to do anything to make the hotel look bad.'

Like I keep doing, for instance.

Hunter watches me silently for a moment.

'Well, I hope you're right, Rosie,' he says, clearly unconvinced.

'I am,' I reply, with a confidence I don't particularly feel. 'No one's going to post anything about turnips. Well, other than me, obviously, and I took that video from yesterday down. And tonight we're going to the village fair, so that'll definitely distract them all. They'll be too busy taking photos of Ferris wheels and carousels, and whatever else there is there, to think about who might have stolen my clothes for a few hours.'

'Aye. You're probably right,' he says, still sounding unsure. 'I was planning to take Hannah to the fair tonight, myself, as a matter of fact,' he adds, looking at me almost shyly. 'She's been bugging me about going ever since she heard about it.'

'Oh. Right. So I guess I might see you there, then?'

I grin, unable to ignore the prickling of excitement that's started up in my stomach at the thought of getting to see him again – and hopefully without the accompaniment of an angry mob this time.

Much to my relief, though, Hunter responds with a smile. A small one, true, but still – a smile.

'Aye, you might,' he says, a familiar twinkle in his eye, then looks at his watch. 'I have to do some more work on the maze before the grand opening. I'll, er, maybe see you later?'

I nod, not quite trusting myself to speak. I watch him stride off towards the stairs, then, realising I've left my phone in the library, I turn and duck quickly back into the room, stopping short when I find Dante still standing there, flicking through a book he's taken from one of the shelves.

'Whoops, sorry, I didn't know anyone was in here,' I mutter, darting forward to snatch up my phone, not exactly relishing the thought of being alone with Suspect #1.

'I was just leaving,' Dante says stiffly, quickly putting the book he's holding back. He pauses for a second, as if he's considering saying something else.

'I know you're enjoying your little game of Cluedo,' he says at last. 'But this isn't a game to us, Rosie. Me, Hunter, the rest of the staff. You'll be going home in a couple of days, but we have to stay here and make this place work. You might want to think about that before you start accusing people of being out to get you all the time.'

I swallow nervously, hot tears prickling the backs of my eyes; tears of guilt, shame, and . . . is that *anger*?

'It's not a game to me either, Dante,' I reply, confirming that the emotion lurking behind the others is, in fact, anger. 'It's actually *happening*. Someone's been trying to scare me. I'm not imagining it, or making it up. And you can't seriously expect me to pretend nothing's going on, can you?'

Dante looks at me as if that's exactly what he expects. Then he gives an almost imperceptible shrug.

'I'll speak to the staff,' he says. 'I'm sure there's a simple explanation for . . .'

'The goings-on?' I supply helpfully.

Dante doesn't bother to dignify this with an answer. Instead, he just gives a small nod, then goes stalking out of the room, looking like a man with the weight of the entire world on his shoulders. Or the weight of the hotel, at least.

I wait for a moment to make sure he's not coming back, then quickly cross the room to the bookshelf he was standing next to. One of the books is sticking out from the rest slightly, as if whoever read it last didn't take the time to replace it properly, and I slide it out, looking at it curiously.

A History of Glenmuir Castle, says the title on the hardback cover, above an old black-and-white photo of the castle, looking much the same as it does today, only without any of the cars that are normally parked outside it.

The book was published in 1950, according to the flyleaf, so it doesn't go up to the present day, but I flick through it anyway, pausing to look at some of the sepia-toned photos, which show a selection of people in old-fashioned clothes, posed around the castle and grounds, their faces bleached to a ghostly pallor thanks to the age of the paper and low-quality photography.

It's kind of creepy, actually.

I'm just about to put the book back again, when my eye falls on a photo of a group of young men, all standing in front of the castle, wearing clothes that look stiff and uncomfortable to my modern eyes.

'*Glenmuir Castle, 1925*' says the caption underneath. It's not the *year* this photo was taken I'm interested in, though; it's the tall man standing in the middle of the group, with his pale face and shiny black hair.

Dante.

He looks *exactly* like Dante.

Which means one of two things: either Dante actually *is* a vampire, who's lived here for hundreds of years, or . . .

. . . he's somehow related to the Glenmuirs.

Which is a far more likely explanation, really.

I scroll frantically back through my memory, trying to recall everything I've found out about the hotel manager since I arrived here. His mother came from Italy, Hunter said; and fell in love with a Scotsman. It obviously wasn't the man in this photo (Well, not unless we're going back to the 'vampire' theory, which is a stretch even for me), but maybe one of his descendants?

Dante and the Laird are as thick as thieves, Izzie's voice says in my head. *Ideas above his station, that one.*

Oh, my God. Could *Dante* be the Laird's nephew?

And, if so, could he be trying to scare me away from the hotel because he knows my poor attempts at influencing people to come here might ruin his chances of selling the place one day?

I stand clutching the book, my breath coming in shallow gasps as I consider this.

I have to find Hunter. I have to run this theory past him, and find out what he thinks. And I have to do it *now*.

I rush out of the room, and go running down the stairs and out into the grounds.

The maze. Hunter said he was going to do some work on the maze.

I set off at a jog, making my way around to the back of the castle, and past the beautiful, mirror-like lake, until I spot the entrance to the maze, the little tree Hunter was cutting down in front of it now reduced to just a stump.

The weather has changed again since this morning, a fog blowing in from the sea and shrouding the castle grounds in mist, while a cold breeze rustles the leaves on the trees. Given the kind of luck I've been having, it's probably not the best idea to get myself lost in a maze right now, but, as I approach, I can hear the steady thud of Hunter's axe, which tells me he's not too far from the entrance.

All the same, I hesitate before going in, wishing I had a ball of string or something I could unravel as I go, Famous Five style, so I could find my way back out easily.

Still, it's not a particularly big maze. It can't be *that* hard to find a way through it, surely?

That familiar feeling of foreboding hanging heavily over me, I take a step inside; then another, and another. Nothing bad happens, so I speed up a little, following the sound of the axe falling; a stead thud, which would be ever-so-slightly ominous, if I didn't know what – or rather *who* – was behind it.

All I have to do is find Hunter; then he'll be able to help me find my way back out again.

The trees which make up the maze are taller than they looked from my bedroom window, the paths between them only wide enough for two people to walk abreast. The fog from the sea hangs wispily over us, giving the whole place a surreal, nightmarish quality, and I've only been walking for a couple of minutes when I hear the sobbing. It's low and unearthly, and makes goosebumps stand out on my arms, my entire body vibrating with fear.

This was a very bad idea.

My legs are trembling too much for me to run, so I open my mouth to scream, instead closing it abruptly as a familiar voice drifts over from the other side of the row of trees.

'Yes, I know,' says Sabrina Bates, in a voice so shaky I almost fail to recognise it. 'But if you could just give me another few days, then this hotel campaign will be wrapped up, and the payment we get for it will have us back in the black again. That's *if* we get paid for it. It's not going particularly well, to be honest.'

She starts crying again; a sound so incongruous that I almost find myself doubting that it's really her.

I take a step forward, trying to get closer without her seeing me.

'No, I can't do that,' she's saying now. 'I don't want to have to lay off any of my staff. I'll . . . I'll try harder with this campaign. If I can just make sure the launch goes well . . .'

She must be walking now, because her voice is getting fainter, and I can no longer hear her clearly. But, from what I did hear, it sounds like Sabrina's business really *is* in trouble, like Hunter said. It sounds, in fact, as if she has everything hanging on the Chrysalis launch. The one I'm currently in the process of completely messing up.

My heart starts hammering wildly in my chest.

This is all my fault. Ever since I got here, it's been one disaster after another; and now it's not just the hotel staff who might lose their jobs if the launch doesn't go well, it's Sabrina and Luna, too.

I have to fix this. I have to make it right.

First, though, I have to find Hunter.

I turn to walk away, but I manage to step on a twig, which snaps loudly, the noise seemingly amplified by the quiet of the castle grounds.

'Who's there?' calls Sabrina tremulously, still on the other side of the trees. 'Is there someone there?'

I step cautiously backwards, grateful for the grass underfoot, which muffles the sound of my footsteps. I can't let Sabrina catch me in here. I don't want her to know I overheard her conversation.

I continue walking backwards for a few more steps, but a sudden rustling sound tells me Sabrina's started to follow me, so I turn and run, sprinting down through the long columns of trees, not really thinking about where I'm going.

This, of course, is *another* mistake.

A big one.

A very *Rosie* one.

It doesn't take long for me to realise I'm hopelessly lost. The avenues of trees twist and turn, leading to dead ends and forks in the path, forcing me to choose routes at random, with absolutely no idea where I'm going. I can't hear the thud of Hunter's axe any more, but I can't hear Sabrina either; which would be reassuring, if it wasn't for the fact that I have a horrible feeling that Sabrina Bates isn't the *only* person lurking in this maze, chasing me down the long avenues of trees. The wind in the leaves makes them whisper as if they're alive – as if they're telling each other secrets – and, as I run between them, my breath coming in sharp gasps which hurt my chest, I feel as if I'm never going to get out of here. I'll just keep running around this maze forever, lost and alone, and . . .

WHUMP.

I come to a sudden stop as my body slams into something tall and solid; something which smells like woodsmoke and pine cones.

Something that makes me sob with relief when I recognise it as Hunter.

'Rosie?' he says, his voice registering surprise as his strong arms come around me. 'Rosie, what are you doing here? What's wrong?'

* * *

Hunter leads me to a wooden bench in the middle of the maze, which it turns out I'd almost reached, and listens patiently as the whole sorry story comes spilling out: how I recognised Dante – or one of his ancestors, at least – in the book he was reading in the library; how sure I was that he must be Lord Glenmuir's nephew, and therefore the person who's been trying to scare me since I got here . . . right up until I heard Sabrina Bates talking on the phone just now in the maze.

'And now I'm thinking it's just as likely to be Sabrina,' I say, the words sounding wild even to me. 'Her business is failing, Hunter. She really needs this campaign to be a success. And *I'm* the main reason it isn't.'

Tears trickle down my face, and Hunter reaches out and wraps his arms around me again, pulling me into the comfort of his chest.

'Shhh, Rosie,' he says, his lips brushing my hair. 'You have to try to calm down. No one's out to get you. And even if they were, I'm here; I won't let anyone hurt you. I promise.'

I can't seem to calm down, though. Instead, I keep on crying, all of the built-up tension of the last few days overflowing at last, until Hunter reaches around my body, and pulls me onto his knee, where I sit, burrowed against his chest, until my breathing starts to return to normal.

'I'm sorry,' I say at last, embarrassed by the state I've let myself get into. 'I'm sorry, Hunter, this must all sound absolutely crazy. You must think *I'm* crazy.'

He pulls back slightly, so he can look into my eyes.

'I don't think you're crazy, Rosie,' he says quietly. 'And I'm the one who's sorry. I should have taken you more seriously. I should have tried harder to figure out what was going on so I could reassure you.'

'It's not your fault,' I tell him, very aware of how close our faces are, and how awful I must look after all of those tears. 'But what do you think? About Dante, and Sabrina, and . . . everything?'

There's a short silence as he strokes my hair, and I lean into him, comforted by his closeness and strength.

'I don't know what to think, Rosie,' he says, his voice oddly husky. 'I'm as confused as you are. About a lot of things, really.'

'It's all very confusing,' I agree, with another sniff.

He reaches up and brushes the hair carefully about my eyes.

'One thing I'm not confused about,' he tells me, 'is that none of this is your fault, Rosie. It really isn't. You have to stop blaming yourself. All you did was post one video by mistake. That's hardly going to bring down the hotel, is it?'

'I suppose not,' I reply, not sure if I can believe this.

'Seriously,' Hunter says, his fingers grazing my lips in a way that makes my entire body tingle. 'Things are rarely as bad as they feel when you're right in the middle of them. And I definitely don't think any of this is your fault.'

'But . . .'

'I'm going to do everything I can to figure out what's been going on,' he says firmly. 'I promise. But, for now, I think you should go and get ready for the funfair. I seem to recall we had a date?'

'Um, did we?' I smile in spite of myself. 'Was it a date?'

'Well, I was hoping it might be,' he replies.

He pulls me closer, his lips close to mine, and I lean into him, half of me still anxious about everything that's just happened, while the other half just wants him to kiss me again, like he did last night.

Which is exactly what he does.

Hunter's lips meet mine, and he doesn't just kiss me like he did last night; he kisses me as if none of this matters – not Dante, or Sabrina, or dirks in turnips or any of the rest of it. He kisses me like it's just me and him in the whole world; like we don't live hundreds of miles away from each other, and as if I'm not going home in two days' time, never to see him again.

The last thought lurks unpleasantly at the back of my mind; a shadow hanging over this otherwise perfect kiss, which starts off with him cupping my face tenderly in his hands, but quickly escalates until his hands are in my hair, and I'm not thinking about anything anymore but him.

We sit there and we kiss, completely lost in each other, until Hunter pulls away at last.

'Rosie,' he says, his expression unusually serious. 'I—'

But I never find out what he was about to say, because the rustling sound of leaves underfoot intrudes into this little private world we've created, and we leap apart, me almost throwing myself off Hunter's lap just moments before Sabrina Bates appears through a gap in the trees, looking significantly less well-groomed than she usually does.

'Oh, er, hi,' she says, looking too dazed to even question what we're doing here, in the middle of a maze. 'I don't suppose one of you could show me how to get out of this thing, could you?'

Chapter 24

Hunter walks Sabrina and I out of the maze and back to the hotel, where Sabrina, who's been silent the entire way back, her eyes red from crying, mutters a quick thank you before leaving us alone in the lobby.

I turn to Hunter to speak to him, but, before I can even figure out what it is I want to say, Agnes appears, a wide smile on her pretty face.

'Oh, there you are,' she says. 'I've just left a tray in your room. The bus for the funfair leaves in an hour, so there's no formal dinner tonight. I left you some scones, too; I noticed you liked the last lot I brought you.'

I smile gratefully at her.

'Thanks, Agnes,' I say. 'I, er, guess I'll see you later, then?' I add, looking up at Hunter, who hesitates, as if he's about to say something, but just nods silently, before heading off in the direction of his apartment.

I'm disappointed not to have any more time to talk to him, but I'm feeling much better after our encounter in the maze, so I go upstairs to my room, where I find that, as well as leaving me considerably more food than I suspect she was supposed to, Agnes has also run me a bath and turned down the bed, ready for my return.

I shiver slightly at the sight of it. Agnes has carefully laid my pyjamas out on the quilt, and put a foil-wrapped chocolate on the pillow, but the thought of sleeping in here tonight is something that no amount of chocolate is going to make me feel good about. I'm so nervous, in fact, that I wedge a chair under the door handle, like people do in horror movies, before getting into the bath.

Well, you can't be too careful, can you?

Despite my fears, though, the hour until the bus leaves passes without incident, and I head back down to the mini-bus, which I manage to board this time *without* grabbing anyone's head.

So far, so good.

The village fair turns out to be not so much a fair as it is a few food trucks and stalls grouped around the same little square the market was held in yesterday, which is now also home to a handful of fairground rides, including a slightly perilous-looking Ferris wheel, and one of those old-fashioned carousels, from which music rises and falls in time with the painted horses.

I jump down from the minibus, and immediately look around for Hunter and Hannah, who're nowhere to be seen. Instead, I follow the other influencers across the square, which has been strung with fairy lights. They twin-kle merrily against the dark sky, giving the place a magical feel, even in the face of the increasingly strong wind, which makes the lights and bunting sway to and fro above us.

The scent of cinnamon and toffee fills the air, and over in a corner next to the Waltzer, I spot Ian presiding over the same market stall he was manning yesterday, which now has the words 'Ian's Tatties' painted above it in a very slapdash manner that suggests Ian probably did it himself – possibly while under the influence.

'Hi, Ian,' I say, waiting for a gap in customers before I wander over. 'I didn't know you'd be here tonight.'

'No choice, Rosie,' he says sadly, ladling something pale and lumpy into a cardboard container. 'The farm just isn't making enough money on its own, so I'm having to moonlight. Izzie's the same.'

He points across the square to where a little tent has been set up, with a rather terrifying photo of Izzie herself on the front of it. A sign next to the door advertises tarot readings and fortune telling, and I briefly wonder if I should pop over and ask her if she thinks there's any possibility of a future for Hunter and me. Then it occurs to me that Izzie hasn't exactly been doing a great job of predicting anything else that's happened this week, and decide to stay put.

'Now, what can I get you, Rosie?' asks Ian, bringing me back to reality. 'We've got tattie scones, skirlie tatties, tattie hash, or stovies. Or I could do you a baked tattie, if you'd prefer?'

I'm not remotely hungry after all that food Agnes left me, but I know Ian needs the money even more than I do right now, so I decide to buy something anyway.

'Um, I'll take the stovies, thanks,' I reply, choosing the one thing on the menu that appears not to involve 'tatties', only to be handed a dish of the same pale slush I saw Ian ladling out earlier, which turns out to be surprisingly delicious – and very much potato-based.

'How are you getting on with your letter to the Laird?' I ask, tucking in to the stovies. 'Have you made a start on it yet?'

'Och, we're leaving that to Callum,' Ian replies, handing another customer a tattie scone in a paper bag. 'He's got a real way with words, that one. Could talk the hind legs off a donkey, so he could.'

'Right.' I take another forkful of food to hide my surprise at this. 'Well, I hope the Laird at least agrees to read it, once it's done.'

'That's if the Laird's still alive,' says a gloomy voice from behind me. I turn to see Yasmin, still with her sunglasses perched on top of her head, even though it's not at all sunny, standing eating a toffee apple. 'We shouldn't assume that he is.'

'Wh—why wouldn't he be *alive*?' I stutter.

'Well, none of us have actually *seen* this "Laird", have we?' she says, unperturbed. 'And that handyman guy was being really cagey about him earlier, didn't you think? It was like he didn't want us to speak to him. It made me wonder if he's bumped him off or something?'

She licks delicately at the side of her toffee apple, completely oblivious to the horrified stares Ian and I are exchanging over the tatties.

'Why would Hunter want to "bump off" the Laird?' I hiss, glancing around to make sure no one overhears me. 'That's ridiculous, Yasmin.'

'Well, probably so he can get his hands on the fortune, I would imagine,' she replies, her brow wrinkling as she considers this. 'I mean, there must be a fortune, right? And why else would he keep refusing to let the village people – or Fleetwood Mac, or whoever they are – see the Laird, if he was alive and well? Don't you think that was a bit suspicious?'

I look helplessly at Ian, hoping he'll step in and answer this for me, but he just shrugs then continues stirring his stovies, not even bothering to address the Fleetwood Mac comment.

I guess it's up to me to defend Hunter's honour, then.

'Look, Yasmin,' I say, taking her by the elbow and steering her away from the food stalls. 'You can't go around accusing people of stuff like that, OK? It's not fair. Well, actually, it's worse than not fair; it's completely unhinged. Hunter's a good man; he wouldn't hurt anyone.'

To my horror, Yasmin's Bambi-sized brown eyes immediately fill with tears.

'Sorry,' she mutters, pulling her sunglasses over them. 'I just thought . . . Well, you don't really know him, do you? None of us do.'

She turns to walk away, and I have to reach out to grab her to stop her walking into a passer-by.

'Yasmin, take off the glasses,' I tell her, turning her around to face me. 'It's too dark, you'll end up hurting yourself. Or someone else. What's wrong with you?'

She pushes the glasses reluctantly back up.

'Nothing's wrong with me. I'm just *awkward*, OK?' she says, folding her arms defensively. 'I get nervous around people I don't know, and I end up saying something stupid. Like when I blurted out that thing about the massacre earlier, in the hot tub.'

'What's that? A massacre in a hot tub?' says a woman who happens to be walking past, clutching her two children protectively to her side. 'Where?'

'Nowhere,' I tell her, smiling reassuringly as I grab Yasmin again and pull her away from the crowd. 'Everything's fine! Enjoy the fair!'

I turn and walk quickly away, still holding onto Yasmin, who follows me meekly, until I find us a quiet-ish spot just next to Izzie's fortune-telling tent.

'Yasmin,' I say gently, turning to face her. 'Are you . . . Do you have anxiety or something? Is that what you're saying?'

Yasmin's brow wrinkles again.

'I don't *think* so?' she says. 'I think I'm just weird. That's what everyone always says, anyway. I'm really bad with people. I never know what to say. Then, any time I try to force myself to get involved in a conversation, I end up just blurting out something stupid. Like that time I started going on about Hansel and Gretel, and the witch trying to cook children into a stew.'

A young woman who's just come out of Izzie's tent with a baby strapped to her chest gives a small gasp, then rushes away.

'I was just trying to join in,' Yasmin says. 'I thought it was interesting. But I always get it wrong. Always.'

Her eyes fill with tears again, and I impulsively reach out and take her hand.

'It *was* interesting,' I tell her firmly. 'And you're not weird, Yasmin. Everyone feels a bit shy or awkward sometimes. Everyone says stupid things now and then. I know I do.'

'You do, don't you?' Yasmin says, brightening slightly. 'I do it *all* the time, though,' she goes on, sniffing. 'It's as if I can't help myself.'

She raises the toffee apple and starts licking it mournfully, which is quite an achievement when you really think about it.

'I don't understand,' I say. 'You always seem so confident. Weren't you supposed to be doing some kind of reality TV show at one point?'

Yasmin shudders theatrically. 'God, no,' she says. 'I turned that down. Can you imagine me on TV? No, I'm going to just stick to social media. You can hide in front of a camera, you know. People say they never lie, but that's not true. Cameras lie all the time. They let you pretend to be anyone you like. And, in my case, the camera lets me pretend to be normal. Well, as long as I don't try to talk in my videos.'

She shrugs, as if this is no big deal.

'That's why I try not to talk *at all*, actually,' she goes on, examining the shiny surface of the apple like the witch in Snow White. 'It's just much easier not to, even though it means I have no friends, and everyone thinks I'm stuck-up.'

I stand there watching her. To me, Yasmin is the epitome of sophistication: someone so beautiful and apparently self-possessed that she appears not to even *need* anyone to be her friend. And, to be totally honest, I *did* think she was a bit stuck-up; that her silence and refusal to get involved with anything meant she thought she was too good for the rest of us – even Bex. And yet, here she is, revealing herself to be totally human after all; and with exactly the same insecurities and anxieties I have myself.

Who would've thought it was all just an act?

'You *do* have friends,' I tell her, touching her softly on the arm. 'You have us. Well, *me*, anyway. I don't care if you start talking about . . . about massacres, or Hansel and Gretel, or whatever. Seriously. Be as awkward as you like; I can guarantee I've done worse myself. But you can't go around saying the Laird is dead, though,' I add gently. 'And you definitely can't go around suggesting the handyman killed him.'

'*What?*'

Izzie's head pops out of the tent door, her eyes ringed with sparkly blue eyeliner, and surrounded by glittery, press-on stars. After a second, Millie's surprised face appears beside her – also decorated with stars, for some reason.

'The Laird's *dead*?' Izzie says, in a voice that somehow seems to echo across the little square, cutting through the music and laughter.

'And Hunter Stuart *killed* him?' adds Millie, even louder.

'No! No, that's not what I said,' I begin, but it's too late: Izzie's eyes have gone round with horror, and as I watch, she reaches out a bony finger and points it at someone behind me; someone I know without even having to turn around can only be Hunter Stuart himself.

Chapter 25

'MURDERER!' screams Izzie, although she only gets as far as 'murd—' before Yasmin leaps forward and clamps a hand over her mouth to stop her. There's a short scuffle as Izzie tries to bite her hand and Yasmin drops what's left of her toffee apple on the ground, but eventually Izzie quietens down, leaving me free to face Hunter.

'So. I'm a murderer now, am I?' he says in a conversational tone that's completely at odds with the fierce look in his eye, and the defensive stance he's adopted. 'Anyone care to explain who I'm supposed to have murdered? Rosie?'

'But Rosie's still alive,' says Millie, frowning. 'That's her right there. How could you have murdered *Rosie*?'

'He hasn't murdered anyone,' I say, my chest tightening uncomfortably at the sight of Hunter's tense expression. 'No one has. At least, not as far as I know. This is just a misunderstanding, that's all. You misheard us, Izzie.'

'No, she didn't,' replies Millie. 'I heard you too. I was in there having my palm read – I'm going to meet a tall, dark stranger soon, apparently. Exciting! – and I heard you say something about Hunter killing the Laird, Rosie.'

'And something about Hansel and Gretel,' adds Izzie, who's managed to wrestle her way out of Yasmin's grasp. 'But I didn't quite catch that bit.'

Hunter lets out a sharp, humourless laugh, his eyes filled with hurt as they find mine.

'Well, this is fascinating,' he says. 'I'm not just a murderer, I've apparently found my way into a fairy story, too.'

'Oh, "Hansel and Gretel" is no fairy story, trust me,' mutters Izzie darkly, but Hunter wisely ignores her.

'Do I at least get to know how I'm supposed to have committed this crime?' he asks, addressing the rest of us. 'Poisoned turnip, perhaps? Lead pipe in the drawing room? Or is there something even more fantastical I could possibly be accused of?'

'No one's accusing you of anything,' I say firmly. 'Like I said, this is just a stupid misunderstanding, and we've cleared it up now. Haven't we, Yasmin?'

I stare at her meaningfully, trying to communicate that if ever there was a time for her to speak up, this would be it.

'Well, whatever it is, I've had more than enough of it,' says Hunter, in a tone that suggests he's had enough of all of us – me included. 'I need to go and collect my daughter from the ghost train. I'll leave you lot to your scurrilous gossip.'

He attempts to turn and storm off, but Yasmin darts forward to stop him, finally getting the message I've been trying to send her with my eyes.

'This is all my fault,' she says, grabbing his arm. 'I was the one who said you might be a murderer. Rosie was just defending you. She said there was no way you'd murder a defenceless old man. She said you were a good man, and she didn't say you were hot, but I could tell she was thinking it. Sorry,' she adds, glancing at me. 'But it's true, isn't it?'

'I . . . um. I *did* say he wouldn't kill anyone,' I begin. 'Although not in those *exact* words, Yasmin.'

'Please don't be angry with Rosie,' she tells Hunter. 'She didn't do anything wrong. She was being a good friend to you, actually. You should be thanking her.'

She lets his arm go and stares up at him challengingly. This is definitely the longest speech I've ever heard her make, and I'm starting to wonder what, exactly, I've unleashed by telling her I'll be her friend.

There's a short silence, broken only by the sound of Millie scrabbling around on the ground for the dropped toffee apple.

'I really need to go and get Hannah,' Hunter says, clearly relieved to have an excuse to get away from us all. 'I don't want her to think I've abandoned her. Are you coming?'

It takes me a few seconds to realise the last sentence is directed at me and, by the time I do, he's already striding off across the square to where a little ghost train ride has been set up, a small crowd of parents standing patiently outside it, waiting for their offspring to emerge.

'Look,' I say, catching up with him. 'I'm really sorry about . . . that. It wasn't what you're thinking. Well, I mean, it probably *was* what you're thinking, if what you're thinking is that I'm an idiot who keeps getting herself into trouble. But I wasn't—'

There was something else I was planning to say to him, I'm sure of it. But every word I've ever known goes flying out of my head as Hunter stops and turns to face me, and now all I can think about is the way his lips are turning up ever so slightly at the edges, and how Yasmin was absolutely right when she said I think he's hot.

Because right now, even when he's facing accusations of murder from a fortune-teller and a fashion influencer, Hunter Stuart is nothing if not *hot*.

As if to prove it, he takes a small step forward, shortening the distance between us, and making me gasp in surprise by cupping my face in his hands and kissing me – slow, and deep, as if this is the most important and natural thing to be doing in the middle of a crowded village square. For several long, delicious seconds, the sounds of the fairground and the smell of cotton candy and . . . well, tatties . . . fade away, and all that's left is me, him, and the way his lips move softly against mine, sending little jolts of electricity vibrating through my body.

'That was for standing up for me back there,' he says, pulling away at last. 'I'm still not totally sure what happened, but I know you were on my side, and that your pal's right: I should thank you for that.'

'No thanks necessary,' I reply, slightly breathlessly. 'Although, if that's how you normally thank people, I might have to see if I can do you another favour soon. Maybe I could—?'

Hunter chuckles, his eyes darkening in a way that makes my stomach flip.

'You talk too much, Rosie Winter,' he says softly, interrupting me. 'Has anyone ever told you that?'

Then, before I can respond, his lips are on mine again, slower and softer this time; my arms are around his neck, and this moment is absolutely, positively *perfect* . . . until Hunter pulls abruptly away, releasing me just in time for the little train to come bursting out of its tunnel, with Hannah sitting in the front seat, grinning widely at the sight of us both.

'Daddy, where were you?' she demands, jumping out and running over to us. 'I went round three times. The man said you can pay him later. Hi, Rosie,' she goes on, without waiting for an answer. 'Will you come on the Ferris wheel with us?'

'Oh. Um, I'm not sure,' I reply, struggling to catch up with the abrupt transition from what was shaping up to be one of the best kisses of my life to . . . this. 'I'm not great with heights.'

Or with being snapped rudely back to reality when I can still feel the heat of Hunter's lips on mine, actually. In fact, I would really, really like to rewind to that moment. I wonder who I can speak to about that?

'It's OK,' Hannah assures me, slipping her little hand into mine, completely oblivious to the way my stomach is fluttering, for reasons that have absolutely nothing to do with fairground rides. 'Daddy will look after us. Won't you, Daddy?'

'Aye. Why not?' says Hunter, falling into step beside us, and behaving so normally that I briefly wonder if I might have imagined our kiss – both of them. Then he turns and gives me one of those winks of his over the top of Hannah's head, and the blood instantly rushes to my cheeks.

'I still really want to talk to you about what happened back there,' I say in a low voice, as Hannah drops my hand and goes running on ahead. 'The murder thing, I mean, not the . . . other thing. Although I suppose we should probably talk about that too at some point. Um, shouldn't we?'

Hunter sighs and rubs his eyes.

'I have other ways to get you to stop talking, Rosie,' he says dryly. 'But I don't think any of them would be particularly appropriate with so many kids around. I have to admit, though, I'm curious about what led your pal in the sunglasses to decide I must have killed Lord Glenmuir. I'm grateful you had my back, though. What was it you said again? Something about me being "hot", wasn't it?'

'I *didn't* say that,' I protest, my heart racing so much at the thought of the 'other ways' and what they might be, that I almost forget how to speak again. 'That was Yasmin. She . . . well, she thinks you were being "cagey" earlier;

you know, when Ian and Izzie wanted to see the Laird? And I guess she let her imagination run away with her a bit.'

Kind of like I'm doing now, actually, although for very different reasons.

'Sounds like someone else I know,' Hunter comments dryly, making my cheeks flush. 'There's a lot of *imagination* going around this week, for some reason. It must be infectious.'

'Hey! I haven't accused anyone of murder,' I reply, nudging him in the side, mostly just as an excuse to touch him again. 'And I'm being serious, Hunter. I feel really bad about what happened with Izzie and Yasmin. I know you wouldn't hurt anyone.'

'I'm glad to hear it. I'd hate to think *everyone* was going around assuming the very worst of me,' he says with a frown that tells me he's definitely not as OK with all of this as he's trying to pretend he is.

'So, um, why *wouldn't* you let them see him? The Laird, I mean?' I ask, speaking quickly so I can get this out before we have to get on board the Ferris wheel with Hannah. 'Wouldn't it have been easier to just let them sort it out between themselves? It's not like it's your fault the hotel isn't buying goods from the village anymore.'

'It's not the Laird's fault either, though,' Hunter replies, raking his hand through his hair. 'He might still own the castle, but he doesn't run the hotel. And he's in his eighties, Rosie. It wouldn't be fair to let the village people over there bother him. Not that he'd let them get much of a word in, mind you.'

'I suppose not,' I reply, still puzzled. But before I can say anything else, Hannah gives an excited little squeal as we reach the front of the line, and I realise I have a much more time-sensitive problem to deal with than Dante and his stress levels; or Hunter and his need to gatekeep the Laird from the villagers.

That's going to have to wait for a moment when I'm *not* worried about falling to my death from a Ferris wheel.

'I wasn't joking about not liking heights,' I tell Hunter in a whisper as he helps Hannah board the little carriage, which is bucket-shaped, with lights around the outside, and a cheerful red umbrella over the top. 'I *really* hate them, actually.'

'Ach, it's not that high,' he replies, holding out his hand to me. 'And you heard what Hannah said, didn't you? You can trust me to keep you safe.'

He winks at me again, in a way that makes me think I might not actually mind just a *little* bit of danger right now – and I'm not talking about the kind that comes from swinging high above the earth on a Ferris wheel.

'Just for the record, Rosie,' Hunter whispers, his lips brushing my ear. 'I think you're pretty hot, too.'

I grin back at him, excitement fizzing in my stomach, and then we're in the carriage, which is every bit as tiny and precarious as it looked from the ground. It lurches horribly from side to side as we take our seats, Hannah tucked between us, and chattering so loudly there's absolutely no opportunity for me to respond; or to do anything, in fact, other than cling onto the metal rail at the side of the carriage and try not to think about Agnes's comment about 'Danger Night' earlier this week.

Please let this not be Danger Night.

I really don't think my nerves can handle it.

The wind seems to intensify as the carriage rises into the air, leaving my stomach somewhere down below.

I want to ask Hunter if it's safe to be riding this thing when there's supposed to be a storm on the way, but I don't want to scare Hannah, so I squeeze my eyes shut tight and concentrate on the light drizzle that's dusting my skin; rain so light you can barely even feel it.

'Look, Rosie! Look at the lights!'

Hannah's voice, a few minutes into the ride, prompts me to open my eyes again.

'Oh, wow,' I breathe, risking a glance down to the square below us, which has been transformed into a magical little model village, with lights cobwebbed above it, and music drifting faintly up through the damp air.

'I thought you said it wouldn't go too high,' I gasp at Hunter, who laughs, and then reaches for my hand.

'You're fine, Rosie,' he says, reassuringly. And, miracle of miracles, I realise I *am*.

I'm perfectly safe, up here in the sky, with this lovely man and his little girl. Far below, I can see the throng of people in the square, while, just beyond the funfair, the streetlights of the village stretch down to the sea, like strands of gold leading to its inky dark blue.

This place is wild and wonderful, and only occasionally scary; and, even in the short time I've been here, it's somehow already wormed its way into my heart.

It's just a shame I'm leaving soon.

The thought bursts into my happy thoughts like a firework into the night sky; only, instead of leaving me excited and filled with awe, it just makes my stomach plummet abruptly – although that could also be because the carriage we're in has reached the top of the wheel.

'You OK?' Hunter says quietly, squeezing my hand.

'Sure,' I reply brightly, smiling over at him in spite of the dull ache that's started up in my chest at the thought of never seeing him again. 'Never better.'

And yet, I definitely *could* be better, couldn't I? Because, at the exact moment I'm starting to get close to him – and to Hannah, and to everyone else I've met here in the Highlands – I'm about to go home, to my very average life, my money worries and the problem of finding somewhere to live other than my sister's sofa.

I may not be the wrong Rosie, but I'm definitely living the wrong life.

'Could you take a photo for me?' I ask impulsively, handing Hunter my phone.

'Still trying to win that competition, are you?' he says, taking it reluctantly.

'No. I don't care about the competition. I wanted you to take a photo of all three of us,' I tell him shyly. 'I'd do it myself, but your arms are longer.'

He hesitates for just a moment, then a slow smile spreads across his handsome face.

'Aye,' he says, holding up the camera. 'Aye, why not?'

Hannah and I both lean in to him, all three of us grinning cheesily at the camera as Hunter presses the button to take the shot.

And that's the exact moment the lights go out.

Chapter 26

It seems this is, in fact, Danger Night after all.

'What's happening?' says Hannah, leaning over the side of the carriage as the square below us erupts into chaos. 'Is it fireworks? Is that what that bang was, Daddy?'

'Er, no. No, I don't think so,' replies Hunter, grabbing her coat to pull her back to safety. 'Here, sit still. Let me try to figure out what's going on.'

The Ferris wheel stopped moving at the same time as the lights went out, and our carriage hangs there, rocking gently from side to side in the wind, as Hunter peers over the side, while Hannah and I shuffle carefully towards each other for safety.

'What *is* going on, Hunter?' I ask, my voice shaking as Hannah crawls onto my lap. I hug her tightly to me, not quite sure who's comforting who.

'It looks like a power cut,' says Hunter, pulling his head back inside the carriage. 'As far as I can see, all the power in the village is out. There's not a light to be seen.'

My fingers tighten around Hannah's body. The lights being out isn't too much of a problem for now, given how late the sun sets here at this time of year. The power, on the other hand . . .

'What does that mean?' I ask, trying not to sound as scared as I feel, for the benefit of the seven-year-old on my lap. 'How will we get down from here without electricity?'

In spite of my best efforts at self-control, my voice wobbles dangerously at the end of that sentence, and Hunter reaches out and wraps a comforting arm around both me and Hannah, pulling us into the reassuring warmth of his chest.

'It's OK,' he tells us. 'We'll be fine, I promise. They're bound to have a back-up generator to get us moving again. We'll be on the ground in no time. We're just taking a little break up here, that's all.'

Hannah shifts uneasily on my lap.

'What's a generator?' she asks, her small voice breaking the uneasy silence. 'And what if they don't have one? How will we get down then?'

'Are you kidding me?' says Hunter, in a cheerful tone that hopefully only I can tell is completely fake. 'A funfair as cool as this one, without a generator? No chance. This is just an extra adventure for us, Hannah. And look, we've got the best view of the village now – haven't we, Rosie?'

He nudges me hard in the side, and I reluctantly look down at the square, which is a scene of pure chaos: people shouting and yelling as they try to exit stalled rides and figure out what's going on. Somewhere in the general commotion, I can hear Sabrina's voice rising above everyone else's while, off in the distance, dogs are barking as if they know something the rest of us don't.

It's not much of a view to be honest, but I coo dutifully over it anyway, seeing the way Hunter keeps glancing worriedly at Hannah, and wanting to help reassure her.

Fake it till you make it; isn't that what I've been doing here all along?

I hug the little girl tighter, whispering into her ear about what a great story she'll have to tell her friends.

Hannah looks up at me doubtfully, just as a strange, mechanical noise comes from somewhere below us, and the Ferris wheel jolts back into action, creaking horribly as it goes.

'See?' says Hunter smugly. 'Back-up generator. I told you they'd have one.'

Sure enough, the carriage is on the move again, and although the lights are still out, and this whole episode feels a lot like the opening scene of a disaster movie, it's not long before we're safely back at ground level, and Hannah's doing her best to insist that she wasn't scared *at all*, she was just pretending.

'Me too, Hannah,' I tell her, taking her hand as we exit the ride at last, my legs still wobbly from the tension of the last few minutes. 'Me too.'

Hunter disappears to find out what's going on, and I take a moment to stand there, enjoying the reassuring feel of the ground beneath my feet again, as I take in the mayhem of the funfair. The crowd has started to thin out now – I guess most people have decided to head for home now that nothing's working – but there's still plenty of confused fair-goers milling around, trying to figure out what to do next.

'Rosie! There you are!' says Bex, coming bouncing up to me with Daniel trailing behind her, still meticulously documenting everything with his two cameras.

'We were wondering where you were,' Bex says, beaming down at Hannah, whose eyes get even wider at the sight of the 'princess' she saw in the castle grounds. 'Are you ready to go? Sabrina wants to get everyone back to the bus. We can't get any decent photos here now that nothing's working, so we may as well head back to the hotel.'

'I can't go now,' I tell her, my heart sinking with disappointment at the thought of going back to my lonely hotel room without Hunter there to protect me. 'I have to look after Hannah. I'm not sure where her dad's gone.'

'I'm here,' he says, appearing at my elbow. 'And you should go with the minibus, Rosie. I've just been talking to some folk from the village, and it doesn't look like the power's going to be back on here anytime soon; probably not tonight. They haven't been able to figure out what the problem is yet, and the generator was only for the Ferris wheel, so everything else is still out.'

'Will the hotel be OK, though?' I ask, reluctant to leave him and Hannah. 'Will it have power, I mean?'

'Aye. Aye, the hotel should still have power,' he replies distractedly. 'It's on a different grid from the village. We'll be fine.'

'Oh, ye will, will ye? And what about the rest of us?' demands a voice from the crowd. 'What are we supposed to do while you lot are up there at the castle, feasting and carousing like Henry the Eighth?'

A moment later, Izzie appears, clutching a large crystal ball, which she brandishes before her like a weapon.

'Maybe your crystal ball could give you the answer to that?' says Hunter bluntly. 'I'm surprised it didn't warn you about this in advance.'

'That's not how it works,' replies Izzie sharply. 'The force moves in mysterious ways.'

'The force? Are we in *Star Wars* now?' Hunter says, amused. 'You couldn't get this "force" of yours to get the power working again, could you? That would be a lot more helpful than whatever it is you're trying to do with it right now.'

'OK, smart arse,' replies Izzie, glaring at him. 'Are ye seriously all just going to head back to your swanky castle and leave us here to starve?'

'Och, we won't starve, Izzie,' says Ian, joining us. 'I still have a full pot of stovies back there. And there's quite a few tattie scones left over, as well. I've nothing to warm them up with now, mind you, so we'll have to have them cold.'

'I suppose we could build a fire,' Izzie muses. 'Although if the storm's as bad as they're saying it's going to be, it'll probably just blow it out again.'

She looks up at the sky accusingly. I somehow don't think even a storm would dare defy Izzie, but I'm moved to help her, all the same.

'Why don't you come back to the hotel for a bit?' I say impulsively. 'All of you? Hunter says they'll still have power there.'

Hunter's disgust at this suggestion is so strong I can almost feel his eyes burning into me; and the Fosters don't look particularly thrilled at the idea either. Hannah, how-ever, starts jumping up and down with excitement, and Ian looks like he's about to join her.

'That's certainly what the ball told me would happen tonight,' Izzie says, nodding. 'Thank you, Rosie, lass; we'd be pleased to accept your kind invitation.'

'Hold on,' says Hunter. 'It's not really up to Rosie to invite anyone to the—'

'I'll go and find Callum and tell him where we're going,' Ian interrupts. 'We'll meet you at the minibus, Izzie. Unless you want to take your car?'

'Aye, probably a good idea,' she replies thoughtfully. 'I can get at least four people in it; and if you bring the van, Ian, that'll be even more.'

'No, wait, you can't—' Hunter begins, but it's too late; Izzie and Ian have already darted off in different directions, leaving the rest of us standing there, open-mouthed; me in particular, given that I'm the one who started all of this, and I can already tell from the grim look on Hunter's face that it's not going to go down as one of my better ideas.

'Um, sorry?' I venture cautiously, risking a glance at him. 'It's just, you said it could be a while before the power's back on, and it's starting to get cold now. It didn't seem fair to just leave them to get on with it when there's an entire hotel they could shelter in.'

'It's a power cut, Rosie,' Hunter points out. 'Not a natural disaster. I hardly think we need to start thinking about setting up shelters. They do all have homes to go to, you know.'

'Homes that won't have any heat or light,' I reply. 'Plus, don't you think it would be a good opportunity to build some ties between the hotel and the community? It's just a few extra people; and maybe it'll make them less likely to want to complain to the Laird?'

'You're always saying we should try to help people when we can, Daddy,' adds Hannah, coming unexpectedly to my rescue. 'And this'll be so fun!'

'Aye. Well. I suppose it's done now,' Hunter replies, his jaw tightening with thinly suppressed annoyance. 'We'll just have to hope they don't bring too many people with them. And that the power comes back on sooner rather than later.'

'Oh, I'm sure it will,' I say, with the confidence of someone who has absolutely no idea what she's talking about. 'And, like Hannah said, it'll be fun. Kind of.'

'Just promise me one thing,' replies Hunter, as he takes Hannah's hand, ready to leave. 'Promise me you're going to be the one who tells Dante about this?'

Oh yeah. *So much fun.*

Chapter 27

Dante is, unsurprisingly, even less enamoured with the idea of hosting a group of villagers in his precious hotel than Hunter was.

'Are you kidding me?' he says, his eyes narrowing dangerously when I present him with the idea, having accepted a lift back with Hunter and Hannah so we could give the hotel manager at least a bit of warning. 'Since when was it your job to invite people to stay at the hotel?'

'It's just two or three people,' I reply soothingly, wondering if he's planning to speak to the actual paying guests like this, too. 'And they're not going to be staying here; just, you know, hanging out for a bit, until the power comes back on. You'll hardly even know they're here. And it'll be a great opportunity for publicity, too; the Chrysalis coming to the rescue of the poor villagers in their hour of need. It's perfect, actually, when you really think about it.'

Dante looks at me with suspicion; which is fair enough, really, considering everything I've put him through since I got here. I wouldn't trust me, either. And I don't trust *him*, so I suppose, in that respect at least, we're even.

'It's not that Fleetwood Mac lot again, is it?' he asks. 'Isobel Lamb and her strange sidekicks? Because I've had more than enough of that bunch for one day. Or one lifetime, actually.'

I blink nervously, noticing the way his shoulders keep twitching. I guess he really is feeling the pressure of making this launch a success. I just hope I haven't gone and ruined it for him yet again.

Fortunately for me, I'm spared the horror of having to answer his question by the crunch of tyres on the gravel outside, heralding the arrival of the bus.

'That'll be them now,' I say, heading gratefully for the door, followed by Hunter, who's been ominously silent since we left the funfair.

Sure enough, the hotel's minibus is pulling up outside, and we all line up on the steps as the passengers start to disembark.

'I thought you said it was just going to be a couple of people?' Dante splutters, his face paler than ever as he watches the villagers pile out of the bus, some of them carrying what looks suspiciously like overnight bags.

'Er, I said two *or three*,' I reply weakly, my heart sinking as a purple VW Beetle appears at the bottom of the drive and begins bumping its way towards us, with Izzie at the wheel. Behind it is an old Transit van being driven by Ian, and by the time they've pulled up next to the bus, I'm pretty sure Dante is going to require medical attention for the quivering rage he appears to be experiencing.

'Hiya, Rosie,' says Izzie, climbing out of the Beetle. 'We'll just park here, will we?'

Hannah goes running down the steps to meet her, and I quickly follow, leaving Hunter to deal with Dante. By the time I look back up at the hotel's entrance, Hunter's steering him carefully back inside, so he misses seeing Ian and Callum climb out of the van, followed, to my surprise, by a small girl with a cloud of dark curls, and a Barbie in her arms that looks a bit like Millie.

'My wee sister, Rowan,' Ian calls over to me. 'She's looking forward to getting a look inside the castle.'

'Ian's mam and dad died when Rowan was just a toddler,' says Izzie in a low voice, coming to join me. 'Bad accident. Ian was at college at the time; he had to give it up to raise Rowan and Callum, and take over the farm.'

'But that's awful,' I whisper, my heart contracting with pity for them all. 'Poor Ian. Poor all of them.'

'Aye, he's some boy,' Izzie replies. 'There's not many young men who would rise to a challenge like that. We all rallied around, of course, to help them, but it was a tough time for them, there's no mistaking it. And now the farm's at risk too, thanks to His Highness up there.'

She gives a jerky nod in the approximate direction of the castle, presumably referring to the Laird. My resolve to use tonight to try to rebuild relationships between the hotel and the village goes up a notch.

I wasn't lying when I told Dante this could be a good thing for everyone; it's just going to take a bit of careful management, is all.

It's a good job managing things is my job, and although I'm more used to managing an office full of marketing executives than a Highland hotel and a group of disgruntled villagers, how different can it really be?

'Well, this is lovely,' says Ian, rubbing his hands together cheerfully as he approaches me and Izzie on the drive. 'It was right good of you to invite us all, Rosie. Now, if you wouldn't mind giving us a hand with this stuff . . .'

He walks round to the back of the van, where he and Callum start unloading trays of food; most of it potato-based, but I notice quite a few other vegetables too, including an entire box of turnips, which I give a wide berth.

'If you could show us where the kitchens are, Callum and me can heat up the soup we've brought,' Ian goes on, lifting yet another tray of produce out of the van. 'And there are some lassies from the village bringing some baking as well.'

I have no idea where the hotel kitchens are, but Hannah does, and she leads Ian and Callum into the castle, me trailing along behind them and trying not to notice the fact that a group of children are attempting to slide down the main stairs on trays.

Hunter is nowhere to be seen, and neither – to my relief – is Dante, so I follow the sound of voices along the hall and into a vast room with polished wooden floorboards, which I assume is the ballroom Hunter mentioned a few days ago. The room looks straight out of an episode of a Regency drama, with crystal chandeliers, velvet curtains and even a grand piano positioned in one corner, as if it's just waiting for someone to come along and strike up a tune. Instead, the place is currently filled with confused villagers, all milling around wondering what to do with themselves.

'If this is what you call a few extra people, I'd hate to see what you'd describe as a crowd,' says Hunter's voice from behind me, a few minutes later. 'There must be at least half the village in here.'

He steps up to join me, a frown line etched between his eyebrows.

'It won't be for long,' I reply, trying to sound confident. 'The electricity in the village will come back on, and they'll all go home with stories about how lovely and welcoming the staff at the Chrysalis were.'

I shoot him a meaningful look, and the frown line gets deeper.

'I wish I could be so sure,' he tells me. 'I've just been on the phone to the electricity company and they still haven't managed to figure out what's caused the fault. And the wind's getting stronger, which'll make it more difficult for them. I'm worried these folks will end up being here all night at this rate.'

'Did you hear that, everyone?' yells a man standing nearby, who's obviously overheard us. 'We're going to be here all night, apparently. Good job we're in a hotel, eh? And a five-star one at that!'

A murmur of excitement rumbles around the room as everyone takes in this fresh piece of news.

'We don't actually *know* that's going to be the case,' Hunter protests loudly, but his voice is lost in the general hubbub as everyone starts talking at once.

'A free stay in a spa hotel! I bagsie the best room!' shouts one voice.

'I bagsie first go in the Jacuzzi,' yells another.

'Right, that's the soup ready,' says Izzie, appearing in the doorway of the ballroom with a large cauldron, which she's stirring with a wooden spoon. She carries it over to a long table that's been set up under one of the tall windows which line one side of the room, and puts it carefully down.

'Soup's up, everybody,' she shouts, her voice cutting through the commotion. 'Come and get it while it's hot!'

Dozens of pairs of feet go thundering across the wooden floor, the hungry villagers momentarily distracted from the spa by the promise of hot food. With Agnes's help, Izzie starts ladling the broth into bowls which someone's brought in from the kitchen, while Ian recruits some more surprised staff members to help him carry in the rest of the spread; plus some more tables and chairs, which have soon transformed the grand ballroom into something resembling a school cafeteria.

'Dante isn't going to like this,' Hunter mutters darkly, the line between his eyes now in danger of becoming a permanent feature. 'In fact, he's going to hate it.'

'Dante isn't here,' I point out reasonably. 'And what he doesn't know . . .'

'. . . could definitely hurt him,' Hunter finishes for me. 'Ach, look,' he adds, relenting slightly at the sight of me twisting my hands together nervously. 'It's done now. I suppose we'll just have to make the best of it. It's not as if we can kick this lot back out into the storm that's coming.'

The expression on his face suggests that's exactly what he'd like to do, but before he can change his mind about 'making the best of it', his phone starts ringing, and he scowls down at the caller display, before excusing himself to answer it. For once, I'm actually relieved to see him go.

The evening wears on, and the wind picks up, roaring around the castle and occasionally finding its way down the giant chimney, much to the delight of the children present, who try to convince each other the eerie howling noise it makes is coming from a ghost.

The 'lassies' from the village turn out to be the owners of one of the little cafes by the seafront, and they supply not just a few cakes, as Ian had led me to believe, but also a huge selection of pastries, along with filled rolls and sandwiches, which go nicely with Ian's various tattie-based goods, none of which ever seem to run out.

'This seems to be going well,' he says, pausing beside me as he swaps out a tray of tattie scones for one of baked potatoes. 'Good idea to throw a party, Rosie. Everyone's having a great time.'

'I didn't actually say we'd have a *party*,' I protest, but he's already gone, handing out foil-wrapped potatoes as he goes.

'Want me to take some more photos for you, Rosie?' Agnes says, seeing me standing there uncertainly on the edge of the room. 'All the other influencers are busy filming each other.'

'No, that's OK, Agnes, thanks,' I say gratefully, not wanting to take her away from her work. All the same, she's helped remind me about the publicity I promised Dante this would give the hotel, so I pull out my phone and start to make my way around the room, taking photos and videos of everything, from the delicious-looking food to the rain that's started lashing the large windows that line the ballroom.

Ian was right: this *is* going rather well. So well, in fact, that by the time I've finished uploading my content, I've almost convinced myself that this *was* a really good idea of mine, after all. And I'm sure Hunter, and Dante, and maybe even Sabrina will think so too once they realise what great – and, most importantly, *authentic* – publicity the villagers are creating for the hotel.

On my second lap of the room, I find Daniel Foster sitting on the floor in a corner, looking so miserable that it doesn't feel right to just keep walking, no matter how much I want to.

'Hi, Daniel,' I say, stopping in front of him. 'Everything OK down there? Where's Bex?'

'Upstairs, getting changed into something more suitable for a ballroom,' he says, picking moodily at a frayed spot on the leg of his jeans. 'So we can take some more *fucking* photos. I've been dismissed until then. I'm surplus to requirements, apparently.'

'Oh. Right. Well, that's . . . Would you like some potatoes?' I ask brightly, realising he's more than a little bit tipsy. 'There's lots of potatoes. It might do you good to, er, line your stomach.'

'You've no idea what it's like, being an Instagram husband,' Daniel says, ignoring me. 'I feel like I'm invisible sometimes. No one cares about the guy behind the camera, do they? All they care about is Bex. She's the talent. I'm just—'

'Ken?' I venture, slapping my hand over my mouth as soon as the words are out. 'Sorry,' I whisper. 'I didn't mean . . .'

'No, you're right,' Daniel says stoically. 'That's exactly how it is. They even refer to me as Mr Bex, like I don't even have a *name*. I think you're the only one who understands me, RR.'

'Um . . . RR?' I crouch down beside him, wincing as the alcohol fumes on his breath hit me full in the face, confirming that he's been sampling some of Ian's home brew. Quite a bit of it, it would seem. That explains why he's slumped against the wall, his face looking strangely naked without a camera attached to it.

'RR? Wrong Rosie?' he clarifies, looking at me as if I must be particularly slow not to have got this.

'But "wrong" doesn't start with an . . . actually, that's beside the point,' I tell him, sitting down beside him and doing my best to angle my face away from the stench of alcohol. 'I do understand what it's like to feel invisible, actually,' I go on. 'But you can't complain about the way people treat you when you go around calling them names like Wrong Rosie, Daniel. And I thought you enjoyed taking photos, anyway?'

'Sorry, RR,' he says quickly, looking up at me with puppy dog eyes. 'I mean *R*. And I *do* enjoy it, mostly. I'm just sick of everything having to be a photo opportunity, though. *Everything*. I just want my wife to smile at me sometimes when I don't have a camera in front of my face. Is that really too much to ask?'

'I guess not,' I reply carefully. 'I think Bex is the one you should be speaking to about this, though. Do you want me to go and find her for you?'

I start to get to my feet, but Daniel's hand darts out and he grabs hold of my forearm.

'No! Don't tell her what I said,' he says hoarsely. 'Please, RR. Just forget it. Bex needs to win this competition. The Face of the Chrysalis thing. We need the money. And if this sale goes ahead, then the contract could be worth even more than we thought. Sabrina hasn't been being honest with us,' he goes on, leaning earnestly towards me, his special-brew breath almost making me gag. 'We can't trust her, RR. You hear me?'

'I hear you,' I assure him, trying to speak and hold my breath at the same time. 'And I *don't* particularly trust Sabrina, to be honest. But what do you mean "if the sale goes ahead", Daniel? What sale?'

A familiar flutter of excitement starts up in my chest at the sound of the word 'sale', although I'm pretty sure he's not talking about shopping.

'The sale of the hotel,' Daniel hisses importantly, glancing over his shoulder as if he's worried someone might be listening in. 'To WanderNest. I heard Dante talking about it on the phone a couple of days ago. It's all very hush-hush, apparently – well, you can imagine; the place isn't even open, yet. But he said that if the launch goes well, they'll probably make an offer.'

'*WanderNest?*'

I sit back on my heels, dumbfounded. WanderNest is one of the biggest hotel chains in the world. If they buy the

Chrysalis, I can't help but think they'd be even *less* likely to want to trade with the village than the Laird does.

A cold knot of anxiety replaces my earlier feeling of hope.

'Are you sure about this, Daniel?' I ask, hoping this is just some kind of alcohol-induced fever dream he's been having.

'Of course I'm sure, R. What do you take me for?' he replies indignantly, his face flushed. 'I told you, I heard Dante talking about it. He said they're just waiting to see how the launch goes before they finalise their offer.'

I rock back on my heels, trying to take this in.

So Izzie and Ian were right; the Laird's nephew *is* planning to sell the hotel after all.

And it sounds to me as if I was right about his identity, too.

I have to tell Hunter.

There has to be something we can do to stop this.

I squint harder at the faces in the crowd, wishing yet again that my eyesight was better, because I'm sure Hunter must be here somewhere, but I still can't see him. Just as I'm about to go and see if he's in his apartment, though, there's a commotion from the hallway outside the ballroom, and a small boy comes bursting through the double doors, his eyes wild with terror.

'Ghost!' he screams, his voice surprisingly loud for his size. 'There's a ghost in the lobby!'

Chapter 28

Without hesitating, everyone rushes for the doors, piling out of the ballroom in a way that's really quite strange to me, because shouldn't we all be running *away* from this ghost – or whatever it is – rather than *towards* it?

But, then again, there are no such things as ghosts; and I, of all people, should know that, after my encounter with Hannah just a few days ago. So, as the last person goes thundering past me, a foil-wrapped jacket potato clutched firmly in his hand like a grenade, I give myself a quick shake, then follow along behind them all.

I reach the hotel lobby a few seconds behind everyone else, and am just in time to see a tall, ethereal figure in a long, bloodstained silk dress, come gliding down the wide staircase, its dark hair cascading down its back in a way that's eerily reminiscent of . . .

'Bex?' says Zara, pushing her way to the front of the crowd, who've all stopped short at the sight of the apparition. 'Bex, what on earth's happened? Is that *blood* on you?'

Bex – because it's blindingly obvious even to me, without my contact lenses, that the ghost is none other than everyone's favourite influencer, Bex Foster – takes a step towards us, making someone behind me scream.

'Shhh, Millie,' says Yasmin's voice reassuringly. 'It's just Bex. It's OK.'

'It is *not* OK,' shrieks Bex, in a tone that sends the children in the crowd rushing for the safety of their parents' arms. 'Look at my dress! It's ruined! It's completely ruined!'

Sure enough, the pale green silk of her dress is splattered with something red and sticky that looks *exactly* like blood. It's the prom scene from *Carrie* come to life. It's every Gothic horror movie I've ever seen. It's . . .

'Ketchup,' says Zara, dabbing at it with her finger, and then licking it experimentally. 'Yeah, that's definitely ketchup. What happened, Bex? Were you trying to open a new bottle or something?'

'Of course not,' replies Bex sharply. 'Why would I be trying to open a bottle of ketchup in my room? No, I laid the dress out on the bed, ready to change into it after my shower, and when I came out of the bathroom, it looked like this.'

'So . . . you put it on and came downstairs in it?' says Zara, sounding like she's in a courtroom drama. 'I mean, *why*? Why wouldn't you just, I dunno, wear something else?'

Bex glares at her. 'For your information, *Zara*,' she snaps, 'I *had* to put it on because all of my other clothes were covered in this . . . whatever this is . . . too.'

'Ketchup,' supplies Zara again. 'It's ketchup. But wait – seriously? *All* of your clothes are covered in ketchup?'

'Yes! I just said that. Someone must have crept into my room while I was in the shower. And now it's ruined! It's all ruined!'

Bex's voice breaks on the last word, and Zara pats her comfortingly on the arm as, all around us, people start talking again; some of them wondering aloud what's going on, and others mildly disappointed that the ghost drama has turned out to be just some woman in need of a washing machine and a bottle of stain remover.

'Where's Sabrina?' says Zara, looking around the packed lobby. 'And Dante? We're going to have to get to the bottom of this; it's getting out of hand now. And I really want to go and check my room, too, just in case whoever's doing this is going after all of us.'

'Oh, right, *now* it's getting out of hand,' I blurt, annoyed. 'It was fine when it was just *me* being targeted, but now that Bex is involved, we're "going to have to get to the bottom of it"?'

Zara gives me a steely kind of look that makes me think she'd make a great cop; or maybe a high court judge.

'You only told us about your turnip thing a few hours ago,' she points out, sounding annoyingly reasonable. 'And we've been out at the fair since then. But, yeah, we're going to have to get to the bottom of it for sure. Look at the state of her.'

Everyone looks at Bex, who obligingly does a slow pirouette, showcasing the ketchup-stained dress in all its glory.

'I'll go and find Hunter,' I say quietly. 'He'll know what to do.'

I turn around on the spot, trying to find him, but although most people have started to drift back to the ballroom and the feast that awaits them there, the lobby is still too crowded for me to be able to make much headway.

'What is the meaning of this ruckus?'

The room falls quiet as a loud voice goes booming across the lobby, silencing even Bex. Standing at the top of the wide staircase is an elderly gentleman looking dapper in an old-fashioned velvet dressing grown and a pair of smartly pressed pyjamas. He's leaning on a walking stick, and his pure white hair is standing on end, as if he's just got out of bed.

'Oh, my God,' says Millie in a squeaky voice. 'That one really *is* a ghost.'

'That's not a ghost,' says Hannah, scornfully. 'That's just Dougie.'

To everyone's surprise, she goes bounding up the stairs and takes the old man by the hand. 'Ah, Hannah,' he says, beaming down at her. 'You're here. Good. Now, where's that nephew of mine? I need him to get all of these intruders off my property. Damn nuisance they are. Shouting and arguing loud enough to wake the dead.'

He attempts to shake his walking stick at us all, but ends up wobbling so dangerously he has to grab hold of Hannah's shoulder to steady himself.

'Is that the Laird?' says Ian from the back of the crowd. 'We've been wanting a word with him. Let me through, will ye . . .'

'The Laird?' yells someone. 'I thought the Laird was dead? I heard a rumour that the handyman murdered him?'

'Aye, I heard that as well,' says someone else. 'The murdering bastard!'

Outrage fizzes through the crowd like electricity, everyone shouting at once about how we should call the police, or, at the very least, barricade the doors to make sure no one can escape until justice can be served.

I shiver, despite the heat from the fire.

'Are you all daft?' pipes up Izzie, as if it wasn't her who started the rumour in question. 'The Laird's alive and well, as you can plainly see. Well, he's alive, anyway. Now let's all pipe down and hear what he has to say. Is the bawbag nephew here too, though? I thought he was in Glasgow?'

The entire room seems to hold its breath, and I *definitely* do, staring up at Lord Glenmuir as he stands at the top of the stairs, and feeling quietly smug about the fact that he looks almost exactly as I imagined him: magnificently cantankerous, and just a tiny bit like Albert Einstein.

'Is the nephew in Glasgow meeting with the people from WanderNest?' says Daniel Foster, obviously forgetting that this whole WanderNest thing is supposed to be a big secret. 'Is the sale of the hotel going ahead, then?'

'Sale? What sale? What are you talking about, camera boy?' Izzie elbows her way towards us, her sharp eyes focused on Daniel, who seems to sober up a little under the force of her gaze.

'Ask him.' He shrugs, nodding in the approximate direction of the Laird. 'He'll know more than me. It's his nephew who's trying to sell the hotel. That's why he's in Glasgow. At least I *think* that's why he's in Glasgow. *Is* he in Glasgow? Dante'll know. Where's Dante?'

He turns around on the spot, then promptly falls over, stumbling into the arms of Callum, who manages to catch him just before he crashes to the floor.

'Where's this nephew, more like?' says someone else. '*That's* who we need to speak to, surely?'

I bite my lower lip, telling myself not to get involved; that it's none of my business, really, and unmasking Dante would be the very worst thing I could choose to do right now. Then I catch sight of Bex, in her 'bloodstained' dress. I remember the knife sticking out of the turnip.

Zara's right. This is all getting out of hand – and now it's time to put a stop to it.

'It's Dante,' I blurt out, unable to contain myself any longer. 'Dante *is* the nephew. *He's* the one who's been speaking to WanderNest.'

There's a painfully long drawn-out silence, then Izzie starts laughing.

'Dante Romano?' she says incredulously. 'The Laird's nephew? Have you been on Ian's special brew, Rosie?'

I open my mouth to tell her what I know, but, before I can speak, the crowd around me parts, and Dante himself appears, his dark hair dishevelled, as if he's been raking his hands through it.

'What's going on?' he demands, looking from me to Izzie, and then up at the Laird, who's still standing on the stairs, looking as bemused as everyone else. 'Did someone say my name?'

'Aye,' says Izzie. 'It was Rosie. She reckons you're the Laird's nephew. Have you been telling people you're related to royalty again, Dante? Because I know your mother's had to speak to you about that before.'

She glares at him sternly.

'I was *eight* when I used to say that, Izzie,' Dante replies, looking uncharacteristically flustered. 'I haven't said it for *years* now. And I'm not the Laird's nephew, as you very well know.'

'But . . . but Daniel heard you on the phone to Wander-Nest,' I say tremulously, still sure my theory must be right, although I'm growing less certain with every moment that passes. 'And there's a photo of a man who looks just like you in the library. He . . . he must be a relative of yours. I saw you looking at it earlier today.'

'Aye, he is,' Dante says, his eyes so narrow it's a wonder he can see out of them. 'He's my great-great grandfather – or something like that, anyway. My mum told me about the photo in that book; she'd seen it when she used to work here. I was just curious about it, that's all. It's not a crime, is it?'

He folds his arms across his chest defensively.

'So he *is* related to you?' I reply, wondering why none of the people around me seem as surprised by this admission as I am. Can't they see what it means? Can't they see that Dante is . . .

'Aye,' he says again. 'He's related to *me*. He's not related to the Laird, though.'

I suddenly realise I've lost the power of speech; and of breathing properly, it would seem, if the weird, light-headed feeling that's creeping over me is anything to go by.

'Look, the man in the photo was the fifth Laird's valet,' Dante says, looking a little bit annoyed to be having to admit this. 'And his good friend, apparently. He wasn't one of the family, he just worked here – like my mum did. Like I do. It's a family business, almost, running this place. Well, sort of.'

My mouth opens and closes uselessly.

This feels even worse than when we all briefly thought Bex had been stabbed.

'Oh, and I have spoken to someone from WanderNest a few times,' Dante adds, almost as an afterthought. 'But just to take a message for the Laird's nephew. Who isn't me, by the way. I mean, *obviously*.'

He utters the last word in a tone so frosty I'm surprised I don't freeze to death on the spot.

If ever there was a time for a *real* ghost to appear, this would be it.

Instead, Ian steps forward.

'So, where is he, then?' he says bluntly. 'This nephew who wants to sell the castle to some chain who'll just destroy the place, and make it the same as every other hotel they own. Or *who* is he, rather?'

The crowd quietens down, everyone straining to hear Dante's answer.

'Oh. Um, I'm not sure I should say,' he begins, tugging uncomfortably at the collar of his shirt. 'I said I wouldn't. He's—'

'Here,' says a familiar voice from just behind me. 'I'm here.'

The room falls silent, the only sounds coming from the steady *tick tick* of the grandfather clock next to the reception desk, and the sharp click of Steve's claws as he comes padding across the tiled floor at the sound of his master's voice.

Like Stevie, I don't even need to see him to recognise that voice. I've only known it a few short days, but I'd already know it anywhere. And that's why I can't bring myself to turn around just yet, even though, all around me, people are shuffling and straining to get a look at him; scandalised whispers breaking the stillness of the room as everyone nudges their closest neighbour, urging them to turn around and look at Hunter Stuart: the bawbag heir of Lord Glenmuir.

Chapter 29

'Ouch!'

I reluctantly turn around just as the first foil-wrapped jacket potato hits Hunter square in the chest. It's quickly followed by another, then another, and before anyone knows quite what's happening, potatoes are raining down on us all, most of them thrown more or less at random, because the people standing at the very back of the room don't have a good enough view to know who they're supposed to be aiming at.

And I'm not sure they particularly *care*, either.

In the middle of it all, Hunter stands, his hands raised to protect his face from the flying veg, and his eyes locked pleadingly onto mine.

I'm sorry, he mouths, ducking out of the way of a particularly large spud. *I'm sorry.*

I turn my back on him, my entire body trembling with shock as I look at the scene in front of me.

Over by the doors, Callum is still cradling Daniel Foster in his arms, like a baby. Next to them, Bex is dabbing tearfully at the stain on her dress, while, a few feet away, Sabrina viciously slings potatoes at Dante, with a devastatingly accurate aim.

I push my way through the crowd, opening the first door I come to, which turns out to lead down to what I'm assuming is the castle's wine cellar.

Or possibly the dungeon.

It's definitely creepy enough, with its low ceiling and uncovered stone walls.

Just as I'm about to turn and leave again, though, there's a low, fizzing sound, and the lights come on, making shadows jump into the corners of the long, underground room, which is, reassuringly, lined with bottles of wine rather than the skeletons of long-dead prisoners.

'Rosie? Are you down here?'

A moment later, Hunter's feet appear on the stairs I've just climbed down, followed by the rest of him.

'I can explain,' he says, holding up both hands as if he thinks I might shoot. 'I promise I can explain, Rosie.'

'Bet you can't,' I reply, annoyed by his confidence, and how much it reminds me of my gaslighting ex. 'But you can give it a try. I can't wait to hear it.'

I lean back against the rough wall of the cellar, my arms folded across my chest.

'OK. Right. Well. Where to start?'

Hunter sits heavily down on top of a barrel and scratches his head, looking lost.

'How about starting with you being the Laird's nephew,' I say helpfully. 'And then you could move on to the bit where you've been scheming to sell the hotel behind everyone's backs?'

He looks at me warily.

'I wouldn't call it "scheming", exactly,' he says, in a tone that suggests he knows he's not off to a strong start here. 'I'm just trying to do the best I can for everyone, Rosie. This deal with WanderNest – *if* it happens, and that's still a pretty big if, mind – is worth a fortune. Way more than we could ever hope to make without them. It would—'

'So it's all about the money, then?' I interrupt, struggling to reconcile the man who sneered at the so-called materialism of influencer culture with the one in front of me, who's apparently willing to sell his family's inheritance to the highest bidder. 'You just want to make as much as you can, then go back to Glasgow with your . . . your spoils?'

'No,' he protests, stung. 'No, it's not like that at all. I don't care about the money. I've never cared about the money. It's Dougie I worry about.'

'Dougie?' I blink, wondering if he has another child he's neglected to mention.

'Douglas. Lord Glenmuir,' he explains. 'He's the one who needs the money. God knows, there's none of it left.'

He rubs his eyes, and I somehow get the feeling this is an old worry of his; one he's used to poking at, and prodding, and turning around in his hands without ever really solving.

'Do you have any idea how much it costs to run a place like this, Rosie?' Hunter says quietly, looking at me through his fingers. 'I don't just mean as a hotel; I mean the building alone. The heat, the light, the non-stop maintenance.'

I shrug, thinking about the flat I used to rent in London, and how extortionate everything connected to it was. I can only imagine what the upkeep a place the size of the Chrysalis must be.

'It's a lot,' Hunter goes on, without waiting for an answer. 'And Dougie . . . well, let's just say, he hasn't always stayed on top of things, financially speaking. There's . . . well, there's debt. Quite a bit of it, actually.'

'I know the feeling,' I mutter, surprised to find I have something in common with Lord Glenmuir. 'That doesn't mean selling up is the only option, though. Especially when you haven't even given the place a chance. You never know, the launch could go really well. The hotel could take off *without* WanderNest and their money. You haven't even tried, Hunter. How can you give up on it without even trying?'

'Think about it, Rosie,' Hunter says. 'People don't want boutique hotels anymore. We're right on the route of the North Coast 500. We're competing with people in camper vans and tents. With glamping pods and budget hostels. And here we are, trying to market ourselves as a luxury five-star spa hotel. I've done my best to cut as many costs as I can, but I had to take out a loan for the renovation and the extension, so now I need to cover that, too. It's not going to work. I can already tell it's not going to work.'

He shakes his head despairingly, and I'm tempted to go over and shake *him* right along with it.

'You don't know that,' I tell him stubbornly. 'You're being ridiculously defeatist about it. The only way you can know for sure that it won't work is if you don't even try.'

'I've run the numbers, Rosie,' Hunter says, as if I haven't spoken. 'Over and over again. We have fifteen bedrooms; all of them huge. WanderNest could triple that easily.'

'How?' I ask. 'By taking everything that's unique and special about the place and turning it into something ordinary? That's going to be your gimmick, is it?'

I take a deep breath, aware that I'm starting to sound like Millie.

'No. No, that's not what I'm talking about,' Hunter says, his voice rising to match mine. 'What do you take me for, Rosie? I'm not some vandal, willing to destroy the place for the sake of a few pounds. I'm trying to *save* it. I don't know why you can't see that? And I'm from Edinburgh, by the way,' he adds, almost as an afterthought. 'I don't know where everyone's getting this Glasgow thing from.'

'Sorry,' I reply, flicking my hair over my shoulder. 'I didn't know. Just like I didn't know you were the Laird's nephew, say. I'm starting to think there's a lot I don't know about you, actually.'

'You've only known me for a few days,' he points out, not unreasonably. 'I'm sure there's probably a lot I don't know about you, either.'

I pause, momentarily wrong-footed.

He does have a point there, actually.

'I know we haven't known each other long,' I say, slightly less confidently. 'But, even so, that seems like a pretty big detail to leave out, don't you think?'

'Not really,' Hunter says. 'I haven't even known about it myself for long, so it's not the first thing that occurs to me to blurt out to a pretty girl I've just met, and who's only going to be here a few days. And Dante and I had agreed not to tell the staff who I was just yet. I didn't want them to feel like the owner of the hotel was breathing down their necks all the time, *and* I wanted to be able to get to know them all without them thinking of me as "the boss". So it wasn't just you I kept it from, Rosie; it was everyone.'

I take a ragged breath, my mind desperately trying to latch onto the 'pretty girl' comment, but snagging instead on the bit about me only being here for a few days.

Does that mean he was never really interested in getting to know me? Was all of this just a bit of fun to him?

'What do you mean you haven't known about it for long?' I ask, choosing to concentrate on a question I actually *want* to know the answer to, other than the one that could break my heart.

'Exactly that.' He raises his shoulders as if this explains everything. 'I'm not the Laird's nephew, for one thing; I think I'm actually his great-great-nephew, once removed, if you want to get technical. Or twice removed, maybe. Whatever it is, I only found out a few months ago, when Dougie's solicitor contacted me to let me know he was planning to name me as his heir, and that he wanted to meet me. I mean, you can imagine what that felt like, finding out you're one day going to inherit a sodding *castle* in the middle of nowhere.'

He chuckles mirthlessly.

'It just so happened to come along at the same time Hannah's mum had accepted a big contract in New York,' Hunter goes on, looking like he could be doing with a dram of that whisky he likes so much. 'She was going to be away for months, which meant there was nothing keeping me and Hannah in the city. So I thought: what the hell, why not come up and meet the old guy? I thought it would be a bit of a laugh, I suppose – something to tell people about when I got back. And, to be totally honest, I wasn't convinced it wasn't some kind of wind-up.'

'But it wasn't.'

'No. No, it was all real enough; a bit *too* real, actually, because once I got here, and Dougie told me what a mess he'd managed to get himself into, I realised it wasn't quite the windfall his solicitor had made it sound like. At first, I thought the only option was going to be to sell up and use whatever we got for the place to pay off the debts.'

He shakes his head again, but this time I don't feel quite so frustrated by him.

'Was it really that bad?' I ask instead. I have no idea what a Highland castle is worth, obviously, but I'm guessing it's a lot more than even *I* could run up on my credit card, which means . . .

'It was that bad,' Hunter replies bluntly. 'Loans, gambling, you name it. He's had quite the life, has Dougie; I have to hand it to him. But he's not stupid. Reckless, yes, but still – he knew he was going to have to find some way to pay it all off by that point, so I guess that's why he got his lawyer to track me down. It wasn't so much that he wanted to leave me the castle; it was more that he knew he'd be leaving me everything that went with it, and he wanted to at least give me the chance to fix it.'

'So, whose idea was the Chrysalis?' I ask, still trying to make sense of all of this. 'Yours?'

'Dougie's,' he says, surprisingly. 'Well, he didn't come up with the idea of it being a *wellness* retreat, obviously. He wanted it to be a hunting lodge. I managed to talk him out of that idea, but I couldn't persuade him to sell up. He only grudgingly agreed to let me turn it into a hotel, and that was bad enough for him. It's his family home, Rosie. He's lived here his entire life. He couldn't stand the thought of losing it.'

'Which he will anyway if you sell it to WanderNest,' I exclaim, any sympathy I was starting to feel for him evaporating as I realise the truth of this. 'Poor Dougie! I mean Douglas. Lord Glenmuir.'

'No,' says Hunter, leaning forward intently. 'No, that's just it; Dante got it wrong. I was never planning to *sell* the place. WanderNest would have a stake in it, that's all. A large one, sure, but Dougie would still be the owner. Hannah and I would still get to stay here, which . . . well, you know how much I want that. I fell in love with the place, Rosie. I wasn't expecting to, but I did. It gets under your skin – you must feel that too? In fact, I know you do.'

His golden eyes bore into mine, and I focus my gaze on a rack of dusty wine bottles behind him, avoiding the question.

He's right, of course. I've only been here a few days, but I can feel the magic of the place, the same way he does. If I were him, I wouldn't want to leave either. I *don't* want to leave. But . . .

'In the maze, earlier,' I say, in a small voice that sounds like it's being dragged out of me. 'I told you I was sure Dante was the Laird's nephew, and you didn't say anything. You let me believe it. You let me make a complete fool of myself, accusing him like that. And in front of all those people.'

The cellar suddenly goes blurry, my eyes filling with tears of both shame and sadness. Hunter makes a move as if he's about to reach for me, but I step sharply back, and he lets his arm fall uselessly to his side instead.

'I was going to tell you, Rosie,' he says hoarsely. 'I promise. But you were so upset; so scared. I wanted to calm you down first, but . . . well, then we got a bit distracted, didn't we?'

He tries a smile, but I can't bring myself to return it. I just keep thinking of the way I stood there in the lobby, like some kind of budget Nancy Drew, accusing Dante of being someone else.

I wish *I* could be someone else right now. Someone who has even the foggiest idea what to do about all of this.

'In fairness, I didn't think for a second you were going to accuse him like that,' Hunter points out. 'And I was about to tell you in the maze, but then Sabrina turned up. After that, there was always someone around, so I didn't get the chance. But I *was* going to tell you, Rosie. You have to believe me.'

He holds up his hands in a gesture of helplessness, and we both fall silent.

'I honestly don't know what to believe, Hunter,' I tell him at last. 'I know you didn't owe me an explanation of who you really were . . . we barely even know each other, like you said. But it still hurts that you didn't tell me. And it's going to hurt everyone if you end up selling the hotel to WanderNest. That would . . . well, it would really, really suck.'

'Would it, though?' he says, his eyes bright in the dim light of the cellar. 'Would it really be worse than having to sell up altogether? Probably to some property developer who'd turn it into executive apartments? Trust me, I know what I'm talking about here. '

Something tugs gently at my memory.

'A property developer,' I say slowly. 'That's what Ian said the Laird's nephew is – what *you* are.'

'That's what I *was*.' He nods. 'And that's how I know what'll happen if the castle ends up being sold outright. This partnership idea seems like the lesser of the two evils.'

He watches me carefully, waiting for my reaction. He doesn't *look* any different from the Hunter who kissed me at the funfair just a few hours ago; which makes it almost impossible for me to believe that *this* Hunter is not the rugged, tree-chopping, outdoor man I thought he was, but actually a cut-throat property developer.

No. I definitely didn't know him at all, did I?

Everything that's happened between us has been based on a lie; or, if not a lie, exactly, then at least an omission of truth. He's no better than Bex, really, pretending to be younger than she is, or anyone else who lets people think they're something they're not.

No wonder he didn't make a big fuss about me pretending to be Rosie Summers when I first arrived here. How could he, when he was pretending to be someone else, too?

And he's been pretending the entire time.

My shoulders sag in defeat as I lean back against the cellar wall.

'Could you say something, please?' Hunter says, his voice raw. 'Tell me what you're thinking?'

I consider this carefully. What I'm *actually* thinking is that there's no chance of a future between us; and there never really was. Even if Hunter had been honest with me from the start, he'd still live hundreds of miles away, and there's just no way around that.

Plus, he said it himself: I've only known him for a few days. It's nothing, really. It was silly of me to think it could be something more; just as silly as it was for me to think I could come to the Chrysalis as myself and emerge as someone else.

Nothing's going to change.

'What I'm thinking is that we barely know each other, Hunter,' I say softly. 'We're from completely different worlds; and in a couple of days, I'll be going back to mine. So I think it's probably best that we just end this – whatever this is – between us now, don't you? It'll be easier that way.'

A flash of emotion crosses his face, too quickly for me to be able to identify it. Then he nods, just once, not looking at me.

'Can we at least still be friends?' he says, his voice cracking on the last word. 'I know you don't want it to be any more than that, and I get that – I do. But . . . well, I don't know about you, but I could definitely use a friend around about now.'

I pause, one foot on the first step.

Friendship isn't what I want from him; and I'm not sure it's what *he* really wants, either. But we don't always get the things we want in life – isn't that what he told me?

And isn't it the truth?

'I'm not sure,' I say honestly. 'I don't know if I can trust you anymore . . . even as a friend.'

Then, before he can say anything else, I open the door and walk away.

Chapter 30

The hotel lobby is empty, with just one solitary potato sitting on top of the reception desk as a reminder of the events of earlier.

The ballroom, however, is still filled with people, and there's a low hum of excitement in the air as they crowd around the room's tall windows, watching the rain falling outside. The wind whistles through the trees that line the driveway, making them bend precariously, and, as I watch, there's a sudden loud roll of thunder, that makes the smaller kids – and Millie – shriek in alarm.

'I don't suppose you've seen Dante, have you?' Zara says, coming hurrying over as soon as she catches sight of me. 'Or Sabrina? No one knows where they are, and this lot are getting restless. None of them want to risk driving back in this weather, and apparently the power's still out in the village, so they don't want to leave, even if they could.'

As if on cue, lightning lights up the room with a loud crack that makes me jump, and Millie scream again.

This is going to be a very long night.

'I haven't seen either of them,' I tell Zara, my mind still struggling to process everything that's happened in the last few hours; and the last few days. 'If Dante isn't around, though, I guess that leaves the Laird in charge?'

Zara and I look over to where Lord Glenmuir is sitting in a wingback armchair in front of the fire, looking rather lordly with a glass of whisky in one hand and a jacket potato in the other, which he's eating as if it's an apple. There's a couple of villagers around his age sitting on each side of him, and the entire scene is strangely reminiscent of something from *Game of Thrones* – which isn't particularly reassuring, all things considered, although the fact that he's apparently decided to make peace with the 'intruders' can only be a good thing.

Thunder booms around the room once more. Just a few seconds between it and the lightning, which means the storm must be almost overhead.

'Er, you should ask him,' I say, nudging Zara forward. 'You seem to know what you're doing. And also, I'm a bit scared of him.'

Zara sighs loudly, sounding a lot like my oldest sister when the kids have asked her to do one too many things simultaneously. But, after a moment's hesitation, her instinct to take charge kicks in, and she goes striding confidently towards the Laird; me trailing much less confidently along behind her, fighting the urge to drop a quick curtsy as we arrive in front of him.

'They can stay here,' says the Laird, when Zara finishes explaining the situation with the storm and the villagers, having to raise her voice so he can hear her over the sound of the rain, which now sounds like it's attempting to break through the windows. 'If there aren't enough rooms, some of them can sleep in the ballroom. It'll be just like in the war, when we were requisitioned. Soldiers in every corner. Limbs falling off and everything. Blood everywhere. Marvellous time it was, though. Proper Dunkirk spirit.'

For once, not even Zara knows quite what to say to that, and I'm just glad Yasmin isn't within earshot.

'So . . . what, we just hand out room keys?' she manages. 'Shouldn't someone from the hotel be doing that kind of thing?'

'I *am* "someone from the hotel", young lady,' the Laird growls, glaring at her from underneath a pair of very bushy eyebrows. 'Although it's really that nephew of mine you want to get on the case. Where is he, anyway?'

Zara glances at me, and I shift uneasily from foot to foot.

'Did you know?' she asks in a low voice. 'That it was Hunter?'

'No,' I confirm miserably. 'No, I found out at the same time as everyone else. I . . . look, I don't know where he is. We're just going to have to manage without him.'

Zara briefly closes her eyes, as if she's trying to make up her mind about something.

'Right,' she says, opening them again. 'Here's what we do: we . . . Oh, thank God, here's Dante.'

Dante comes sidling silently into the room to the accompaniment of a particularly dramatic bolt of lightning. The Laird imperiously beckons him over, and I shrink back behind Zara, willing him not to notice me.

I'm going to have to apologise at some point for trying to call him out like that in front of everyone; and being wrong about it, into the bargain.

'We don't have enough rooms for everyone,' says Dante, snapping back into manager mode once Zara's explained the situation for a second time. 'So I'd suggest we allocate the rooms we do have to the people who need them most, then we can get blankets and pillows from the laundry for everyone else. If you're sure you really *want* all of them to stay here, that is?'

'Yes, yes,' says the Laird impatiently. 'They must all stay. Wouldn't put a dog out in weather like this. Not that one, though,' he adds, pointing at me. 'That one has to go.'

I blink rapidly, then look quickly over my shoulder, just to make sure there isn't someone standing behind me.

But there isn't. And from the way the old man is glaring at me, it seems pretty obvious who his ire is directed at. My stomach gives a nervous little gurgle which, unfortunately for me, sounds freakishly loud, even with all the background noise.

'Rosie?' says Zara, with a confused frown. 'You don't want *Rosie* to stay? But . . . why?'

'Well, because she's a spy, of course,' the Laird says, his eyebrows shooting up towards his fluffy head. 'I'm not having a spy on the property one moment longer. Go on, get off with you,' he adds, shaking his whisky tumbler in my direction, and making the liquid inside spill out on the floor. 'Off you go.'

'I . . . I'm not a *spy*,' I say shakily, aware of everyone's eyes upon me. 'I'm not *anyone*, really. I'm just Rosie.'

'That's right,' says the Laird, as if this confirms it. 'Rosie the spy. That's what I said, didn't I?'

'But Rosie isn't a *spy*,' Zara says soothingly. 'You're not, are you?' she adds, under her breath.

'No! Of course not,' I gasp, more and more convinced that this is some kind of weird nightmare, and I'll wake up from it soon. 'I don't know what he's talking about.'

'I think I do,' says Dante, a small flush of colour spreading unexpectedly across his high cheekbones. Before he can go on, though, there's a loud crashing sound from somewhere outside the window – the kind of sound you just know doesn't mean anything good.

As one, we all dash for the windows, cupping our hands against the glass in order to see out.

'Shit,' says Dante, running an exasperated hand through his dark hair. 'I think there's a tree down in the driveway. I need to find Hunter.'

He disappears out through the double doors and, a few minutes later, we see his shadowy form, accompanied by the familiar (to me, at least) figure of Hunter appear on the front steps, both of them holding the collars of their coats up to shield them against the wind and rain. We all stand there watching as they make their way down the driveway, to where we can just see the hulking form of something black and huge blocking the gates.

This does *not* look good.

Sure enough, when the two men finally rejoin us in the ballroom, their hair plastered to their foreheads and water dripping from their clothes, I can tell by Hunter's face that I'm not going to like what he has to say.

'There's a tree down just in front of the gates,' he announces, directing his words to Lord Glenmuir, and carefully avoiding looking at me. 'One of the big ones. It hasn't hit anything, thankfully, but it's going to take a bit of work to move it. I'll make a start on it first thing tomorrow, but it might take me a bit of time. It's going to have to be chopped up before it can be moved, and nothing's getting through those gates until it is.'

There's a low murmur of discontent from the assembled villagers, who seem less keen on being forced to stay in the lap of luxury now that it's the bawbag nephew who's telling them about it.

I guess I'm not the only one who feels let down by him right now.

'We'll worry about that in the morning,' says Dante firmly, before the complaints can get out of hand. 'For now, we need to just concentrate on finding everyone somewhere to sleep. Where's Agnes?'

He turns to look for her, and Hunter reluctantly meets my eyes.

You OK? he mouths cautiously in my direction. I nod slowly. I'm *not* OK, as it happens. Someone's trying to scare me, there's a red warning in effect over the entire area according to Google and the Laird has just accused me of being a spy.

So, no, I'm pretty far from OK right now.

But Hunter is no longer the person I can turn to about all of this, so I just settle for that tiny nod, then turn quickly away, almost walking into Zara in the process.

'Here,' she says, dumping a pile of blankets into my arms. 'Start handing these out, will you? It's going to have to be all hands on deck for a bit while we get everyone settled.'

I do as she says, and the next half an hour or so passes in a blur of pillows and blankets, and last-minute requests for hot chocolate and directions to the spa, where the new guests have been told they can use the showers, but not the other facilities, much to their disappointment.

Finally, though, peace descends on the ballroom, punctuated only by the occasional rumble of now-distant thunder, and the rather more regular rumble of people's snores. The worst of the storm seems to have passed, but the rain is still doing what Izzie describes as 'pishing it doon', and, upstairs, every vacant room in the hotel is now filled; including my own, which I offered to Ian, Callum and Rowan, begging Zara to let me bunk in with her instead, so I don't have to worry about any more goings-on. As I settle into one side of the fourposter bed, though, all I can think about is Hunter, in his room just a few doors away.

Despite everything I found out tonight, I still can't bring myself to think of him as the bad guy the villagers seem convinced he is. The fact that he hid his identity from me is a whole other matter, of course, but I believe him when he says he's doing his best to save the hotel, under circumstances I can't even begin to imagine. And even though I wish he'd trusted me enough to tell me who he really was, I guess I can sort of understand why he didn't – especially once I got rolling with the 'arsehole nephew' comments.

I cringe, remembering the things Izzie and Ian told me that I mindlessly repeated to Hunter, not knowing *he* was the person I was talking about. The stupid jibes. The *cucumber video*.

I *really* wish he hadn't seen the cucumber video.

But he did. And he still decided to kiss me, even though my attempts at influencing could've cost him his business.

So I'm upset, sure, but I can't bring myself to hate him. And even if there's no future for the two of us, I still wish there was one for the hotel – and for the villagers, too.

But we don't always get to do the things we love most in life.

Isn't that what Hunter told me?

It is.

And, most of the time, I suppose it's true.

But what if this time it didn't have to be?

Chapter 31

By the time we wake up the next morning, after a night which is thankfully free of goings-on (unless we're counting Zara's surprisingly loud snoring), there's a message on all of our phones from Sabrina, summoning us to a breakfast meeting in the orangery, and confirming that, after the chaos of yesterday, today's theme is going to be back to business.

Literally, I mean.

'Today's theme is "Back to Business",' she's written. 'Last night's plans might have been disrupted, but we can't allow ourselves to be distracted from our mission to promote the Chrysalis. The competition has just one day left to run. Let's all have our best content ready to upload.'

'Today's *actual* theme is "how the hell is anyone getting out of here anytime soon?"' says Zara, pulling back the curtains to reveal a scene which is startlingly reminiscent of a post-apocalyptic movie. The tree blocking the gates isn't the only one to have been blown down in last night's storm: the long driveway is littered with leaves and branches, plus what looks like quite a few of Ian's baked potatoes. As Zara said, it's hard to see how anyone is going to get past the huge trunk that lies across the road, though, the sheer size of which I completely failed to appreciate while peering at it through the wind and rain. In the cold light of day, however, I can see that Hunter wasn't exaggerating when he said it would take him a while to clear it; and, until he does, the only way anyone's going to be leaving the castle is on foot.

I quickly pop back to my own room to put on some clean clothes, then make my way to the orangery, which is filled with lush greenery and tasteful wicker furniture, giving it an almost tropical feel, in stark contrast to the grey skies that are visible through the window.

The rest of the influencers are already there, along with Sabrina and Luna, who are hunched together over a laptop. Daniel is wearing a pair of sunglasses and wincing in pain every time a weak shaft of sunlight filters through the many windows. Bex is in a soft cream jumper which looks like cashmere, and which I'd be totally coveting if it wasn't for the large ketchup stain she hasn't quite managed to remove from it. It's positioned right over her heart and makes her look like she's been stabbed.

'I can't stay,' says Dante, bursting importantly into the room. 'I have a few dozen hungry guests to feed. *Non-paying* guests,' he adds, glancing pointedly at me. 'Then I need to figure out how we're going to clear that tree and get them all back to the village, *pronto*. So you're going to have to deal with this contest on your own, Sabrina. Oh, Hunter, there you are – good.'

He addresses the last words to Hunter himself, who pushes the door open, looking rumpled and bleary – although still unreasonably gorgeous – as if he hasn't slept at all. Everyone except me stops what they're doing to stare at him with open curiosity, all of them clearly struggling to recast him in their minds from handyman to heir. I do my best to focus on the sugar cubes I'm busy dropping into my cup of tea, but, after a minute or so, I can't resist a quick peek at him over the top of the steaming mug.

Hunter's standing by a potted palm, talking to Dante, who keeps waving his hands at the devastation, as if he can't quite believe it has the audacity to exist. He doesn't look up, or in my direction. It's as if I'm not even here at all.

Back to being invisible, I guess. Although the Laird certainly noticed me last night, didn't he? Which reminds me . . .

'Er, wait a minute, would you?' I call out as the two men finish their conversation and head for the door. I get up and follow them, really wishing I could speak to Dante in private, but knowing there's no way he's going to agree to that; not with how much he still has to do today.

'Dante, I, er, wanted to apologise,' I begin, my entire body cringing with awkwardness as I feel everyone's eyes on me. 'For what I said yesterday. I got everything wrong—' I allow myself a quick glance at Hunter here '— and I'm really sorry. I shouldn't have told everyone you were the Laird's nephew. I was just . . . well, I guess I was more freaked out by everything that's been going on than I realised. The ketchup attack felt like the last straw.'

As apologies go, it's not a great one, so I'm not surprised Dante looks uncomfortable rather than grateful for it.

'Um, about that—' he begins awkwardly, but, before he can go on, the orangery door opens and the Laird himself appears, Agnes hovering behind him with a tray of breakfast things.

'Ah, Hunter, there you are,' the Laird barks, waving his stick in the direction of his great-great-nephew once removed – or whatever Hunter's relationship to him is. 'Been looking for you everywhere. Damn place is overrun with people. I need you to send them back to wherever they came from.'

'You know where they came from, Dougie,' says Hunter patiently. 'You invited them to stay here yourself. Or so Dante's just been telling me.'

'Yes, yes,' says the old man impatiently, stopping next to the seat Daniel Foster is sitting in, and prodding him with his stick until Daniel takes the hint and reluctantly gets to his feet. 'I said they could stay overnight,' he goes on, taking the seat for himself. 'It's morning now, though. Time for them to go, I think. And this one too,' he adds, catching sight of me sitting opposite him, trying my best to sink into the cushions and out of sight. 'I don't know what she's still doing here. Didn't I tell you to remove her last night, Dante?'

'I was just about to say—' Dante begins, but Hunter cuts in.

'What's this?' he asks, his eyes narrowing. 'Why d'you want Rosie to leave, Dougie?'

He looks from the Laird to Dante, and then back again. The atmosphere is so tense that even Sabrina looks up from her laptop to see what's going on.

'So, it's a funny story, really,' Dante says, shuffling his feet on the tiled floor. 'Remember a few weeks ago, when you'd gone down to Inverness for supplies, Hunter? Well, the WanderNest rep called while you were gone. They said they'd be sending a mystery guest. It's like a mystery shopper, but, well, for hotels. Anyway, they wanted to send someone to review the place as part of the process of deciding whether they wanted to make an offer.'

He looks around at us all, as if to make sure we're following this.

'I don't get it,' says Millie, puzzled. 'How's that a funny story?'

'I assumed it would be one of the influencers who were booked in to stay,' goes on Dante, ignoring her. 'So I googled you all, and I saw that Rosie Summers had just got a contract with WanderNest. Well, it was obvious it was her, wasn't it? It was obvious she was the mystery guest. And I, um . . . I might have mentioned it to Lord Glenmuir.'

'There's no "might" about it,' the Laird says. 'You most definitely did mention it; while you were bringing me my elevenses, it was. I remember it well. The toast was slightly burnt, as I recall.'

'It was just a throwaway comment,' says Dante desperately. 'I didn't think he'd remember it.'

'There's nothing wrong with my memory,' says the Laird, sniffing. '"It's a girl called Rosie Summers," you said. "She's coming to review the hotel," you said. "And if she gives us a good review, the deal's as good as done," you said.'

Dante stares rigidly at the floor and doesn't bother to reply.

'But Rosie Summers didn't turn up,' I say, the pieces falling into place at last as I turn to face Lord Glenmuir. 'I came instead. And I guess you thought if you made my stay as difficult as possible, I'd report back to WanderNest that the hotel was awful, and they wouldn't buy it. That's it, isn't it? That was the plan. I guess you didn't realise I was . . . well, the wrong Rosie.'

'And a jolly good plan it was too,' says the Laird staunchly. 'Get rid of this Rosie person; save the hotel from the invading forces. Just like the war.'

'And you didn't think to mention any of this to me?' Hunter asks Dante, his expression fierce. 'You didn't think a mystery guest was something I might want to know about?'

Dante shuffles his feet miserably.

'I wanted to handle it myself,' he admits, raising his chin defiantly. 'My family's been running this castle for generations, Hunter. It means as much to me as it does to you. And I would've told you about the mystery guest, but, of course, Rosie Summers was replaced with Rosie *Winter*. And I knew Rosie *Winter* wasn't likely to be the mystery guest, so—'

'Why not?' I blurt out. 'I *could* be a mystery guest. Any one of us could be.'

'I couldn't,' says Millie, blonde hair flying as she shakes her head. 'I'm a terrible liar. And you probably couldn't either, Rosie; you only have about two thousand followers, don't you?'

Dante nods, confirming that this was, indeed, the reason he didn't suspect me of being this mystery guest. I actually have 4,912 followers now, having gained some more thanks to Luna's photos of me on the beach, but I don't bother mentioning it; there doesn't seem to be much point.

'But what about me?' wails Bex, who still looks like she's been involved in something unspeakable, thanks to the ketchup stain on her chest. 'What did *I* do to deserve my clothes being ruined?'

'Well, this one didn't seem to want to leave,' says the Laird, pointing a bony finger at me. 'So I started to think she might *not* be the spy after all. But it had to be one of you, so I decided to hedge my bets. We don't want hotel chains here in the Highlands. No, we can manage perfectly well on our own, I think. That was the original plan, and I'm damn sure we'll be sticking to it, no matter what Hunter here has to say about it.'

'Wait a minute,' Hunter puts in, his tone ominous. 'You're seriously telling me *you* did all of this, Dougie? The turnip? The missing clothes? The *sauna*?'

'Hang on. You said the sauna was an accident?' I inter-ject, my stomach lurching at the thought that it might not have been. Hunter meets my eyes for the first time since he walked into the room, and I'm annoyed with myself for the way his glance makes my skin tingle, even after everything that's happened.

'Oh, I didn't have anything to do with the sauna,' says the Laird with a shrug. 'That really was an accident. You want to get that looked at, Hunter,' he adds sternly, look-ing at his nephew from under his bushy eyebrows. 'Can't have people getting stuck in saunas. Could seriously hurt someone. Keep up, man, would you?'

'But . . . you did the rest?' replies Hunter incredulously. 'You? On your own? Just because you didn't want the WanderNest deal to go ahead, and you thought Rosie had some kind of influence over it?'

There's a loud crash as Agnes drops the tray she was hold-ing, sending pieces of crockery careering over the tile floor.

'I didn't want to do it,' she wails, putting her hands over her mouth. 'I swear I didn't. But we've all been so worried we might lose our jobs if the hotel gets sold.'

'You mean . . . you mean you're behind the . . . *goings-on* . . . Agnes?' I say, swallowing hard in an attempt to hide how hurt I am by this little revelation. 'You took my clothes? And stabbed my turnip?'

'I took the clothes,' the girl admits, her eyes downcast. 'But I brought them all back again,' she adds, looking up at me eagerly. 'The Laird wanted me to hide them until you left, but, well, you were so *nice*. I just couldn't do it. And I've been trying to make up for it ever since, by taking your photos for you, and stuff. I even brought you extra scones, I felt so guilty about it all, but I just . . . I need this job, or I'll never save up enough for my course.'

She looks at me pleadingly, but I can't quite meet her eye.

Not until I've had some time to process all of this, at least.

'I stabbed the turnip myself, though,' says the Laird proudly. 'And, by God, I'd do it again. So don't blame Agnes: she was just doing as I asked. And she didn't want these WanderNest people in the hotel, either. None of the staff do. Well, other than Dante, here, but no one listens to him, anyway.'

Dante hisses like a snake.

'I wish I'd brought my camera,' says Daniel Foster. 'This is all turning out to be quite entertaining.'

'I'm glad you're enjoying it,' I tell him sharply. 'I've been thinking someone was seriously out to get me.'

'Someone *was*, though,' says Millie. 'Him!' She points at the Laird, who waggles his eyebrows devilishly at her. 'So you were right, Rosie!'

She beams at me as if I should feel pleased about this, but the only emotion I can make sense of right now is anger. Burning, righteous anger, that starts at my toes and spreads all the way up to my head, where it joins forces with its friend, betrayal.

I *was* right. Someone *was* deliberately targeting me, and all because they thought I was someone else.

I can't even get people to *hate* me for myself. What does that say about me? I wonder.

'I think I'm going to go upstairs and pack,' I say, my legs a little wobbly as I stand up. 'I just want to go home now. It's pretty obvious I'm not going to win the competition, or influence anyone, so I'll leave you all to it.'

Hunter starts towards me, his arm outstretched, as if to stop me, but Zara gets there first.

'Hold on,' she says, grabbing me by the arm and making me spin around on the spot. 'If you're not the mystery guest, then who is?'

'I'd like to know that too, actually,' says Sabrina shrilly. 'Because if one of you has been lying to us, by failing to disclose that you're being paid to be here by someone else, then I can assure you, there will be serious consequences. I will sue. I'll—'

'No, you won't, Sabrina,' says Zara. 'Calm down. I just want to know who it is. Someone here's been lying to us, all this time.'

'Well, I'm sure you can see it's not me,' says Bex, sniffing down at her stained jumper. 'Or Daniel.'

'It's not me either,' adds Millie, eagerly.

'Or me,' puts in Yasmin, sounding slightly disappointed to have to admit this. To be fair, she would've made an *excellent* mystery guest.

'Well, it's definitely not me,' says Zara, folding her arms in a businesslike manner. 'So that just leaves—'

'It's me,' says Luna, her voice barely audible.

Everyone jumps. I think we'd all forgotten she was even in the room with us – I know I had. Luna shuffles forward, as if pushed by some invisible force, her eyes rather watery as she blinks around at us all.

'I'm really sorry,' she says in a squeak. 'But I think this is all my fault.'

Chapter 32

'You?' Sabrina says, looking at her assistant as if she can't quite remember who she is. 'What do you mean, it's *you*?'

'I'm the mystery guest,' replies Luna miserably. 'From WanderNest. They contacted me a few weeks ago and asked me if I'd be interested in a one-off job for them. I guess they must have somehow found out I'd be coming here anyway with you, so they figured it would be an easy way for them to get some feedback on the hotel. It, um, seemed like a good idea at the time?'

Now it's Sabrina's turn to explode, which she does in typical Sabrina fashion: by turning very pale and twitching slightly.

'So you've been working for someone else while you're supposed to be working for me?' she says, her face a mask of tightly controlled emotion. 'And you didn't think that might be just the *tiniest* conflict of interest?'

'Not . . . not *working* for them exactly,' replies Luna, blushing. 'They just asked me to take some notes while I'm here; and photos, of course. Then, once we leave, I'll have to fill out a questionnaire, I think. It hasn't interfered with my work for you, Sabrina. I promise.'

She widens her eyes appealingly, but it's no use; if Sabrina had a better nature that could be appealed to, I'm sure we'd have seen some sign of it by now.

'Right. Well, you're fired, obviously,' she says briskly, closing her laptop with a snap. 'And you can forget about getting a reference, too. This is intolerable behaviour. I've never felt so betrayed.'

It's hard to imagine Sabrina feeling anything at all, really, but, then again, it's not nice knowing someone you thought you could trust has been lying to you, or going behind your back – trust me, I would know – so I can't help but feel the tiniest twinge of empathy with her.

I'm starting to wonder if anyone in this hotel is who they say they are?

'*You*, of all people,' Sabrina goes on, sniffing. 'You knew how important this was to the business, Luna. How important it was to *me*. And you've gone and ruined it.'

If I didn't know better, I'd think she was about to cry again; and Luna almost definitely is.

'Hang on,' Zara interrupts. 'You can't just fire her like that. It depends what her contract says. You don't have a copy of it with you, Luna, do you? I'll take a look at it, if you like.'

'What are you, a lawyer?' says Sabrina, raising her eyebrows as high as she can, given the lack of movement in her face.

'Well, not yet,' Zara replies, shrugging. 'I will be once I've finished my training, though. I'm not going to be an influencer all my life, am I? I'm going to do something that's actually worthwhile.'

And now Zara turns out to have a secret of sorts, too.

Millie's eyes widen in admiration. 'Wow, that's amazing. Will you have to wear one of those little wigs, Zara? Could you get me one, d'you think?'

'I'm serious,' Zara insists, going to stand next to Luna, who looks at her the same way I've seen Stevie the dog looking at the treats Hunter keeps in his pocket for him. 'I can't promise anything, because it's . . . well, it's a bit of an unusual situation, really, but if you come and find me later, Luna, I'll go over the contract with you. You never know, you might still be able to keep your job.'

Luna takes a deep breath, as if she's trying to summon her courage.

'Actually,' she says, pushing her hair out of her eyes, 'I don't think I *want* to keep my job. I . . . I hate it. I've hated it since I started. I hate *you*, Sabrina,' she adds, her cheeks turning even redder as the words burst out of her, as if she's been saving them up for a long time and can't hold them in any longer. 'Well, I mean, I don't *hate* you. I just hate the way you treat me. You're a horrible, horrible boss, Sabrina. Just . . . the very worst. And your reaction just now proves that. So you don't have to fire me – I quit.'

Luna raises her chin defiantly as she finishes, but her cheeks are bright red, and she keeps blinking as if she's trying to hold back tears. I somehow get the feeling this is the first time she's ever stood up to anyone in her life, and I have a sudden urge to applaud her for it.

A log falls in the fireplace, making everyone jump. Sabrina's mouth opens and closes uselessly, like a toy that's lost its squeak. Then the Laird starts clapping loudly. One by one, we all join in; even Dante, who claps louder than anyone, even though he, of all people, should probably be on Sabrina's side on this one.

'Bravo,' the Laird says loudly, as the applause dies down. 'Well said, young spy. I'm going to have to ask you to leave, though, I'm afraid; I can't have any more of this undercover nonsense on the premises. It's not on. Hunter, kick this one out, would you? The other one can stay.'

Hunter doesn't move. Instead, Bex stands up, revealing another large ketchup stain on the seat of her cream-coloured jeans. It really is unfortunate for her that she's such a big fan of neutrals; if this had happened to Yasmin, say, whose entire wardrobe consists of black, no one would even notice the difference.

'Are we done with the Cluedo stuff?' Bex asks plaintively. 'Because I don't really care who's spying on who, or who wears a funny wig to work, or whatever else is going on here; I just want to get on with the contest so we can go home. That's why we're all here, isn't it? To win . . . I mean to work?'

Everyone looks at Sabrina, who appears to be wrestling with her emotions.

'OK,' she says at last, making a visible effort to regain her composure. 'The contest. Sure. Let's get back to business, shall we? That's the theme for the day, isn't it? Yes. The theme. For the day.'

She sits abruptly back down at the table and starts rifling through some papers that are lying there, apparently without really seeing them. From where I'm sitting, I can see her shoulders shaking under her impeccably tailored jacket.

'Here, let me,' says Dante, going over and plucking a piece of paper from her hands. 'Today's agenda involves a tour of the local attractions,' he reads. 'Well, that's definitely not going to be happening with the road still blocked. And then there's the launch party tonight, which will only be going ahead if we can get all of these bloody villagers out of the hotel first. So, if you'll excuse me, I'm going to get on with that, and if anyone wants to come and give me a hand, you're more than welcome.'

He turns on his heel and marches off, and, after a few seconds in which he tries to catch my eye and I determinedly ignore him, Hunter follows.

'Sabrina?' prompts Bex, as the door closes behind them. 'What do you want us to do now that the bus tour's off? It's just, I was really hoping to get some more photos before we leave tomorrow.'

Sabrina drums her fingernails on the laptop thoughtfully.

'You know what?' she says, looking up at us with suspiciously damp eyes. 'You can do what you like. I'm going back to bed.'

Then she picks up her laptop, slings her handbag over her shoulder, and goes marching off, to the accompaniment of surprised stares from everyone in the room (with the exception of the Laird, who appears to have fallen asleep).

'Does that mean we should all go back to bed, too?' says Millie, after a short pause. 'Like, do we have to?'

I look out of the window. The rain has stopped at last and, as I watch, a ray of sun appears from a gap in the clouds. Somehow, it reminds me of my plan.

'We should go out there and help clear the road,' I say, turning back to the rest of the group. 'And we should get the people who stayed last night to help, too. If we all work together, we can have that tree moved in no time.'

And hopefully get Hunter and the villagers talking in the process.

'Help?' says Millie, as if she's trying to speak a foreign language. 'But . . . what can *we* do to help? I don't think I'd be much use with an axe.'

'I think *I* would be,' puts in Yasmin, thoughtfully. 'Count me in, Rosie.'

'I was just thinking we could spend the morning in the spa, actually, if Sabrina isn't going to give us some direction here,' puts in Bex. 'There's nothing else to do, and I wasn't really happy with the photos you got the last time we were there, Daniel. I'd like to get some more before we leave.'

'Bex,' I say patiently. 'We can't spend the day in a spa while everyone downstairs is stranded here. We have to help them try to get home.'

Bex looks like she's about to argue with this, but a glance from Daniel silences her.

'Rosie's right,' says Zara, coming to join me at the window. 'And the fact is, none of us will be leaving here tomorrow if we don't get the road cleared. You don't want to end up stuck here for days, do you, Bex?'

'No.' Yasmin nods. 'We don't want that. Because if the hotel runs out of food, we'd have to eat each other. They must be running low already, after last night.'

She takes a long look around the room, as if she's trying to decide which one of us would be the tastiest, and that's all it takes to spur Millie and Bex into action. Daniel follows them out of the room, still looking a little green around the gills, and I pause in the doorway to quickly check my Instagram account, where @cosmicsprinkles1995 has commented on my last selfie to ask what's wrong with my face, and Jim from Canterbury has sent me a photo of his flaccid penis, which reminds me of one of the chipolata sausages my sister served last Christmas.

One thing's for sure: my stay at the Chrysalis might not have changed my life, but it has, at least, proved beyond doubt that I'm not cut out to be an influencer.

And, honestly? I don't think I *want* to be one anymore.

I don't want to have to spend the entire day snapping endless photos of myself in a selection of unrealistic outfits that I can't really afford, and don't even like. I don't want to spend my evenings editing content when I could be out dancing with friends. I don't want to have to eat all of my meals cold because I have to spend so much time photographing them first. And I *definitely* don't want to have to spend my life pretending to be something I'm not – which, as far as I can see, is all anyone's doing in this place.

Actually, I think I want to go and chop up a tree.

Chapter 33

After a quick stop at the reception desk to speak to Dante (who's surprisingly amenable now that his role in Turnip-gate has been exposed) I head outside, where a large group of villagers have gathered on the hotel driveway, Izzie and Ian among them.

'Mornin', Rosie,' says Ian, as I come walking towards them, enjoying the feeling of the sun on my skin after all the rain we had yesterday. 'Looks like more bad weather's on the way; we're going to have to try to get ourselves out of here soon if we're going to make it back home today.'

Izzie nods, squinting as she peers up at the sky. I follow suit, seeing a few dark clouds, but nothing that suggests another storm.

'Aye, there's more rain coming,' Izzie says. 'Ach, look out,' she adds, looking beyond me to the hotel entrance. ' And a bawbag coming too, by the looks of things.'

A few seconds later, Hunter joins us, Stevie at his heels as usual. I straighten my shoulders almost subconsciously, steeling myself for our first real interaction since all of last night's – and this morning's – revelations.

'Bad news, I'm afraid,' Hunter says without preamble. 'I've just had a message from the power company, and the power to the village is still out. It seems they've managed to find the problem, but we're not the only ones who sustained some damage in the storm last night, so they're having trouble getting to the part that needs to be repaired.'

There's a rumble of discontent from the crowd around us.

'Well, if it's a problem they were looking for, I could've helped them with that,' retorts Izzie sharply. 'There's one standing right in front of me.'

'Now, that's not fair, Izzie,' Ian says in a soothing tone. 'It's not this lad's fault the power went out. We can't blame him for that.'

'No, but we *can* blame him for everything else that's gone wrong around here,' replies Izzie tersely. 'I knew he was up to no good as soon as I saw that Black Shuck o' his. You're a Good Boy, though,' she adds, ruffling Stevie's ears. 'It's not your fault you're a harbinger of doom.'

'If we could get back to the issue at hand,' says Hunter, who's clearly aiming for a neutral tone, although his expression tells a different story. 'As I said, the power's still out, and there's no telling when it'll be back on. In the meantime, you're all stuck here until this tree's out of the way. I'm going to make a start on trying to clear it now, but it might take me a while; the chainsaw's broken, so I'm going to have to make do with an axe.'

'I'll help,' says Ian promptly, just as I thought he would. 'Then, as soon as it's cleared, we'll be on our way.'

'I'll help, too,' says a man standing next to Ian.

'And me,' says someone else.

A few more of the villagers volunteer their services, and Hunter gives a sharp nod.

'Fine by me,' he says. 'I'll go and get some tools, and we'll make a start on it.'

Seeing the opportunity I've been waiting for, I clear my throat importantly.

'The thing is,' I say brightly, 'even if you can get past the tree, there's no point in heading back if the power's still out, is there?'

'Oh, there is,' says Izzie immediately. 'We'll no' stay where we're not wanted.'

'But . . . but it'll be dangerous,' I protest, seeing my grand plan start to fall apart before I've even got started on it. 'This won't be the only tree that came down in the storm last night, will it? What if there's more of them on the road to the village?'

There's a short silence from the crowd.

'Well, we'll cut them down, too.' Ian shrugs, not looking particularly thrilled at the prospect.

'Rosie's right,' says Hunter reluctantly. 'There are power lines down all over the place, apparently. The road might be dangerous.'

'Maybe to you, city boy,' says Izzie. 'But me and Ian grew up on these roads, and so did everyone else here. Well, other than the ones who moved here, obviously, but they're still one o' us. Unlike some I could mention.'

She fixes Hunter with the kind of glare that leaves us in no doubt who she means.

'She's talking about you,' Ian tells him, helpfully.

Hunter sighs.

'Why don't you all stay another night?' I put in, trying to make it sound as if the idea's just occurred to me. 'There's no point in going back until the power's back on, is there? And there's plenty of room here; isn't there, Hunter?'

'Now, hold on,' Hunter begins, but Ian gets in first.

'No, we'll be leaving as soon as the road's cleared,' he says staunchly. 'We've trespassed on his lairdship's hospitality for long enough, so we'll be heading home, power or none. If the castle's to be sold to this WanderNest chain,

I suppose us villagers will have to get used to fending for ourselves, anyway, without the support of the Laird.'

'Oh, for goodness' sake,' says Hunter. 'You're talking like it's the Middle Ages and Dougie's some kind of feudal overlord. He's just an old guy with a house that's far too big and expensive for him to run. And I'm just the mug who got saddled with a problem he didn't ask for, and who's doing his best to solve it, in impossible circumstances. You could try cutting me some slack here. I'm not some toff who was born into this, you know. I'm not a *laird*.'

'That's as may be,' says Izzie, pulling her cloak a little tighter around her tall frame. 'But it doesn't change the fact that the village has suffered since you've been here, and it'll suffer even more if this sale you're so keen on goes ahead. Bawbag,' she adds, obviously judging the rest of her short speech to have been too polite.

They glare at each other, like two gunslingers in a spaghetti western, and I experience an almost irresistible urge to grab them and bang all of their heads together.

'Look,' I say instead. 'You're all being completely ridiculous.'

I look around, wondering what I can do to convince them to stay. Hunter's Land Rover is parked a few metres away from me, its roof covered in a light scattering of leaves that have been blown from the surrounding trees. Before anyone can stop me, I run over to it and scramble up onto the bonnet.

'Listen up, everyone,' I yell, my voice shaking. 'Um, I mean, if you could all just give me a second?'

'Rosie, what are you doing?' Hunter says, starting towards me, his expression almost comically surprised.

I hold up a hand to stop him, surprised by my own daring.

'Um, right. OK,' I say, looking down at the sea of surprised faces in front of me. People jostle forward, so they can hear better, and I notice a few of them holding up their phones and filming me, presumably hoping for a viral TikTok moment later.

Well, good luck with that; the only time I go viral is when I do something wrong – and this time I'm absolutely certain I'm in the right.

'I know you were all angry when you heard about the Hunter's plans to go into partnership with WanderNest,' I say, my legs now as wobbly as my voice is. 'But, the thing is—'

'To sell it, you mean,' shouts a woman in a jumper with a picture of a cat on the front. 'Partnership my arse!'

'It *is* a partnership,' I reply firmly. 'The hotel wouldn't be sold *if* the deal goes ahead. But it might not. And until we know for sure what's going to happen, I think you should all stop being so mean to Hunter and . . . and throwing *tatties* at him. It's . . . *absurd*.'

'You're absurd,' comes a voice from the crowd, mimicking my English accent.

'Hey! That's enough,' Hunter yells back, glaring at whoever it was. He looks like he's about to say something else, but another voice cuts in first.

'Can we throw tatties at him if this partnership *does* go ahead, then?' shouts a man with long hair and an equally long beard. 'Because we all know he only cares about himself and his money. He doesn't care about us.'

There's a murmur of agreement from the crowd.

'That's not fair,' I shout over the top of it. 'I suppose you lot know *exactly* how you'd run a castle this size, if you were in his shoes, do you? I suppose you've all got tons of ideas on how to pay the bills with . . . with tatties and leeks?'

Silence.

'We'd do a better job than yer man from Glasgow, anyway,' mutters the woman in the cat sweater. 'That's for sure.'

There's no conviction in her tone, though, and no one tries to speak up in support of her.

'Edinburgh,' Hunter mutters in a voice no one hears. 'I'm from *Edinburgh*.'

'Look,' I go on, wishing I hadn't started this, but feeling like I have to see it through now that I have. 'I get that you want the hotel to do more to support the village, but surely you can see this isn't the way to do it?'

More silence; although this time there's also a shuffling of feet that suggests the crowd isn't *quite* as sure of themselves as they were before.

'Would you please get down from there, Rosie?' Hunter says, stepping forward and holding out his hand. 'You're making me nervous.'

'I'm not getting down until everyone here's agreed to stay and talk this through like adults,' I say stubbornly. 'We're stuck until this tree's cleared. The power's still out, and there's no guarantee when it'll be back. The road's impassable. Even if you make it back to the village safely, you'll have no electricity to go back to. But we have plenty of food here, and I'm sure Hunter would be more than happy to let you stay another night if you have to – which should give you all more than enough time to listen to his point of view, and figure out some way to help him, rather than just attacking him all the time.'

Below me, Hunter's brow creases in alarm.

'I wouldn't be more than happ— I mean, sure, yeah, you're . . . welcome to stay until the power's back on,' he mumbles, catching the glare I send in his direction. 'If you want to.'

'You heard the man,' I say, straightening my shoulders like an army general. 'You're all welcome to stay, and I, for once, think you should. Now, who's with me?'

Chapter 34

Most of the villagers, it turns out, are *with me*.

Izzie, Ian and a few others, however, are still hell-bent on heading back to the village as soon as the tree can be removed; which, they say, they're going to make happen, even if they have to haul it out of the road themselves with their bare hands.

'Come on,' says Hunter, reaching up and putting his arms around my waist. 'Let's get you down from there.'

He lifts me down from the Land Rover as easily as he lifted me onto the pony a few days ago, and I try not to think about how good it feels being close to him as I slide down his chest until my feet are back on the ground.

'So, that was quite some speech,' he says as my eyes draw level with his. 'What on earth were you thinking, Rosie?'

I shrug, not entirely sure of this myself.

'I thought I was trying to help,' I say. 'I thought if I could just make sure they knew how hard it's been for you, and that you're not this horrible, penny-pinching city boy they seem to think you are then maybe they'd understand. That's . . . that's what friends are for, isn't it?'

Hunter's eyes crinkle with amusement.

'I *am* technically a city boy,' he says. 'I'm only a country one in my heart.'

'That's the only place it counts,' I say stubbornly, very aware of the fact that his arms are still around my waist, and that he's making no move to step away.

'Ach, Rosie, I wish that was true,' he says sadly. 'I wish wanting something was enough to make it happen. You have no idea how much I wish that.'

He looks deep into my eyes, and I'm not totally sure if he's talking about the city versus the country . . . or something else.

'You *could* make it happen, though,' I point out, breathlessly. 'You could be whatever you want to be.'

Our faces are almost touching. Not far away, Izzie and Ian are arguing over whether or not it might be possible to cut up the tree with one of the bread knives they brought with them, and two of the other men who stayed behind have started a 'sword' fight with two of the fallen branches. But, to me, there's only the two of us: me and Hunter and the utterly undeniable spark between us that's making it almost impossible for me to pull myself away from his arms, even though I know I have to.

'And so could you, Rosie,' Hunter replies, his voice soft. 'Have you not worked that out yet?'

He leans towards me, and I jump back as if I've been burned, remembering at the last second that he might be the most beautiful man I've ever met, but there's no hope of a future between us; even if he hadn't neglected to tell me who he really was. Which means kissing Hunter Stuart – again – will only lead to heartbreak.

And I'm going home tomorrow, anyway. So, walk away, Rosie Winter, before you get hurt.

'Um, I wanted to check in with you, anyway,' he says, flinching slightly at the speed with which I move away from him. 'To see how you are after all that stuff about Dougie and Agnes? It must've been a shock.'

'It was,' I reply, remembering the guilt on Agnes's face when she apologised to me. 'I still can't believe they did all of that. I'm OK, though,' I add, seeing his eyes cloud with worry. 'I actually feel a lot better now that I know who was doing it, and why. And now they know I'm not spying for WanderNest, I guess I'll be able to have my first decent night's sleep since I got here.'

It's just a shame it'll also be the last.

'I'll be having a word with them both,' Hunter says quietly. 'It's horrible, what they did to you, Rosie. Dougie in particular. And as for Agnes . . .'

'Please don't sack her,' I say quickly. 'I know she shouldn't have moved the clothes, but she *was* only doing what the Laird told her to do, Hunter. She's probably terrified of him. I know I would be. And she really needs this job.'

I look up at him pleadingly, and an expression I can't quite read briefly crosses his face.

'I won't sack her,' he says at last. 'I will be having strong words with her, though, Rosie. I can't have staff members messing with the guests' stuff like that. Not if this hotel's going to be a success.'

'Is that still what you're aiming for, then?' I ask, my heart filling with hope. 'To make it a success? Or are you still considering the WanderNest offer?'

Hunter looks at me, as if he's considering how to answer this.

'I'm considering everything,' he says, his eyes on mine. 'All options are still on the table as far as I'm concerned.'

I nod slowly, wondering if I'm one of the options he's talking about; although I don't see how I possibly can be.

'Um, anyway,' I say, trying to speak as if this is a perfectly normal conversation we've been having, and my heart isn't hammering wildly in my chest just from being close to him. 'If the rest of the villagers are determined to leave today, we're going to need a plan. Here's what I think we should do . . .'

* * *

I send Hunter off to the tool shed to rustle up everything he can find that could be used to cut up a tree, and Ian to the hotel to muster some more volunteers.

For a split second, I think they're going to refuse to cooperate, but then I point out that if they don't at least *try* to work together, no one's going to be going anywhere, at which point they both do as I've asked.

'Come on, Izzie,' I say, taking her by the arm and steering her back towards the hotel. 'We're going to need some more of that amazing turnip soup of yours, to keep everyone's strength up.'

'It was leek and tattie soup,' she protests. 'And I don't think we've any leeks left. Plenty o' tatties, though, so I suppose I could sort something out for you, Rosie.'

'Great,' I reply, privately relieved that I'm not going to be confronted with any more turnips. 'See if you can round up some helpers; there are a lot of people to feed.'

Izzie nods her agreement, her eyes lighting up as she catches sight of Yasmin, coming wandering towards us.

'You'll do,' she says, taking the surprised influencer by the arm, and frogmarching her towards the kitchen. I follow them down to the long, whitewashed room in the castle basement, where I push open the door to the pantry, looking for some other snacks I can take to the workers outside.

'Oh, my God!'

I let out a shrill squeal as my foot makes contact with something soft and squishy.

'Rosie? Is that you?'

The voice from the floor is a familiar one, and I force myself to look down, gasping in surprise when I spot Sabrina crouched in a corner, her legs folded neatly underneath her as she tucks into a large chocolate cake, which is smeared around her lips in a way that reminds me of my niece at her first birthday party.

'Um, Sabrina?'

It's obviously her, but the sight in front of me is so *unlike* her that I feel I have to check.

'Close that door behind you, would you?' she orders, sounding more like her usual self. 'I don't want Dante to find me in here.'

'Er, sure.'

I push the door shut, then turn back to her.

'Are you OK, Sabrina?' I ask cautiously. 'It's just, I've never seen you . . .' I'm about to say 'eat', but change my mind at the last minute. 'I've never seen you *like this* before,' I say instead.

'Oh, Rosie,' she sighs, sticking the fork she's holding into the cake. 'Of course you haven't. I've been on a diet since I was in my early twenties. That's when I started the business. That's how long I've been trying to make a success of my life; to stay in control of it all. And now I don't know why I even bothered, because I'm going to lose everything I've worked for anyway. So now I just think I might as well have eaten the bloody cake when I had the chance. You know? Always eat the cake,' she adds, offering me the fork. 'Don't be me, whatever you do.'

'If this is about Luna, and what she said earlier,' I say carefully, crouching down until we're at eye level, and pushing away the fork she's holding out to me, 'you could just, you know, apologise to her, instead of . . . well, this.'

I gesture towards the cake, and Sabrina stares down at it miserably.

'She said she hates me,' she says, her voice wobbly. 'I think everyone hates me, Rosie. I probably deserve it, to be honest. But this business has been my entire life, and it's just so hard to watch it fail that I suppose it was easier to blame Luna than blame myself. And now I've lost Luna too, which is awful, because she was a really good assistant. And she was my best friend.'

She sniffs loudly, and I reach over and awkwardly pat her on the arm, feeling a bit like I'm petting a lion who might turn on me at any second.

'Luna doesn't hate you,' I remind her. 'She took that bit back, remember? She said it was the way you'd been treating her she hated, not you personally. I think maybe if you just tried talking to her? Maybe you could figure something out together?'

I let the suggestion hang in the air for Sabrina to consider. She sniffs again, but doesn't try to argue, which I take as a good sign.

'Just have a think about it,' I suggest. 'Luna's still here. Only because the driveway's blocked so she can't leave yet, obviously, but still . . . you have time to fix this, Sabrina – the thing with Luna *and* the campaign. You can do this.'

I straighten up again, uncomfortable with my new role as motivational speaker and life coach.

'That's just it, though,' says Sabrina quietly. 'I don't think I *can* do it.'

She reaches for the cake again, and I pull it quickly out of reach.

'Of course you can,' I say firmly. 'You're Sabrina Bates. You're . . .'

I'm about to say 'terrifying', but stop myself just in time. 'You're really good at what you do,' I say instead. 'Anyone can see that. You're just having a bit of a wobble, that's all. You'll be back to your usual, confident self in no time.'

'But I'm not confident at all, Rosie,' she replies. 'I just pretend. And now I'm about to be caught out, because I planned this big, elaborate party for the hotel launch tonight – you know, the one I was telling you all about, with the countdown to midnight?'

I nod, vaguely recalling something about a countdown.

'I invited all these people,' she goes on. 'Mostly from the hotel industry, but some local celebrities, too. Important people, you know? And I'd booked this great band – well, Luna had. They were supposed to be the best ceilidh band in the Highlands, she said. But I've just had a message saying all flights into Inverness have been cancelled because of the storm. The rail lines are down, too, apparently. So now none of them can make it, and everything's ruined.'

Her voice breaks on the last syllable, and I risk another quick pat on the arm as I consider the fact that, for all her bravado, Sabrina's turned out to be yet another one who's faking it until they make it. In Sabrina's case, though, she actually *has* made it; she just needs a bit of help remembering that. And I think I know someone who can help with that.

'Um, I think you might have to forget about the band and the celebrities,' I tell her, not wanting to add to her distress by telling her about the tree currently blocking the hotel driveway, on top of everything else. 'I'm not sure it matters, though. No one cares about celebrities, and all of those other people you mentioned, though, Sabrina. They're not the "important people" you think they are. So I think you should go ahead with the party. It's just the guest list you might need to think about changing.'

Sabrina listens carefully as I outline my plan to her, and, a few minutes later, I leave the pantry with a fresh list of party-planning tasks on top of my existing villager-mediation duties, and the spark of an idea making my heart beat a little faster.

I might not be leaving the Highlands as the best version of myself, like I was promised, and I might not ever see any of these people again after tonight, but I can at least make sure we all go out with a bang. And if I can help mend some bridges between Hunter and the villagers in the process – and make up for whatever damage I might have caused with my stupid video – then so much the better.

I just might need a little bit of help is all . . .

Chapter 35

I find Luna in her room, packing her suitcase, and not looking remotely like the daring, undercover spy Lord Glenmuir accused her of being just a few hours ago.

Still, she *is* technically the reason he's spent the last few days attempting to terrify me, and I'm hoping she feels just guilty enough about that to help me out with tonight's launch party.

'But, I don't understand,' Luna says, a few minutes later, once I've finished explaining my plan. 'I don't work for Sabrina any more. She fired me. I quit. Well, she fired me *and* I quit, I suppose. I was just about to try and walk to the village to see if any of the trains are running, so I can get out of everyone's hair.'

'Oh, they're not running today,' I say, remembering what Sabrina told me. 'The trains are all cancelled because of the storm. And you won't be able to get to the village, anyway: the road's blocked by the fallen tree.'

'But there are people out there clearing it now,' Luna protests, glancing out of the window. 'I can see them.'

I quickly flick the curtain shut.

'I know,' I say sympathetically. 'But they're all mad as brushes, Luna. You've seen them. They're determined to get home at all costs, but you can't seriously try to follow them.'

'Maybe,' Luna says doubtfully. 'But I can't stay here, Rosie. Sabrina must hate me for all those things I said to her. And I don't expect Dante and Hunter will be particularly impressed either, now they know I'm . . .' her voice drops to a whisper '. . . a *traitor*.'

'Oh, Dante and Hunter will be fine about that,' I lie. 'And Sabrina doesn't hate you at all. She said you're her best friend, in fact.'

This part, at least, is true. But it sounds so unbelievable that for a moment I think Luna's eyes might pop out of her head.

'Her *what*?' she says, astonished. 'Her *best friend*? She called me Linda for the first six weeks of my contract. I'd be amazed if she even knows what my surname is.'

'I, er, don't think she has a lot of friends, somehow,' I say quietly. 'And I think she's genuinely upset to have lost you as an assista— friend.'

'An *assistafriend*?' Luna frowns, clearly unconvinced.

'Luna, she was eating chocolate cake,' I tell her. 'Without even cutting it into slices, first.'

'Whoa.' Luna puts down the jumper she's holding, and sits down on the edge of the bed. 'Chocolate cake? Really.'

'Really.'

I take a seat beside her.

'Look, there's no excuse for the way she's been treating you,' I say truthfully. 'We've all seen her, and you're absolutely right; she's a terrible boss. But I think she's genuinely sorry. So . . . maybe if you just gave her a chance to apologise?'

A ghost of a smile flits briefly across her face, igniting a tiny spark of hope in my chest.

'I *was* a really good assistafriend,' she says, picking at a thread on her jeans. 'Sabrina was lucky to have me, really.'

'She was. Maybe you should just talk to her?' I suggest. 'I'm sure Zara would help you draw up a new contract. If Sabrina apologises, that is.'

Luna nods, almost imperceptibly.

'The thing is,' she says shyly, 'I do like the job. I want more responsibility, though. I want to have my own projects and teams, and not just spend all my time making Sabrina's coffee and buying her verruca cream. I think I'd be good at it.'

'I'm sure you would,' I reply, hoping she doesn't have to apply the verruca cream as well as buying it, although nothing would surprise me. 'But you won't know unless you try, will you?'

This is *almost* what I said to Hunter last night, but luckily Luna's a bit more receptive to my pep talk.

'You're right,' she says, getting up. She walks over to the window and flicks the curtain open again. 'About that, *and* about me not being able to leave today, with the weather like this; it still looks pretty wild out there, doesn't it? So maybe I will have time to help you plan this party, Rosie. If Sabrina doesn't insist that I leave anyway, that is.'

'I don't think she will, somehow,' I reply. 'Why don't you go and find Zara? She'll know how to deal with Sabrina.'

I leave Luna to unpack her suitcase again and head back downstairs, where I find Hunter in the lobby.

Time to put the next part of my plan into action.

'Bad news,' I tell him, trying to sound as normal as I can, even though just being close to him makes my heart flutter dangerously in my chest. 'The power company are saying they definitely don't think they're going to be able to repair the fault tonight after all. The weather's really hampering their progress, apparently.'

'Really?' says Hunter with a frown. 'It looks like it's clearing up to me. Who told you this?'

'Luna,' I say, crossing my fingers behind my back. Well, she *did* say it looked wild out there, didn't she? Which is *kind of* the same thing. 'She must have called them.'

'Maybe I should speak to them myself?' says Hunter doubtfully. 'It seems strange that it'd take them so long to repair the fault, even with all the damage the storm caused. I'll try calling the person who messaged me earlier.'

He pulls his phone out of his pocket and I leap forward and snatch it out of his hands, knowing perfectly well that if he tries to make that call, it's my phone that'll start ringing – because I'm the person who messaged him this morning pretending to be someone from the power company, responding to his earlier enquiry.

'Er, no, don't do that,' I say quickly, as he blinks at me in confusion. 'I'll call them for you. From my own phone,' I add, passing his back as quickly as if it's one of Ian's hot potatoes from last night. 'You've got enough on your plate right now with the tree. And, well, the angry mob.'

'Yeah. I don't think they're going to welcome the news that the power's staying off,' replies Hunter, still looking vaguely bewildered by my erratic, phone-grabbing behaviour. 'Well, if you're sure you don't mind double-checking with the power company, I guess I'll go and speak to the mob. Might as well get it over with, I suppose.'

'Oh, I'll do that too,' I offer quickly, spotting an opportunity to do some more of that bridge-building. 'They'll take it better coming from me.'

This isn't, as it turns out, strictly true. When I squelch my way down the rain-soaked driveway to where the giant tree trunk lies straddling the road, Ian snorts in disgust at the news, Callum lets out a strange, wolf-like howling noise and the men they're with all immediately start bickering over whose fault it is, while making plans to boycott the power company.

'Well, we'll just have to make the best of it,' says Ian, once the shouting has died down. 'As soon as this road's cleared we'll be heading home, as planned.'

'But that's just silly, Ian,' I point out. 'Especially when Hunter's offered to let you all stay here in the hotel. Where there's electricity. And food. And a swimming pool and hot tub at your disposal.'

The men standing next to Ian visibly brighten.

'The lass has a point,' says one of them.

'I was never in favour of trying to make it back in this weather, anyway,' says another. 'I was just going along with it because everyone else was.'

'Can we really use the spa?' asks Callum eagerly. 'What about the treatments? I could really use a deep tissue massage.'

'We all could,' says the first man, who doesn't look like he's been near a massage table in his life.

'Well, you're in the right place,' I reply brightly. 'I've sampled the spa treatments myself, and I can tell you, you're in for a treat. A free one, too.'

'No, we're not,' says Ian in a decisive manner. 'We're going home. All of us.'

'Who put you in charge, Ian McBride?' says the man who wants a massage. 'We don't all have to do what you say, you know.'

'Um, did I mention there's stovies?' I say quickly, before things can get out of hand. 'Izzie's got the hotel staff making them. I'd hurry if I were you, or there'll be none left.'

The two men immediately throw down their tools and head for the hotel, passing Hunter on the way. He watches them go, then comes over to join us, his expression guarded.

'What's going on?' he asks, looking from me to Ian, then back again.

'Some of the villagers have decided to stay after all,' I tell him, choosing not to mention the bit where I offered them free spa treatments as a bribe. 'Now that they know the power's not going to be back on for a while.'

'Right.' Hunter looks less than thrilled by this.

'Some of them have small children, or elderly parents,' I add, when he doesn't say anything else. 'So we obviously don't want them going home without power.'

'Well, no. Obviously not. And you?' He directs his question at Ian, who pretends to have found something very interesting to stare at on the ground.

'My family and me will be leaving as planned,' Ian says stubbornly. 'Even if me and Callum are the only men left to clear the tree.'

'Speak for yourself,' says Callum. 'I'm going for a massage. My back's killing me after all that chopping.'

'Massage?' says Hunter, as Callum follows in the footsteps of the other men, towards the hotel. 'Who does he think's giving him a massage?'

'Millie,' I reply, improvising. 'I think she likes him,' I add in a voice I hope is low enough for Ian not to hear. Ian, however, is too busy glowering at Hunter to listen to anything I have to say.

'So,' he says gruffly, the axe he's still holding making him look a lot like Jack Nicholson in *The Shining* – a comparison that doesn't exactly set my mind at ease. 'It's just you and me, then. That's if you're still willing to help me get my family out of here, Yer Lordship?'

'I will if you stop calling me that,' says Hunter, squaring his jaw. 'It's Hunter, thanks. And I have to clear the road whether you're planning to use it or not, so if you helping gets it done faster, then you'll get no objection from me.'

'Right then, Laird Hunter,' Ian replies, with a smirk.

'Um, how about we make things a bit more interesting?' I suggest, seeing my plan start to fall apart before my eyes. 'Why don't you have a competition?'

'A competition? What do you mean?'

It's Hunter who asks the question, but both men look equally confused.

'Er, yes – a chopping competition,' I say, making something up on the spot. 'First person to chop all the way through the tree trunk is the winner? What d'you say?'

'I say, what's the prize?' Ian says, his voice loaded with suspicion. 'What am I supposed to be winning?'

I think quickly.

'If you win, Ian, Hunter will sit down with you and discuss how the hotel could work more closely with the village,' I say. 'Buying your produce again, that kind of thing.'

'And if *I* win?' asks Hunter, his mouth a thin line of displeasure that makes me doubt for a minute whether I should really be pressing ahead with this hastily concocted idea.

'If you win, the villagers have to accept whatever decision you make about the hotel,' I tell him. 'And stop calling you a bawbag.'

'I feel like they have a lot more to gain here than I do, somehow,' Hunter says wryly, reaching up to push his hair out of his eyes in a way that makes my heart give a traitorous little flutter.

'Do you want to make it up to me for not telling me who you were or not?' I reply, hoping the answer to this will be yes – and not just for the sake of the 'competition'.

Hunter's throat bobs as he swallows. 'Fine,' he says gruffly. 'Let's get it over with, then.'

Ian uses the blade of his weapon – I mean axe – to cut a small line in the middle of the tree trunk.

'You take that side o' the line,' he says, pointing. 'And I'll take this. Rosie, if you wouldn't mind timing us?'

I pull my phone out of my pocket, open up the timer and hold my finger above the start button.

'OK, on three,' I say. 'One . . . two . . . three . . . GO.'

Without another word, Ian and Hunter start chopping as if their lives depend on it, and I take the opportunity to slip away.

My work here is done – for now, at least.

But there's still more to do.

Chapter 36

Two hours later, the sun bursts through the drizzle that's been falling on and off, creating another one of those shimmering rainbows that seem so common in this part of the world. As the influencers all rush to photograph it, a single ray lands on Hunter's head, making him look briefly like he has a halo as he and Ian toil away at the end of the drive, two solitary figures who don't stop chopping, even though the rainbow is, as Millie says, 'fire'.

Beside them, Hannah and Rowan stand huddled under a bright red umbrella, cheering both men on simultaneously, apparently not caring which one wins. Right now, Hunter's slightly in the lead, but Ian's not far behind him, and one of the men from the village has started taking bets on who's going to finish first, while a handful of others stand drinking beer and adding their expert commentary.

If it wasn't for the fact that we're all trapped in a castle by a tree, it would feel almost like a party.

Which is, of course, exactly what I was hoping.

'OK,' says Luna, joining me on the front steps of the hotel, where a small group of us have gathered to watch the two men hack away at the tree. 'So, the bad news is that the band I'd booked definitely aren't going to make it. The storm caused absolute chaos on the railway network, apparently.'

I nod in resignation. I'd expected this, but it's disappointing, nevertheless.

'The good news, though,' she goes on, with a grin, 'is that I've managed to find three guitarists among the villagers, one pianist and a woman who says she once sang backup vocals for the Bay City Rollers.'

I smile back at her, delighted.

'There are no drums, unfortunately,' she adds. 'But there's a ton of booze in the cellar, so hopefully no one will notice.'

'Great,' I reply. 'And the rest?'

'Tables have all been taken into the ballroom,' Luna replies, taking a list out of her pocket and consulting it. 'The kitchen has enough food to feed an army. And Dante's in the attic.'

'The attic?' I raise my eyebrows, convinced I must have misheard her.

'Yeah. I had to get him out of the way so he didn't try to stop us, so I told him Sabrina was lost up there. He's gone to find her. She's actually in her room, putting together a presentation for the end of the contest, though, so he'll be looking for a while.'

'Good work, Luna,' I say admiringly, trying not to think about the competition, and how badly I've performed in it; not that it matters now. 'And did you manage to speak to her about your job?'

'I did,' Luna replies, her face glowing. 'I took Zara with me, and she talked Sabrina into renewing my contract. And she's going to give me more responsibility from now on, too.'

'Wow! That's amazing.'

'It's strange, though.' Luna wrinkles her nose. 'It was almost like she was expecting me to ask; she didn't even put up a fight. Then she said she acknowledged that she hadn't been the boss I deserve, and that she'd aim to do better from here on out. So she didn't actually say the word "sorry", but . . . I think that's what she meant?'

'Well, we can't expect miracles,' I reply. 'As long as her behaviour changes now she knows how it's been affecting you, I guess that's the main thing.'

'Absolutely,' Luna replies, nodding vigorously. 'Anyway, I better get on; there's still loads to do.'

I glance at my watch. It's just past four o'clock, which gives us a few hours before the launch party's scheduled to start; with just a *few* more guests than Sabrina had originally planned to be in attendance.

I twist my hands nervously together, hoping we're going to be able to pull this off. It's not like I've ever tried to organise a party in a castle, after all, let alone one for a couple of hundred people.

'Look,' says Millie from behind me. 'I think they're almost there!'

Sure enough, Hunter and Ian have both almost chopped their way through their respective sections of the tree trunk; it's hard to see who's in the lead from here, but it doesn't really matter, because, as we stand there watching them, they both suddenly stop what they're doing, and put down their axes.

'What's going on?' says Yasmin, who's standing next to Millie. Both of them are wearing chef hats, having been roped into helping Izzie in the kitchen, and both of them look ridiculously cute in them. 'What are they doing?'

I squint in the direction of the fallen tree, wishing for the twentieth time that I had my contact lenses with me. Hunter and Ian are still standing in front of the tree, talking. From what I can see, it doesn't *look* like a particularly heated conversation, but you never know with those two, and a familiar bubble of anxiety starts to work its way up my chest.

As I watch, though, Hunter raises his arm and holds a hand out towards Ian; after the briefest of seconds, Ian takes it and shakes it firmly, while Hannah and Rowan dance around them, cheering loudly. Then all four of them move back towards the tree trunk, and start pushing. At first, nothing happens, and then, with another shriek of joy from Hannah and Rowan, the middle section of the trunk rolls away, leaving the gates of the castle clear.

I stop the timer on my phone, feeling smug.

'Hunter technically won,' says Ian, as the two men come walking towards us. 'But he's agreed to sit down with us and have a talk about how we can all work together anyway, so I've agreed to stop referring to him as a bawbag. I can't speak for Izzie, though, unfortunately. She still thinks he's a Nuckelavee.'

'I think he might have won over Izzie too, actually,' I say, with a grateful smile in Hunter's direction.

'I'll still need to move the rest of the tree, obviously,' he says, smiling back at me. 'But at least the gates are clear now, so people can leave whenever they want.'

'So . . . will you?' I ask Ian. 'Leave, I mean? Now that the road's cleared?'

'Er . . .' Ian glances at Hunter, who steps forward.

'I've managed to persuade him to stay until the power comes back on in the village,' he says. 'Well, actually, it was these two who did the persuading.'

He gestures at Hannah and Rowan, who're both sporting matching grins.

'We're going to have a sleepover,' Hannah says importantly. 'Rowan's going to stay with me and my stuffed animals, and we're going to have a midnight feast. Daddy said it was OK.'

'The road out of the castle's clear,' adds Ian, looking slightly abashed. 'But the roads back to the village aren't. And Hunter's right; there's no point heading back if the power's still out. If it was just me and Callum, I'd give it a go, but I don't think Rowan would enjoy going back to a house with no power.'

'Well, that's great,' I exclaim, noting Ian's use of 'Hunter' rather than 'Bawbag'. That's definitely progress. 'And now you'll all be able to stay for the launch party.'

There's a murmur of excitement from the assembled crowd, and slowly everyone starts to drift back inside the hotel.

'So, what happened?' I say, falling into step beside Hunter. 'To change your mind about talking to them, I mean?'

Hunter doesn't look at me.

'Ian's a good man,' he says to the ground beneath his feet. 'A good man, who's had a rough deal of it, and now he has a little girl depending on him; and a younger brother, too. So, you could say we had quite a bit to chat about.'

'And a bit more in common than you realised?' I suggest.

He stops walking and turns to face me.

'Don't push your luck, Rosie Winter,' he says softly. 'I could still throw them all out, you know; you too, if I really wanted to.'

'You'd never do that, though,' I point out, grinning. 'Because you're a good man, too, Hunter Stuart. Even though you do your best to hide it.'

He pulls a face at me, and I respond by sticking out my tongue, like a child.

'Does this mean you've forgiven me?' he asks, his expression suddenly serious. 'For not telling you sooner that *I* was the Nuckelavee, whatever that is? I did try, Rosie, when we were in the maze. I should have said something sooner, though.'

'You were in a difficult position,' I reply, having had a lot of time to think about this over the last few hours. 'You didn't really know me; and I don't suppose I made it easy for you, with all of the things I said about you, before I knew it was *you* I was talking about.'

'You're forgiven,' he says instantly. 'And you were right – I *was* being a bit of an arsehole by trying to change the way things worked without speaking to anyone about it first. I didn't really consider the effect it would have on the village. I was just trying to figure out how to make sure the castle didn't have to be sold.'

My heart gives an uncomfortable little lurch at the reminder that it still might be.

I still have so much to do if we're going to make sure the launch goes well.

'Um, I should go and help Luna,' I say, looking away before this conversation can go any further. 'There's still tons to sort out before tonight.'

Hunter eyes flicker with disappointment, but he just nods, and gives me a sad smile as he turns to walk away, me following a few steps behind.

I'm glad he managed to find some common ground with Ian. I really hope it helps him figure out what to do about the hotel, and this deal he's been so hell-bent on pursuing. But as I follow the sound of voices along to the ballroom, where the hotel staff are busy setting up for tonight's party, my feet feel as heavy as my heart, and I have to force a smile as I join the other volunteers.

Because, assuming the trains are running again by morning, I'll be going home tomorrow, along with everyone else. Which means tonight is my very last chance to turn myself into a butterfly.

I think it's time to break out my magic sweater.

Chapter 37

It's only been underway for a couple of hours, but I can already tell the launch party at the Chrysalis is going to go down in history as one of the best parties the village has ever seen.

As I'd asked, the tables from the restaurant have been arranged in two long lines at one end of the room, with an area at the top left free for dancing. Izzie and the kitchen staff have outdone themselves with the food (it's surprising just how many dishes you can make with potatoes and veg . . .), and delicious scents waft up from the heaped plates and serving bowls which have been set out on each table, so the diners can help themselves.

Hunter, meanwhile, has, somewhat reluctantly, given up the keys to the wine cellar, and the result of that is a raucous, festive atmosphere that's only slightly marred by Callum and Izzie's terrible singing, as they stand by the grand piano and treat us to their rendition of 'Super Trouper'.

('You'd have thought they'd be better, really,' says Millie thoughtfully. 'What with all the albums they've released.')

After dinner, though, the woman who'd told Luna she'd been a backup singer takes over, and turns out to be pretty good; especially once Hunter's been talked into fetching his guitars from the apartment and offering them to the musicians among the crowd.

'First wine, now musical instruments,' I say teasingly, as we watch two men from the village strike up a jaunty little folk tune. 'You're going to lose your reputation as a complete bawbag if you're not careful.'

'That sounds really weird in an English accent,' Hunter comments, taking a large swig of his beer. But when I glance back over at him, he's watching the people on the dance floor with a smile on his face which does nothing to disprove my comment.

'It's OK,' I say, leaning over so I can shout into his ear above the sound of the music. 'Your secret's safe with me. I won't tell them you're a teddy bear, deep down. You can continue pretending to be the aloof laird.'

'I'm neither aloof nor a laird,' he points out, his face very close to mine as he turns to grin at me, looking more relaxed than I've seen him since I got here. 'That title definitely belongs to Dougie, and Dougie alone.'

I tear my eyes away from his face and follow his gaze to where Lord Glenmuir is seated at the head of one of the tables, barking orders at everyone who happens to be within earshot. He seems to be enjoying himself; everyone does, actually. Well, everyone except me.

I've been so wrapped up with the goings-on in the hotel that my own problems have been pushed to the back of my mind. Now, though, as it gets closer to midnight, and the day I'll be leaving this place, those problems are back again, all jostling for position at the very front of my mind.

The credit card debt.

The job I hate.

The fact that I still have nowhere to live when I leave here, and no real prospect of being able to afford anything better than a shabby room in a flat-share somewhere on the outskirts of town.

Hunter.

It's always Hunter.

It's funny how a man I've only just met has somehow managed to worm his way into my head, until there are moments when he's all I can think about.

It's funny how just four days away from 'real' life can leave you feeling like a completely different person; and one who has no idea how she'll somehow manage to fit back into the life she left behind.

It's funny, yes, but it's also crazy, because one thing I do know is that, no matter what happens next for either of us, it can't happen for us *together*. There are too many miles between us, and too many unknowns for us to make even the slightest bit of sense.

But I wish it could.

I wish we could at least *try*.

I wish there was more time; time to find out if that spark between us could ever turn into something more, or time to just *be together*, without a looming departure date hanging above our heads.

I just need more time.

Time, though, is running out; as evidenced by the grandfather clock in the hall, which announces each hour with a DING-DONG, so loud we can hear it in the ballroom. By the time that clock strikes twelve, my time in the Chrysalis will be almost over, whether I'm ready for it to end or not.

'Come *on*,' I say, looking down at the magic jumper, which I'm wearing over the top of the same sequinned number I overdressed for dinner in. 'If you're planning to work some magic here, this would be a *really* great time to do it.'

But tonight, the sweater seems to be all out of magic. So the night goes on, and the clock keeps striking, no matter how much I will it to stop. Much to my relief, however, there's no trace of animosity between the people from the village and those from the castle. Villagers dance with hotel staff. Hannah and Rowan go skidding across the polished wooden floorboards in their socks, with a small gang of children following close behind them. Izzie offers to read the Laird's palm, and the Laird is only mildly rude in his response.

At one point, Dante comes staggering into the room, his dark suit draped with cobwebs, and a sprinkling of dust on top of his glossy head, like dandruff.

'You!' he says, pointing a shaking finger at Sabrina, who's sitting with Luna, each of them treating the other with exaggerated politeness. 'I thought you were supposed to be locked in the attic?'

'I beg your pardon?' replies Sabrina frostily, a semblance of her old self returning at the sight of her arch nemesis. 'What would I be doing in an *attic*, of all places? Haunting it?'

'I've been up there for hours,' Dante splutters, ignoring the question. 'I thought you might have gotten lost, or hurt. I've been beside myself!'

'Gosh, how romantic,' says Millie, sipping a cocktail in exactly the same shade of pink as her dress. 'Look how worried he was about you, Sabrina! I wish *I* could get locked in an attic so someone could come and find me.'

'I was worried she'd sue us if she'd fallen over and hurt herself,' Dante snaps. 'That's all. I don't care what happens to her other than that.'

'I don't care what happens to you either,' Sabrina retorts, tossing her head like a capricious pony as she gets up to walk away. 'I didn't even notice you weren't here.'

'That reminds me,' says Millie, touching me on the arm. 'We never found out about that invisible woman you mentioned, Rosie? Was it a ghost, do you think? Izzie says sometimes the souls of people who didn't do the things they were supposed to in life can become trapped, they can't move on. So they just keep doing the same thing over and over, and no one can even see them doing it. Isn't that wild?'

'Pretty wild,' I agree, staring at the bubbles in my champagne glass. 'That would be . . . that would be terrible.'

That *is* terrible, I mean.

And I would know, because she's literally describing *my life*. But maybe it doesn't have to be anymore.

Maybe it's time I took Sabrina's advice to eat the bloody cake while I still have the chance.

'Whoever she was, I think she's gone now,' I tell Millie. 'I haven't seen any sign of her in days.'

Which is true, actually. I've organised this party, haven't I? I've rescued a woman from a runaway horse. I've done my very best to build bridges between Hunter and the villagers.

I haven't been invisible, is what I'm saying.

Actually, I think I've been pretty damn *visible* for once in my life.

And I think I've quite liked it, too.

'Oh, that's good,' Millie says, relieved. 'She must have figured out whatever it was she had to do to be free.'

'Yes,' I say slowing, my mind whirring as I put my champagne glass back down. 'I think she did. It's just whether or not she's brave enough to actually *do* it that's the question . . .'

Millie looks at me questioningly, but before she can ask what I mean, the sound of someone tapping a glass with their knife cuts through the air.

'If I could have your attention, everyone, for just a few minutes,' says Sabrina, who's standing at the front of the room, in front of the fireplace, with a laptop set up in front of her. 'It's time to announce the results of our exciting influencer competition, and find out who's going to be the face of the Chrysalis hotel.'

She says this in the enthusiastic tone of a children's TV presenter, but her words are met with a groan of disappointment from the villagers, most of whom have no idea what she's talking about, and who just want to get back to the party.

'Four days ago,' Sabrina begins, pretending she can't hear them, 'five women entered the Chrysalis.'

'And one man,' yells Daniel Foster indignantly. 'Why does everyone keep forgetting about me?'

'Five women *and one man* entered the Chrysalis,' Sabrina goes on. 'Their mission? *Change.*'

She pauses, as if to give the audience a chance to react to this, but everyone just stares at her blankly.

'Change comes in many forms,' says Sabrina, tapping a key on her laptop, which makes a large screen come to life behind her, with a photo of the hotel on it. 'Physical. Mental. *Spiritual.* The Chrysalis aims to facilitate them all, with its holistic approach to self-care, combined with the utmost in luxury accommodation.'

The screen behind her flicks through a series of slides showing various parts of the hotel, along with the dramatic landscape surrounding it, which I guess is supposed to represent the mental and spiritual changes Sabrina mentioned.

'Over the last few days, our exclusive influencer team has experienced these changes for themselves,' says Sabrina, tapping another key. 'And just look at the results!'

She stands back to allow us a clear view of the screen, which now starts scrolling through some of the photos we've been posting while we've been here. There's 'princess' Bex floating through the misty castle grounds before going back to her room to cry; Yasmin pretending to drink champagne in a cold bathtub; Zara and Millie looking gorgeous in bikinis I now know they almost froze to death in, although you wouldn't know it to look at them. There's even one of me stroking Bramble on the nose, and looking like I'm having the time of my life, when, in fact, I felt lonely and pushed out by everyone around me.

Every single photo is stunningly beautiful . . . and completely fake.

'Can we get on with this?' says someone plaintively from the direction of the dance floor. 'This free bar isn't going to last forever, is it?'

'Although all of our influencers have produced amazing work,' says Sabrina, pretending not to hear this, 'only one of them can become the face of the Chrysalis. And, in order to decide who that should be, my assistafriend Luna and I have been carefully analysing the number of likes, shares and referrals they've managed to generate. We've also been sharing some of our favourite photos and videos on the Chrysalis's Instagram account, and the influencer with the best overall engagement will become the face of the hotel for the next twelve months.'

'What's that? Is somebody getting engaged?' asks Lord Glenmuir, holding a hand to his ear. 'Speak up, woman. What's she talking about?' he adds, turning to Ian, who's sitting next to him.

'Don't ask me,' replies Ian, taking a swig of beer. 'I don't even know what an "assistafriend" is. I'm just here for the free booze.'

'Luna,' calls Sabrina, glaring at them both. 'Could you pass the envelope, please? And Dante, you should be up here too.'

Beside me, Millie leans forward in her seat, but I just tap my fingers impatiently on my chair. It's obviously going to be Bex who wins the contest – and just as obvious that it's *not* going to be me – and now that we're about to find out, I really don't care anymore. I just want to get it over with, so I can speak to Hunter.

That's the only thing that matters to me.

Luna gets hurriedly to her feet and hands her boss a large gold envelope. After a moment, Dante follows her to the front of the room, where he takes his place next to Sabrina, looking like he's there at gunpoint.

'This is just like the Oscars,' observes Izzie, who's somehow managed to get Stevie the dog onto her knee, and is hugging him as if he's a teddy bear. 'I wish we'd thought to make some popcorn.'

Sabrina takes her time opening the envelope, drawing out the moment for full dramatic impact.

'And the winner is . . .' She pulls a card from the envelope and holds it up to the light, only for Dante to snatch it rudely out of her hand.

'Surely this must be a mistake,' he says, squinting at the piece of paper. 'This can't possibly be right? You'll have to do a recount.'

'There's no mistake,' says Luna, two spots of colour appearing on her cheeks. 'I counted it up myself. Twice, in fact. This is one hundred per cent the correct result.'

Stepping quickly over to the laptop, she presses another few buttons, and the hotel's Instagram page appears on the screen.

'As I mentioned,' Sabrina says smoothly, 'we've been sharing some of our favourite photos from the last few days on the account for the hotel. Luna added some today, in fact.'

She scrolls down the page, and I gasp in horror as a video of me standing on top of Hunter's car appears.

'I sent them that,' says Callum excitedly. 'It's good, isn't it? I'm going to put it on TikTok, too.'

I daren't look at Hunter as the video starts to play; and, by the time it ends, I'm cringing so hard I'm in danger of disappearing into my seat. But the number of hearts at the bottom of the post shocks me into sitting upright again, sure I must be seeing things.

But no. It's still there. Which means . . .

'What we found,' says Sabrina, 'is that followers of the hotel's account responded best to the rawer, more natural content we posted. They loved this video, for instance, which not only showcases the, er, unique relationship that exists between the hotel and the local community, but also shows the change that Rosie here has experienced as a result of her stay at the Chrysalis.'

She beams over at me, and I slide down my seat, horribly aware of the curious stares I'm getting from everyone in the room. The video definitely does not show anything even close to what Sabrina's just described; but some members of the crowd have recognised themselves in the background now, so they're fully invested.

'Rosie entered the Chrysalis a mere shadow of the woman you see standing on top of this car,' says Sabrina. 'Mousy. Shy. Scared of her own shadow.'

I attempt to slide even further down in my seat, wondering if hiding under the table is a viable option, or if she'll just come over and pull me back out.

I wouldn't put it past her.

'But now look at her,' Sabrina goes on, pressing another button on the laptop.

A video of the beach appears on the screen, the sea almost completely blending into the pouring rain. Then a black pony emerges from the spray, mane and tail flying, as I thunder along the sand to the rescue of Bex.

'Oh, my God,' I whisper, sitting back up so quickly it makes me light-headed. 'That's the video I promised Bex I wouldn't post.'

I get quickly to my feet, barely noticing the chair falling over in my panic.

Bex is going to hate this. She's never going to believe I had nothing to do with it. She's going to hate me.

'This video has only been up for a few hours,' says Sabrina triumphantly. 'But it's already been liked and shared over half a million times. Followers of the hotel's account have loved following Rosie's journey from a mousy little nobody to the woman she is now.'

There's a small ripple of applause from the slightly bemused audience.

I think I'm going to cry. Or throw up. Or throw up while crying.

'Oh, come on,' says Hunter loudly. 'That's a bit much, don't you think? Mousy? Shy?'

He stands up, and the entire room seems to hold its breath.

'Rosie Winter couldn't be *mousy* if she tried,' he snorts. 'And if she was scared of her own shadow, that's only because you lot bullied her mercilessly. Not to mention what you put her through, Dougie.'

At his table, the Laird raises both hands in a *ya got me* gesture.

'As for being a nobody,' Hunter goes on, his eyes searching the crowd for me. 'This woman is not a nobody. This woman, in fact, has more bravery and integrity in her little finger than ten of you combined. This woman is a *some-body*. And I know, because I've seen it over and over since she got here. So if you want to call her any more names, or put her down the way you've been doing for days, you're going to have to go through me first.'

He folds his arms across his chest and widens his stance as the room explodes into a flurry of cheers and applause, which Sabrina silences by tapping a knife against her glass again.

I'm so busy staring at Hunter – slightly blurrily, thanks to the tears that are filling my eyes – that it takes me a moment to focus on her instead and, when I do, I'm surprised to find that, instead of the fury I expected to see on her face as the recipient of this rousing speech, she's actually *smiling*.

'You're absolutely right, Hunter,' she says, smugly. 'Rosie is all of those things, and more. Which is why it gives me the utmost pleasure to announce that the first ever face of the Chrysalis is . . . Rosie Winter!'

Chapter 38

All around me, people are clapping and cheering, but I don't care. I know this can't possibly be happening – and, if it is, it's only because of that stupid video of me on the beach.

That video is the only reason I got enough likes to win; and it's a video that should never have been posted.

That means that, as far as I'm concerned, there's only one true winner here, and it's not me.

'Where's Bex?' I yell, pushing my way through the crowd of people who're all gathering to congratulate me. 'She's the person who should've won the stupid competition, not me.'

'Oh, no,' Sabrina assures me, the crowds parting to allow her and Luna to get to me. Luna's smiling at me too, as if this was their plan all along.

This is obviously some strange kind of fever dream I'm having; and I really need to figure out how to wake up from it now.

I need to find Bex.

I need to speak to Hunter.

Oh, God, I really, really *need to speak to Hunter.*

'No, Rosie,' Sabrina goes on, reaching me, *'you're* the winner. Oh, Bex's content was amazing, obviously; everyone knows that.' She waves a hand dismissively. 'But Bex was *already* a butterfly. So were the rest. You were the one who *changed*, Rosie, and that's what we were looking for.'

I stare at them, nonplussed – and not particularly convinced this is the compliment Sabrina seems to think it is.

'We *all* changed, though,' I protest, frantically scanning the room for Bex, who's nowhere to be seen. 'Yasmin became more confident; Bex stopped being horrible to everyone. Even you, Sabrina, you changed, too. And you.' I turn towards Luna, who pats me comfortingly on the shoulder.

'Your journey is the one our followers responded to the most,' she explains. 'And I don't know if you've looked at your Instagram page lately, but I think you'll be surprised by how many new followers you've gained in the last twenty-four hours.'

I shake my head, overwhelmed. I don't care about Instagram. Not anymore.

'I need to find Bex,' I say firmly. 'She's going to be devastated by this. Where is she? Daniel?'

I spot him lurking behind Sabrina, but he just shrugs, still looking painfully hungover.

'I've been looking for her too,' he says, croakily. 'But I can't find her. I think she must be—'

'I'm here.'

Everyone falls silent at the sound of Bex's voice.

She's standing in the doorway of the room, her eyes wild.

'I'm here,' she says again, sounding faintly hysterical. 'And I don't give a crap about who won the stupid competition – oh, congratulations Rosie, by the way. I'm being serious, Daniel,' she repeats, addressing her husband, who looks every bit as confused as the rest of us. 'It doesn't matter. We don't need the money anymore.'

She holds a small plastic stick in the air, her eyes swimming with tears. It takes me a hot minute and a collective 'Oooh!' of appreciation from the assembled crowd to understand what's happening.

And then my heart is beaming for Bex.

She's *pregnant*.

'Has she *peed* on that?' says Millie, spoiling the moment somewhat.

Bex doesn't even register the comment. Her face is shining with joy, her eyes locked on her husband.

'Daniel, we're going to have a baby!'

Daniel picks her up and swings her around, his face buried in her dark hair. Then he puts her back down and starts sobbing.

'It's OK,' he assures us, as a hush falls on the room again. 'They're happy tears. I know no one ever cares what the man in the relationship thinks, but I'm just . . . I'm just so happy.'

He starts sobbing again, and I catch sight of Sabrina dabbing at her eyes with a napkin and then looking at it if she can't quite understand what's happening.

Within seconds, the party atmosphere is restored; champagne corks pop ('Did none of you notice I was on the non-alcoholic stuff, just as a precaution?' says Bex gleefully. 'It tastes like cat's piss, but who cares, right?'), the music starts back up and the dancing recommences, everyone chatting and laughing as if nothing particularly important has happened.

But it did.

I just somehow won a competition that could change my entire life. That could let me clear my debt, and start over, with a brand-new career as an influencer. If Luna's right, I might even already be well on my way to that, with all the new followers I've apparently picked up.

Oh, and as the face of the Chrysalis, I'll be coming here for one weekend of every month to create my content, too. Wasn't that part of the prize?

I asked the magic sweater for more time, and it looks like the sweater has delivered.

This thing was definitely worth *way* more than I paid for it.

'Ahem!'

The sound of a knife against glass tings through the air again, and a collective groan goes up at the prospect of yet another speech. This time, however, it's Hunter who's standing at the front of the room, holding a glass of whisky as if it's a prop.

Around me, people nudge and hush each other. 'That's my daddy,' Hannah can be heard saying to Rowan, who high-fives her in excitement.

'I wonder how Bex knows what cat's piss tastes like?' Millie whispers loudly, a few steps behind everyone else, as usual.

'I'm not a man known for his way with words,' Hunter begins – somewhat inaccurately, given the speech he made to Sabrina just a few minutes ago. 'So I'm going to get straight to the point.'

He clears his throat, nervously.

'I've just got off a phone call with the person I've been dealing at WanderNest,' he says, ignoring the gasp of horror that goes up at the mention of the dreaded name. 'I've told them we're pulling out of the proposed deal. I'm not selling the hotel – not to them, and not to anyone.'

'I knew it,' yells Izzie. 'I saw it in the cards!'

Ian shushes her, his eyes fixed firmly on Hunter, who isn't done yet.

'One thing the last couple of days have shown me is how much we all need each other,' he says. 'And how much this place has come to mean to me. So, Hannah and I will be staying on in the castle. I've already agreed to sit down with Ian – and Izzie, and anyone else who feels they have something to contribute – and talk about how we can better support each other; how the hotel can help the village, and vice versa. It's not going to be easy; there's a lot of work ahead of us all, in fact. But I know no one here's afraid of hard work, and neither am I. So, I suppose what I'm trying to say is that I'm willing to give it a go if you are.'

There's a short pause, during which the air in the room seems to hum with tension. Then Ian gets to his feet.

'I'll drink to that,' he says simply, holding up his glass.

Hunter raises his in response, and then everyone's on their feet, glasses clinking in a toast that goes on for so long I start to worry they'll still be at it by the time my train leaves tomorrow, and I'll never get the chance to talk to Hunter.

'Ten minutes to go until midnight,' Dante yells, as the noise finally dies down. 'Which means there's just ten minutes until the Chrysalis is officially open for business. Charge your glasses, everyone.'

I frantically scan the room for Hunter, finding him at last, his tall shape almost hidden by all the people around me, who're hurrying to refill glasses and find the person they want to be standing next to when the clock strikes midnight, and this new era of the Chrysalis begins.

For me, it's definitely him.

So let's just hope he feels the same.

'Hunter!' I call, my voice lost in the general buzz of the crowd. 'Hunter! Over here!'

His eyes swivel towards me, and he smiles, his face lighting up in a way that suggests he might just have been looking for me too.

We swim towards each other through the packed room, carried on the sea of people, none of whom have even the slightest clue how incredibly important it is that we reach each other.

'Hi,' I say shyly, when I'm standing in front of him at last. 'Nice speech.'

'I'm glad you liked it,' he replies, grinning down at me. 'Because I'd never have said any of it if it wasn't for you. You were the one who made me see what was right in front of my face. You were the one who persuaded me to stay here and try to make a go of this place, rather than selling up and running away.'

'Oh, I'm sure you'd have got there in the end,' I reply. 'In fact, I know you would have. I just gave you a tiny little push.'

'It was you who messaged me about the power being out, wasn't it?' he says, smiling to show he's not angry with me. 'I thought there was something odd about that, but Ian told me he called one of his farmhands not long ago to find out how they've been coping without power, and they said it's been back on for ages now. You wouldn't know anything about that, would you?'

'Sorry.' I grin, not feeling remotely sorry at all. 'I know I shouldn't have done it, but I knew if you just had a bit of time to get to know them all, you'd be able to put aside your differences. I just wanted to give you that extra time. I could do with some myself, to be honest.'

We look into each other's eyes, both of us tongue-tied now that we finally have the opportunity to speak.

'I think I want to move to the Highlands,' I blurt out, surprising even myself.

'I think you should come and work for the—' Hunter starts to say, almost at the same time.

We stare at each other, both of us red in the face, neither one of us wanting to break the fragile spell that feels like it's been cast over us.

'You first,' I say quietly. 'What were you going to say?'

'I, um, I was just saying that I think you should consider coming to work for the hotel,' Hunter replies, scratching his head bashfully. 'I know you've won this influencer contest thing, so you'll be up here anyway sometimes, but—'

'I don't want to do it,' I interrupt, my heart almost leaping out of my chest as it thumps frantically in my chest. 'I don't want to be an influencer, Hunter. I think I'd hate it. I *know* I'd hate it. I do want to . . . spend more time here, though,' I add carefully. 'A lot more time, really.'

'Which is why you should come and work for us,' he says, his grin wider than I've ever seen it. 'You might not want to be an influencer, Rosie, but . . . well, look at how you've influenced *me*. Look at how you've influenced all of us.'

He nods in the general direction of the room, where the party is back in full swing, now that all the interruptions are over.

'You're good at organising things,' Hunter says. 'At managing people. You know how to get things done, and you have a way of doing it without ruffling too many feathers, the way I seem to. I think we need you here. I don't think we can do without you, actually. I know I can't.'

'Are you offering me a job?' I ask cautiously, wanting to make sure I'm getting this right. 'Or something more?'

'I'm offering you everything, Rosie,' Hunter says, without hesitation. 'A job. A home. *Me*.'

His face is open, his eyes filled with hope.

I take a deep breath to steady myself, my mind skimming over the hundreds of miles between here and my life in London. My friends. My family. My job. Everything I know.

Can I really leave it all behind, just like that?

'That's if you want it,' he adds, his eyes darkening as he watches the conflicting emotions play across my face. 'It can just be a job, if you . . . if that's all you're interested in. It's a big move, I know that better than anyone. And we've only known each other for four days, so I'll understand if you say no. I promise I'll understand. But—'

He swallows, his eyes shining in the dim light of the busy room.

'But I really hope you'll say yes,' he says, so quietly I have to lean into him to hear the whispered words. 'It's what I want more than anything, Rosie. *You're* what I want, more than anything. I don't want to be friends. I want to give this a chance; see where it goes. I can't stand the thought of these being our last moments together.'

'*Ten!*' yells someone behind me, as the countdown begins, almost as if it's been waiting for Hunter's words to cue it in.

'*Nine!*' roars the crowd, enthusiastically taking up the chant.

I gaze around the room, at the crowd of people I didn't even know existed this time last week, but who've already come to feel like old friends. Well, *some* of them, anyway.

'*Eight!*'

Over on the dance floor, Bex and Daniel sway together slowly, their arms wrapped around each other, dreaming of the family they'll have this time next year.

'*Seven!*'

Millie and Callum are standing by the drinks table, edging their way towards each other in a way they presumably think is subtle, but which leaves no one in any doubt who either of them will be kissing at midnight.

'*Six!*'

Izzie is carried past on the shoulders of the red-bearded man I briefly argued with outside the hotel earlier, her hair and cloak flying behind her.

'*Five!*'

Lord Glenmuir follows her, held aloft by two burly-looking villagers, who seem to be taking both him and his chair to the dance floor.

'*Four!*'

Yasmin is dancing in a circle with some of the kids from the village – Hannah included – who all look equal parts impressed and terrified by her.

'*Three!*'

Zara and Luna join them, both of them pointing and shouting excitedly at something on the other side of the room, where . . .

'*Two!*'

. . . Sabrina and Dante are kissing in a corner as if both of their lives depend on it.

'*One!*'

The clock in the hallway booms into life, as streamers and champagne corks erupt into the air. All around us, people are hugging and kissing, while here in the centre of it all, Hunter and I stand perfectly still, both of our lives teetering precariously on the edge of this brand-new opportunity, and the myriad opportunities it brings.

Change.

That's what I came here for, after all. Isn't it? And what was it I said to Hunter just yesterday?

The only way you can know for sure that it won't work is if you don't even try.

Maybe it's time I took my own advice on that.

'Well?' Hunter says softly, as someone strikes up a tune on the piano. 'What do you say, Rosie? Do you want to give it a go? With me, I mean, not just with the job?'

I look up at him, my eyes swimming with happy tears.

'Oh, I made up my mind about you ages ago,' I tell him with a grin that makes my face hurt. 'Long before you offered me a job, or made a speech about how much – what was it? "Bravery and integrity"? I have?'

'I said you were a *somebody*,' he replies, touching my lips softly with his thumb. 'But what I really meant to say was that you're special, Rosie. And I know we haven't known each other for very long, but I can assure you, I meant every word of it.'

'Then I think I'm going to accept your offer,' I reply, a thrill of excitement running through my body like electricity at the thought. 'But on one condition.'

'And what's that?'

'Could you just kiss me already?' I say. 'It's way past the stroke of midnight.'

Hunter chuckles, then puts his lips on mine, his strong arms winding around my waist as he lifts me right off my feet and spins me around. He kisses me again and again, and as I kiss him back, I feel that cloak of invisibility I've been carrying around fall from my shoulders at last.

Just like Millie said, the invisible woman finally figured out what she had to do to set herself free.

Acknowledgements

This book came about almost entirely by accident.

Back in February 2024, I was considering quitting writing altogether, when, completely out of the blue, I got an email from my now-editor, Clem Flanagan. It would probably be an exaggeration to say that message changed my life, but . . . it kind of *did*? So my thanks go first of all to Clem, who not only pulled me back from the brink, but who also worked her editing magic to turn *Highland Getaway* from a very rough first draft into the book you've just read. It's definitely *not* an exaggeration to say I wouldn't be here without her, and the rest of the amazing team at Black & White, who've been so incredibly supportive and welcoming, right from the very start of this journey.

Within a few weeks of meeting Clem, I signed with my fantastic agent, Kate Nash, who has held my hand, patiently explained how everything works, and even once pulled over while driving to reply to a message. She is the agent I couldn't even have imagined being lucky enough to have, and I'm so grateful to have her on my side.

My thanks also go to my friends and family; particularly my parents, who have never once faltered in their belief that they would one day see my books in actual *shops*, and whose endless support and encouragement (not to mention the babysitting!) is the number one reason I've ever managed to write anything at all.

About the Author

Amber Eve started her career in journalism before spending over a decade exhaustively documenting her life for her award-winning blog, ForeverAmber.co.uk. After the pandemic, she traded personal stories for fictional ones and now spends her days writing romantic comedies from her home in Scotland, where most of her books are set.